EMMERDALE AT WAR

Can the nation's favourite village make peace with each other? It is a must for fans of ITV's *Emmerdale*, and readers who love heart-warming and heart-breaking stories set during war-time. Pamela Bell's book transports us to the Yorkshire Dales in the midst of World War II, exploring the lives of Emmerdale's much-loved families. Will the nation's favourite village overcome adversity to deal with the loves and lives lost?

PAMELA BELL

♦

EMMERDALE AT WAR

Complete and Unabridged

MAGNA
Leicester

First published in Great Britain in 2019 by
Trapeze
an imprint of The Orion Publishing Group Ltd
London

First Ulverscroft Edition
published 2020
by arrangement with
The Orion Publishing Group Ltd
An Hachette UK company
London

A catalogue record for this book is available
from the British Library.

ISBN 978–0–7505–4747–5

Published by
Ulverscroft Limited
Anstey, Leicestershire
Set by Words & Graphics Ltd.
Anstey, Leicestershire
Printed and bound in Great Britain by
T. J. International Ltd., Padstow, Cornwall

This book is printed on acid-free paper

My thanks go to Alasdair Gordon for his help with the manuscript, John Whiston for his help with the story lines, and Shirley Patton for making this all happen.

January 1940

1

'You pick first.' The tips of two straws poked out of the top of Jacob Sugden's clenched fist as he thrust it towards his brother.

Annie Pearson twisted her fingers in her apron as Edward grinned and rubbed his chin, pretending to debate which straw to draw. Pretending that it was a joke. As if it came down to anything more than luck anyway. Draw the long straw, and he would stay at Emmerdale Farm, with her. The short one, and he would go and fight.

Please pick the long straw, Edward, she pleaded silently. *Pick the right one. Please, please, please get it right.*

Beside Annie, Maggie Sugden stood rigidly, her face set in grim lines as she watched her younger son larking around. 'Get on with it, Edward,' she said, the snap in her voice revealing the tension she shared with Annie.

They had been equally appalled when Jacob and Edward had announced over dinner that they had been talking about the war and had decided that one of them should enlist now that conscription was being extended.

'You'll do no such thing,' Maggie had said with a frown. 'What do you want to do a daft thing like enlist for? Farming's a reserved profession, and a lot more use than fighting. You should both stay here and make yourselves useful doing something you know about.'

'It doesn't feel right for both of us to stay,' said Edward while Annie, afraid that she would do something stupid like burst into tears, got up to clear away the plates. 'I know it doesn't feel like much is happening at the moment, but we're at war. They need fighting men, or they wouldn't have brought in more conscription. We agreed that one of us should go and do his duty for both of us.'

'Duty!' Maggie spat out the word. 'If you'd lived through the last war you wouldn't talk to me about duty,' she said. 'Your dad did his duty, and look what thanks he got for it!'

Annie hadn't been able to help glancing at Joe Sugden as she bent to pick up his plate. One side of his face was so hideously scarred that the evacuee children who'd been billeted at Emmerdale Farm the previous September had screamed in terror at the sight of him.

She herself scarcely noticed. She had only ever known Joe after the terrible injury that had blown away half his head. He had come home from war a changed man, slow of speech and mind, they said, although Annie didn't think Joe was as stupid as other people thought. Her pa, Sam, remembered the bitter, brutal man who had gone away to fight. 'Who says nowt good comes out of war?' he often said. 'It changed Joe Sugden for the better, didn't it?'

What if Edward changed? What if he came home horribly scarred or embittered? Annie's hands were unsteady as she put the plates in the sink to rinse. She didn't want anything about Edward to change. She had loved him her whole life.

4

Edward had looked at his father, too. 'No disrespect to you, Pa. We know you suffered, but you did your duty and we have to do ours. We've talked about it and we both feel the same, don't we, Jacob?'

Jacob nodded, as usual letting Edward do the talking. The two brothers were nothing alike. One dark, one fair; one sunny-natured, one prone to moodiness. Jacob was good-looking, better-looking than Edward if the truth be told. He was loyal and steadfast, but because he was taciturn those who didn't know him as well as Annie did tended to assume that he was just a typically dour Yorkshire farmer.

It was hard to believe that he was related to Edward, with his wheat-coloured hair and clear blue-grey eyes. Edward wasn't as handsome as his brother — Annie could admit that — but his expression was bright and good-humoured, and he had a warmth and a steadiness and an openness to him that meant everybody liked him.

Except for the Skilbecks, of course; but then, they didn't like anybody and nobody liked them, so that was only fair.

'We did think we should both enlist,' Edward had gone on, 'but that didn't seem fair to you, Ma. I know you're more than capable of running the farm by yourself. It's not as if you haven't done it before, and there's Pa and Sam — and Annie, of course,' he'd added, including her in his smile.

Annie's heart normally warmed at being considered part of Emmerdale Farm. She had been working there since she was fourteen, helping

5

Maggie in the house and the dairy, and willingly turning a hand to milking the cows or gathering in the harvest if necessary. It was Maggie Sugden who had saved the Pearsons after an accident left Annie's father badly injured. The Pearsons' farm had been lost to Clive Skilbeck, but Maggie gave Sam a job at Emmerdale Farm even before he could work properly again, and let them have the old shepherd's cottage to live in. It was not what they had been used to, and Sam was bitter still about the Skilbecks, but but at least they had a home.

Suspecting that Maggie had taken her on out of the goodness of her heart, Annie worked hard and was grateful. Other girls sometimes wondered that she wasn't bored, or asked if she wouldn't rather get a job in a city, but the thought filled Annie with horror. She loved Emmerdale Farm, and not just because it meant she could see Edward every day.

But what would Emmerdale Farm be without Edward? How could he talk so easily about the prospect of going away?

Edward was still trying to reassure his mother. 'Still, the farm's bigger now, so Jacob and me, we reckon one of us should stay. Drawing straws seems the only fair way to do it. Come on then, Jacob,' he said to his brother, 'let's do it now.'

So Jacob had found a couple of straws and now there they were, all staring at Edward as he reached out for a straw, almost pulled one, then snatched his hand back, changing his mind at the last minute.

'Ma's right, hurry up, Ed.' Annie could hear

the tension in Jacob's voice. He must want the decision made as much as the rest of them did, she thought.

'Righto, then. Here goes.' Edward took a breath and all at once Annie couldn't bear to look. Biting her lip, she stared out of the kitchen window while her heart thudded anxiously against her ribs.

The sky was an iron grey pressing down on the monochrome landscape. It had been the coldest winter Annie could remember. The snow piled up in great drifts against the stone walls that slanted across the fells, and the lane to Beckindale was impassable in the farm truck. It had been a struggle to get down to the village with the farm's ration books the day before, and several times she had sunk knee-deep in the snow.

Now it looked as if more snow was on its way. It was warm enough in the farm kitchen, with its fire and the great range that Annie had to clean out and light every morning when she arrived, but it would be a hard trudge back up the track to the old shepherd's cottage where she had lived with her parents ever since the Pearson farm had been lost to Clive Skilbeck and, oh, when would Edward pick a straw? She couldn't bear this waiting!

The thought had barely crossed Annie's mind before she heard Maggie suck in a breath, and knew without looking which straw Edward had pulled.

It was Edward who would be going to fight.

Oddly, it was Jacob she saw first as she turned her head. He was staring as if in disbelief at his

7

hand where a single straw still poked free. The straw Edward didn't pick. The long straw that meant Jacob would stay safely at home and Edward would go to war.

'No!' Annie cried without thinking, and Jacob's eyes lifted to hers. She saw his expression blaze with a strange mixture of relief and shame before he looked away at his brother.

Annie followed his gaze. Edward was holding the short straw aloft, and he couldn't hide the excitement in his face. *He's pleased*, she thought dully. *He wants to go.*

'Don't look like that,' he said, glancing from his mother to Annie. 'I'll be a hero. I'll be the one getting all the glory, while poor old Jacob here has to stay at home. No hard feelings, brother?'

A strange look crossed Jacob's face. 'None,' he said after the tiniest of pauses. Taking a breath, he tossed his straw into the fire so that he could shake Edward's hand. 'None at all.'

'I'm going to join the Navy,' Edward said jubilantly. 'I'd already decided, if I pulled the short straw.'

'The Navy?' Maggie echoed in disbelief. 'You've never even seen the sea!'

'I have! We had a Sunday School outing, and once me and Annie got the bus to Scarborough. Remember, Annie?'

'Yes, I remember.' Edward had loved it but she had found the sea frightening. There was something remorseless about its heaving waves, the way it stretched grey and sullen to a dauntingly wide horizon. She remembered clinging to Edward's hand as they stood on the beach and shivered in the salty wind. She hadn't been able to wait to get home to the familiar fells, to the long stone walls and the wooded dales, where the buildings were grey but the grass was lush and green.

'All those U boats . . . ' Maggie sank into a chair, smoothing her hair back, distressed. 'What hope will you have if a torpedo hits while you're out at sea? Oh Edward, I wish you'd reconsider.'

Edward pulled out the chair next to her. 'Ma, it's going to be dangerous wherever I serve. That's what war's about.'

'Don't tell me what war's about,' Maggie said tightly. 'I know. I lived through four years of it. You think it's going to be exciting, don't you? Well, it won't be, I can tell you that now. It'll be dreary and hard and it will grind us all down, whether we go to fight or not. Your friends will be injured and they'll die. *You* might be injured or die, and we'll have to sit here and wait for news, not knowing if you're alive or dead or having your leg amputated or your brains blown out, and all for what?' She broke off with an exclamation of frustration. 'Oh, what's the use of talking to men about war?'

'I know it's hard, but I couldn't live with myself if I stayed at home while others risked their lives to keep us all safe.' He glanced at Joe. 'Pa, tell her.'

Joe had been listening intently without saying anything but now he nodded slowly, looking from one son to the other. 'Proud,' he said. 'Both of you.'

Edward's face relaxed. 'Thanks, Pa. So no

tears now, Ma, nor none from you, Annie,' he added as she lifted a hand to cover her trembling mouth. 'You understand, don't you?'

'No,' Annie heard herself say. 'No, I don't understand.' Her eyes blurred with tears. 'Excuse me, I'll just . . . I need to . . . ' Unable to think of an excuse but knowing she had to get out before she started howling, she grabbed her heavy coat from beside the door and walked out of the kitchen, ignoring Edward's demand for her to wait.

The cold hit her as soon as she stepped outside, and she gasped for breath as her chest tightened. She looked around blindly. She would freeze to death if she stood out here, but she couldn't go back to the kitchen, not yet. She headed for the stable instead, wading through the snow to pull open the heavy wooden door and stepping into the familiar fusty smell of straw and manure. The two carthorses, Daisy and Dora, greeted her with a whicker as they stood placidly chewing. Even Neddy the donkey had been brought inside to shelter from the cold with Bessie, the pony who pulled the trap that they were using more, now that petrol was rationed.

Edward found her there, rubbing the donkey between his furry ears. He didn't say anything immediately, but patted Neddy absently on his rump.

'He's getting fat.'

Annie knuckled tears from under her eyes. She didn't want to make this too hard for Edward, so she tried to steady the wobble in her voice.

'He's looking better than he did.'

10

'That's not hard. Remember what a state he was in when we brought him back?'

Annie had been out blackberrying a couple of years earlier when she had come across Oliver Skilbeck tormenting a frail donkey. Edward often teased her about how soft-hearted she was, but Annie couldn't bear the thought of anyone hurting an animal and when she saw what Oliver was doing, she hadn't stopped to think. Marching over, she had pushed him away from the donkey and shouted at him to stop being a cruel bully. 'And don't think I'm going to leave him here for you to start teasing him again as soon as I've gone! I'm taking him with me.'

Oliver had been so surprised at quiet Annie Pearson standing up to him that he had gaped at her as she snatched the rope from his hand. 'Have him if you want,' he sneered, recovering himself. 'He's just a waste of grass. I was taking him to the knackers anyway.'

'In that case, I'll definitely take him.'

'Hey, don't I get something in return?'

'No, you don't!' Annie's face was pink with temper, and Oliver's eyes sharpened with interest.

'Give me a kiss, and you can have him for free.'

She had recoiled in horror. 'I'm not kissing you! I hate you!'

'That's not very nice now, is it?' Oliver dodged round to block Annie's attempt to lead the donkey away. 'It's not like you don't kiss. Everybody knows you do it with Edward Sugden.'

'Leave me alone!' she cried when he grabbed her and she beat at him with her fists, but that

11

only seemed to excite Oliver.

'I always thought you were a mousy little thing, but there's a bit of spark to you, isn't there? Come on, just one kiss!'

'Take your filthy hands off her!'

Never had Annie been so glad to hear Edward's voice. He had pulled Oliver off her and the next moment the two lads were grappling on the ground. Edward had come away with a black eye and cut lip, but Oliver had fared even worse. He had never forgiven either of them for his humiliation. Not that Annie cared about that.

She and Edward had led Neddy back to Emmerdale Farm, where he had been enjoying retirement in a field with Bessie and the carthorses ever since. Her parents couldn't afford to keep animals, but any strays she rescued had to find a home at Emmerdale Farm. A tiny black kitten rescued from a sack thrown into the river was the one animal she had been able to take to the cottage, and that was only on the understanding that Sooty would feed himself on the mice in the outbuildings and other wildlife.

'It's all we can do to feed the three of us,' her father, Sam, had pointed out.

Annie scratched Neddy's nose. He was such a patient, sweet-tempered animal, she couldn't understand how anyone could have wanted to hurt him. 'You fought Oliver Skilbeck for me,' she reminded Edward.

'He made you cry.' Edward paused. 'And now *I've* made you cry. I'm sorry, Annie.'

'You wanted to get the short straw, didn't you?'

He hunched a shoulder. 'It's just ... I've

never been anywhere, or done anything. I don't want to be the one who stays here while the war happens somewhere else. At least this'll be a chance to see somewhere other than Beckindale.'

'What about me?' she asked, without looking at him.

'Annie, you know I love you, and I know you love me too.' He ducked his head, trying to meet her eyes and make her smile. 'We've always belonged together. The war won't change that. I'll come back to you, I promise, and we'll get married — if you'll wait for me.'

Annie looked up at that, her heart in her eyes. 'Of course I will, Edward. It's just . . . I'll miss you.'

'It won't be for ever, and meanwhile, let's make the most of the time we have together.'

'All right.' Sniffing unromantically, Annie offered a watery smile. 'I'd better get back to the dishes.'

'Ma said she'll do them. She gave me a right ticking off for not talking to you before all this, and told me to take you out for the rest of the afternoon. Come on,' he said grabbing her hand buoyantly and towing her towards the stable door. 'Got your gloves?'

'Where are we going?'

'I found the old sledge in the barn earlier. The snow's perfect right now. Let's go tobogganing and have some fun while we can.'

2

'Be *quiet*, children!'

Meg Warcup sighed and glanced yet again at the clock on the classroom wall. The children had been wild all day, poking at each other and chattering and crashing around like animals. She should just let them out, she thought. It was hopeless trying to get them to concentrate when it was snowing outside and the hill behind the Post Office was just begging to be climbed and slid down.

Through the window she could see Edward Sugden and Annie Pearson dragging a toboggan. In earlier years, she and Rosie would have been with them, and Jacob. They had all been part of a gang who had played and fought together for as long as Meg could remember.

And she had been the leader in most of the mischief, incredible as it seemed now. Old Miss Atkinson, the schoolmistress in their day, had sucked in her teeth whenever Meg's name was mentioned. 'She's a little devil,' an exasperated Miss Atkinson had told Robert Warcup more than once. 'She leads Rosie and the other children astray. Can't you and Mrs Warcup do anything to control her?'

How Miss Atkinson would stare if she could see Meg now! Meg caught a glimpse of her reflection in the schoolroom window: sensible shoes, obstinately straight dark hair drawn

14

severely away from her face, a stern expression.

Rosie would hate what she had become.

Meg felt her face twitch at the thought. Perhaps she could put all the children out of their misery and let them go early — but that would be rewarding them for their bad behaviour, wouldn't it?

Turning from the window, she saw Ruby Dubbs sliding out of her desk. 'Ruby, please sit down and open your book,' she said sharply.

'I've finished it,' said Ruby with one of her sullen looks.

Meg gritted her teeth. Ruby was an unattractive child, sour-tempered and sallow-faced. She and her little brother Stan were evacuees from Hull. They had been sent away from the city in the first wave of evacuations, part of a contingent of exhausted children, pregnant women and those nursing small babies who had ended up in Beckindale the previous autumn.

As schoolmistress, Meg had been the obvious choice as billeting officer for the village. She had spent many evenings cycling around trying to persuade the people of Beckindale to take in the evacuees. It was amazing how many had turned out to have palpitations or heart problems, which meant they couldn't offer a bed or two, but eventually Meg had found homes for all the evacuees, and at the end of a bewildering session when the hosts had descended on the village hall to pick up their reluctant guests, only two had been left without anywhere to go.

Ruby and Stan.

It was hardly surprising that no one had

wanted to give them a home, with scrawny Ruby glowering ferociously as Stan, even smaller and scrawnier, scratched the lice in his hair.

Meg had had the cottage to herself since her father had died. The last thing she wanted was to take on two children, let alone two as dirty and difficult as Ruby and Stan, but she could hardly leave them standing there in the middle of the village hall.

'You'd better come with me,' she had said with an inward sigh.

She had moved out of the tiny room she had shared with Rosie and now slept in her parents' old bed. After a battle royal, she had given both Ruby and Stan a good scrubbing in the tin bath in front of the fire, and combed the lice out of their hair. She fed them as best she could on their limited rations and made sure they were warmly dressed.

Of course it was right. Of course it was sensible. It was war, and everybody had to get on with things. But still Meg hated seeing Ruby sitting in Rosie's seat, hated knowing that she was sleeping on Rosie's side of the bed. Although she should be glad that the children were using the bed at all, Meg knew. When they had first arrived, she had found them curled up underneath the bed. It turned out they had never slept in one before. Stan was still wetting the bed at night, which meant Meg was constantly washing sheets when she had lessons to prepare and meals to cook and clothes to mend and a house to keep clean. Was it any wonder she was short-tempered?

To be fair, Ruby wasn't any happier with the

situation. She complained incessantly about being made to live in the country. It was too quiet, it was too dark, it was too smelly. She had never seen cows or pigs or even hens before, and Meg suspected she found the fells frightening. At the first opportunity, ten-year-old Ruby had taken Stan and headed back to Hull, though the village policeman, Jack Proudfoot, had come across them marching along the road to Ilkley and had promptly brought them back to Meg.

Ruby tried again a week later, and that time she and Stan made it all the way home. Meg was relieved to hear that they were safe, but was glad to have the cottage to herself again. The other evacuees were drifting home, too, as the threatened bombings never happened and the war seemed increasingly phoney.

The next day, though, Ruby and Stan were back, brought by their mother, Beryl Dubbs, a wiry, sharp-featured woman who had handed her children over to Meg as if they were parcels. 'You two bugger off,' she had said to them, her sharp eyes darting around the cottage. 'I want a word with Miss Warcup here.'

'But Mam — '

'I said *bugger off!*' Beryl screeched, rounding on Ruby. Stan flinched, but Ruby pressed her lips together and took his hand to lead him out of the room.

Meg felt obliged to offer Mrs Dubbs a cup of precious tea.

'Don't mind if I do.' She settled herself at the table and looked at Meg hopefully. 'Got a ciggie?'

'I'm sorry, I don't smoke.'

'Shame.' Beryl dug in her handbag and produced a cigarette of her own, lighting up and inhaling deeply, only for her thin frame to be shaken by a deep, phlegmy cough. 'Don't worry, I've given them both a good hiding for coming back the way they did,' she told Meg when she had recovered. 'I've told them they're to stay put.'

Meg was aware of an unexpected pang of sympathy for Ruby, who had gone to so much trouble to get back to this woman, who was clearly only too ready to get rid of them again.

'I think they were homesick,' she said carefully as she poured the tea.

'Ruby, she just likes to make trouble,' said Beryl dismissively. 'I can't be doing with them under my feet all day, not with my job in the munitions.' She blew smoke over the table, waved it carelessly away and coughed again. 'And now it's cost me an arm and a leg to bring them back here. So, what I was thinking was, how would you like to keep them?'

'Keep who?'

'Ruby and Stan. I reckon they'd be comfortable enough here. Better'n back in Hull.'

'I'll try to look after them while they're evacuated,' Meg said stiffly.

Beryl squinted at her through the cigarette smoke. 'I was thinking more like for good.'

'*For good?*' Meg goggled at her. 'You want me to *adopt* Ruby and Stan?'

'We don't need to do nothing official, like. They just stay here with you when the war's over. I daresay they'll be used to it by then, anyway.'

'What about their father?'

Beryl gave a crack of laugher. 'Him? He's not around to care. Buggered off after I had Stan, didn't he?'

Poor Ruby, Meg found herself thinking. Poor Stan. Unwanted and unloved by those who were supposed to care for them most. At least she knew what it was like to be part of a family, even if she had never been able to comfort her own parents after Rosie's death.

Now she looked across the table at Beryl Dubbs. 'There's no question of me adopting Ruby and Stan,' she said clearly. 'I'm sure they wouldn't want that, and I don't want it either. I'll look after them for as long as there's a need for evacuation, but after that I'll be sending them home to you.'

'Oh, well, it was worth a try.' Beryl stubbed out her cigarette in the saucer and eyed Meg's scraped-back hair and drab outfit dismissively. 'Sure you don't want to think about it? Could be your only chance to have kids, you know. You're not going to get a husband looking like that.'

'Quite sure, thank you,' said Meg tightly.

'Well, I'd better be getting back.' Beryl hauled herself to her feet and headed for the door.

'Aren't you going to say goodbye?'

Beryl rolled her eyes. 'Bye, kids,' she shouted up the stairs.

Ruby and Stan came clattering down the wooden stairs. 'Mam, take us with you,' Ruby begged, throwing her arms around her mother's waist. 'Please!'

'Give over, Rube,' said Beryl, impatiently

19

pulling Ruby's clinging arms away. 'You and Stan are going to stay here and no more running away. I don't want to see you at home again.'

'Mam — '

But Beryl was gone, shutting the door firmly behind her. Meg couldn't see Ruby's face, but her slumped shoulders told their own story.

'I'm sorry, Ruby,' she said.

Ruby was scowling when she turned. 'What did she want to talk to you about?'

'She just wanted to make sure I was looking after you and Stan properly,' Meg lied, but Ruby still looked suspicious.

'It isn't fair! We don't want to be here.'

'I know.'

'You don't want us here either.'

Meg sighed. 'Well, we're all just going to have to make the best of it, aren't we?' she said. 'Your mam's right, Ruby. You mustn't run away again. It's too dangerous. We're at war, and everyone's got better things to do than look for you.'

That had been just before Christmas, and Ruby had sullenly submitted to staying in Beckindale. Perhaps even she had realised it would be lunacy to run away when the whole country was gripped by freezing weather. It would be too soon to say that they were getting used to each other, but they had fallen into a certain routine at the little cottage by the bridge where Meg had been born.

She made the two children help with some of the chores. Ruby's effort was always grudging, but Stan was more willing. He was a very quiet little boy, too quiet for a six-year-old, and Meg suspected he didn't miss his mother nearly as much as his sister did, although Ruby was continually reminding him about her. 'Mam wouldn't want you to do that,' she would say the moment Meg suggested anything. 'Mam doesn't like that.' 'Mam would give you a skelping if you said that.'

Even so, Meg was glad to see that Stan was gradually coming out of himself, and would be making more friends if Ruby didn't drag him away from a group as soon as she saw that he was enjoying himself. 'We don't belong here,' she reminded him constantly. 'We hate the country.'

Unsurprisingly, she made no friends of her own. Part of the trouble was that she was intelligent, and far ahead of the others of her age. Meg remembered how that felt.

If Ruby said she had finished her book, she probably had.

Meg drew on her last reserves of patience. 'In that case, I'll find you a new book to read.'

'I don't want to read any more stupid books. What's the point of books? I want to go home! There isn't going to be any war. Everybody else has gone home to Hull. Why can't Stan and I?'

'I'm not having this argument again, Ruby,' Meg said tiredly. 'If you can't be polite, you can stay in after school and write out 'I must not speak to the teacher in an insolent way' a hundred times.'

Ignoring Ruby's glower, she turned to search along the bookshelves. Perhaps it was time to give nine-year-old Ruby a proper book to read. The school library was limited, but Meg pulled out *Five Children and It*, a book she had loved herself. In fact, this was probably the same book she had borrowed to read out loud to Rosie.

She dropped the book on Ruby's desk. 'Try this,' she said. 'It might be too hard for you, though,' she added casually, knowing that Ruby would be determined to prove her wrong. Sure enough, Ruby snatched up the book and opened it with such a defiant toss of her head that Meg almost smiled.

Quickly she wiped the amusement from her face and fixed the rest of the class with a glare. 'The rest of you, settle down and get on with your own reading.'

Oh dear, when had she turned into such a dreary schoolmarm? Meg rubbed her temples. Her head was aching and she longed to tell the children that school was over for the day, to throw open the doors and run outside with them, to grab whatever she could find and run up the hill so she could slip and slide down over the snow, laughing, the wet stinging her cheeks, her stomach clutching at the speed.

But of course she couldn't do that. How the children would gape to see her behave so foolishly! Their parents would complain. She wasn't madcap Meg any longer, she reminded herself sternly. She was respectable Miss Warcup, the schoolmistress, and her days of behaving badly were over.

3

'What's with the mardy face?'

Lily jumped at the poke on her arm. Huddled into her heavy coat and lost in her thoughts, she hadn't even noticed Jed as she trudged past the Woolpack.

'Don't do that!' she said, rubbing her arm and eyeing him crossly. 'You gave me a fright!'

Jed Dingle was the closest thing she had to a brother. Their fathers were cousins, and she and Jed had grown up together. The two families were very close — or had been, Lily thought bleakly, until her mother had died so suddenly five years earlier. Jonah and Dot Dingle had done their best to support Lily and her father through that terrible time, but since Mick had taken up with the scandalous Nina Lazenby relations had become frosty. Dot disapproved of Nina as much as Lily did.

Now Jed failed to look apologetic. 'You won't be much use to the Army if you get frightened by a poke in the arm,' he pointed out.

Lily had recently joined the ATS and was pleased as punch with her khaki uniform. She had grown up in a garage, and her father proudly introduced her as a first-rate mechanic, skills that she was now putting to good use at the new military training camp on the outskirts of Beckindale.

'At least I'm doing something useful,' she

retorted. 'Why haven't you joined up, Jed? You're nearly nineteen.' Jed might have been six months older, but Lily had always been more sensible, even before Rose Dingle's death had forced her to grow up sooner.

'It's my heart.' Jed tapped his chest and winked. 'Got an exemption, didn't I?'

'There's nothing wrong with your heart!'

'Got a paper that says different, Lil,' he said virtuously.

Lily sniffed her disapproval. 'And how did you get hold of that?'

Jed lowered his voice and glanced over his shoulder to make sure no one was listening — not that anyone else was out on the street in the freezing weather. 'A mate of mine rents out his doctor's certificate,' he said. 'Ten quid a pop, and cheap at the price, I say.'

'You should be ashamed of yourself,' said Lily, frowning. 'Everybody else is doing their bit for the war effort.'

Jed shrugged, unperturbed. 'Uncle Mick was the one who said that war is overrated,' he reminded her.

A shadow crossed Lily's face at the thought of her father. 'Do Auntie Dot and Uncle Jonah know you haven't joined up?'

'I'm doing my bit for morale in Beckindale by keeping the Woolpack going in their absence.'

Lily snorted. 'I don't know what they were thinking, leaving you and Larry in charge! It was asking for trouble!'

★ ★ ★

Larry was one of innumerable Dingle relations who had come over from Ireland armed only with a roguish charm and an entrepreneurial spirit, which he had used to the full since Jonah and Dot had taken their two youngest children travelling. Quite why Jonah should want to take his family to South Africa nobody in Beckindale understood, but Lily knew that Jonah's feet had grown increasingly itchy over the past few years, and he was keen for his children to see something of the world. Not that there was any question of luxury. Dot wrote wry letters about the cargo ship that had taken them down to the Cape of Good Hope, with Jonah determined to recreate his earlier travels.

Jed had refused to go, pointing out that Jonah had left home to make his own way at sixteen and that he too should be given the chance to be independent. It was hard for Jonah to argue against that, and in any case, it would clearly be more restful for everyone if Jed, who clashed frequently with both his parents, stayed at home.

Larry's arrival just when Jonah was planning the adventure seemed providential, and Larry leapt at the chance to keep an eye on Jed and the Woolpack. Lily wondered, though, if Jonah and Dot had any idea of the bad influence Larry was having on Jed. She was fond of both of them, but between the two men, they were giving the Dingles a bad reputation for shady dealings. The Woolpack was still the centre of the village but increasingly, too, it was the place you went if you wanted to get round the restrictions of rationing.

'You should say something to Uncle Jonah, Dad,' she had pressed her father, but Mick Dingle had shaken his head.

'I'm not getting involved, *asthore*, and neither should you. No one likes a tattletale. And it's not as if Larry or Jed are going to listen to me.'

'But what about our reputation?'

Mick had thrown his head back and laughed at that. 'Our reputation? We're not gentry, Lily. We're just an Irish family trying to get by. You worry too much about what people think. You do what you think is right, and let everybody else live their lives the way they want to. That's all you can do.'

Sometimes Lily thought her father was too easy-going for his own good. She wished he cared more about what other people thought. If he did, he would never have got involved with Nina Lazenby.

Jed noticed her scowl at the thought of Nina. 'Why are you looking so glum, anyway?'

'Oh . . . nothing,' said Lily, digging her hands deeper into her pockets. She might be fond of Jed, but there was no way she would confide in him.

'Why don't you come tobogganing with me?' he said, and for the first time she noticed the sledge he was holding. It was spanking new with gleaming runners.

'Where did you get that?' she asked, and he grinned.

'Fell off a lorry, didn't it? I've got more out the back,' he said, jerking his head at the Woolpack behind him. 'Thought I'd go up the hill and show it off, see if anyone fancies a new toboggan.'

'Don't you ever stop trying to do business, Jed?' she sighed.

'Come on, Lil, it'll be fun. You look like you could do with cheering up, and it's too cold to stand still.'

'Oh, all right,' she said, turning to walk with him. It wasn't as if she had anything to go home to. Nina Lazenby would probably be there, and it turned Lily's stomach to see her father with someone who was as different to her mother as could possibly be imagined.

Jed was right. It was fun to be back on a toboggan. Edward Sugden and Annie Pearson were there, too, and it was almost like old times to be skidding down the hill just as they had done when they were children with Meg and Rosie and Jacob.

Lily was breathless and laughing by the time Jed's demonstration of the toboggan's abilities had caught the attention of Oliver Skilbeck. 'I wish you hadn't sold it to him,' she whispered to Jed. 'He's such a creep!'

'He's a rich creep,' Jed pointed out, patting his pocket. 'And there's plenty more toboggans where that one came from.'

'I'd better get back, anyway,' Lily said. Her woollen gloves were clogged with ice, and they had tumbled off the toboggan into the drifts so many times that snow clung to her coat in great clumps. Jed brushed it off her back and turned so that she could return the favour.

Amicably, they trudged back through the snow

towards the village, but at the top of the street, Jed tensed at the sight of a figure ahead. 'Back me up, Lil,' he said out of the corner of his mouth.

'What for?'

'Just do it, okay?'

As they came closer to the figure, Lily recognised Sergeant Proudfoot, Beckindale's new policeman. Word in the village was that Jack had been a big-shot detective in Leeds before he had been invalided out to the country. The exact nature of his injuries, and whether it had been an accident or something more sinister had never been established, in spite of much speculation and swirling rumours about some unspecified tragedy in his background. Jack himself was close-mouthed on the subject. All that could be said for certain was that he walked with a limp still and had been sent to a quiet Dales village to recuperate after Constable Bates had enlisted.

'You'd think he'd be wanting a quiet life,' Larry had exclaimed in disgust when it became clear that far from resting up, Jack Proudfoot would be taking his job very seriously. It hadn't taken him long to get the measure of the Dingles.

Now Jack touched the peak of his cap to Lily but addressed himself to Jed. 'Jed Dingle, just the person I wanted to see.'

'Why's that, Sergeant?' asked Jed with a winning smile.

'I was wondering if you knew anything about a lorry that skidded off the Ilkely Road on Tuesday night?'

Jed pursed his lips and looked innocent. 'News to me.'

'Because by the time the driver got back with some help, the entire lorry had been emptied.'

Jed changed his look to one of concern. 'I'm sorry to hear that. What did it have in it?'

'Cans, mostly. Canned fruit, tins of meat, that kind of thing. All meant for the training camp.'

Jed tutted, and the policeman's eyes narrowed. 'Would you mind telling me where you were on Tuesday night?'

'Me?' Feigning surprise, Jed turned to Lily. 'Tuesday, let me see . . . Wasn't that the night you came round to have a read of Ma's letter, Lil?'

Put on the spot, Lily found herself the focus of Jack Proudfoot's uncomfortably shrewd gaze. He had been pointed out to her from a distance before, and she'd had the impression of a slight man with nondescript features, but close to, he seemed almost . . . dangerous.

What could she say? Jed was infuriating, but he was family. 'Yes, I think it was Tuesday.'

'Think?'

The corner of Lily's mouth twitched nervously but she made herself meet Jack's cool grey eyes. 'No, I'm sure it was Tuesday. That's the day I do a late shift at the camp. I'm in the ATS,' she said, even while she told herself to stop talking. Years ago, Jed had taught her that the key to successful lying was to keep your answers short and simple.

Typical Jed advice.

'And how long did you spend together?'

'Oh, well, it was quite a long time.' Lily

banged her frozen gloves together, her skin prickling with awareness of her lies. And something about Jack Proudfoot's penetrating gaze was making her conscious of her unpowdered face, without so much as a swipe of lipstick, and her bedraggled hair beneath her ATS cap.

Lily's one vanity, her hair, was a shimmering gold, and she rolled it carefully every morning. For no reason that she could explain, she wished Jack could see how neat and composed she could look. Perhaps it would make her lies more convincing, too. While her hair was inherited from Rose Dingle, Lily's dark blue eyes were her Irish father's, although in her case they were painfully transparent. She had always been a hopeless liar, as no doubt Jack Proudfoot could tell.

'We talked about family,' she floundered on. 'My aunt and uncle — well, they're not really my aunt and uncle, but I call them that — ' Jed's nudge brought her back to the point and she cleared her throat. 'Anyway, they're in South Africa. They went off to see something of the world, and then war broke out, so they've decided to stay there with my younger cousins, so whenever Jed gets a letter we share it round and then, you know, we talk about what they're doing and how much we miss them . . . '

Horribly aware that she was babbling again, Lily trailed off.

'I see,' said Jack. 'And am I right in thinking that Mr Larry Dingle was part of this cosy family chat, too?'

'He was indeed,' said Jed. 'We Dingles like to stick together.'

'I don't doubt that for a minute,' said Jack in a dry voice. 'You look cold, Miss Dingle,' he added. 'You'd better get home.'

'Yes, I am a bit cold,' said Lily, who had been shifting her frozen feet miserably in the snow. 'Thank you for your help.' Touching his cap once more, Jack moved off.

'That was sarcastic, in case you were wondering,' said Jed.

'Oh, Jed, how could you make me lie like that?' Lily whispered furiously. 'I'm sure he knew I wasn't telling the truth.'

Jed shrugged. 'What can he do about it?'

'Please don't ask me to do that again!'

'Oh, come on, Lil, it was just a little white lie. You did pretty well, I thought, and I think our sergeant fancies you, which wouldn't be a bad thing.'

In spite of the cold, Lily stopped dead and stared at Jed. 'How on earth can you say that?'

'Oh, I don't know,' said Jed vaguely. 'It was just something in his expression, that's all.'

'I thought he looked at me as if I was an . . . insect!'

'I might be wrong,' Jed allowed. He dug his elbow into Lily's side. 'So, do you want a tin of peaches?'

'Jed! Please don't tell me you do know about the missing tins!'

'What can I say?' Jed spread his hands. 'The lorry was just sitting there. Finders, keepers and all that.'

Lily pressed her lips together and shook her head. 'Sergeant Proudfoot's no fool. You'll go to prison if you're not careful, Jed.'

'I'm always careful,' he said gaily, which was completely untrue. His recklessness had caused his parents many a sleepless night.

'You might think about the rest of us. You're giving the Dingles a bad name,' she said, wincing inside at how stuffy she sounded. 'We've only just recovered from Uncle Caleb.' The village still liked to revisit the scandal of her father's brother, who had been a profiteer in the Great War and had eventually crashed to his death on the steep, twisty back road over Tegg's Hill. Rose Dingle had been tight-lipped on the subject of Caleb. Respectability had always been important to her, which was another reason Lily was uncomfortable with her father's friendship with Nina Lazenby.

'Yeah, well, if we're going to talk about bad names, mebbe you'd better have a chat to Uncle Mick, eh?' said Jed nastily. 'If he keeps carrying on with that slut Nina Lazenby, nobody will want owt to do with your side of the family, either.'

4

'We don't want women like Nina Lazenby in Beckindale,' Janet Airey announced, the click of her knitting needles as firm as her opinions.

There was a general murmur of agreement. The scandalous Mrs Lazenby was a popular topic of discussion at the WVS knitting circle. The stalwarts of the circle were the older women of the village, who could knit without so much as glancing at their needles, while Annie was constantly dropping stitches. She was a better cook than she was a knitter, but she had wanted to do something for the war effort, so she came along to the weekly sessions in the blacked-out village hall with her mother.

Grace Pearson always rolled her eyes at what she called the 'old cats' who enjoyed the chance of a good gossip, but Annie had to concentrate so hard on her stitches that she rarely caught much of it. She knew Nina Lazenby's name came up more than most, though. Mrs Lazenby dressed like a trollop and had a laugh that was downright rude. Mrs Lazenby held wild parties, widely suspected to be no better than (lowered voice) *orgies*. Mrs Lazenby didn't care what anyone thought. Mrs Lazenby had pictures of naked people on her walls. She was rumoured to have painted an actual naked *man* in her studio.

'She's an artist.' Meg Warcup was the only one who ever spoke up in Mrs Lazenby's defence.

'She's unconventional, that's all.'

'Oh, Meg dear, you are so easily taken in,' Mary Ann Teale always replied, patting her knee in a way you could just see set Meg on edge.

Annie admired Meg's willingness to say whatever she thought, even if it did sometimes put people's backs up. She had developed a brusque manner that could be intimidating at times. Strange to remember that when they were all growing up, Meg had been the leader, the naughtiest girl in the school by far. But when her twin sister had died, all the light and merriment had leaked out of her and she had retreated behind a prickly barrier that none of them had managed to penetrate.

Poor Meg, Annie often thought, knowing how lucky she herself was to have both her parents — and Edward, of course. As if losing Rosie hadn't been bad enough, Meg's mother had died soon after, it was generally agreed of a broken heart. Bob Warcup had lived another ten years but he too had died the previous year, leaving Meg all alone.

A sharp knock at the door was followed by Sergeant Proudfoot limping in and shutting the door quickly behind him as the conversation broke off and they all turned to stare at him, knitting needles paused mid-stitch.

'Sorry to interrupt,' he said in a remote voice, and nodded at a window in the corner. 'You've a light showing.'

'So there is,' tutted Janet Airey. 'Annie, you fix it, will you?'

Obediently, Annie jumped up and tugged the

blackout blind into place. She found the new policeman rather fearsome, and was glad she didn't have to have much to do with him.

'You're working late, Sergeant,' said Janet. 'The ARP wardens usually do the rounds when it gets dark.'

'I was on my way home when I spotted the light, that's all.' Jack Proudfoot clearly had no intention of telling Janet what he was doing out so late. 'Thank you, Annie,' he said curtly when she had finished, and, turning, he left with an abrupt nod to acknowledge the others.

'Well!' huffed Mary Ann Teale as soon as the door had shut behind him. 'What a rude man! Constable Bates was always so friendly and helpful. He would never have spoken to us like that.'

'Aye, he's a closed-mouthed one, that's for sure,' said Janet.

'What difference would a tiny chink of light make, anyway?'

'You don't want to be bombed, do you, Mary Ann?'

'Nobody's being bombed,' snapped Grace Pearson. 'And if Herr Hitler does ever get round to sending any planes over, he's not going to be bothered with Beckindale, is he? I can't stand this blackout business. I can't breathe in the evenings!'

Annie picked up her knitting and tried to remember where she had got to before Sergeant Proudfoot had come in. Her mother always seemed to be irritable at the moment, but then lots of people were nowadays. Since the

Germans had invaded Poland and war had been declared in September the previous year, life in Beckindale had gone on just as before, apart from the discomfort of the blackout and the inconvenience of rationing. They had all heard on the wireless about the terrible loss of HMS *Royal Oak* at Scapa Flow, of course, but no bombs had fallen in the Dales and people were on edge, wondering what, if anything, would ever happen.

But now young men like Edward were volunteering or being conscripted, and it felt as if the war was moving remorselessly onwards.

'If you ask me, that Sergeant Proudfoot is a bit too big for his boots,' Betsy Middleton, the butcher's wife, declared. 'He certainly seems to be taking his job very seriously,' she added with a sniff, and everyone knew she was thinking of the way he had confiscated several packets of sausages that Arthur Middleton had been keeping under the counter for friends and family.

'There's no sign of a Mrs Proudfoot,' Peggy Summers announced, apropos of nothing. Peggy ran the Post Office with her husband, Len, and was clearly in a position to know.

'I heard he was married but his wife died,' said Mildred Barlow. The Barlows were the village grocers and nearly as important a hub of gossip as the Post Office. 'It was a terrible tragedy.'

'Yes, wasn't that how he got his limp, too?' said Mary Ann. 'He survived and she didn't.'

'Perhaps that's why he's so short with everybody. Eaten up with grief, he is.'

'Unless he feels guilty?'

'*I* heard she was shot by gangsters,' Brenda Lane put in. 'And it wasn't his wife, it was his fiancée.'

There was a silence broken only by the click of knitting needles while they all considered the story.

'It doesn't sound very likely,' Janet decided in the end.

'None of it sounds likely,' said Meg sharply. 'Why can't he be an unmarried policeman recovering from an injury?'

'Why doesn't he just say, in that case?'

'Maybe he doesn't want everyone knowing his business.'

'Aren't you the least bit interested, Meg?' Sarah Barlow asked. After Edward, Sarah was Annie's best friend, a cheerful bleached blonde generally considered to be 'flighty'.

Meg frowned. 'I'm interested in him making sure people don't break the law.'

The old Meg would never have said anything so stuffy. Lifting her gaze from her knitting, Annie studied her, trying to see the tousle-haired girl in the rigid figure sitting across from her in the circle. Rosie had been the pretty twin, the sweet one, the good one, while Meg was the opposite: sharp where Rosie was soft, her pale grey eyes a striking contrast to her dark, straight hair and soaring brows. Not that she was ugly. Annie thought Meg could be really attractive if she loosened her hair and let her mouth relax into a smile.

Janet Airey was still talking about Sergeant Proudfoot. 'If he's going to uphold the law, he'd better keep an eye on the Woolpack. Those Dingles are a disgrace! I hope Dot doesn't know what her lad is up to. It would break her heart!'

'What do they want to go to Africa for, anyway?' grumbled Mary Ann. 'Africa, I ask you! I thought Dot was too sensible for that kind of carry-on.'

'That Jonah Dingle always did have strange ideas,' Janet agreed. 'If you ask me, all those Dingles are an odd lot. Remember that Caleb?'

Meaningful looks and nods all round, even from those who, like Annie, had been born after his notorious death.

'Mick Dingle's all right,' Grace said.

'I used to think so, too,' said Peggy, 'until he took up with that Lazenby woman.'

'Dear Rose must be turning in her grave,' Mary Ann sighed.

'And as for Lily . . . whoever heard of a female mechanic?'

'Only anyone who's ever heard of the ATS,' said Meg, obviously exasperated. 'At least Lily is doing her bit for the war effort.'

'We're all doing what we can, Meg,' Mildred Barlow reproved her. 'Why do you think we're all here? We're not knitting socks for the troops for the fun of it.'

As the talk turned to the usual grumbles about rationing, Annie went back to her knitting. Her bottom lip was caught between her teeth as she tried to concentrate on her needles, but she was thinking how well they all knew each other. The gossip always ran on well-worn tracks, but there was something comforting about that. It must be awful to live in a city, she decided. She couldn't imagine choosing to live amongst strangers instead of in the country, where you knew exactly who everyone was.

Beside Annie, Sarah Barlow gave her a nudge. 'Well, I think he's dishy,' she confided in a whisper.

'Who?'

'Sergeant Proudfoot, of course. I wouldn't mind consoling him for the loss of Mrs Proudfoot, if she ever existed!'

'Really?' Annie looked dubious. 'But he's so . . . aloof.'

'I like a challenge,' said Sarah with a wink. 'There's something about that my-work-is-my-all kind of thing that's quite exciting, don't you think?'

'No,' said Annie frankly, and Sarah rolled her eyes.

'Oh, you! I might have known you wouldn't understand! You've only got eyes for Edward.'

Annie couldn't help smiling. 'True.'

'When does he leave for training?'

Her smile faded. 'Tomorrow.' She had been trying not to think about Edward going. It was ten days since he had drawn the short straw, and even now she couldn't quite believe he would actually leave Beckindale. Would actually leave *her*.

Sarah squeezed her hand sympathetically. Everyone knew about the bond between Annie and Edward and they were always spoken of together, as if they were one unit, not two separate people. Annie was so used to being half of Edward-and-Annie that she wasn't sure how she was going to manage on her own. What was the point of her without Edward? she wondered. She kept getting an image of herself lurching uselessly to one side without him, just waiting for him to come back and pull the world back into place.

★ ★ ★

The stars were so bright when they left the village hall that Grace switched off the torch she had brought with her. 'I don't know why we bother with a blackout on a night like this,' she sighed, shoving the torch into the pocket of her coat and tightening her belt. 'Any bomber could see exactly where he's going.'

Annie didn't answer. Absorbed in her thoughts about Edward and the dread of saying goodbye to him the next day, she walked next to her mother in silence, broken only by the squeak of snow beneath their boots.

'Grace? Annie? Is that you?' The way back to the shepherd's cottage took them through the Emmerdale farmyard. Maggie Sugden must have been listening out for the creak of the farmyard gate because she opened the kitchen door a crack and beckoned them in.

'Is everything all right, Maggie?' Grace pulled off her gloves as they stepped into the familiar kitchen. A paraffin light hissed gently on the table but the atmosphere in the room was anything but peaceful. Joe was sitting by the fire, his head bent and his hands between his knees. It was never possible to read an expression in the ruined features, but his body language was eloquent of distress. Maggie, too, was visibly upset. She was pacing up and down, twisting her fingers together, and there was no sign of either of her sons.

Annie looked around, instinctively searching for him. 'Where's Edward?'

'That's why I wanted to catch you. He's gone out.'

'Out? It's freezing out there!'

'I know. I want you to find him, Annie. He only left a few minutes ago, and he didn't take anything with him. He just stormed out . . . ' Maggie's voice broke.

It didn't sound like Edward at all. 'But why?'

'I . . . I was trying to persuade him not to join up after all. I wanted him to know there's no shame in not fighting, but he wouldn't listen. I was desperate,' Maggie went on. 'He's leaving tomorrow. Once he's done his training, there'll be no way back. I had to try, and the only way I could think of was to tell him something I've kept secret from him a long time. It was a mistake, I can see that now,' she said. 'I should have told him years ago, but there never seemed a reason to before. I never dreamt he would volunteer to go and fight.'

Beside Annie, Grace lowered her voice. 'Did you tell him about Hugo?'

'Yes.' Maggie glanced at Joe, but he seemed lost in his thoughts beside the fire. 'I told all of them.'

'Told them what?' asked Annie, baffled.

41

Maggie and her mother seemed to be speaking in riddles.

Grace ignored her. She was looking at Maggie with concern. 'How did they take it?'

'I told Joe last night. He knew. He's always known.' She swallowed. 'I wasn't sure. We never talked about it. There didn't seem any point. I was just glad he was ready to accept it.'

Annie looked between Maggie and her mother in frustration. Accept what? And who was Hugo?

'And the boys?' Grace asked, and Maggie shook her head, her face crumpling.

'Not good. Jacob just turned on his heel and went upstairs. He didn't say a word. And Edward . . . ' Her voice broke. 'Edward's so angry with me. I'm afraid he'll never forgive me.'

She turned to Annie. 'You'll know where he's gone, Annie. Please, can you find him and talk to him? Get him to come home. I understand if he doesn't want to talk to me, but I can't bear to think of him out in the cold.'

'I don't understand,' said Annie, baffled. Edward adored his mother. What had made him so angry?

Maggie hesitated. 'I think Edward should tell you. It's his secret now.'

The barn in the West Field had always been their special place. Annie went straight there, following Edward's footsteps but at times still sinking up to her knees in snow. She found him lying in the hay, an arm thrown over his face.

'Did she tell you?' he asked without looking at her.

'No.' Annie sat down beside him, pulling her

42

coat more closely around her. 'I don't understand what's happened. Mum said something
about a Hugo. Who's he?'

'My father, apparently.'

'Your *father*? But Joe . . . '

Edward dropped his arm and propped himself
up on his elbows. His normally good-humoured
face was bleak. 'Yes, it turns out that Joe isn't
my dad after all. I'm not a real Sugden. No: not
only am I a bastard, but I'm the son of a
conscientious objector in the last war.' He
practically spat out the last words as Annie's
mouth dropped open. 'My father was a coward,
and Ma thinks that should make me think twice
about joining up! She said I should be *proud* of
him, can you imagine that?' He gave a mirthless
laugh. 'She didn't even sound ashamed!'

Annie could hardly take it in. Together with
her parents, the Sugdens were the constants in
her world, the solid pillars that she had taken for
granted all her life. She had thought she knew
them all inside out, and now it appeared that
Maggie, sturdy, straight-backed Maggie, had
taken a conscientious objector to her bed . . .
and Annie's mother had known. It was a secret
she had kept close.

Realising that the two women who meant the
most to her had kept such a secret from everyone
was making Annie's head reel. It was nothing to
do with her, she knew, but she couldn't help
feeling betrayed. And if she felt like that, how
much worse must Edward feel? Annie didn't
know what to say, but she knew he needed
comfort.

'Oh, Edward!' She opened her arms and he buried his face against her breast, clinging to her.

'What am I going to do now?' he said, muffled against her coat. 'I don't know who I am any more. Thank God Jacob didn't pull the short straw. Imagine if he'd been going to fight and I was the one staying at Emmerdale Farm, not even a real Sugden.'

'You are a Sugden, Edward. You've grown up as a Sugden. That's not going to change.'

'Isn't it? I'm going off to war tomorrow and I don't even know if I'll have a home to come back to.'

'Of course you will,' said Annie, stroking his hair. 'You'll come back to me, Edward. I'm your home.'

'Sweet Annie.' Edward lifted his head to kiss her. 'At least I know you'll never change.'

'Never,' she promised. 'I'll always love you, Edward.'

Letting out a long sigh, Edward rested his head back on her breast. 'I'll never forgive Ma for this,' he said in a low voice. 'Never.'

Summer 1940

5

Sunshine dappled through the trees as Lily drove to the station through the familiar fells, criss-crossed with slanting grey stone walls. The hedgerows were tangled with long grass and wildflowers, and sheep grazed high on the lush green hills. It was such a tranquil scene that she could almost persuade herself that the country wasn't at war.

But braking at a junction, she realised that the signposts had been taken down, and when she walked onto the platform, the familiar sign announcing ILKLEY had been blacked out. The sight gave Lily a queer feeling in the pit of her stomach. The blackout was a bore and rationing tiresome, but blacking out destination boards brought home more than anything else the real prospect that the Germans might invade.

Lily tried to imagine what that would be like. She wanted to think that it couldn't happen, but in May Hitler's forces had overrun Norway and Denmark, and then Belgium and Holland . . . the Channel was all that stood between Britain and the same fate.

The station was busy, and the number of people in uniform was another sign of the reality of war, Lily thought. She was glad that she was wearing her own uniform and she tugged her jacket into place, proud of the stripes on her sleeve that showed she had been promoted to corporal.

Only the night before, she had sewed the

second stripe onto her jacket, and when she appeared in her uniform that morning, Mick's eyes had filled with tears.

'Ah, *mavourneen*, I'm so proud of you. You look so like your mother . . . I wish she could see you now.'

Then Lily had wanted to cry, too. Rose Dingle had dropped dead five years earlier. A brain aneurysm, the doctor had said sombrely. There had been nothing anyone could do. One minute Rose had been standing at the sink, humming to herself. The next she was dead on the floor. Lily had been thirteen at the time. She would never forget coming home from school to the sound of her father sobbing on the stairs.

It had been the two of them from then on, and Lily had missed her mother every day. She loved working in the garage with her father, but it was Rose she had idolised. Rose had been a vicar's daughter, and was widely considered in Beckindale to have 'married down', although Rose herself had never regretted marrying Mick for a moment. Lily remembered her mother as beautiful and gentle and loving, and in the years since her death that memory had become burnished into perfection. Rose was refined. She had taught Lily her table manners and how to behave properly. She never raised her voice or argued, and always seemed to know the right thing to say or do. Lily would look at her school friends, whose mothers were roughly affectionate at best and more likely to clip their children round the ear than gather them into a perfumed hug, and she would thank God for Rose.

It had been a golden childhood. Rose and Mick adored each other, and Lily was the centre of their world, innocently taking her happiness and good fortune for granted. Rose's death had put an end to that. In their grief, Lily and Mick had clung to each other for comfort, slowly building a new life, although Rose's absence was still raw.

And then Nina Lazenby had arrived in Beckindale.

Lily loved her father and wanted him to be happy. After five years of widowhood, he was entitled to look for someone new, she told herself endlessly, but why did he have to choose Nina Lazenby of all people?

Nina was an artist, or so she said. Lily presumed that explained the trousers Nina wore and the bohemian way she tied her hair up in garish scarves. She had moved to the village three years earlier and had proceeded to scandalise her neighbours, who soon discovered that Nina had been divorced not once but *twice*. That hadn't gone down well in Beckindale.

Nina didn't seem to care what anyone thought of her. She invited friends to stay and they took over the Woolpack in noisy groups. With her red hair, her lush figure and her smoky, raucous laugh, it was hard to imagine anyone more different to Lily's beautiful, elegant mother.

'What do you *see* in her?' she had asked Mick once, genuinely baffled.

'She makes me laugh,' Mick said. 'She doesn't try to be anything she's not. I like that. You should give her a chance, Lily. You've got more in common than you think.'

Lily couldn't imagine that she and Nina could possibly have anything in common. She resented the way the woman had so casually annexed Mick. Nothing had been the same since Nina had sauntered into Beckindale nearly a year ago.

Mick was as affectionate as ever, but Lily felt as if she had lost him. She was lonely and jealous. It wasn't a good feeling, and not fair on her father, Lily knew, but she couldn't seem to get over it. The war at least had given her a new focus, and she was determined to make a new life for herself so she wasn't as reliant on Mick.

When war had been declared, Lily had leapt at the opportunity of joining the ATS. Thanks to her father, she knew how to drive and was already a skilled mechanic before she joined the service. She hadn't enjoyed basic training, Lily had to admit, but she had stuck it out and been posted back to the training camp that had been built, like the one in the previous war, in the fields of Emmerdale Farm. As accommodation was in such short supply, she had continued to live at home with Mick, though she hated going home to find Nina there or, worse, to find the garage empty and knowing that Mick was with Nina.

But now she had been promoted, she was a staff driver and her first assignment was to pick up Derek Mortimer, the new commander of the training camp. Lily was determined to impress him.

Between the training camp, evacuees, refugees and the new prisoner of war camp being constructed beyond the Skilbecks' farm, the area was much busier than normal. Most of the men on the platform were in uniforms of one kind or another. The majority were in khaki, but Lily could see the pale blue of the Royal Air Force and, unusually, the darker blue of the Royal Navy. Craning her neck, Lily recognised Edward Sugden. She had seen him in the Woolpack, on leave after his training, but it looked as if he would be going to join his ship today.

Edward glanced up and caught Lily's gaze. She smiled but didn't go over, as he had his arm around Annie, who looked as if she was struggling not to cry. Poor Annie, Lily thought. She would miss Edward terribly.

Lily's mother had been a romantic. She had always told Lily that one day she would meet someone special, someone she could love as deeply as Rose and Mick loved each other, and Lily was longing for that to happen. She might envy Annie's contentment with Edward, but she herself was looking for something more. She wanted passion, she wanted excitement. She wanted to be swept off her feet.

Not that there was much sign of that happening yet, Lily had to admit with an inward sigh. With the ratio of men to women in the training camp, she got lots of attention, of course, but there was no one she really liked, and she didn't want to get a bad reputation. She was holding out for someone really special.

And that was not going to be the private sauntering over to her on the platform.

'What about a last kiss, Corporal?' he said with a wink.

'Good luck to you, but I'm out of kisses.' Lily tried to make a joke of it, but the soldier wouldn't take the hint and kept pestering her.

She gritted her teeth and did her best to be nice without encouraging him, but she was growing more and more flustered until suddenly the private seemed to be being lifted bodily away to be deposited at some distance on the platform. Lily's intense relief turned to mortification when she realised that her saviour was none other than Jack Proudfoot.

'Take yourself off,' he said to the soldier. 'The lady said no.'

The private scowled and jerked aggressively at his jacket, but after a look at Jack's uniform and another at his face, he slunk off, muttering under his breath about frigid virgins.

Jack turned back to Lily. 'Are you all right?'

'I'm fine.' Her cheeks burned as she straightened her hat. Why did he always find her at a disadvantage? 'Thank you,' she added belatedly.

'You shouldn't have to put up with that kind of behaviour.'

'He's just an ass,' Lily tried to dismiss the matter. The way he was watching her with those penetrating eyes was making her feel guilty. 'What are you doing here?' she asked to change the subject, but even to her own ears she sounded peevish.

'We've had reports of goods being pilfered from trains locally,' he said. 'I don't suppose you've been offered any sugar or cheap cigarettes recently?'

'I'm not in the habit of dealing on the black

market, Sergeant,' said Lily stiffly.

'That's not something that can be said about all the members of your family, is it? I haven't been in Beckindale long, but Dingle is the name that usually comes up when I'm investigating. Tell me,' Jack went on while Lily was still searching for a quelling reply, 'why isn't Jed in the Army?'

Oh, God, now she was going to have to lie some more! Lily flushed, remembering Jed telling her how he had avoided conscription. 'He, um, he has a bad heart.'

Jack raised a disbelieving eyebrow. 'He doesn't look like an invalid to me. Has he had this condition long?'

'I believe it only came up in his medical. Why the interest in my family, anyway?' she asked, deciding to go on the attack. 'Shouldn't you be dealing with more important things?'

'Like what?'

'What about all these German spies parachuting into the country?'

'Have you seen one?'

'Of course I haven't. I would have reported it at once if I had!'

'You seem very well informed about them.'

'I heard a farmer on the other side of Ilkley had found pieces of parachute stuffed down rabbit holes,' she said. 'And wasn't there a dentist discovered with a transmitting set hidden in his chimney? Those are the people you should be chasing, not Jed,' she told him crossly.

'I think you'll find that reports of spies dropping from the skies are no more than rumours,' said Jack. 'I can assure you that if there was any evidence at all of traitors operating in the area, I would be pursuing them,' he went on, and Lily was perversely pleased to have nettled him. 'As it is, the black market is much more of a threat to law and order than exaggerated gossip, which is why I'm keeping an eye on the Dingles, and on Jed Dingle in particular.'

To Lily's intense relief, the train was drawing into the station with a confusion of steam and hissing brakes. Mindful of her role, she stood to attention while she waited for Colonel Mortimer to alight, but she wished Jack would go away. She was very aware of him standing next to her, scanning the crowd with his eyes, and she edged off, not wanting it to seem as if they were together.

An officer tossed a case onto the platform and descended from the train. Surely he was too young to be a colonel? But wait . . . Lily checked the pips on his shoulders. This must be him!

Ignoring Jack, she marched over to him and saluted smartly. 'Colonel Mortimer?'

He returned the salute. At closer quarters he wasn't as young as she had first thought — in his forties, she guessed — but he turned out to be even more attractive than her initial impression. Tall, lean-limbed and clean-jawed, he had slightly pouchy eyes fanned by laughter lines and a smile that creased his cheeks in a way that made Lily's heart stumble.

'Corporal Dingle, sir,' she said. 'I'm your driver.'

'Excellent.' His smile widened appreciatively

as he looked her up and down and Lily felt colour creep into her cheeks. 'A local girl, I take it from your accent?'

'Yes, sir.'

'So you'll know your way around?'

'Yes, sir. The jeep's just outside, sir.'

'I'm beginning to feel better about my appointment already,' he said and bent to pick up his case. 'Lead on, Corporal.'

Lily spun on her heel only to find herself nose to nose with Jack Proudfoot, and they had to do one of those dances where each one tried to dodge past, only to find that the other was trying to do exactly the same thing.

Jack raised his brows. 'Goodbye, Lily,' he said with what Lily thought was deliberate provocation. Then he nodded at Derek Mortimer. 'Colonel.'

'Sergeant.'

Derek Mortimer had watched the awkward little scene with amused interest. 'Friend of yours?' he asked.

Lily scowled as she led him outside to the jeep. 'Absolutely not,' she said.

6

Out of the corner of her eye, Annie saw Lily Dingle leaving the station with a senior-looking officer. Someone who was staying, not going. The way Edward should be staying.

To Annie's dismay, Edward had gone off to naval training the day after the revelation about his real father without saying a word to his mother. He had left in mid-February when the snow was still on the ground, and returned on a glorious June day. Four months, he had been gone, and then all he had was a week's leave before being posted. It hadn't been nearly long enough as far as Annie was concerned.

'Please try and get him to understand,' Maggie had begged Annie before Edward came back. 'I know it was a shock to him, and perhaps I shouldn't have told him, but it was the only way I could think of to persuade him to stay on the farm.' She sighed and looked straight at Annie. 'I lost the two men I loved in the past war. I can't bear the thought that I might lose Edward, too.'

Two men? Annie had always been in awe of Maggie, who was so strong and straight-backed, and she was struggling with the idea of her as a young, passionate girl.

'But what about ... ?' she had asked awkwardly.

'Joe?' Maggie understood instantly. 'I didn't love Joe. You don't know what he was like before the war, Annie,' she said.

The two women were in the dairy, making butter. Annie worked the churn, while Maggie weighed the previous lot of butter they'd made into pounds and rolled into cones.

'He was brutal,' she went on. 'He beat me. He killed my dog,' she said, glancing to where her faithful collie, Ben, lay panting in the shade of the elder bush planted at the door to keep the flies away. 'And he nearly killed me. When he went to fight, he raped me and left me to run this farm on my own while I was expecting Jacob.'

Annie's arm was tiring and she slowed the churn, wiping her sleeve across her forehead. She was shocked at what Maggie had told her. To Annie, Joe had always been a gentle giant. It was hard to imagine him being violent to Maggie, and the thought of him killing a dog made her feel ill. 'I didn't know,' she said inadequately.

'No one knew, or if they did, they wouldn't help me. The only one who did was a Quaker whose beliefs wouldn't allow him to fight but who wanted to do his bit in spite of all the abuse he got. Just like now, it was important for farms to keep producing food, so he came to do the hard labouring for me.'

'Was he Edward's father?'

'Hugo.' Maggie nodded, her face softening as she said the name. 'I wish Edward could have known him. He was so . . . You know that shining quality Edward has? The way you just feel that he's honest and kind and . . . and *good*?'

Annie couldn't help smiling as she nodded.

She knew exactly what Maggie meant.

'Well, he gets that from Hugo. Hugo was the bravest man I've ever known, and the best.'

Did a good man sleep with another man's wife? Annie wondered. Then cursed her expressive face as Maggie glanced at her with a faint smile.

'I know what you're thinking, but for two years we were just friends, whatever anyone thought. We loved each other, but I was married to Joe. I'd made my vows to him in church, and I wasn't brought up to break a promise I'd made. But so many men were dying, so many decent men, it began to seem as if Joe would surely die too. I hoped he would,' Maggie confessed, her hands still busy rolling out the butter. 'It was wrong of me, I know, but I hated him for what he'd done.'

'But he didn't die.' Caught up in Maggie's story almost against her will, Annie took hold of the handle of the churn once more. She couldn't believe that she hadn't heard all this before. What was it she had thought at the knitting circle? That in a village like Beckindale, they all knew everything there was to know about each other?

'No, he didn't die. He came home, but he was different. It's a miracle that he survived an injury like that. For a long time, he couldn't speak. He wasn't really alive. He just sat and looked at nothing. Hugo said it wasn't right for him to stay then, so he went to drive ambulances at the front. We agreed that it would be wrong to write to each other, so it was another goodbye.'

'Did you miss him?'

'Do you miss Edward?'

With every painful beat of her heart, Annie thought. She nodded.

'That's how I missed Hugo.' Maggie's expression was sad as she remembered those bleak times. 'But I had a farm to run and a sick husband to care for. And I had a child to live for.' She looked up from the butter. 'I know everyone thinks Edward is my favourite, but I love Jacob just as much. He hasn't forgiven me either,' she added with a sigh. 'He hasn't said anything, but I know he resents me now. He doesn't understand that everything I did, I did for him. When you have children, Annie, you'll understand.'

'What happened to Hugo?' Annie asked after a moment.

'After he was demobilised, he came back one cold winter night to tell me that he had survived — and, I think, to see if Joe was still alive. Which he was, but barely. So Hugo said he would emigrate, that it was wrong to come between a man and his wife. He said he would go the next day. I made him a bed in the little room above the stable.' Maggie glanced through the open door of the dairy to the stable across the farmyard. 'We just had that one night to say goodbye.'

Sighing, she laid down the last pat of butter. 'Your mum was here then,' she told Annie. 'She looked after Jacob and Joe, and I went to say goodbye to Hugo. That was the night Edward was conceived.'

'Mum never said anything about this to me!'

'Grace has been a good friend,' said Maggie. 'She didn't judge me. I've always been grateful to her for that. I'm not ashamed of what Hugo and I did together that night. We loved each other, and that was our one and only chance to express it. And how could I regret anything that gave me Edward?'

Annie took another rest from the churning, shaking out her tired arm as she digested what Maggie had said.

'Does Hugo know about Edward?' she asked. 'Where is he now?'

'Here.'

'*Here?*'

Maggie pressed her lips into a firm line to steady them. 'He had Spanish flu. Sometimes it was like that. You'd be fine in the morning and dead by nightfall. He died in the stable and we buried him down by the river. I still go and sit there sometimes in the summer,' she said. 'I talk to him and I tell him about Edward. I know he would have been proud of his son.'

'Why didn't you tell Edward about all this before?'

'What would have been the point? He's grown up thinking Joe's his father. Joe's different now. I didn't want to tell Edward — or Jacob — what Joe used to be like. If it hadn't been for this *bloody* war . . . ' Maggie burst out, slamming her hand down on the newly rolled butter, squishing it out of shape and making Annie jump. 'How many more men have to go off and die before they'll stop fighting?' she demanded. '*How many?* And now Edward is going to go and fight too, and because I tried to stop that, he hates me.'

Maggie's voice broke at last. 'I wish I hadn't told him now. I drove him away. He'll go, and I won't even be able to hold him when I say goodbye.'

Annie's eyes filled with tears of sympathy. She put an arm around Maggie's heaving shoulders, thinking about the times over the years that Maggie had comforted her for a scraped knee or a sore tooth, for losing a childish game or a harsh word. Maggie had always seemed invincible, so strong and stoical that seeing her weep knocked one of the corners of Annie's world askew.

'I'll talk to Edward,' she promised. 'When he comes back, I'll make him understand.'

★   ★   ★

It hadn't been that easy, though. When his training ended, Edward had a week's leave before joining his ship. On the face of it, he was his usual cheerful self, but he spoke to Maggie with a rigid politeness that clearly broke her heart. The weather was glorious, and although there was work as always to do on the farm, by tacit agreement Annie and Edward were spared, and they spent every minute they could together.

Their favourite place was down at the beck, where the holm oaks leant over the water and the grass grew long and sweet. This was where Hugo had been buried, Annie realised, although there was no trace of him now. As a Quaker, he'd had

61

no cross or stone to mark his grave, but perhaps his spirit lingered. Perhaps that was why Edward had been drawn to the spot so often over the years.

She wanted to ask him if he knew about his father's resting place, but Edward turned aside all her attempts to coax him into talking, diverting her with a joke instead or rolling her beneath him to kiss her. 'Let's not talk about boring old history now,' he would say. 'Let's just make the most of this week. Let me tell you how pretty you are instead.'

But the day before it all came to an end, Annie could let it go no longer. She was paddling barefoot in the cool water while Edward lounged on the bank in the dappled shade. He was chewing a piece of grass, and staring up through the leaves at a sky so blue and beautiful it made Annie's chest ache. In the distance, they could hear the tractor as Jacob took advantage of the weather to cut the hay and, even further afield, the faint sounds of gunfire and barked commands from the training camp.

Edward's expression was brooding, and Annie waded out of the water to sit beside him, curling her damp toes in the grass.

'You need to talk to me,' she said.

'I don't know how to,' said Edward. 'When Ma told me, it was like she'd kicked my legs out from underneath me. I don't know who I am any more.'

'You're Edward,' she said gently. 'Knowing who your real father is hasn't changed who you are.'

'It feels as if it has.' He threw the grass away. 'How could she do it, Annie?'

'She loved Hugo, Edward. Really loved him. It wasn't just a fling because she was bored.'

'Does that make it better?'

Annie hesitated. 'I think it does. If I had to marry . . . I don't know, Oliver Skilbeck, say . . . it wouldn't stop me loving you.'

Edward reached for her then, pulled her down to lie against him. 'Don't even say that, Annie. You're not to marry anyone but me,' he said. 'I need you.'

'Not as much as I need you,' she said.

He brushed a curl away from her face. 'You think that, but you're wrong. I know it seems like I can go anywhere and talk to anyone, but I can only do that because I know you're here, waiting for me. You don't realise how important you are,' he went on, dropping a kiss on her lips. 'You're stronger than you know, Annie love. I may be going on a big ship, but you're my anchor.'

Dropping his forehead to hers, he looked deep into Annie's eyes. 'I wish we'd had time to get married. The first time I have leave, let's do it. We won't wait until we can afford it.'

Annie wound her arms around his neck. 'Let's pretend we're married now,' she whispered. 'Let's pretend the war is over and that you're back safe and that this is our honeymoon. We don't need to go away or to have a fancy bedroom. We just need this beck and this patch of grass.'

'Here?' Edward began to smile as he realised what she meant and she smiled back at him.

'There's no one around,' she said. 'Here. Now.'

'You sure, Annie?'

She thought of Maggie and the one night she had spent with Hugo, of how Edward's mother had never once regretted what she had done. Of course she and Edward had kissed and petted, but Annie had always assumed they would wait until they were married before they went all the way. But now they were at war, and they couldn't count on anything beyond the moment.

'Oh yes,' she said, squirming pleasurably as Edward's hands slid urgently up her bare leg, still damp from the beck. 'I'm sure.'

Afterwards, Edward held her close, and she rested her cheek on his bare chest while his hand gentled up and down her back. Slowly she drifted back to reality, feeling the tickle of grass against her skin, the stickiness between her thighs. Jacob was still driving the tractor; she could hear the grumble of the engine as he changed gear at the top of the field. Strange to think that nothing momentous had happened in his world, while hers had changed completely.

'No regrets?' Edward asked, and Annie pulled herself up to look down on him. Her curly hair tumbling around her flushed face, her mouth curved in a smile.

'Not one,' she said. 'I didn't know it would feel that good. Do you reckon that's because we love each other?'

'I reckon so,' he said with a grin.

She hesitated. 'Please, Edward, talk to Maggie before you go. She was in love, too. She's still your mother. You can't undo the last twenty years, and who knows what's going to happen in this war? I'm afraid you'll regret it terribly if you leave things the way they are. She doesn't expect you to forgive her, but she needs to be able to say goodbye to you properly.'

Edward's grin faded, but then he nodded. 'I'll talk to her.'

★   ★   ★

Annie didn't know, what had been said, but she had watched with relief as Edward gave his mother a farewell hug that morning and climbed into the ancient farm truck Mick Dingle had sold them many years earlier. A grim-faced Jacob drove Edward to the station, Annie squeezed in the middle. Edward's arm was behind her head, but as the truck jolted down the farm track, she kept being thrown against Jacob.

Since Maggie's revelations, Edward's brother had been more taciturn than ever. The Sugdens had never been demonstrative, but they'd always been a unit. The truth about Edward's birth seemed to have cracked the family apart. Meals were always going to be more silent after Edward left for training, but when he'd come home on leave, the atmosphere jangled still between the brothers, and between the sons and their mother. Discovering that his mother had been unfaithful might have been a blow to Jacob, but it had surely been much harder for Edward, Annie thought, and she was glad that he and Maggie had managed a proper goodbye.

Jacob was holding out a hand. 'Good luck, Ed,' he said briefly.

'Thanks.' Edward wrung his brother's hand. 'Look after Annie for me.'

Jacob glanced at Annie and nodded. 'And Ma?' he asked, and Edward sighed.

'I talked to Ma last night after you'd gone to bed. You should too, Jacob. She told me what it was like for her in the last war. What Pa was like. It was hard to hear, no doubt about it, but I reckon I understand a bit better now.'

Jacob hesitated, then nodded again. 'I'll talk to her,' he said.

Now it was Annie's turn to say goodbye. The train was gathering steam. Doors started to slam, whistles were being blown. Jacob stepped back, leaving Annie alone with Edward. This was it, she thought in a panic. She wasn't ready, she would never be ready. Waving him off to training had been hard enough, but this, this was far worse.

Edward took her face between her hands. 'You know I love you, Annie. Wait for me. We'll be married as soon as I get home.'

'Of course I'll wait,' she said, tears trembling at the ends of her lashes. 'But I'll miss you so.'

'And I'll miss you,' he said, but she knew there was a bit of him too that was excited and keen to get on the train.

Edward threw his case into a compartment, kissed her, one long, hard kiss, and climbed in.

Annie clung to the door as he yanked down the window and leant out to kiss her again. 'Please be careful, Edward. Please, please be careful!' she called, but the train was tooting and the guard was blowing his whistle as the carriage started to move inexorably forward.

'Goodbye!' Edward waved his seaman's hat as the train gathered speed. Annie ran along the platform beside him as far as she could, but he was moving away too fast, and when the platform ran out, she could only stand, weeping and watching as he was borne away and out of sight.

When there was only an empty track to see, Jacob came to put a comforting arm around her shoulders. 'Oh, Jacob,' Annie sobbed into his chest. 'When will I see him again?'

'Ed'll be all right, Annie,' he said, and after a moment's hesitation, he pulled her closer so that she could lean against him. 'You know him, always lands on his feet.'

She cried for a little while, then pulled back, sniffing, to offer him a watery smile. 'Thanks, Jacob. I'm glad you're here, at least.'

A muscle in his jaw twitched. 'I'm always here for you, Annie,' he said. 'You know that.'

'I know. I don't need a brother when I've got you,' she sighed gratefully, and with a last look down the track after Edward, she took his arm. 'Come on, let's go home.'

7

'Who's this, then?' Unembarrassed at having been caught intruding in Meg's bedroom, Ruby picked up the framed photo taken when Meg and Rosie were ten.

Meg took it from her and put it back on the chest of drawers. 'What are you doing in here, Ruby?' she asked sharply. 'This is my room.'

'I'm bored.'

'Read a book.'

'I've finished my book.'

'Well, then, go outside and play. It's a beautiful day.'

'I don't want to. I hate the country. There's no one to play with and nothing to do.'

'There's no one to play with because you won't make any friends,' Meg pointed out.

Ruby hunched a sullen shoulder. 'The other children hate me.'

Meg bit back the obvious retort. 'Do you like them?'

'No, I hate them.'

'Well, then, why should they like you?' Meg knew that she should be more sympathetic to Ruby when she was clearly homesick and unhappy, but it was hard when the child was so surly and rebuffed any attempts to befriend her.

'I want to go home,' Ruby said, folding her lips into a mutinous line.

'Ruby, we've been through this. Your mum

thinks you're safer here while the war is on. I'm sure you'll be able to go home once it's over. Until then, she wants you to be safe.'

The truth was that Meg had no idea what Ruby and Stan's mother wanted. Since Beryl Dubbs had brought the children back, there had been no word from her. Ruby and Stan penned stilted notes to her which Meg dutifully posted, but as far as she knew they had had no reply. She had seen Ruby seize the post when it dropped through the door, only to throw the letters back onto the mat and turn away, shoulders drooping.

'I hate the Germans!'

Meg picked up her gloves and hat and held the door open. 'None of us is very fond of them at the moment,' she said. 'But we're at war, and this is just the way things have to be. Now, please leave my room and don't come in here again, Ruby.'

Ruby slouched past her and Meg shut the door pointedly. 'Where's Stan?' she asked, following the girl down the stairs.

'Hiding.'

'Hiding? What from?'

'He doesn't want to go outside in case a German spy catches him. The other kids are all talking about the horrible things they do to you if they get you. Sometimes they take you back to Germany and keep you a prisoner.'

'Is that why you don't want to go outside either, Ruby?' Meg asked gently.

'Course not.' But Ruby wouldn't meet her eyes. 'I know they're just being stupid.'

'They are.' Meg dropped her gloves on the

rickety old hallstand that had stood by the cottage door for as long as she could remember. Its mirror was speckled with age but it was good enough for Meg to squint at her reflection in as she stooped to put on her hat. 'Look, nothing's going to happen to you in Beckindale,' she said, adjusting the angle. 'This is the safest place you could possibly be. Safer than Hull, I promise you.'

She turned from the mirror and pulled on her gloves. 'Now, will you keep an eye on Stan, wherever he is?'

'Where are you going?'

'There's going to be another evacuation of children from the cities, and as I'm the billeting officer for Beckindale I have to go round and find somewhere for them all to stay.'

She wasn't looking forward to it.

Since the Germans had invaded Belgium and Holland in May it felt as if the phoney war was over at last. Tensions were running high and rumours about enemy spies being parachuted into the country were rife. Meg wasn't surprised that the children had heard something and had spun it into a tale to frighten each other. France had capitulated in June and Churchill vowed to fight on, but a German invasion was expected almost daily. Only the previous day Meg had opened a newspaper to read the headline: 'Hitler to Invade Us Next Friday'. The threat of imminent bombing had led to a hasty dusting off of the original evacuation plan, too, and now in July more children were being sent to safety in the countryside again.

It would be Meg's job to make sure all those due to arrive in Beckindale the following week would have a bed, and persuading her neighbours to open up their homes again wouldn't be an easy task. It had been hard enough last time.

'Can we come?' Ruby asked, and Meg looked at her in surprise.

'It'll be very dull,' she warned.

Ruby shrugged. 'I don't care.'

'Will Stan want to come?' Meg asked dubiously.

'He will if you're there.'

Meg wasn't sure she really would be much use if a German spy jumped out on them, but she was queerly touched that Ruby and Stan might be coming to trust her.

'Well, if you want to . . . ' Perhaps it would be a chance to show them that it was perfectly safe to be outside, and the presence of two children might even make some people think twice before refusing. 'All right, then.'

Ruby ran to find Stan. In spite of her sullen manner, Meg had noticed that she was very protective of her brother. Stan himself allowed his sister to boss him around, and he had evidently not hidden himself very well because it was not long before he came trotting obediently behind her.

* * *

Fully expecting them to get bored and decide to go home after a while, Meg took her bicycle as she had planned. Pushing it was easy; it was only the moment she set her foot on the pedal that her stomach would dip sickeningly.

Come on, Rosie, let's go for a bike ride.

I'm reading!

Oh, please . . . I'm bored!

Rosie shut her book with a sigh, but was smiling as she clambered to her feet. You are such a pest, Meg.

Meg pushed the memory aside, dropped her notebook into the bicycle basket and grimly took hold of the handlebars. 'Let's start on this side of the river. We'll try Emmerdale Farm first.'

They set off up the lane leading away from the bridge, past the turning to Miffield Hall and then up the rough track winding to Emmerdale Farm. It was hot and dusty in the sunshine. Cow parsley frothed along the grassy verges and sheep grazed peacefully on the fells, but Stan and Ruby's eyes kept flicking nervously from side to side, and when a cow stuck its head over the grey stone wall, they both shrank towards Meg.

'That's not a German spy,' she said. 'It's a cow. She's just nosy.' Propping the bicycle against the wall, she scratched the cow between its ears, watched by a wide-eyed Stan.

'Won't it bite yer?'

Meg laughed. 'No, she's eating grass, see?' It was hard to miss as the cow was noisily chomping and dribbling bits of grass out of the side of her mouth.

Ruby eyed it nervously. 'It's big.'

Meg wanted to laugh again, until it occurred to her that the countryside she found so familiar might be a frightening place for children who had only ever known city streets. What if Ruby's sullen defiance masked fear rather than rudeness? If anyone knew anything about putting up a prickly front to disguise her real feelings, Meg realised shamefaced, that would be her.

So instead of making a joke of it, she just nodded. 'She is big, yes, but she's very gentle. She won't hurt you.' She glanced down at Stan. 'Remember that song I taught you about Old MacDonald and his farm?'

Stan nodded eagerly. He was a quiet child, but Meg had noticed that he came to life with music of any kind. 'Old MacDonald had a farm,' he sang in his clear voice, 'E-i-e-i-o.'

'And on that farm he had a cow,' Meg joined in, pointing at the cow.

'E-i-e-i-o,' Stan sang back. 'Here a moo, there a moo, everywhere a moo-moo . . . '

Even Ruby joined in after a few more lines, and they set off up the track once more, all singing. It was the nicest time Meg could remember having with the two children, and she was sorry when a loud boom from the direction of the training camp made them break off in the middle of 'a neigh-neigh here'.

'What's that?' Ruby demanded in a high voice, and Stan clutched at Meg's skirt.

'Is it the Germans?'

'No, it's not the Germans.' Gently Meg disentangled her skirt from his grubby fingers. 'That's the sound of our soldiers training to fight the Germans.'

'I wish *I* could fight them,' Ruby said fiercely.

'Girls don't fight,' Stan pointed out. 'Only

boys can be soldiers.'

'I wouldn't mind. I would kill lots of Germans.'

Meg was a little disturbed at the turn the conversation had taken. It seemed a big leap from happily singing nursery rhymes to threatening to kill the enemy. 'Neither of you is going to kill anybody,' she said firmly. 'You're children.'

'I'm ten,' said Ruby. 'I'm old enough. I could do it. I hate the Germans.'

'That's enough, Ruby.' Meg was glad they had reached Emmerdale Farm. She pushed open the gate to the farmyard and checked that Ruby had closed it properly behind them before leading the way to the farmhouse. The bicycle juddered over the rough cobbles of the yard and she paused when she saw that they were not the first visitors to Emmerdale Farm that day.

Maggie and Joe Sugden were sitting on the bench in the sunshine outside the kitchen door, while Annie Pearson hovered, wiping her hands on her apron, and Jacob lounged against the doorway. They were all listening to Jack Proudfoot, the new policeman, who was talking to them seriously about something. Meg hoped that what he was saying wouldn't frighten the children even more.

Maggie spotted Meg first and waved her over. 'Meg! I haven't seen you in a while.'

'I've been busy.' Meg bent to kiss her godmother's cheek. Maggie and Rose Dingle had helped her mother give birth that snowy Christmas Eve twenty-five years earlier, and Polly Warcup had named the twins after them.

As it happened, Meg had grown up dark and formidable just like her namesake, while Rosie and Rose shared the same sweet temperament. Meg had often wondered what it would have been like if she had been named after Rose instead; would she have been the good, pretty one, while Rosie got a reputation as the prickly, naughty twin, too clever for her own good? Had she and Maggie grown into the hard edges of the name Margaret, while Rose and Rosie adapted to the soft sounds of their name?

Meg nodded at everyone else and introduced Ruby and Stan, who were hanging back, looking wary.

'We've got some kittens in the barn,' Annie said. 'Would you like to see them?'

'Yes, show them the kittens, Annie,' Maggie said when the children nodded, 'and Meg, you sit down.' She shifted sideways, pushing Joe further along the bench.

Meg sat down, noticing without surprise how Jacob's eyes followed Annie. She and Rosie had been born less than a month earlier than Jacob and the three of them had grown up together. She understood Jacob in a way few people did, and she knew that most people in Beckindale assumed she and Jacob would end up together one day. But because she knew him, Meg had known for a long time that Jacob was hopelessly in love with Annie Pearson.

Hopeless was the word. Annie had only ever had eyes for Edward. Meg was fairly sure that Annie had no idea what Jacob felt for her, although it seemed obvious to Meg. So it had never occurred to her to think herself in love with him.

She couldn't imagine being in love with anyone, in fact. She just wasn't that kind of girl. Sometimes Meg wondered if Rosie would have had a sweetheart if she had lived. She had been so pretty and sweet, there would have bound to have been boys queuing up to ask her out.

Rosie would have been married by now, Meg was sure, with a baby or two. Her twin had loved children. Meg had only become a schoolmistress because that was what Rosie had wanted to do. It was the only way she could think of to make up to her parents for the fact that the wrong twin had died.

Nobody ever said as much, but Meg knew in her heart that it was true.

With an effort, she brought her attention back to what Jacob was saying.

'Sergeant Proudfoot here has just been inspecting our stables.' His sardonic expression was even more pronounced than usual. 'It seems Clive Skilbeck thinks we might be harbouring German spies!'

'I'm obliged to follow up all information received,' the policeman said mildly.

'I can tell you now no spies will be welcome here. My parents lived through the last war. Look at my father,' said Jacob, scowling. 'Do you think he'd help a German?'

'I'm not accusing you of anything,' said Jack Proudfoot. 'I'm just doing my job and checking. Needless to say, if you do see anything suspicious, send for me. Don't try any heroics.'

'If you want something suspicious, you should check out the Skilbecks!'

Jack was unperturbed by Jacob's anger. 'I already have.'

'Is there any truth in the rumour that spies are being parachuted in?' Meg intervened before Jacob got any angrier.

'Frankly, I think it's unlikely, but we can't rule anything out,' said Jack. 'Everyone's on edge at the moment. I'd just as soon people kept calm instead of looking for Germans under every hedge.'

Meg felt distinctly snubbed.

'He doesn't have a very cosy manner, does he?' she said crossly as they watched Jack take his bike and cycle off, and Jacob grinned.

'Didn't take to him, Meg? He doesn't seem fussed about making friends, I'll give that to him.'

'He's just doing his job.' Maggie got up and brushed down her apron. 'What can we do for you, Meg?'

'I've got my billeting officer hat on, I'm afraid.' She had almost forgotten why she had come to Emmerdale Farm. 'We're getting another lot of evacuees, and I need to find them beds. Can you take any here?'

Maggie pulled a face. 'Afraid not, Meg. We've applied for some help from the Land Army, and we really need to keep any spare beds for them.'

'I understand,' said Meg. 'I thought it was worth asking. I'm pretty sure I'll get the same answer at the Skilbecks' farm.'

Jacob snorted. 'Good luck with getting

anything out of a Skilbeck!'

'How are you getting on with your two?' Maggie put in.

Meg sighed, thinking of how difficult Ruby could be. 'I keep reminding myself there's a war on, and that things could be worse,' she confessed, and Maggie smiled.

'You're doing a good thing, Meg. Those bairns need you more than they know.'

8

Lily pulled on the handbrake. 'Here you are, sir.'

'Thank you, Corporal.' Colonel Mortimer shifted so that he was facing Lily and threw his arm over the back of the seat.

He didn't actually smile, but his eyes crinkled in a way that always made Lily's heart miss a beat. In the month since he had arrived, practically all the ATS girls at the camp had fallen in love with Delicious Derek, as they called him amongst themselves. As his driver, Lily got to spend the most time with him, much to the envy of the others.

'You lucky thing, Dingle!' Connie Jones sighed. 'He's *such* a dreamboat.'

'Aren't you madly in love with him?' Sylvia Dawson added. 'I know I am.'

'Don't be silly,' Lily always said primly. 'I'm just his driver.'

Although of course she *was* more than halfway in love with him. It was so hard not to be, especially when she saw so much more of him than the others did. Lily hugged to herself the certainty that Colonel Mortimer thought of her as different to the other girls. She loved the way he called her Corporal Dingle, so formally but with a smile in his voice, as if it was a secret between them. It always gave her a little thrill. He was coming to rely on her, she was sure of it.

'I've learnt the hard way that you don't get

anything done without a reliable driver,' he had said as Lily had driven him to the camp for the first time.

'You can count on me, sir,' Lily had promised. She would do anything for him now.

In just four short weeks Derek Mortimer had turned the camp around, Lily thought admiringly. He had an easy manner with the men, but they all obeyed him unquestioningly. The colonel had all the assurance and sophistication that every other man she knew lacked, and a charm that was frankly irresistible. When Derek looked at you, you felt you were the only person he wanted to be with, the only person who had anything of interest to say to him.

Lily was dazzled by him. Of *course* she was madly in love with him. How could she not be? He was intelligent, humorous, distinguished . . . what had they been thinking, putting a man like the colonel in a billet with *Nina Lazenby* of all people?

She had been appalled when she heard where he would be staying. 'Are you sure?' she had asked when he had handed over the address with amusement. But there had been no mistake. There it was in black and white: Mrs Lazenby, Pear Tree Cottage, Beckindale.

'Is there a problem, Corporal?' Derek had asked that first day.

'It's just . . . I don't think it's very suitable for you. Mrs Lazenby has an unsavoury reputation,' Lily said, tight-lipped, but to her dismay, he had only grinned as he settled himself into the passenger seat.

'There's a war on, Corporal. I'm lucky to have a bed at all.'

He chose to be amused by Nina. Lily had offered to arrange another billet, but he insisted that he was perfectly comfortable. 'Mrs Lazenby's an interesting woman,' he said. 'She's got style.'

So every morning Lily picked him up outside Pear Tree Cottage, and every evening she drove him back there from the camp. His tolerance of Nina was the only flaw in his character, as far as Lily was concerned.

Now, Derek swung easily out of the jeep, turning to rest one hand on the open door. 'Enjoy your evening, Corporal,' he said as he always did.

'Thank you, sir.' Lily pressed her foot on the clutch and put the jeep into gear, but he stopped her with a question.

'What will you be doing?'

What *would* she be doing? Sharing a tense meal with her father? Mending the tear in her blouse? 'Nothing special,' she sighed.

'In that case, how would you like to help me build relations with the locals?'

'Sir?' Puzzled, Lily put the jeep back into neutral and looked at him.

'Having a huge training camp on the doorstep isn't an easy situation,' said Derek. 'It's important to maintain good relations with Beckindale, so that we can deal with any problems that might arise before they get out of hand. And it seems to me that as a local lass, you might be just the person to help me.'

Lily didn't even mind the way he teased her about her Yorkshire accent, and now she glowed at the prospect of spending more time with him.

'Happy to help, sir,' she said. 'What would you like me to do?'

He smiled. 'You can drop the 'sir' when we're off-duty, for a start,' he said. 'I've already met the vicar, but if I want to meet the real locals, I imagine the pub would be the best place to start, don't you?'

'Good idea, s — ' Lily just managed to bite off the 'sir' in time. 'I mean, yes, that's right.'

'I get the impression that the Woolpack is the place to be. Do you know it?'

'I practically grew up there,' Lily confessed. 'It's owned by my father's cousin.'

'Excellent,' said Derek with satisfaction. 'How about coming along and having a drink with me this evening, in that case?'

Lily hesitated. Was he asking her out? But surely not? A colonel would hardly bother with a lowly corporal, would he? She was his driver, that was all. And what would he make of the Woolpack? What if Jed started acting the spiv, or Larry did his over-the-top Irish act?

'Come on, take pity on me,' Derek said with his most charming smile as she dithered. 'It would be nice to have some company.' He shot her a penetrating look as she bit her lip. 'But if you're uncomfortable with the idea . . . ?'

'Oh, no, it's not that,' Lily said hastily. She would rather he hadn't chosen the Woolpack, but she could hardly ban him from the pub, and the lure of spending extra time with him was too great to resist. She would just have to hope that Jed was on his best behaviour. 'I mean, yes, I'd love to help.'

'Good.'

Oh, how could she resist when he smiled at her like that? Warmth uncoiled inside Lily, and she couldn't help smiling back.

'Let's both change into mufti and then I'll come and call for you,' Derek suggested. 'Do you live nearby?'

Lily didn't want him at the garage, and besides, it would be good to show him that she wasn't considering this as a date or anything like that. 'Oh, it's very close. Why don't I meet you there?'

'All right then. Seven o'clock?'

'Lovely.'

Back at the garage, Lily jumped out of the jeep and ran up the stairs to the room she had slept in since she was a child. Catching sight of her reflection in the mirror on the chest of drawers, she checked herself, startled. Was that really her, with that flushed face and eyes bright with excitement? Pressing her hands to her cheeks, she made herself stop and take a deep breath.

This wasn't a date. She mustn't get carried away. It would just be a drink and a chat. Derek was a senior officer who was honest enough to admit that he'd like some company, that was all, and she was a local who could help him make a connection with the village. There was nothing improper about meeting him. In fact, it would have been rude to refuse, Lily decided. There was absolutely no reason to be silly about it.

Still, there was no reason either not to look nice. She pulled off her cap and tossed it onto the bed before stripping, right down to the regulation underwear. It might not be a romantic assignation, but there was no way she was sitting next to Derek tonight in khaki knickers.

What to wear? Lily pawed through her meagre wardrobe, struggling in and out of dresses until eventually settling on one of her older but favourite frocks. It was a little frayed around the collar, but Mick had once told her the blue brought out the colour of her eyes, and she could brighten it with a petunia suede belt. Wriggling into her suspender belt, she pulled on her much-darned stockings and wished now that she had taken Jed up on his offer of some new nylons instead of sanctimoniously refusing to have anything to do with the black market.

Oh well, it was too late now, Lily decided. There was no time to do much with her hair, either. Without much hope of improving things, she pushed back the waves that had been flattened under her cap and pinned them into place. A final powder of her nose and some lipstick, and she was ready.

Mick Dingle was at the kitchen table reading a newspaper. Pausing in the doorway, it struck Lily that her father looked lonely and her heart twisted. How long had it been since the two of them had had a comfortable evening in together? Ever since she had joined the ATS, she had used the excuse of her changing shifts to avoid spending time at home. Too often when she did, she would either find Nina there, which was always awkward, or she would come home to find the garage empty, and that hurt even more. It reminded her too much of those dreadful days when she had come home from school to an empty kitchen, when all the spaces which Rose had filled had ached with her absence.

Well, she had wanted to detach herself from her father, hadn't she, Lily reminded herself. He needed to live his own life, with Nina if he must, and Lily herself had been preoccupied with her life at camp and with Derek since his arrival. Still, she missed her father. They had been so close once.

For a moment she was tempted to go over and hug him from behind the way she had used to do, and when he looked up to see her, his eyes lit with such pleasure that Lily had a sudden urge to pull out a chair and sit down with him. She felt as if she were teetering on the edge of a momentous decision: stay with her father or go out and meet Derek. Ridiculously, tears suddenly crowded her throat.

'You look nice, *asthore*,' he said.

'Thanks, Dad.'

'You eaten yet?'

'No.' Her stomach was too fluttery to be able to contemplate food.

'You should eat something, Lily. Why don't you eat with us?'

'Us?'

As if she needed to ask!

He hesitated. 'Nina's coming round in a bit. She said she'd cook.'

'Thanks, but I'm going out.'

'Right,' he said, not making a very good job of disguising his disappointment. He forced a smile 'Got a date?'

'No, I'm just meeting someone from camp. In fact, I need to go now.' She blew him a kiss across the kitchen, not trusting herself if he wrapped her in one of his warm hugs. 'Bye, Dad.'

9

Meeting someone from the camp. That was *all* she was doing, Lily reminded herself. It didn't stop the fizzing feeling in her belly as she walked quickly up the road to the village. It was another gloriously golden evening, but Lily barely noticed the lush hedgerows or the fells looking soft and green in the drowsy light. She was thinking about Derek Mortimer and the smile in his eyes.

When she reached the Woolpack, she paused outside the door and took a deep breath, smoothing down her frock.

A drink. To talk about local issues.

That was all.

Yanking open the door, she was met by the familiar smell of beer, old wood and sawdust. Low evening sunshine slanted through the window, cutting through the dimness of the interior, and a thousand dust mites danced in the beam of light. The pub was crowded, but Lily only had eyes for Derek, who was chatting to Larry Dingle as he leant against the bar, looking quite at home with one foot casually propped on the rail, and at the sight of him, her heart did one of those unnerving somersaults that left her breathless. In a short-sleeved white shirt open at the neck, and trousers, he looked just like Cary Grant in *Bringing Up Baby*, which she'd seen at the flicks, and all at once she felt hopelessly dowdy in her blue frock.

But it was too late to change. Larry had already spotted her. 'Ah, here she is!' he cried.

Mick Dingle had never lost his Irish lilt, either, but to Lily, Larry always sounded as if he was putting it on. He was a little too jaunty, his brogue a little too broad, the twinkly-eyed Irish charm laid on so thick that she never quite trusted him. That Larry Dingle was absolutely the worst person to be left in charge of Jed, who was so clearly ready to be led astray, was about the only thing on which everyone in Beckindale agreed.

'I've just been telling the colonel here that you're the light of your daddy's life,' Larry boomed, and Lily folded her lips together.

Oh, Lord. 'I'm sure Colonel Mortimer isn't interested in our family,' she said stiffly.

'Oh, I'm always interested in what makes my staff tick,' said Derek, turning to greet her with a smile. 'You look very nice,' he said appreciatively, and Lily tingled as his eyes roved over her.

She shifted uncomfortably, delighted and embarrassed at the same time.

'Now, what can I get you to drink?'

He stepped back as he spoke and Lily realised to her horror that Jack Proudfoot was standing beside him, looking dour as always.

'I didn't realise you were there,' she said without thinking.

Derek looked from one to the other. 'Oh, do you two know each other?'

'No,' said Lily just as Jack said, 'We've met.'

'Sergeant Proudfoot is the village policeman,' Lily added. 'We don't know each other personally.'

'But tonight I'm off-duty.' Jack picked up his glass. 'I'll leave you to it,' he said. 'Nice to talk to you, Colonel.'

'You too, Sergeant.'

Derek turned back to Lily and his smile warmed. 'So, Lily . . . can I call you Lily, as we're both off-duty?'

'Of course.' Did that mean she could call him Derek? Lily wondered. She wasn't sure she would have the nerve.

'Let's get you a drink. What will it be?'

Lily would have liked to order something sophisticated, but she could just imagine Larry's teasing if she asked for a martini or even a port. She was also burningly aware of Jack, who had moved away along the bar but was still well within listening distance.

'Just an orangeade, please.'

'An orangeade, and I'll have another pint of your best,' Derek said to Larry. 'And one for yourself.'

'Thank you kindly, sir. You're a gentleman.' Larry winked at Lily as he pulled Derek's pint. 'You've got a generous one here, Lil.'

Lily coloured. 'I'm sorry about that,' she muttered when Derek carried their drinks over to a table, but he only laughed.

'Don't worry about it. We've all got embarrassing family members.'

'Even you?' She found that hard to believe.

'Even me,' he said cheerfully.

They sat side by side on the bench, facing the bar, and Derek lifted his glass. 'Cheers! Here's to associating with the locals!'

Lily could feel his thigh pressing against hers, but couldn't decide whether it was deliberate or not. Should she move further along? But then that might make him think she was offended. Less embarrassing to pretend she hadn't noticed, she decided.

'Cheers,' she echoed, still distracted by his closeness.

'Larry was telling me how close you are to your father.'

'I was.'

'Not any more?' Derek probed gently.

Lily studied her orangeade. 'My mum died when I was thirteen.'

'I'm sorry, Lily. That's a hard age at the best of times. You must miss her.'

'I do, yes.' She swallowed. 'She was lovely.'

'I'm sure she was.'

'So after that it was just me and Dad. But now he's met someone new, and it just doesn't feel right.'

'You're jealous,' said Derek, but so compassionately that she couldn't resent him.

'I suppose I am. I mean, I know he's entitled to a life of his own, but I just wish he'd chosen someone more like Mum. It's like he's forgotten all about her.'

'I lost my mother, too, when I was young,' Derek said. 'We lived in Ceylon — my father was a district commissioner there — and I was sent to boarding school in England when I was six. I only got home once a year,' he remembered. 'When I was nine, my mother came back on the ship with me, took me to school and kissed me goodbye. I never saw her again. She died of typhoid, and by the time I went home the next summer, my father had remarried and there was a new woman where my mother had been.'

'That's awful.' Lily's eyes filled with tears as she imagined him as a little boy finding that his mother had been replaced so easily.

'Don't cry, Lily.' Derek put his hand over hers on the table. 'It was a long time ago.'

His fingers were warm on hers. It would be so easy to turn her palm upwards so that their fingers could entangle. The temptation to do just that trembled down Lily's arm, but when she glanced up, she saw Jack Proudfoot watching sardonically, and for some reason she flushed and drew her hand away.

Derek had followed her gaze. 'I think there's something between you and the policeman,' he teased.

'Absolutely not!' said Lily, horrified. 'I don't even like him!'

'I think he likes you.'

'He doesn't. He looks at me like I'm some kind of insect!'

Derek threw back his head and laughed. 'I doubt that. Policeman or not, Sergeant Proudfoot is a man, and believe me, he'll have noticed that you're a very beautiful young woman.'

A blush prickled up Lily's neck and across her cheeks. 'I don't think so.'

'You've got no idea, have you? You're so very sweet, Lily.' He smiled at her and then pulled his mouth down ruefully. 'But I shouldn't talk to you like this. I'm old enough to be your father,

91

and I'm a senior officer. It's just . . . no, I don't want to make you uncomfortable.'

'It's all right.' Lily stammered a little, dazzled by the warmth in his voice, by the look in his eyes. Was it really possible that he could be attracted to her, to shy Lily Dingle? 'I . . . I don't mind.'

'Really?'

A smile trembled on her lips. 'Really,' she said.

She looked at him then. His eyes were brown and so warm, she felt her bones dissolving into a delicious rush of honeyed gold. His thigh was hard and lean against hers, burning through the thin material of her frock, and her hand throbbed where it had lain beneath his palm. His gaze seemed to be drawing her irresistibly into him. Lily felt herself begin to lean towards him, her lips already anticipating his kiss . . .

'Lily?'

She jerked upright to see Mick standing over the table, Nina Lazenby beside him.

'Dad! What are you doing here? I thought you were eating at home.'

'We decided to have a drink first. I thought *you* were meeting a friend at the camp.' Mick's normally cheerful face was dark with suspicion as he looked from his daughter to Derek, who had risen gracefully to his feet.

'Nina, how nice to see you.'

'Derek,' Nina said with a cool nod. She was a tall woman with bold features and long red hair that she refused to have curled and set like everyone else. Today it was tied up in a vibrant purple scarf and she wore wide flapping trousers and a lime-green blouse. Next to her, Lily felt colourless and dull in the demure blue frock she had been so pleased with earlier.

'You haven't met Colonel Mortimer, have you?' Nina said, turning to Mick. 'The new camp commander. I told you he's billeted with me.'

'And very comfortable I am there too,' Derek put in.

'Is that so?' Mick's gaze was hard. 'And how do you come to know my daughter well enough to buy her a drink?'

'Lily's my driver,' said Derek.

'She's not driving now,' Mick pointed out.

'Stop it, Dad!' Lily was furious. 'I'm not a child! I'm in the ATS and I don't need to tell you where I go or who I'm meeting.'

'It's only natural your father should feel protective,' Derek said smoothly. 'I would feel the same if I had a daughter. But please, join us,' he went on, gesturing to the stools on the other side of the table.

Mick looked as if he were about to demur, but Nina sat down, and after a moment, he followed, his dark blue eyes still full of suspicion.

'Hello, Lily,' Nina said with a smile as she put her glass on the table.

'Hello,' Lily muttered. She felt ridiculously like a child who had been caught doing something she shouldn't.

Derek was the only one who seemed entirely comfortable. 'I'm glad you're here, actually, Nina. This was your idea, after all.'

Nina's dark brows shot up. 'It was?'

'You were telling me at breakfast that I should

get a sense of the local community and build relationships. Lily here kindly agreed to give up her evening to introduce me to the pub. I must say, she's been invaluable.' Derek turned to Mick. 'Your daughter is the best driver I've ever had, and the best mechanic. I've never met a woman who knows so much about engines.'

Mick was obviously determined not to be charmed. 'She grew up in a garage,' he said curtly, but when his eyes rested on Lily's face, she wondered if he was remembering how fascinated she had been even as a very small girl. She had been happy to spend hours squatting beside him as he worked on an engine, proud of being allowed to hold a spanner at first, and then learning to use it. Rose was always pretending to complain about the way Lily would end up covered in oil. Lily remembered her wiping the smudges from her face. 'You're just like your father,' she would sigh, but she would be smiling.

Lily's throat ached at the memory and she took a gulp of orangeade.

Why had Derek invited her father and Nina to sit down? He had called her beautiful. He had said she was sweet. He had been about to kiss her, she was sure of it, and she wouldn't have cared that everyone was watching. Now, the three of them were sitting there making small talk while Lily sat feeling awkward and left out.

I'm old enough to be your father. Lily looked from Derek to Mick and realised with something of a shock that it was true. But Derek didn't seem like a father. She didn't care that he was older. She was in love with him, and there was no use denying it. Derek was exactly the kind of man she had imagined falling in love with, a little older perhaps, but so intelligent, so assured, so devastatingly attractive, she couldn't possibly be expected to resist him any longer.

But then her father had come in and she had gone from feeling like a beautiful, desirable woman to a sulky adolescent.

Mick was glowering, clearly finding the situation as awkward as she did. Only Nina and Derek seemed unperturbed. Shifting as subtly as she could away from Derek, Lily glanced around the pub to find the other customers watching with undisguised interest. They were all clearly hoping that Mick would cause a scene. Between Lily having a drink with a man old enough to be her father, and Nina Lazenby strolling in bold as brass, the regulars must have thought they were in for a ringside seat on the latest gossip.

Jack Proudfoot was observing them coolly, too, no doubt ready to step in if needed, and Lily lifted her chin defiantly. She couldn't answer for Nina, but she wasn't going to be embarrassed about having a drink with Derek.

'What's this? Nobody told me there was a family gathering.' For once, Lily was glad of Jed's interruption. He came sauntering over in his cocky way and pulled up a stool without waiting for an invitation.

'All right?' he asked the table as a whole, and without waiting for an answer turned to Lily and lowered his voice. 'What's Jack Proudfoot doing here, Lil?'

'I have no idea, Jed.'

'I don't like the way he keeps sniffing around.'

'That's probably what he thinks about you,' said Mick sourly and Jed held up his hands.

'I've got nowt to hide, Uncle Mick.'

'Then what's your problem with Sergeant Proudfoot?'

'He just makes me uneasy. Hey, Lily, why don't you go and find out what he's up to?'

'Why me?'

'Cos he fancies you.'

'He does not!'

'Oh, go on!'

Mick drained his glass and put it down with a bang. 'That's enough, Jed,' he said and got to his feet. 'Ask your own questions, and don't involve Lily in your shady business. We're leaving now, anyway. Come on, Lily, Nina.'

Lily toyed briefly with the idea of objecting, but her pleasure in the evening was spoiled anyway. Besides, she wanted to be alone to absorb the incredible, wonderful idea that Derek wanted to be with her, and to remember the look in his eyes.

'I'd better go,' she said to Derek with an apologetic glance.

'Of course.' He stood too. Giving the hand she held out a meaningful squeeze, he lowered his voice. 'Another time, perhaps?'

Lily cast a defiant look around the pub. Nobody was looking at her, but she was sure they were all straining to hear her conversation. 'That would be lovely,' she said.

10

The brambles scrambling along the sides of the lane were heavy with blackberries. Annie stopped to help herself to a particularly juicy-looking one.

She should come and pick some properly, she thought. They would make lovely jam — not that she even wanted to think about jam again after the WI's mammoth jam-making session at the village hall the previous week. The call had gone out to help deal with the glut of plums, and Annie had volunteered to help. It had meant a whole day of stoning plums, but they'd managed to produce a huge quantity of jars of jam and bottles of preserved fruit to send to hospitals and canteens across Yorkshire instead of letting the fruit rot.

Right now, Annie never wanted to see another plum. Ever.

Absently, she picked another blackberry while her gaze rested on the familiar view. The dale stretched away, looking a little raggedy around the edges after a long, hot summer. The verges of the lane were snarled with nettles, docks and collapsed cow parsley, but to Annie it was still the best view in the world.

It was nice to have a few moments to herself. Late summer was always a busy time at Emmerdale Farm, and they were all working long into the evenings to get the harvest in.

Being sent down to Beckindale to do the shopping made a welcome change. The air was muggy and purplish clouds were brooding behind the far fell, but it was quiet apart from the bleating of sheep in the distance. Strange to think that the country was at war. Annie could almost believe that when she got back to the farm Edward would be at the kitchen table, ruddy after a day in the fields, fair hair tousled, looking up to greet her with the smile he kept just for her.

Instead, he was in the middle of the Atlantic somewhere, surrounded by that grey, unforgiving sea. Annie hated to think of Edward with nothing to look at except that bleak, empty horizon. He wrote cheerful letters that she read and reread until they were creased and worn, but they didn't tell her much, just that he was well and thinking of her. He said that he had seen plenty of 'action', but what that meant or what it was like to live on a ship knowing that a torpedo could strike at any time, Annie could only imagine.

Thinking of Edward, she sighed. She was doing her best to keep her spirits up as they were constantly being urged to do by the authorities, but it was hard when missing him was a constant ache in the pit of her stomach. At least she didn't need to worry about being pregnant any more. At the time, the consequences of making love hadn't crossed her mind, but Annie had to admit that afterwards she had been a little anxious. Not that she didn't want to have Edward's baby one day, but she would like to be married first. Opinion in Beckindale could be unforgiving of those who anticipated their marriage vows.

Oh, if only she and Edward had been married already! Annie could picture him so clearly that her heart twisted painfully. Determinedly blinking back tears, she sucked blackberry juice from her fingers and headed towards the bridge into Beckindale.

The reality of war hit Annie the moment she turned into the high street and saw the queue outside Barlow's the grocers. She quickened her pace. After walking all the way down from Emmerdale Farm in the heat, she didn't want to go back empty-handed.

Rationing had really started to bite lately, although in Beckindale they were not nearly as badly off as in the cities. Most people had a vegetable patch as well as a pig or a few chickens, and if they didn't, they were likely to know someone who did. Bartering had soon become a way of life, but there were still staples that everybody missed. Only the previous week a rumour that the Barlows had taken a delivery of oranges had led to a queue stretching down the street.

Today, Annie had ration books for everyone at Emmerdale Farm tucked into her pocket. Maggie had sent her down to get their weekly allowance of sugar and tea. 'See what else they've got while you're there,' she'd added. 'We could do with some dried fruit, and some soap if they've got any. What I wouldn't give for a fresh bar of soap!'

Annie took her place in the queue behind Mary Ann Teale, nodding a greeting and exchanging the obligatory conversation about the likelihood of rain. A minute later old Janet Airey joined the queue with much puffing and panting.

'Would you like to go ahead of me, Mrs Airey?' Annie offered.

'Bless you, love, but you don't want to start that. A queue's a queue. Maggie Sugden wouldn't be too happy if I went ahead of you and got the last bit of sugar, would she?'

As it was, the two elderly women passed the time talking around Annie. Between grumbles about shortages and the blackout and the grubbiness of the new lot of evacuees, they caught up on all the gossip, although surely they had discussed it all at the jam-making session in the village hall.

Certainly none of it was new to Annie: Lily Dingle had been seen practically on the lap of the new colonel from the camp. Nina Lazenby was said to be furious. She had her eye on him, too, and as he was billeted in her house, it was generally felt that she stood a better chance with the colonel.

'He's a very handsome man,' Mary Ann acknowledged, but Janet only sniffed.

'Handsome is as handsome does.'

The Ministry of Food man had fined Arthur Middleton for keeping packets of sausages under the counter, and Len Summers had managed to get his fingers caught in a mousetrap while groping for his torch in the middle of a blackout.

Pausing for breath, the two women watched Jack Proudfoot limp down the other side of the street.

'I heard it from Betsy Allen — her daughter

lives t'other side of Ilkley now — that he never had no accident.' Mary Ann leant round Annie to make sure Janet was listening. 'She says he was sick.'

But Janet wasn't having that. What did Betsy Allen's daughter know about anything? No, Constable Bates had told her himself that criminals in Bradford had crashed into his car.

Mary Ann was miffed at having her story so comprehensively routed, and she preserved an offended silence as the queue shuffled forward. Annie was glad of a few moments' peace, but the two women were soon at it again, tutting at the news that Larry Dingle had been watering down the beer in the Woolpack, and the rumour that Oliver Skilbeck was walking out with Elizabeth Barlow.

It was a relief when Annie reached the front of the queue at last. She was greeted by Sarah, who was behind the counter with her younger sister, Elizabeth, she who was said to be being romanced by Oliver Skilbeck. Annie wished her the joy of him.

'There's a dance in the Drill Hall next Saturday,' Sarah told Annie as she weighed out the sugar ration. 'They're going to have a real band! Why don't you come?'

'I don't really like dances where I don't know people, Sarah,' she said.

'Come on, it'll be fun,' said Sarah, deftly wrapping the sugar in brown paper and stamping the ration books. 'There'll be lots of soldiers from the training camp all looking to have a good time, and they'll need someone to dance with. You can't be so cruel as to deny them a last dance before they go to war. Think of it as your contribution to the war effort.'

Annie thought of the back-breaking work at Emmerdale Farm, of the plums and the endless knitting. 'I think I'm doing my bit. You go with Elizabeth,' she said, nodding at Sarah's sister, who was serving Mary Ann.

Sarah leant forward over the counter to whisper confidentially, 'She's taken up with Oliver Skilbeck. I don't want to play gooseberry to them.' Straightening, she turned to find the bar of soap Annie requested.

'I don't know . . . ' said Annie reluctantly, but Sarah wouldn't give up.

'Edward wouldn't want you to mope for the whole war. Oh, please say you'll come!'

'Annie, could you please just give in and say you'll go?' Meg Warcup's brusque tones came from further back in the queue, where she had evidently just managed to get in the door of the shop. 'Then the rest of us might have a chance of getting served!'

Annie blushed and stammered an apology, but Sarah was unrepentant.

'Keep your hair on, Meg! Can't we have a chat with our pals any more? God knows, we've got few enough pleasures with the war on.'

'The war will be over before I get to the front of this queue,' snapped Meg, at which point, Janet Airey decided to wade into the fray.

'You always were an impatient one, Meg Warcup!' she said, turning round to stare accusingly at Meg behind her.

'Well, I'm sorry, Mrs Airey, but I'm thinking of you too,' said Meg through gritted teeth. 'If we're going to have to stand here for hours, the Barlows could at least provide a chair or two for their elderly customers. Then you could sit down while you're waiting.'

'Here, who are you calling elderly?' Janet objected, and Meg rolled her eyes.

'Sorry I tried to help!'

'There's no need to get snippy with *me*. I'm not the one making you stand in a queue.'

'No, that would be Sarah trying to get Annie to go to a dance,' said Meg crossly.

Annie took her ration books back from Sarah and finished packing the tea, sugar and tins she'd managed to buy into her basket.

'Tell you what,' she said to Meg. 'I'll go if you will.'

'If that's what it takes to move this queue, then fine!'

Sarah clapped her hands together. 'I can't wait!'

Picking up her basket, Annie squeezed out of the shop. Now she would have to go to the dance, and she had made poor Meg agree to go too. She really would much rather stay at home, but nobody would ever believe that.

* * *

Jacob had taken her to the flicks once or twice, and that had been nice. The last time they'd seen Greta Garbo in *Ninotchka*. He'd bought her a half-pound box of chocolates and an ice and they'd sat in the balcony, which was a real treat. Jacob was clearly taking Edward's request to look after her seriously, and for Annie it was like having a brother of her own. She was comfortable with his silences. She had never been a chatterbox either, and she liked being with Jacob, who only talked if he had something to say. The Sugdens felt more like her family than her parents, who were still snapping at each other over Grace's decision to work for Clive Skilbeck. It was strange to think about Maggie having had an affair, and even stranger that Joe had once been so brutal; so hard to imagine, in fact, that Annie had decided it was ancient history and put it from her mind. All she cared about was Edward, and it was comforting to be with Jacob, who knew him as well as she did.

She felt sorry for Jacob sometimes. It couldn't have been easy hearing that your mother had loved a man who wasn't your father, and that your brother was a bastard, but when she'd tried to talk to him about it, he had shrugged it off.

'It explained some things,' was all he'd said.

'Did Joe know?'

'I think he suspected. But you know Pa. It's hard to tell what he's thinking.'

There was something solitary about Jacob, in spite of his knowing everybody in Beckindale, just like Annie did. He and Meg had always been friends, for instance. Why didn't he take Meg out, instead of her?

'Ed told me to look after you,' he'd say whenever she suggested it.

Maggie was in the dairy when she got back to

Emmerdale Farm, and it was not until later that afternoon that Annie confessed that all she had been able to get in the shop, aside from the tea, sugar and soap, was a couple of cans of sardines.

Maggie pulled a face. 'Joe's always hated tinned fish. I don't know what he'll say if I give him sardines on toast for supper ag — ' She broke off at the sound of an engine coughing and spluttering. 'What's that?'

'It sounds like a plane,' said Annie, confused at first and then fearful.

'We don't get planes over here.' But Maggie glanced up at the ceiling as if expecting something to fall through it.

'You don't think it's a bomber, do you?' Annie bit her lip as the noise got louder and lower.

'Whatever it is, I think we'd better get out of here,' said Maggie, abandoning the sardine tins as the roar threatened to overwhelm them. 'It sounds too close for comfort. Come on, Annie, outside, quick now!'

They rushed outside, craning their necks to find the source of the noise. A plane was lurching across the sky above the farmhouse, smoke pouring from one of the engines.

'Oh my goodness,' Maggie gasped, pointing at the swastika on the tail. 'That's a German plane!' It was higher than they had imagined from the sound, but the ugly sign of the Nazi regime was unmistakable.

Annie gaped at the plane, terrified and yet unable to look away. It seemed to fill the sky. All this time the war had seemed so distant, and now it had come to them, making them cover their ears at the noise. Maggie's dog, Ben, was barking furiously.

'It's going to crash!' Annie said, pointing at the smoke.

'It had better not crash into the farmhouse,' said Maggie grimly, but it looked as if the pilot was trying to steer away from the buildings. The wings wobbled precariously and the nose of the plane dipped and then rose again while black smoke continued to stream from one of the engines.

'Look!'

Annie followed Maggie's pointing finger to see two figures jump out of the plane in the distance, their parachutes opening to let them descend with an eerie slowness as the plane stuttered onwards.

A few moments later a third figure leapt from the plane and they watched tensely until the parachute snapped open. Meanwhile, the plane was rapidly losing height.

'There's no way it's going to clear the fell,' said Maggie, her hands twisted together anxiously.

The words were barely out of her mouth before they saw the plane crumple into the hillside with a loud bang.

Annie's hand was pressed to her mouth and Maggie's face was grey. 'Oh, dear Lord, they've crashed!'

Jacob and Joe came running from the home field. 'It's gone down over the Skelder field,' Jacob said. 'It better not have taken out any of my tups!'

'What if there was someone in there?' Annie's

voice quavered with shock. 'They couldn't have survived that, surely?'

Jacob shook his head. 'Looked to me like the crew bailed out.'

'Jacob, take the truck and get Jack Proudfoot,' said Maggie, who was back in control, but Jacob shook his head.

'I'm not leaving you and Annie with Germans around.'

'Your pa's here.' Maggie nodded at Joe, who had disappeared into the house only to emerge with a shotgun.

Joe's ravaged face looked unusually grim. 'Go,' he said to Jacob in his strange, effortful voice. 'I . . . here. Maggie and Annie . . . safe with me.'

11

It was late by the time Meg made it back to her cottage from the shop. All she had to show for the effort of queuing was two measly cans of potted tongue, some macaroni and a jar of fish paste — and as if that wasn't reason enough to feel irritated, she had been manoeuvred into promising to go to that stupid dance.

Scowling, Meg studied the unappetising selection on the kitchen table. She was supposed to make sure Ruby and Stan got all the nourishment they needed, but it was hard on such limited rations. They both remained deeply suspicious of vegetables, in spite of her efforts to disguise them.

Morosely, she leafed through the booklet of ideas about how to save food and fuel. Tripe and Liver Hot-Pot? She couldn't see Ruby and Stan going for that. Perhaps they'd like an oatmeal sausage? But when Meg looked at the recipe, she didn't have the energy to set about mixing and stirring and rolling into sausage shapes and then frying . . . No, it looked as if it would be the potted tongue. She would dig up some potatoes from her father's vegetable patch and see if she could find some salad.

She managed to dig a few potatoes and found a couple of tomatoes and a tired-looking lettuce before forcing herself to pull up a few weeds while she was there. She was lucky to live in the country, she knew. Maggie often slipped her a cheese or a pat of butter, or Jacob would bring her a couple of rabbits he had shot to vary their diet.

Stan and Rosie didn't appreciate her efforts to make a nourishing meal for them, making faces about the potted tongue and pushing the salad around their plates.

'Eat it all up,' Meg told them. 'You're lucky to have anything at all. You're not leaving the table until you've eaten everything on your plate.' And when that didn't make them tackle their food with any greater enthusiasm, she added: 'If you eat everything, we'll do something nice this afternoon.' She had hoped to write a letter to one of her friends from teacher training college, but nowadays it was just a matter of getting over one hurdle at a time.

'Can I learn to ride your bicycle?' said Ruby instantly.

Meg sighed. Ruby had been persistent about wanting to ride the bicycle for weeks now. 'You're too young,' she said, as she always did.

'You're riding a bicycle in that photograph in your bedroom,' Ruby countered and Meg frowned at her.

'I thought I told you not to go into my room, Ruby?'

Ruby ignored that. 'You don't look much older than me,' she pointed out.

It was true. She and Rose had been given the bicycles for their tenth birthday. It had been one of the happiest days of Meg's life. Their father, Robert, had taken their photograph, both of them beaming at the camera. Sometimes Meg couldn't bear to look at that photo, but it was the best likeness she had of Rosie, and she couldn't bear to get rid of it either.

'Who's that with you?' Ruby demanded, obviously unfazed at having snooped.

Meg forced herself to swallow the last piece of potted tongue even though she thought it would choke her. 'My twin sister,' she said when she could.

'You was a twin?' Ruby seemed fascinated.

'What's a twin?' asked Stan, puzzled.

'It means my sister and I were born at the same time.'

'They came out of their mam's stomach together,' Ruby explained, and Stan looked horrified.

'Together?'

'Well, on the same day,' said Meg. She couldn't face discussing childbirth with Stan today.

'You don't look the same,' Ruby objected.

'No, we weren't identical twins. Now, please finish that lettuce, Stan, and Ruby, you've still got that tongue to eat.'

Sulkily Ruby speared a piece of tongue with her fork. She wasn't ready to let the subject drop. 'What's your sister's name?'

It was still so hard to say after all these years. Meg swallowed to ease the tightness in her throat. 'Rosie,' she managed.

'Where is she?' asked Stan.

'She's dead,' said Meg. 'She died.'

'How?'

'It was an accident.' Meg couldn't talk about Rosie any longer. She forced a smile. 'So, what shall we do this afternoon? Tell you what, let's go blackberrying.'

To her relief that distracted Stan at least. He frowned as he pushed his lettuce around his plate.

'What's that?'

'It just means picking blackberries.'

'What are they?'

It was at times like this Meg realised how very different Ruby and Stan s lives had been in Hull. 'You've never picked a blackberry?'

But then, where would they have found blackberries down by the docks in Hull?

'I'll show you the blackberries,' she said. 'It'll do us good to get out, and then we can make a pudding and maybe some jam.'

When the children had moaned their way to the end of their lunch, Meg found some large bowls and gave them one each to carry, while she took a third for herself.

'Can't we take your bicycle?' said Ruby. 'We could put the bowls in the basket.'

'We're going out into the fields,' Meg said. 'There's a place on Emmerdale Farm with the best blackberries. A bike would just be a nuisance. We're going to walk.'

Ruby and Stan trailed along, moaning all the way to the Emmerdale Farm track.

'I wish I could ride your bicycle,' Ruby grumbled for the umpteenth time, and Meg had to grit her teeth.

'I've told you before, Ruby. You're too young, and it's too dangerous.'

'How can it be dangerous? Everybody rides a bicycle!'

Come on, Rosie! Calling impatiently as she waited at the top of the hill. One foot on the ground, one on the pedal. We can freewheel all the way down. It'll be fun.

'You need to be old enough to control it,' said Meg.

It was a long slog up the track and then across the fields to the tangle of brambles where the best blackberries had always grown, and all three of them were panting with the effort. They saw Jacob in the distance at one point. Meg held up her bowl to indicate where they were going and he lifted a hand in acknowledgement.

They were hot and sticky by the time they got there. After lurking for days, the clouds had started to gather and the air was so close that Meg began to worry that they would be caught out in a storm. But having got so far, it seemed a shame to turn back before they had picked any blackberries.

Stan was initially dubious about trying a blackberry, but when Meg persuaded him, he loved it and his mouth and hands were soon stained purple as he ate one for every blackberry that he put in his bowl.

Ruby was less enthusiastic, and soon lost interest. Leaving her bowl in the grass, she climbed onto the gate and perched on the top bar.

'Where does that road go?' she asked.

Meg didn't follow her pointing finger to Teggs Hill. She knew exactly which road Ruby meant.

'Just to the next dale,' she said as casually as she could.

'It looks steep.'

'It is.'

Rosie red-faced by the time she got to the top. I hate this hill, Meg!

I know, but it's worth it when you get to the top. Look, we can go really fast now.

I don't like going fast.

Looking at her twin incredulously. Going fast is the whole point, Rosie!

Pushing off, heart beating with excitement. Race you to the bottom!

Meg, slow down! Wait for me! Rosie's wail lost in the rush of wind in her face.

She hadn't slowed down. She hadn't waited.

Meg's throat burned. 'It's a very dangerous road, Ruby. You mustn't — '

'Look! A plane!' Ruby interrupted, pointing behind the brambles, and Meg turned to see a plane emerging from the clouds. It had smoke pouring from a wing and was flying erratically, lurching and wobbling low over the farmhouse, and was now heading straight for them, its engine spluttering and coughing.

'It's going to crash!'

'Dear Lord!' Meg dropped her bowl of blackberries and looked around frantically. Where could they take shelter? It was too far to get back to the farmhouse. There was a barn near the beck, she remembered. That might be better than nothing. Grabbing a protesting Stan by the hand, she practically dragged Ruby off the gate. 'We need to get out of the way!'

But it was too late. The plane was almost overhead, the sound of the engine so terrifyingly loud that they all clapped their hands over their ears. With what seemed a superhuman effort, it surged higher above them and continued its faltering progress.

Meg saw the swastika at the same time as Ruby. 'It's a German plane!' Ruby cried just as Stan yelled that there were people jumping out. They counted two parachutes and then a third before the plane abruptly lost height and ploughed into the side of the fell in the distance.

'It's a goner!' said Ruby delightedly while Meg was breathing a sigh of relief at their narrow escape. It was ominously dark. Any minute now, the heavens were going to open and they would be stuck outside with nowhere to shelter. They needed to get back to Emmerdale Farm and call for help from there, she decided, but Ruby was more interested in the crashed plane. 'Let's go and see!' she said, and without waiting for a reply, she took off, running over the rough ground in the direction of the crash.

'Ruby, come back!' Meg shouted, aghast, but Ruby ignored her, scrambling up the hillside. '*Ruby!*'

Cursing under her breath, Meg dragged Stan after his sister. They needed to be heading to the farmhouse, not running around the hillside with enemy aircrew who knew where. But she couldn't leave the wretched girl alone.

'What about my blackberries?' Stan protested as she pulled him after her up the hillside.

'We'll get them later.'

Puffing and panting, with Stan still complaining about the lost blackberries, they chased after Ruby, who was faster and more agile, and by the time they reached the plane, Meg had to double over to get her breath back. 'Stay back,' she wheezed. 'It might explode.'

'There's no one in it.' Ruby sounded disappointed.

'Thank goodness for that! Come away, Ruby, we need to report it to the police.'

'I want to get inside it.'

'Ruby, *no!*' Meg grabbed her by the arm and pulled her away from the wreckage. 'We need to get to Emmerdale Farm.'

But as she turned she was hugely relieved to see Joe and Maggie Sugden heading up the hill accompanied by Annie. Meg loosened her grip on the children, who both pulled away, Ruby making a big deal of rubbing her arm.

'I'm so glad to see you!'

As they got closer, she saw that Joe was armed with a shotgun and that made her feel better. Maggie had a pitchfork and Annie a rolling pin. 'It was the only weapon I could find,' she said with an embarrassed grin as Meg raised her eyebrows.

'Well, it's more than I've got.'

'We thought it was going to crash into the farmhouse,' said Maggie with a grimace.

'I know! We were picking blackberries and saw it fly over you. I think the pilot was trying to avoid any buildings, but then it was as if he was coming straight for us . . . ' Meg shuddered. 'We saw the crew bail out before it crashed, but I was afraid there might have been someone still inside the plane.'

'That's why we came up,' said Maggie.

'German or not, we couldn't leave them hurt.'

Annie nodded, her eyes on the crumpled plane with the sinister swastika on its tail. She shivered. 'I can't believe there's a German plane here. It makes the war so real somehow.'

'Luckily it's not a bomber,' said Meg. 'What do you think it's doing over here?'

'Could be a reconnaissance plane,' said Maggie as a rumble of thunder made them all look up. 'Perhaps it was struck by lightning. That could be why it crashed.'

'What do you think we should do now?' Meg asked Maggie, but it was Joe who answered.

'Stay . . . together,' he said firmly.

'Shouldn't we report it?'

'Jacob's gone to get Sergeant Proudfoot,' said Maggie. 'In the meantime, Joe's right. We should stick together.'

Another clap of thunder made them all jump and the next moment the first heavy drops of rain spattered onto the wing of the plane.

'It's going to pour,' said Maggie, hugging her arms together as the temperature plummeted. 'Let's go back to the farmhouse and wait for Jacob. Sergeant Proudfoot will organise the Local Volunteer Force and they'll deal with the Germans. There's no point in us all getting wet.'

That sounded good to Meg. She had no desire to try and tackle the Germans by herself. She looked around for Ruby and Stan.

'Come on, kids, we're going now,' she called, and when there was no reply she walked around to the other side of the plane, expecting to see them there, but there was no sign of them.

116

She blinked the rain out of her eyes. 'Ruby! Stan!'

Nothing. An icy finger poked at the base of Meg's spine as she looked frantically around.

She ran back to Annie. 'Have you seen Ruby and Stan?'

'They were here a minute ago, weren't they?'

'They were . . . but now they're gone!' Meg made herself take a deep breath as the rain doubled in force. Ruby and Stan were all alone on a strange hillside in a thunderstorm with at least three enemy airmen, all of whom were probably armed. 'I have to find them, Annie!'

'They can't have gone far.' Annie had to shout over the sound of the pounding rain and Meg was hit by the memory of wishing for rain earlier, when life had been ordinary and going ahead on a different time zone altogether. Ever since that plane had stumbled out of the clouds, the afternoon had taken on a nightmarish quality. If only she hadn't suggested blackberry-ing . . . blackberrying? Something clicked in her brain.

Annie was gesticulating now to where two figures were emerging through the wet. Meg cupped a hand around her ear. 'What?'

But Meg had stopped trying to listen. She was remembering Stan, and how bitterly he had complained at having to leave his blackberries. What if he had gone back to find his bowl? Ruby might have boasted that she could show him the way. The little devils!

'I know where they are!' She was already running down the hill, sturdy shoes skidding and sliding on the tussocky grass that was already slippery with rain.

'Where . . . going?' Annie shouted after her.

'I've got to get Ruby and Stan,' she called over her shoulder, although she doubted that Annie could hear her. 'I'll bring them to the farm-house.'

'Meg, be careful!'

Meg didn't listen. In her haste to find the children, she stumbled downhill through the rain, barely able to see where she was going. Several times she tripped and fell heavily onto her knees, but each time she forced herself up, wiping her filthy hands on her dress. The moment she found those children safe, she was going to kill them.

12

Meg knew Emmerdale Farm well. She and Rosie had played there as children, larking about in the beck with Jacob and Edward, and later helping with the harvest or the sheep-dipping or digging potatoes. She thought she knew every inch of it, but in the torrential rain she could hardly see where she was going and all at once everything looked alien. She stumbled to a halt, disorientated.

Was this the way they had come? Meg dragged in a panicky breath as she peered through the rain. She had been so intent on chasing Ruby that she hadn't really paid attention, and now she wasn't sure . . . Were the brambles to the left or to the right? Surely she should have found them by now. She had thought she was heading straight for them.

Overhead, thunder was rumbling ominously, and a flash of lightning almost blinded her. Where were those wretched children? She had to get them out of this storm.

Another flash of lightning lit up a barn to the left and Meg's heart jumped in relief. The barn was not far from the brambles. She had overshot the turning in the rain.

Stumbling back the way she had come, she found herself at the brambles but there was no sign of the children. Her bowl lay discarded where she had dropped it when the plane had appeared, blackberries tumbling out of it, but the other two bowls had gone. So Ruby and Stan had come back here . . . but where were they now?

Calm down, Meg, she told herself. *Think.*

Could they have been sensible enough to take shelter? They wouldn't know about the barn, but they might have spotted it. Meg's feet were squelching in her shoes as she pushed her way around the brambles and headed downhill to the barn. The rain was easing at last, thank the Lord, but she was so wet now it made little difference. Her sodden dress clung unpleasantly to her thighs, and —

A sharp cry sliced across Meg's miserable thoughts and she jerked upright as if prodded. Had that been one of the children?

'Ruby?' she called, and all at once fear was drumming along her veins. 'Stan?'

Breaking into a run, she headed down the hill once more.

Breathless and bedraggled, she yanked open the barn door. It was dark inside, and with the sunlight blocked out by the thunderclouds, Meg had to stop in the doorway while her eyes adjusted to the dimness.

The first thing she saw was the bowl she had given Ruby what felt like a lifetime ago. It lay on its side in the middle of the hay-covered floor. Ice pooled in Meg's stomach and her eyes lifted to find her worst fears confirmed.

A young man in a flying suit was holding a struggling Ruby, his hand clamped over her mouth. Ruby's eyes flickered frantically to the right and, horrified, Meg followed her gaze to see little Stan standing stock-still as the airman behind him held a gun to his head.

Meg froze, her heart hammering. Let this not be happening, she prayed. Let this be a nightmare. I'm going to wake up in my bed and Ruby will be sulky and Stan will have made a mess and that'll be fine.

You'll be safer here than in Hull, she had told them.

A small sound from Ruby jerked Meg into action. She raised her hands to show that she was no threat. 'Please,' she croaked. 'Don't hurt him.'

Her mind had gone blank. She had learnt German for a while. How could she have forgotten how to say please?

'*Bitte*,' she snatched the word from her memory. '*Bitte*, don't hurt him.'

The airmen were both very young, she realised. They were obviously shocked from the crash and jittery at Meg's sudden appearance. Keeping her hands high, Meg forced her expression to stay calm.

'It's all right,' she said to Stan with a reassuring smile, and then she turned to Ruby. 'Everything's going to be all right. Just stay calm.'

Dredging up a few more words of German, she looked straight at the crewman holding the gun. It was shaking in his hand and she thought he was nearly as frightened as Stan.

'Let him go,' she said to him, and scratched around for a few more words from those long-ago German lessons. '*Lass ihn gehen. Bitte.*'

The two crewmen began jabbering at each

other in German, much too fast for Meg to understand.

'Stay quite still,' she told Ruby and Stan. 'They won't hurt you. They're just frightened.'

Abruptly, the airman lifted the gun away from Stan's head. The little boy hurtled across the barn to clutch at her and buried his face in her stomach, his thin body trembling. Throat tight, Meg put her arms round him and held him close.

'*Danke*,' she said to the airman, but he lifted his gun and pointed it at her instead. It was wavering alarmingly in his hand and she started to ease Stan behind her.

To her horror, the other man started pulling Ruby away.

'No!' cried Stan, who had seen what was happening, and before Meg could stop him, he had launched himself at his sister's captor, pounding at him with his small fists.

The one holding the gun lifted it uncertainly, and Meg had no choice but to throw herself at him. She had a hazy idea that she might wrest the gun from him, though she had no idea what she would have done with it if she had managed to take it. As it was, the airman lifted the gun easily out of her reach and swung with his fist, hitting her on the face.

Meg's cheek exploded with pain and she staggered and fell to the floor, dazed. Ruby and Stan were screaming and struggling, the Germans shouting, and the rain had started thundering on the roof of the barn again.

A sharp voice broke through all the noise and

panic. The rain continued to drum, but everyone else shut up abruptly and they all turned to look at the man in the doorway. He was dressed in a beige flying suit like the crew, with a leather flying helmet and thick, fur-lined boots, but as he surveyed the chaos with disapproval it was obvious from the way he held himself that he was used to command. He had spoken in German, but even Stan and Ruby seemed to recognise the authority that meant he had raised his voice only to be heard above the rain.

For Meg, sprawled on the hay-strewn floor of the barn, there was an odd moment of relief. Here was the pilot, obviously, and she ought to have been terrified, but all she could think was to be thankful that someone had taken control of the situation and made everyone stop shouting.

The two airmen stood abruptly to attention and released the children, who ran over to Meg as she was still struggling to her feet. Their weight as they threw themselves at her knocked her to her knees once more.

'It's all right,' she said again, putting an arm around each of them. 'Just be quiet now.'

'Are they going to kill us?' Stan whimpered, and Meg raised her eyes to the pilot.

'Are you?' she asked.

'There will be no killing by anybody.' He limped further into the barn and took off his helmet awkwardly. One of his arms seemed to be injured and he held it away from his body. He had a wiry, compact figure and steady eyes in a lean face that was covered in scratches. Ignoring Ruby's glare, he tossed his helmet aside and helped Meg to her feet with his good hand.

'My apologies,' he said. 'My crew aren't thinking clearly. They are nervous and only boys, as you can see.' His grip was firm under her elbow and Meg was sure she could feel the imprint of his fingertips on her skin where he held her. 'Are you hurt?'

'I'm ... all right,' said Meg, completely thrown by his air of cool assurance and how well he spoke English. When he let go of her arm, she lifted a hand to nurse her throbbing cheek, all at once acutely aware of what a mess she must look: mud-splattered and now covered in hay, her thin frock sticking clammily to her body, her hair hanging in dripping rat's tails.

'He hit her!' White-faced and glaring, Ruby pointed to the airman responsible.

The pilot's eyes flicked from Ruby to Meg, and it was almost as if he could see everything: Ruby's truculence, Stan's fear, Meg's grief and guilt.

'I am sorry. In war, people behave badly, but there is no excuse to hit a woman.' He snapped something to the airman, who scowled but managed what Meg assumed was a grudging apology.

The three men held a further conversation in rapid German before the pilot turned back to Meg. 'Our plane crashed, as you saw. We were hit by lightning and I lost control.'

'We did see you,' said Meg. 'We thought you were going to crash into the farmhouse.'

'I was afraid of that, too, but I managed to get the nose up and fly past it. There wasn't any more I could do.'

'We saw you all bail out.'

'Yes. Hans and Walter here landed better than I did.' His expression was rueful and he touched his torn and battered face as if it were tender. 'I came down in a tree and then fell out of it! They came to find shelter as agreed, and were hiding in here when children came in. They . . . what is the word . . . ?' He paused, then answered his own question. 'They panicked. And that is when you arrived. They were just trying to keep the children quiet.'

'By holding a gun to a little boy's head?' said Meg angrily.

When would someone come and look for them? Should she try and keep the Germans talking until the Local Volunteer Force found them, or should she get Ruby and Stan away? The children's safely should be her first concern, but for all the pilot's cool courtesy, Hans (or possibly Walter) was still holding a gun.

'I am sorry for that.' The pilot sounded sincere, but Meg didn't trust him. She gathered Ruby and Stan closer to her side.

'If you're really sorry, you'll tell your crew to put that gun down and let us go,' she said.

He shook his head. 'I'm afraid I can't do that. We need to get away.' A spasm of pain crossed his face and he pressed a hand to his collarbone.

'What have you done?' Meg asked involuntarily.

'I think I have broken this when I fell out of the tree,' he said with another wince, pointing at his collarbone. 'I need to tie it, I think, before I can walk any further.'

There was another quick-fire exchange in German while Meg wondered if they could make a run for it. But they'd have to get past the pilot, and then there was still the gun . . .

The pilot turned back to her. 'I need a . . . what do you call it . . . to support . . . ' He gestured to his arm.

'A sling?'

'Yes, a sling.'

Meg thought quickly. 'I can use my petticoat.'

'Petticoat? What is that?'

For answer, she turned her back and pulled her wet frock up so that she could wriggle discreetly out of her petticoat.

'You shouldn't be helping him!' Ruby spat. 'He's the enemy!'

'The sooner I help him walk, the sooner he'll leave us alone,' said Meg briefly, turning back to hold out the sodden petticoat.

'Your mother is right,' the pilot said to Ruby, whose face whitened with rage.

'She's not our mother!'

He shrugged. 'Whoever she is, she is sensible. She is facing facts. We don't want to hurt you but it is our duty to get away, so the sooner we do that, the better it will be for you.' He glanced at Meg. 'What is your name, you who are not the mother?'

She toyed with the idea of refusing to tell him, but he had just called her sensible. 'Meg,' she said coldly.

'Meg.' He tested her name as if tasting it in his mouth, and for some reason she found herself blushing.

126

Not that he could probably tell in this light, but she scowled anyway, just in case.

'So, Meg,' he said briskly. 'You will make a sling for my arm and my men will stand guard.'

'Why can't one of them do it?'

'Because I am not a fool.' His voice sharpened. 'One man to look after the three of you gives one of you the chance to escape to warn your police. The children are quick. No,' he said, 'they stay on guard. You are the nurse.'

'I don't know anything about nursing,' she objected.

'You look like an intelligent woman. You will work it out.'

Reluctantly, Meg began tearing her poor petticoat into strips. 'We're going to do what he says,' she told the children. 'You sit on the hay there. Walter and Hans won't touch you. They just want to make sure you won't run away.'

'Hurry, Meg.' The pilot eased himself down onto a pile of hay and began to unfasten his flying jacket, but it was a struggle with one arm, and in the end Meg went over with an exclamation of exasperation to help him.

He was very white about the lips by the time she had manoeuvred off the jacket and pulled down the top of his beige flying suit. Beneath it, he wore a vest and Meg could see the bump where the bone had broken. She bit her lip as she assembled the strips of petticoat and knotted them together to fashion a sling of sorts.

The pilot snapped an order and one of the airmen went to the door, obviously to check if there was any sign of a search. The other kept a wary eye on Ruby and Stan.

'I think the bone needs to be properly set,' Meg said.

'We've no time for that. Just tie it up.'

'It's going to hurt,' she warned.

'Meg.' She looked up involuntarily to see his mouth set in an inflexible line. 'Do it,' he said. 'Now.'

Excruciatingly aware of her fingers brushing the warmth of his flesh, Meg tied the sling around his shoulder to provide a support for his arm and then pulled up the flying suit as best she could. She helped him push one arm back into his flying jacket and slung the other side of the jacket around his other shoulder.

'*Gut*,' he said when she had finished. Steadying himself with one hand on her shoulder, he levered himself upright and tested his weight on one leg.

'Is your leg hurt too?' She peered closer at a spreading stain on the flying suit. 'Is that *blood*?'

'It is a cut. It is not a bad one.'

It looked bad to Meg. For some reason she felt close to tears. 'You won't be able to get far like that,' she said, but he only shrugged his good shoulder.

'I will do what has to be done.'

Another barked order and Walter and Hans sprang into action, producing lengths of cord from their pockets. The one holding the gun passed it to the pilot, who calmly pointed it at Meg.

'What are you doing?' Meg asked in alarm.

He ignored her and spoke directly to Ruby and Stan. 'Let Walter and Hans tie your hands and feet,' he said, 'and I won't shoot Meg.'

The children froze obediently while Meg's mouth opened and closed in shock.

'I just helped you!' she accused him.

'You were being sensible, and now I am being sensible,' he said. 'We cannot let you watch which way we go, or shout and warn anyone who might be looking for us. So we will tie you up and leave you in the barn here.'

'You can't leave us here!' Meg was outraged.

He studied her dispassionately. 'You will be warm and dry, and someone will find you eventually. Is there some of that petticoat left? Good.' He took it from Meg's nerveless hand and tossed it to Walter and Hans, who fashioned rough gags to wrap around Ruby and Stan. '*Schnell!*' he snapped.

'The police will catch you.' Meg's voice trembled with fury as one of the airmen tied her hands behind her back with deft fingers, and then bent to tie her feet together. They weren't cruelly tight bonds, but Meg wasn't in a mood to be grateful. He let her hop over to join Stan and Ruby and she half fell into the hay beside them while he hobbled them together.

'You won't get away,' she vowed as the airman bent to fix a gag around her mouth.

'Perhaps not,' said the pilot. 'But we must try.' A faint smile touched his mouth. 'Goodbye, Meg. Thank you for your petticoat.'

A quick burst of orders to Walter and Hans and the three of them moved to the barn door. Cautiously, they peered out. The rain was still drumming onto the roof and cascading past the door in an almost impenetrable sheet of water. The pilot nodded to the two men to slip out. He glanced back once, meeting Meg's furious gaze above her gag with what might have been a look of rueful apology, and then he pulled the barn door to behind him and they were gone.

13

'Slow down, Corporal.'

Surprised, Lily lifted her foot off the accelerator. They were driving back to the camp after a meeting at Divisional Command, and she had taken a shortcut along the unmarked back roads that only the locals knew. Now Derek was pointing at a turning half hidden behind a tangle of long grass and nettles that led up to Teggs Hill.

'Where does that road go?'

'It doesn't really go anywhere, sir,' she said.

He studied the turning. 'It must go somewhere,' he objected.

'It just goes over the hill to some farms in the next dale. It's so steep and winding, especially on the other side, that it's really not used much any more.'

'So it's a quiet road?'

'Very.'

'That sounds like just what I want.'

'You want me to drive you up there?' Lily couldn't quite keep the surprise from her voice.

'If it's not too much trouble, Corporal.'

'Very good, sir.' She turned the jeep into the lane, wondering if he was planning some training exercise. Not that it was her place to ask. Derek was her senior officer, and she was here to do as she was told.

And not just because he was a colonel. Since that evening in the Woolpack, Lily's feelings for him had only deepened. She hugged to herself the memory of that moment when she had been so sure he was going to kiss her, right there in the pub in front of everybody, even stuffy Jack Proudfoot. In hindsight Lily was relieved that he hadn't, but still, it had been a perfect moment.

And then Nina Lazenby had come along and muscled into the conversation, showing off how well she knew Derek, calling him by his first name, treating Lily as if she were a child allowed to sit with the grown-ups . . . Lily ground her teeth whenever she thought of Nina's patronising smile.

As if it hadn't been bad enough, with her father glowering at Derek and Jed and Larry being their usual embarrassing Dingle selves.

Derek hadn't suggested meeting again. Lily could hardly blame him. She had behaved with scrupulous correctness ever since. The last thing she wanted was to embarrass him, and it was always possible that she had misunderstood. She couldn't risk losing her job as his driver. For now, it was enough to see him every day, to thrill at his nearness and to adore him. That was all Lily asked.

The lane was full of suddenly steep hills and tricky bends, but Lily had learnt to drive on roads like these and she kept the jeep moving steadily upwards. She was more concerned about the black clouds in the distance that were rumbling ominously. She would need to get the roof up before it started to rain.

She paused the jeep at the crest of the hill so that Derek could see the dangerous twists and turns of the lane leading down into the next valley.

'Good Lord,' he said. 'What a view!'

'Do you want me to go on, sir?'

'No, stop here, will you?'

Pulling on the handbrake, Lily switched off the engine. Derek got out and strolled to the side of the lane.

'It's beautiful here. Or do you just take it for granted?' he asked with one of his intense looks that always caught her unawares.

'I don't come here often,' she admitted. 'People in Beckindale think of this as a dangerous road more than a beautiful one.' She nodded down the hill. 'My uncle was killed down there, or that's what my parents always told me. He was driving too fast. He came off at a bend and the car somersaulted all the way to the bottom.'

Derek whistled. 'Nasty.'

'And a girl I knew fell off her bike here and died. We were always warned against this road as kids.'

'And yet you drove up here without turning a hair.' Derek eyed her with admiration. 'I couldn't have made it look as easy as you did, Lily. It makes me realise what a good driver you are.'

She couldn't help glowing at his praise. 'Thank you, sir.' The thunderclouds growled in the distance. 'Shall I put the roof up?' Lily asked.

'I'll give you a hand.'

'I can manage, sir.'

'Lily,' he said, 'we're all on our own on the top of a hill. No one can see us. No one's going to mind if we do it together.'

They wrestled the cover into place and then, when the rain still held off, rested side by side against the bonnet, arms touching. Lily was sure she could feel the warmth of his skin burning through his sleeve, through hers and tingling against her skin. They had lapsed into a silence that was freighted with words unspoken, one that lengthened until she was sure Derek must be able to hear the thump of her heart.

'It's hot.' She broke the silence at last, hating how thin and high her voice sounded. 'We could do with the rain to clear the air.'

'Talking of clearing the air,' said Derek, turning to look at her, 'we never did finish our conversation in the pub before your father and Nina joined us.'

Lily flushed. 'I'm sorry my father was so rude to you, sir.'

'Oh, I don't blame him. He could see how I felt about you. He knows I'm too old for you, and you're so young . . . ' Derek pushed himself away from the bonnet, snatching off his cap and raking a hand through his hair. 'I shouldn't say anything at all, but damn it, Lily, you don't understand what you're doing to me!'

'Sir?' she said uncertainly, and he swung round.

'Don't call me sir, Lily, for God's sake! I'm mad about you, can't you see that? I can't think of anything but you. It's been driving me wild, being with you but not being able to tell you how I feel. In camp, there's always someone else around, and it's the same in Beckindale. We never get a chance to be alone, or to talk.'

Striding back to her, he seized her hands in his. 'Tell me you feel the same, Lily, darling. I sense that you do, but I need to hear it.'

'I do! Oh, of course I do!' Lily's eyes were like stars, and with a smothered oath Derek pulled her tight against him for a kiss so long and delicious that when he finally lifted his head, her knees felt weak and she had to cling onto him.

He smiled down into her radiant face. 'We'll find somewhere to be alone soon. Next time you have a day off, we'll — '

The splutter of an engine overhead made them both look up, startled, to see a plane emerge out of the roiling black storm clouds in front of them. 'Good grief!' Derek whistled at the sight of the swastika on the tail. 'That's one of Jerry's.'

The plane was moving in an odd, ungainly way, its wings wobbling as the pilot tried to control it.

'It's going to crash!' said Lily in horror.

'By Jove, I think you're right.' Romance forgotten, they both stared as if mesmerised by the lurching progress of the plane.

'There!' Lily cried, pointing at parachutes that were opening and drifting with an unnerving grace towards the earth. 'They're bailing out!'

A few moments later there was a dull crump as the plane crashed into the hillside. Derek snapped into action. 'We'd better get down there.'

'Won't the police . . . ?'

'I don't think we can ask PC Plod to deal with enemy aircrew,' said Derek. He ran round to the side of the jeep while Lily swung into the driver's seat. 'Can you tell where they're going down?'

'Emmerdale Farm, I think.'

'Step on it, Corporal,' he said, but he put a hand on her thigh and squeezed so that she knew he hadn't forgotten.

★   ★   ★

Heavy drops of rain smacked a warning onto the canvas cover as Lily did a three-point turn on the narrow lane and headed back down the hill. Before long, those first few drops had become a torrent, cascading down from the rumbling clouds in a deafening downpour. The canvas was soon sagging under the weight of the water and leaking into the jeep itself.

The surface of the lane was running with water. It was like driving down a river, and Lily had to inch slowly down in the treacherous conditions. She could feel Derek's impatience, but going faster would be no use if they slid into a ditch.

She was glad of the need to concentrate. It meant there was no time to think about that dizzying kiss. Her heart had been pounding so hard she had been feeling slightly sick, and then the plane had appeared, and now the mood had changed with disorientating speed. If it hadn't been for the warmth of Derek's hand on her thigh, Lily might have wondered if she had imagined it.

As she drove into the yard at Emmerdale Farm, they saw the men from the Local Volunteer Force jogging up the hillside through the rain. Parking the jeep next to their truck, Lily jumped out, but Derek was already halfway across the yard, desperate not to miss out on the action. He left the gate open — obviously not a countryman — and she struggled to drag it shut as she skidded and slipped after him in the mud.

Lily was glad they had the men from the LVF to follow. The rain was pelting so hard that she was almost at the crash site before she saw the fuselage and the people huddled excitedly round it. Holding a hand to the stitch in her side, she studied the scene, which seemed momentarily frozen: Jack Proudfoot the still centre of the group, Annie Pearson gesticulating wildly, and Derek, who had forged ahead of her, leaving her to close every one of the gates they passed, striding forward to take command of the scene.

Lily reached the group in time to hear him address Jack. 'What's the position, Sergeant?'

Jack held up a hand. 'One moment . . . sir,' he added as an obvious afterthought.

'We need to find Meg and the children,' Annie was saying urgently. 'She said they'd go to the farmhouse, but when Maggie and I went back, she wasn't there.'

'Did she say where she was going before that?' Jack asked.

'I couldn't hear . . . I think she just said she knew where the children had gone and that she'd take them to the farmhouse.'

'I saw them blackberrying earlier,' Jacob Sugden put in. 'Was she heading down to the beck?'

'She could have been — but why hasn't she turned up yet?'

'She's sheltering somewhere if she's sensible,' Derek cut in dismissively. 'Why are we wasting time on this, Sergeant?'

'The safety of a woman and two children may be at stake,' said Jack in an even voice. 'That's not *wasting time*.'

Derek was clearly unconvinced. 'It's more important to find the crew. They can't have got far in these conditions.'

'Well, I'm going to look for Meg,' said Annie. 'Lily, will you come with me?'

'Of course,' said Lily, before remembering that she needed to ask Derek's permission. 'If that's all right with you, sir?' she added, uncomfortably aware of Jack Proudfoot's cool eyes on her.

Derek looked irritated. 'If you must. We're wasting time here, Sergeant. We need to get a search party organised for the Germans, pronto.'

'The platoon has already been briefed,' said Jack, not bothering to hide his look of contempt. 'If you'd like to join this section, sir, they're ready to set off now.'

Lily narrowed her eyes at the faint insolence threading his voice. Jack didn't care for Derek, that was clear. She wanted to think that he was jealous of the colonel, but even she had to admit that he was quietly competent, directing the men without fuss and making sure they all knew what they were doing.

Joe Sugden set off with another group, but Jacob Sugden still lingered. 'Annie and Lily shouldn't be wandering around by themselves,' he said. 'It's not safe.'

'They won't be on their own,' said Jack. 'I'll go

with them, and I'm armed.' He patted the pistol at his belt.

Satisfied, Jacob turned to catch up with the final search party, who were to fan out across the hillside.

Jack turned to Annie and Lily. 'Right. Let's find Meg and the children. Where's this blackberry patch Jacob mentioned?'

He was limping badly, but he kept up a good pace. Once, he jarred his leg, and Lily heard him swear under his breath.

'Are you all right?' she asked.

'I'm fine,' he said curtly.

At the bottom of the field, Lily's feet skidded out from beneath her by a gate where the cows had trampled the ground into a quagmire and she fell flat on her back in the mud.

'Here, take my hand.' Jack leant down to help her up and Lily, sodden, floundering and stinking of manure, had little choice but to accept. His grip was cool and insensibly reassuring, and Lily pulled her hand away, jolted in a way she couldn't quite explain.

'Thank you,' she muttered.

Annie led them to a patch of brambles. 'This is where they were,' she said, picking up an abandoned bowl.

'Is there any shelter nearby?' Jack asked.

'There's a barn . . . '

They pushed their way through more brambles and floundered across another sea of mud towards the barn door. The rain was relentless, and Lily couldn't imagine that anyone would have been able to hear their approach, but Jack signalled for silence and gestured her and Annie back before cautiously opening the door.

Ignoring his order to keep back, Lily peered over his shoulder into the gloom. It took a moment before her eyes adjusted and she made out the shapes in the hay.

'Meg!' she cried, rushing forward, evading Jack's attempt to grasp her arm.

'You damn fool!' he snapped. 'What if there'd been a German soldier behind the door?'

Lily ignored him. She was kneeling by the little boy, untying his gag. 'It's OK,' she told him, 'you're safe now.'

Annie was busy releasing the girl from her bonds while Jack, stiff with disapproval at Lily's recklessness, dealt with Meg.

'Oh, thank you, thank you!' Meg spat out her gag and flexed her wrists. 'I have never been so pleased to see you!'

As soon as Lily had released him, the boy flung himself at Meg and she hugged him. 'You've been so brave, Stan,' she told him. 'You too, Ruby.'

Ruby's face was twisted into her habitual scowl. Lily suspected she would have liked to have thrown herself at Meg, too, but pride and stubbornness held her back.

'Meg, you're hurt!' said Annie, alarmed. 'What happened?'

Meg let Jack help her to her feet, Stan still clinging to her, and touched her face gingerly. 'It's not as bad as it looks.'

'It is,' insisted Ruby, rubbing her wrists. 'That German hit her.'

'Oh, my God, Meg!' said Lily, horrified.

'It wasn't as bad as it sounds,' said Meg. She told them about their encounter with the Germans.

'How long ago did they leave?' asked Jack.

'It feels like *hours*, but it probably isn't even one,' said Meg.

'We've got men out searching for them. They should be able to pick them up.'

'Good,' said Meg after an odd moment of hesitation.

'I hope you *shoot* them,' said Ruby furiously.

The corner of Jack's mouth lifted. 'We won't do that. They'll go to the prisoner of war camp.'

'Well . . . good,' said Meg again. Her eyes slid away to the children. 'Can we go home now?'

'If you think you'll be all right on your own.' Jack glanced at Lily. 'Could you give them a lift? I presume you're in a vehicle?'

'Of course.' Lily held out a hand to Ruby. 'Come on, let's get you home.'

By the time she'd seen Meg and the children safely into the cottage and made it back to Emmerdale Farm, the search parties had found the Germans. Lily saw them being prodded, none too gently, into the back of a lorry. Derek was waiting in the farmhouse kitchen, a nerve twitching in his jaw.

'Where have you been?'

Lily explained and he scowled. 'That's a Ministry of Defence vehicle. You should have asked permission.'

'I asked Lily to take Meg and the children home,' Jack Proudfoot interposed.

'The police have no authority over MoD vehicles!'

'I didn't ask her as a policeman,' said Jack. 'I asked her as a human being who could see that Meg and the children were exhausted.'

'I'm sorry you had to wait, sir,' said Lily as Derek got sulkily into the jeep.

'Oh, don't mind me,' he said, his face lightening as they drove away. 'I'm just cross I didn't get a chance to capture those Germans myself.' He laid a hand on Lily's knee so that her skirt rode up when she had to change gear. 'And to be honest, I was more cross at having our conversation interrupted earlier. Next time,' he promised, 'I'll make sure there are absolutely no intrusions.'

14

Annie bent and squinted into the mirror, her eyes almost crossing with the effort of applying lipstick in a steady line. She didn't normally wear make-up, and whenever she did, she always felt like a child let loose with a box of crayons.

Straightening, she blotted her lips with a tissue and examined her reflection ruefully. She had managed some face powder, but the rouge made her look like a clown and she scrubbed at it with the tissue.

'I'd much rather be staying at home with you,' she told Sooty, who was watching Annie with great yellow eyes while he kneaded the eiderdown with his claws.

She wished she hadn't agreed to go to the dance in the Drill Hall, but Sarah had been insistent when Annie had seen her in the shop the day before.

'You promised!' she wailed when Annie made noises about having changed her mind. 'They're going to have a real band from the camp, too!'

'Now I'll have to trek all the way down the track in my best frock,' Annie grumbled as she set boiled potatoes on the table at dinnertime. 'I'll end up at the dance looking like I've been dragged through a hedge backwards! I don't reckon it's worth it.'

'It'll be good for you to have some fun,' Maggie said. 'You can't sit around moping, Annie. Edward won't come home any quicker for you waiting.

You know what he's like,' she went on with a painful smile. Although the rancour felt by both Jacob and Edward when they learnt about her affair with the conscientious objector had died down, it was still a touchy subject. 'He'll enjoy himself whenever he gets the chance, and so should you.'

'I suppose so.' The trouble was, Annie couldn't imagine enjoying a dance without Edward. 'I don't see how I can enjoy myself when I don't know anyone, though.'

'You can dance with me, Annie,' said Jacob.

'Oh, Jacob, you don't need to go for me,' said Annie, piling kale into a dish. 'The last thing I want is to drag you out as well.'

'Mebbe I want to go.'

Annie laughed at him. 'You?' she said affectionately. 'Come on, Jacob, we all know you hate dancing.'

'I'll go for you.'

Maggie had stopped smiling. Her gaze was thoughtful as it rested on her son. 'There'll be plenty of men for Annie to dance with, Jacob. Think of the ratio of men from the training camp to girls!'

'What are you saying, Ma?' The undercurrent of resentment in his voice had Maggie frowning. 'That local men aren't welcome at the dance? It's just a cattle market for those lads to pick out our women, is it?'

'No, I'm not saying that, Jacob,' Maggie said calmly. 'I'm saying Annie should feel she has the chance to dance with anyone she wants.'

'She's just said that it's going to be a long walk

down the track. I could take you in the truck,' he went on, turning to Annie.

'Well, if you're sure . . . ?' Annie had to admit that she would feel better walking into the dance with someone familiar by her side. She would rather it was Edward, but Jacob was definitely her next choice.

'I'm sure,' said Jacob curtly, not meeting his mother's eyes.

Annie's face cleared and she smiled at him with unshadowed affection. 'In that case, that would be grand, Jacob. Thank you.'

Now she patted her curls into place, made a face at her reflection, gave Sooty's furry tummy a farewell tickle and headed down the narrow cottage stairs to wait for Jacob to arrive.

★   ★   ★

After all the excitement of the German plane crashing the previous week, life in Beckindale had returned to normal. The Germans had been taken to the nearby prisoner of war camp, and talk in the village shop had reverted to the dreariness of rationing, the forthcoming dance, Jed Dingle's latest get-quick-rich scheme and the continuing speculation about what exactly had caused Jack Proudfoot to limp, and whether there had ever been a Mrs Proudfoot.

At Emmerdale Farm, they weren't bothered about the gossip. The Sugdens were more concerned about finding extra labour on the farm. They had applied for a licence to employ prisoners of war from the camp who had the option of working if they wanted to. Annie wasn't sure she liked the idea of the enemy at Emmerdale Farm when Edward was away fighting, but it wasn't up to her.

'You look nice,' said Jacob when she hurried out in response to his blast of the horn, waving goodbye to her parents.

'So do you.'

It was true. Shaved and changed into a suit, Jacob was an undeniably good-looking man. He was dark and strong, with big farmer's hands, but he lacked Edward's warmth or humour or lightness of spirit. As always when she thought about Edward, the longing for him rose chokingly in Annie's throat and she had to swallow hard.

But she made herself smile as she climbed into the ancient truck. The cab had hay on the seat and smelt comfortingly of Jacob's dog, Laddie, who usually accompanied him everywhere. The track was badly rutted and Annie had to cling to the door handle as they lurched from side to side.

It was still light when they reached the Drill Hall, but the windows had been blacked out in preparation, once darkness fell, and when Jacob pulled open the door, the lights and music inside hit Annie like a blow. The hall was crowded with dancing couples, and as Annie and Jacob made their way around the edge, the band finished on a flourish and the dancers stopped and clapped. The band had clearly decided to take a break, and a swell of chatter and laughter rose in place of the music.

'Annie! Coo-ee!' Sarah waved excitedly to catch her attention.

Glad to recognise a friendly face, Annie waved back, and along with Jacob she pushed through the crowd to reach her friend.

Standing by Sarah's side was a dazzled-looking recruit. 'This is Ray Merrick,' she said, introducing him proudly to Annie and Jacob.

Ray had a pleasant face with comically large ears. He mumbled a greeting but could barely drag his gaze from Sarah, who was clearly equally smitten.

Annie suppressed a sigh. Having insisted that Annie keep her company, it seemed that Sarah would be perfectly happy with Ray's company now, so Annie might just as well have stayed at home.

Well, she was here now, Annie thought practically. She should make an effort.

Sarah turned to Jacob. 'I hear you captured them Germans single-handedly,' she said.

'Hardly,' said Jacob in his dour way. The search party had found the aircrew huddled by the beck, half drowned according to the men who had crowded into the Emmerdale kitchen afterwards. 'I reckon they were glad to be captured,' he said.

Ray was impressed enough to drag his eyes momentarily from Sarah's generous bosom. 'We heard about the Germans,' he said. 'We were all wishing we'd had a piece of the action. Did you find the pilot, too?'

'No,' said Jacob. 'That were Sergeant Proudfoot. The pilot had made it as far as the waterfall up near Teggs Hill. God knows how he managed it. He had a broken collarbone and a nasty cut on his leg. He could barely walk when they brought him back t'farmhouse.'

'He was cool as a cucumber,' said Annie, who had helped Maggie dress some of the pilot's wounds while they waited for a military ambulance and escort for the prisoners, and had been reluctantly impressed. 'He must have been in agony, but he didn't even wince.'

The band struck up again and there was a general rustle as couples paired up once more. Ray was already turning to Sarah. Annie hesitated. She really didn't want Jacob to feel that he had to ask her to dance as well. She knew how much he hated it, and he had done enough bringing her here. Fortunately one of Ray's fellow recruits came up and demanded with a cheeky smile that Ray introduce him to Annie.

'Like to dance?' he asked, and she smiled a little shyly back at him as she thanked him.

'I was going to ask you,' said Jacob, scowling.

'Oh, Jacob, you don't need to look after me,' Annie said guiltily. 'You go and enjoy yourself. I'll be fine.'

With a reassuring smile at Jacob, she let her partner take her hand and twirl her onto the floor. His name was Bert, he said, and he was flatteringly interested, raising his voice above the sound of the band to compliment her dress, her smile, her eyes.

Annie tried to enjoy herself, but it wasn't the same without Edward. She imagined him walking into the Drill Hall. Hey, he would say to

148

Bert, that's my girl you've got there. Push off. And then he would open his arms and she would walk into them and feel safe at last. They would dance slowly together, their bodies fitting perfectly the way they had always done, and all would be right with the world once more.

The picture was so clear in her head that Annie had to close her eyes against the savage twist of longing.

Bert was reluctant to let her go when the song ended, but another recruit cut in boldly and she was whisked off before he had a chance to object. Girls were in such short supply compared to the number of men at the training camp that a man had to be bold if he wanted to dance. Annie couldn't hear most of their names. She nodded and smiled and gave herself up to the music while she tried not to think of Edward.

It was some time later that Sarah dragged her off to the Ladies, a dingy block at the back of the hall. The two ancient toilets were equipped with rusty pull chains and the sink made an ominous clanking noise when you turned on the tap.

'I like your skirt,' Annie said, trying without success to eke some lather out of the sliver of soap.

Sarah brightened and gave a twirl. 'It's all right, isn't it?' She leant forward confidentially. 'Parachute silk! Dyed, so you can't hardly tell, can you?'

'Where did you get it?'

'Jed Dingle found the German parachutes they'd hidden at Emmerdale Farm, and Mum got a good deal on one of them. She made this skirt for me and a blouse for Elizabeth.'

'It's pretty,' said Annie.

'So . . . ' Sarah went on with a meaningful look. 'What do you think?'

'Think?' Annie echoed, puzzled.

'About Ray, of course! Isn't he dreamy?'

With an effort, Annie recalled Ray's face and those huge ears. 'He seems very nice,' she said diplomatically.

'I think I'm in love!'

Annie laughed at that. 'You've only just met him, Sarah!'

'It just feels right. Like we're meant to be together,' Sarah said, peering into the cracked mirror to pat her carefully permed hair back into place. 'I don't want to dance with anyone else, you know?'

Annie's smile faded, thinking of Edward. 'Yes, I know.'

'You coming back to dance?'

'I'll be along in a minute,' said Annie. 'You go back to your Ray.'

Sarah whisked herself off and Annie dug her lipstick out of her bag, more to have a few moments to herself than because she wanted to make herself look nice. Even the depressing Ladies was more appealing than all the boisterous jollity in the hall.

Her heart sank when the door opened, but it was only Meg Warcup. 'Mind if I hide in here too?' she said.

'I'm not hiding — ' Annie began, only to meet Meg's eyes. 'Well, maybe a bit.'

'Must be hard without Edward,' said Meg.

She was the first person who had understood, Annie thought as she nodded. But then Meg knew what it was like to find yourself alone when you had been used to always being one of a pair.

'Sorry I made you come tonight,' she offered.

'Oh, it's probably good for me.' Meg disappeared into one of the cubicles and raised her voice to float over the door. 'Mrs Airey is looking after the children, and she's more than a match for Ruby so it's nice to get away for an evening.'

'How have they been since the crash?'

'Stan's in a bad way. He's a quiet kid anyway, and having a gun held to your head would be traumatic for anyone. He's got very nervous.' There was a crashing sound as Meg pulled the chain and emerged from the cubicle. 'But Ruby seems to have thrived on all the excitement. She was scared at the time, but now it's given her something to boast about with the other kids, and at last she's making some friends. She's stopped complaining about how boring it is in the country, anyway,' she added with a sardonic look.

She picked up the sliver of soap with a sigh. 'I miss soap. Remember how nice it was to unwrap a new bar and get a lovely rich lather?'

'It's the little things that get you down,' Annie agreed. 'It's like we're not really at war here. It's just a lot of inconveniences, like rationing or the blackout.'

'I felt that too until that German belted me.' Meg squinted into the mirror and touched a finger gingerly to her cheek. 'Can you see the

151

bruise? I tried to cover it with face powder.'

'It's not too bad, and the men are so desperate for partners that no one cares what you look like.'

'I'm not sure that really makes me feel better,' said Meg wryly as the door squeaked open once more.

Lily Dingle came in, stopping when she saw Annie and Meg. 'Hello,' she said in surprise.

'I know, you don't usually see either of us at these affairs,' said Meg. 'I suppose you're always at these dances, are you?'

'Hardly,' said Lily with a huff of laughter. 'Dances aren't really my thing either, but a group of girls from the ATS asked me to come along and I didn't want to seem standoffish.' She glanced at Meg. 'That was quite an ordeal you had with those Germans, Meg. You feeling better?'

'I am, thanks to you and Annie. I might still be sitting in that barn if it hadn't been for you two.'

'That was Annie,' said Lily. 'She was the one who insisted on finding you.'

'It's Jack Proudfoot you should be thanking,' said Annie. 'I always thought he were a bit aloof, but he's nice when you get to know him, isn't he?'

'Nice isn't the word *I'd* use.'

'He wasn't going to have your officer telling him what to do, was he?' said Annie. 'And his leg must have been really hurting, but he kept going. He wouldn't give up until we'd found you,' she added to Meg.

Lily sniffed as she went into the cubicle and

banged the door shut.

Annie and Meg exchanged a look. 'You're just cross because he gave you a skelping for rushing into the barn like that.' Annie raised her voice so that Lily could hear her. 'He was just worried for you,' she added when Lily came out.

'He wasn't worried,' said Lily crossly. 'He just wants to put me in the wrong.'

'Why would he want to do that?'

Lily tossed her head. 'He's decided because my name's Dingle I'm a bad lot.'

Annie didn't think that was how Jack Proudfoot thought of Lily at all, but she could see Lily wouldn't believe her if she said so. She seemed to have taken against the policeman for some reason, although to Annie's mind he was a much better man than the handsome colonel Lily drove around. Personally, Annie wouldn't trust him further than she could throw him.

Lily turned from the sink, decided against the grubby roller towel and shook her hands dry. 'So why are we three lurking in the toilets when there's a whole hall full of men clamouring to dance with us?'

'Annie's missing Edward,' said Meg, 'and I'm having a rest from being manhandled. I only get the desperate ones who know they won't get a look-in with the likes of you two!'

'I saw you dancing with Jacob,' Lily said. 'He's not desperate.'

'He took pity on me.'

'Oh, Meg, that's ridiculous!' said Annie. 'Jacob really likes you. Have you never thought . . . ?'

Meg exchanged an odd look with Lily. 'Me

and Jacob?' She rolled her eyes. 'Annie, Jacob isn't interested in *me*.'

'I wish he'd find someone.' Annie sighed. 'He's been so kind, looking after me while Edward is away, but it's not fair on him. He needs to find a girl of his own. People think Jacob's fierce, but he's lovely really. Any girl would be lucky to have him.'

'Mmn.' Meg glanced at Lily again.

Annie sighed and smoothed down her skirt. 'Well, I suppose we'd better get out there again.'

Pinning a smile back in place, she went back into the hall, but it was a relief that she found Jacob waiting for her. 'Are you ready to go?' she asked.

'We haven't had a dance yet.'

'You don't have to dance with me, Jacob, honestly.'

'I'd like to.' He cocked his head at the band, who had just struck up a slow tune. 'Can't make much of a fool of myself to this.'

'All right then.' Annie smiled and moved into his arms. 'It's a relief not to have to try and chat and make myself sound fun,' she admitted. 'I can be myself with you.'

'You don't need to pretend with me, Annie,' said Jacob gruffly.

'That's what I mean.'

They danced in silence for a while. It wasn't the same as dancing with Edward, but it was comfortable. 'This is nice,' she said. 'I'm glad now I came out, aren't you?'

Jacob's cheek was close to her curly hair, so

close that when he spoke, Annie could feel the rumble of his voice.

'Very glad,' he said.

Autumn 1940

15

'Why do we have to go and pick potatoes? I don't want to!' Ruby wouldn't stop moaning as they trudged up the track to Emmerdale Farm.

'Because there's a war on,' said Meg sharply. 'Farmers need all the help they can get at the moment, and the more of us that help today, the more potatoes there will be to send to the troops and people like your mum in cities who can't grow their own.'

The truth was that there were many things Meg would rather be doing with her precious weekend, too, but when the call went out for help at Emmerdale, she went. That was all there was to it.

She had always liked helping with the harvest, but potato-picking was back-breaking work — although surely not as hard as dragging two whining children up the track, Meg sighed to herself.

They paused for breath halfway up the track. It had rained the night before, and the air smelt of damp earth and wet grass and the coming of autumn. Mist lurked over the river below and the spiders' webs in the hedgerows were spangled with raindrops.

'I want to go and see Edna,' Ruby grumbled. 'She said she'd let me ride her bike.'

Ruby's experience at the hands of the Germans had transformed her. Suddenly she was part of a whole gang of children, and it hadn't taken long for her to become a leader.

Just like I used to be, Meg couldn't help remembering.

She was glad Ruby had found some friends, although she worried about the reckless streak that led her into trouble more often than not. Ruby's eyes were brighter now, her skin flushed with summer colour and she was putting on weight. She still wrote regularly to her mother in Hull, but Meg didn't find her checking the post so often for a reply that never came.

'Edna will probably be there too,' she told Ruby. 'Nobody's riding bikes when there are potatoes to be picked.'

Meg's eyes rested on the view. It was a strangely colourless day, the light dull and milky. The countryside looked tired after summer, as if it had not yet summoned the energy to burst into autumn with its winds and swirling leaves.

A day just like the one on which she had bullied Rosie into getting on her bicycle. *Come on, Rosie, it'll be fun.*

Days like these made Meg scratchy and sad, and when a gunshot broke the stillness of the day, she jumped nearly as high as Ruby and Stan.

Stan shrank into her side. 'What's that?'

'It's just the soldiers at the training camp,' Meg told him, but Ruby wasn't persuaded.

'The training camp's over there,' she said, pointing. 'The shot came from behind us.'

'Well, it's probably someone shooting rabbits.'

'It might be a German,' said Stan nervously.

'It won't be a German, Stan. I've told you,

160

they're all in the prisoner of war camp and they can't hurt you.'

But when they got to Emmerdale Farm, there, waiting in the farmyard with the other potato pickers, was the pilot.

Ruby saw him first. She hissed in a breath and tugged at Meg's sleeve, and, turning to see what the matter was, Meg found herself looking straight into the cool eyes she had last seen as the gag was tied over her mouth.

Her heart gave a great lurch and she glared at him, but he was unfazed. A faint smile touched the corners of his mouth as he gave her a nod of recognition.

'I'm sorry, Meg, but we need the help,' said Maggie when Meg remonstrated with her.

'He's supposed to be a prisoner!'

'He is. The guards drop him off every morning and he's taken back to camp every night.'

'It doesn't sound like much of a prison!'

'Think about it, Meg. What's the point of having young, fit men sitting around in prison when they could be helping us produce food?'

'I know, but — '

'Rolf doesn't have to work but he chooses to, and honestly, we're glad of it. Without Edward, we're stretched.' A shadow crossed her face at the thought of her son. 'Jacob says Rolf Schreiber is a hard worker, and he seems to know what he's doing, so he's made a real difference.'

Meg hugged her arms together, unsettled in a way she couldn't identify. 'What if he escapes? Shouldn't he be guarded?'

'They did send a guard the first few days, but

it seems pointless. There's always one of us with him, and he's got a great circle sewn on the back of his jacket so everyone would know he was a prisoner. He wouldn't get very far,' said Maggie comfortably.

Meg wasn't so sure of that. Rolf, if that was his name, struck her as resourceful and more than capable of getting away if he chose to.

★　★　★

It was a motley group of potato pickers that made their way down to the potato field. Jacob and Rolf were the only young men. Joe Sugden was there, and Sam Pearson, but both were limited in what they could do, and the rest were women and children.

Picking potatoes was dirty work. Ruby and Stan were in shorts and would be filthy by the end of the day, but it couldn't be helped. Meg at least had a pair of trousers to wear. With a heavy sweater and a scarf tied around her head, she had thought she looked practical when she left the cottage, but now, catching Rolf s eyes as they headed out to work, she was sure she saw amusement there, and immediately felt like a scarecrow. Lifting her chin, she looked deliberately away, but she couldn't help wishing that she was wearing something more flattering.

The others were equally wary of the German in their midst. They eyed him askance and kept their distance, while Ruby and Stan stayed as far away from him as possible. Rolf was unperturbed. He worked steadily along the edge of the

162

potato field and made no effort to interact.

Meg was annoyed to find herself glancing over at him frequently. It was as if her eyes had a will of their own, and no matter how hard she tried to ignore him, her gaze would end up being dragged back to him. It must surely be humiliating, to be a pilot and now grubbing around in the earth for the enemy.

But Rolf didn't look humiliated. There was nothing cringing in the way he held himself. Meg imagined that he would have sat in the cockpit of his plane in exactly the same self-contained way.

Maggie brought some bread and cheese out to the field for dinner and Annie brewed up a kettle of weak tea over a fire. Meg was glad of the chance to stretch her aching back. Ruby and Stan seemed to have forgotten about Rolf and were happily squabbling with the other children, so when they'd all had something to eat, Meg decided to indulge her curiosity.

She took her mug back to Maggie. 'Shall I take some tea to the German?' she said, nodding at Rolf, who sat to one side, his eyes on the fells and apparently oblivious to the women and children chattering nearby.

Probably planning his escape, Meg thought dourly.

'Thank you, Meg,' said Maggie, following her gaze. 'Take him some cheese and bread, too. I think he's assumed we won't feed him.'

'It's more than he deserves,' said Meg, but she took a hunk of the cheese wrapped in a napkin and a mug of tea that was all any of them were allowed then and carried them over to Rolf.

163

'Remember me?' she said in a hostile voice.

He stood up as she stood over him. 'I do. It is Meg, is it not?'

'Yes. I'm surprised you remember my name.'

'It was not a day I forget easily,' he pointed out. 'And you gave me your petticoat. That does not happen every day either.'

His mention of her petticoat felt somehow . . . intimate. Meg's pulse quickened and her fingers tingled with the memory of how startlingly warm his skin had felt. Her mouth dried alarmingly and she practically shoved the mug towards him.

'Have some tea.'

He inclined his head courteously. 'Thank you.'

He drank thirstily. Meg realised that she was watching his throat move and jerked her eyes away. What was wrong with her? He was a German, an *enemy*, a man who had tied her up as efficiently as if she'd been a parcel. There was no reason for her senses to suddenly be alert and at attention, but she was excruciatingly aware of him all the same: the hard line of his jaw, the way his hair grew untidily at his temples, the hint of humour around his mouth.

She swallowed. 'How is your arm now?'

'Better.' He flexed it to demonstrate. 'Thanks to your sling it is good enough to pick potatoes at least.' He studied Meg over the rim of the mug. 'And you? Are you better?'

'Me?'

'Your face,' he reminded her.

'Oh, that.' She touched a finger to where the airman — Hans? Walter? — had struck her. 'I had a nasty bruise for a while, but it's gone now.'

His eyes were steady. 'I am sorry you were hurt.'

'Then you shouldn't be at war.'

'True,' he acknowledged. 'War always means people being hurt. Still, I am sorry it was you.'

'Anyway, it wasn't being hit that I minded so much,' said Meg, suddenly wanting him to understand. 'What I hated was the way you tied us up and then put those awful gags on us. I felt so . . . so powerless.'

'I am sorry about that,' he said again, 'but you must see that I had no choice. We could not take the chance of you calling out for help.'

'You were caught anyway,' Meg reminded him. 'I was right about that.'

'That is true, but at least we did our best to get away.'

'And now?'

He drained the mug and handed it back to her. 'Now I'm a prisoner. There is not much I can do about it.'

'I'm surprised you'd want to come and help the enemy,' she said. 'Isn't it a comedown from being a Luftwaffe pilot to digging up potatoes?'

If she had hoped to provoke him, she didn't succeed. Rolf just shrugged. 'I am from Berlin, but we used to spend the summers in the country-side and I liked to help on a local farm.' He glanced around. 'Cutting hay, picking potatoes, just like here,' he said. 'And I would rather be doing something than sitting in the camp looking at the wire. At least here I can breathe fresh air and do something useful and pretend that I am free.'

'So you won't try and escape again? I want to know if you're planning to attack any more children,' she said, aware that she wasn't being entirely fair, but there was just something about him that rubbed her up the wrong way.

'That wasn't me,' he said calmly. 'I am sorry they were frightened.'

'They were terrified! They still are.'

Rolf looked across the field to where Stan and Ruby were running around with the other children. Typically, it was the first time Meg had seen them look happy and relaxed. 'They don't look very terrified to me,' he said.

'Well, they are,' she said, shoving the napkin at him. 'Underneath.'

'Ah, underneath we all feel differently.'

'Even you? You seem so . . . unconcerned,' she said. 'If I were a prisoner in an enemy country, I would be petrified.'

'Perhaps, but you wouldn't show it. You would just lift your chin and glare, like you did to me in the barn. You are a brave woman, I think.'

His voice was matter-of-fact rather than admiring, but still the colour prickled up Meg's throat.

'What about your crew? They don't want to do farm work?'

'They are town boys,' said Rolf. 'They choose to stay in camp for now. I think they are afraid of what the British would do to them.'

'And you're not afraid at all?'

He shook his head. 'We are all ordinary people caught up in this war. You speak a different language, but you are not so different from my sisters,' he told her. 'In fact, you would like them if you met them, and they would like you. No, I'm not afraid of you.'

'I gathered that when you tied me up and gagged me and left me in the barn!' Meg said crossly, and he had the nerve to smile.

'I said I was sorry.'

Ridiculously flustered by his smile, she looked away. 'Eat your dinner,' she said in a brusque voice.

Rolf unfolded the napkin obediently and raised his brows at the sight of the cheese.

'I heard you had rationing here.'

Meg hunched a shoulder, still trying to decide whether she was flattered or irritated by his comment about her glare.

'This is a farm. Maggie makes her own cheese here. Most goes to the Ministry of Food, but there's always some extra that can be found at times like this.'

'But don't tell the Ministry of Food, is that it?'

'Why, were you thinking of reporting the Sugdens?'

'Of course not.' Rolf took a bite of the cheese. 'This is good,' he said. His eyes rested on her face as he chewed. 'You are very . . . like *Igel* . . . a hedgehog, is that right?'

The flush crept up from her throat to her cheeks. 'Prickly is the word you're looking for,' she said in a prickly way.

'Prickly.' Rolf seemed to savour the word as he stored it away for future reference. He smiled at Meg. 'I like that word,' he said.

16

Lily paused at the entrance to the garage, breathing in the familiar smell of oil and rubber. Her father was studying an Austin Seven tourer as he wiped his hands thoughtfully on an oily rag.

'Problem?' she asked.

'Mmm.' Mick glanced over and saw her uniform. 'Are you off to work? Got a minute?'

She glanced at the watch he and her mother had given her when she was twelve. She was due to pick Derek up and take him to the camp as usual, but it was so rare she had a chance to spend time with her father. 'I've got five.'

'Grand. In that case, come and give me your advice on this camshaft.'

Lily peered with him at the engine. 'You've checked the lifters?'

Mick grinned. 'That's my girl — but yes.'

They spent a few minutes discussing the problem until Lily remembered to check her watch. 'I need to go,' she said, reaching for a rag and wiping her hands.

'Ah, that's a shame.' Mick straightened too. 'It was nice to have your help. Just like old times.'

Stupidly, Lily felt the sting of tears. 'I know.'

'What time will you be back tonight? I was thinking we could have supper together,' said Mick. 'It seems like a long time since we've done that. I can rustle up delicious sardines on toast if you're good.'

Lily hated the carefully polite undercurrent to his voice. They had always been so easy with each other, but now . . .

'Will Nina be here?' she made herself ask, and Mick sighed.

'No. I wish you'd get to know each other, though.'

'Dad, I can't . . . ' Her mouth trembled. 'I'm sorry, it's just that I miss Mum so much. Look, I can't talk about this now. I've got to go. Ask Nina to supper. I'm not sure what I'm doing tonight. Don't wait up.'

She felt wretched as she jumped into the jeep, but was careful to rearrange her face into a smile as she waited for Derek outside Nina's house. She could have spared herself the effort.

'What's the matter?' Derek asked the moment he saw her.

'Nothing, sir.'

'Don't 'sir' me, Lily. I know you too well. Something has upset you.'

'It's not important, honestly,' she said, even as she thrilled to the idea that Derek knew her well enough to see past her bright smile. 'Just a silly disagreement with my father.'

'Ah. Fathers often don't like to see their little girls grow up.'

It wasn't that, but loyalty to Mick kept Lily silent. She might not like her father's relationship with Nina, but it felt wrong to tell Derek about it, somehow.

'You need cheering up,' said Derek firmly. 'Let

me take you out to dinner tonight.'

'Oh, no, really, I'm all right . . . '

'I need cheering up, too,' he said and she looked at him in quick concern.

'Have you had bad news?'

'In a way.'

'I'm sorry.'

'So am I,' said Derek, with feeling. 'But if the war's taught us anything, it's to make the most of the time we have. So I say we forget our troubles for a while and go out and have a good time. What do you say?'

Lily chewed her lip, tempted beyond measure.

'Don't you want to come?'

'It's not that,' she said quickly. 'I'd love to! It's just . . . I'm wondering what people would say. With you being a senior officer,' she trailed off as Derek shook his head in disappointment.

'Lily, I didn't have you down as worrying about what people would say. You've always seemed like a free spirit to me.'

Nothing he said could have appealed to Lily more. When her mother had been alive and she had felt secure in the love of her parents, she had been daring and light-hearted, but that happiness had leaked away gradually, leaving her feeling dull and joyless. Now, perhaps, that was within her grasp again. She was in love, with a wonderful man who wanted to take her out to dinner. Why was she even hesitating?

'You're right,' she said with a brilliant smile, and Derek's eyes flared in a way that made her heart beat hard in her throat. 'Where shall we go?'

'How about I drive you for a change, as we'll

both be in mufti?' he said. 'I'll borrow a car. What about an evening on the town?'

'In Ilkley?'

He laughed and Lily instantly felt silly. 'I was thinking of a real town: Leeds or Bradford. It's not that far. There must be somewhere to go to dinner, and where we could dance . . . ' His voice dropped. 'Don't you think it would be nice to go somewhere where nobody knew us?'

'Yes.' Lily's voice was breathless. 'Yes, I do.'

'Good.' Derek smiled at her and put his hand on her knee. 'I'm looking forward to being alone at last, aren't you?'

His meaning was unmistakable, and Lily's heart began to slam against her ribs. Derek wanted to be alone with her! After all her dreaming, it was actually happening. She swallowed and made herself look straight back into his eyes so he couldn't mistake how much she wanted to be with him too. 'Yes, I am, too.'

'Good,' he said again, squeezing her knee before releasing it. 'But first, to the camp, Corporal!'

They were scrupulously proper with each other all day, which only added to Lily's excitement. She hugged the knowledge of their assignation to herself, in a frisson of anticipation. The very air between them seemed charged, and she couldn't help imagining what would happen that night. He would kiss her, of that she was sure . . . and maybe, maybe they would do more than kiss.

If Derek suggested it, she would say yes, Lily decided. He was a dream come true. She was tired of being silly little Lily. She wanted to be the woman Derek made her feel herself to be; to lose her virginity to a man she loved, to a real man who was sophisticated and assured.

She was ready.

She couldn't wait, in fact.

Lily was changing the oil in a jeep when Derek appeared in the garage. 'Everything under control, Corporal?'

'Yes, sir,' she said, suppressing a smile.

'Excellent.' Realising that she was alone, he came over and ran a hand down her back, letting it linger on her bottom. 'I've managed to borrow a car,' he said in a low voice that sent shivers of promise over Lily's skin. 'I'll pick you up at eight, shall I?'

Lily straightened. The last thing she wanted was a confrontation with her father. 'I'll wait for you at the bus stop,' she said, trembling with the awareness of his hand.

'Are you sure?'

'Yes, I'd rather that.'

Derek snatched his hand away as Sylvia Dawson came into the garage carrying a tyre. 'Very good, Corporal,' he said in a louder voice. 'Carry on.'

★ ★ ★

Lily smoothed on her stockings and clipped them to her suspender belt with unsteady hands. She had swallowed her misgivings and asked Jed if he could find her a pair of proper nylons, and he had winked as he produced a packet from beneath the bar.

'Hot date?'

'Nothing like that,' Lily had said primly, but of course it was. She had not mistaken Derek's hand curved over her bottom. He wanted her as much as she yearned for him. This was it: the night she would lose her virginity. Nervousness and excitement trembled just under her skin and churned dementedly deep in her belly. It was going to be perfect.

But on the way to the narrow stairs, she passed her mother's photograph on the old chest, and she picked it up, her chest tightening. What would Rose think of what she was planning? Would she encourage her to be with the man she loved, or to wait until they were married? Never had Lily missed her mother more. Once she would have been able to go and see Dot Dingle, who had stood in as a mother figure after Rose's death. Dot's no-nonsense advice was always helpful, but Dot was in Africa now and there was no one else Lily could talk to. She couldn't talk to her father, that was for sure.

Derek would look after her. There was nothing to worry about. It was going to be perfect, she reminded herself.

Not wanting a conversation about where she was going, Lily called a quick goodbye and let herself out before Mick could answer, but as she turned down the lane she came face to face with Nina. She had forgotten that she had suggested her father invite Nina to supper. It looked as if he hadn't wasted any time hoping that Lily would change her mind.

'Oh.' There was no way to avoid her. 'Hello.'

'Hello, Lily,' said Nina in the sultry voice that

never failed to rub Lily up the wrong way. 'I was hoping to see you.'

'Me? Why?'

Nina hesitated. 'Derek tells me he's taking you out on the town tonight.'

Derek. Lily hated the easy way Nina used his name. 'What of it?'

'He's a charming man, I can see that. Like your father, in fact. I understand. But you're very young, my dear, and I know just how easily an assured older man can bowl you over. My first husband was twenty years older than me.'

Lily stared. 'Your *first*? How many husbands have you had?'

'Just the two,' said Nina with a rueful shrug. 'It took me a while to learn my lesson.'

'I hope you're not planning on making Dad your third!'

Nina's smile faded. 'No, and anyway your father would never consider marrying me if he thought it would make you unhappy.' Lily's eyes slid away at that, and Nina paused before she went on, evidently picking her words with care. 'So I'm not trying to be a stepmother, Lily. I know you don't want that. But I *am* concerned. You don't have a mother to advise you, and Mick, dear as he is, doesn't understand the first thing about what it's like to be a woman dealing with a man.'

'I suppose, after two husbands, you do,' said Lily, unable to keep the tartness from her voice.

'Exactly,' said Nina, refusing to be provoked. 'I've known a lot of men like Derek in my time, and while he's charming company, of course, I

174

wouldn't trust him, and that's the truth. I'm afraid he might . . . take advantage of your innocence.'

Lily was white-faced with anger. 'I may not have your vast experience of men,' she said bitingly, 'but I know Derek, and I *do* trust him, so I'd be glad if you would keep your nose out of my business and your advice to yourself!'

Nina sighed. 'I was afraid you would say that.' She stepped back, holding up her hands as if in surrender. 'Perhaps you're right, and you need to make your own mistakes. God knows, I've made plenty. But I wish you trusted me, Lily. You can, you know. If you ever need any help, I'm here.'

As if she would ever accept help from the most scandalous woman in Beckindale! Lily raged inwardly as she stalked down the lane. How *dare* Nina talk to her like that. If anything was needed to reassure her that she was doing the right thing, that was it!

There was no sign of Derek at the bus stop. Lily hugged her arms together, feeling conspicuous. There were still plenty of people about, making the most of the lighter evenings while they lasted. She exchanged nods with Peggy Summers and Betsy Middleton, and prayed that no one would stop and ask her where she was going.

And then, to make her joy complete, along came Sergeant Proudfoot. That was all she needed, thought Lily resentfully.

'Going out?' he said in his cool way.

'How did you guess?' Lily wasn't in the mood to be polite, and Jack raised his eyebrows slightly at her sarcastic tone.

'I'm a trained observer,' he said, 'and you look particularly beautiful.'

He sounded so sincere that Lily's jaw dropped. 'Well . . . thank you,' she said awkwardly.

At that moment — thank goodness — Derek drew up in his borrowed car and tooted the horn. He made to climb out, but Jack was already there, opening the passenger door for Lily.

'Thank you,' she said again.

'Enjoy your evening.' His eyes rested on her face, and then flicked to Derek. 'Drive carefully, sir.'

'Always, Sergeant.'

Derek put his hand on Lily's knee. 'You look beautiful, Lily,' he said in a warm voice.

She smiled at him, but without meaning to, Lily found herself glancing over her shoulder to where Jack was watching them drive off. Derek had told her she was beautiful, too, but oddly it was Jack's voice she remembered.

You look particularly beautiful. He had said it in that typically matter-of-fact way of his, not as if he was trying to impress her, but as if it were true.

'Lily?'

Derek's amused voice jerked her attention back to him.

'Sorry,' she said.

He put the car into gear. 'We're off,' he said. 'Are you ready to enjoy yourself?'

He's charming company, Nina had said. *I wouldn't trust him.*

You look particularly beautiful.

Unsettled in spite of herself, Lily pushed their voices out of her head and turned to Derek with what she hoped was a seductive smile. She put her hand over his on the gearstick and let it stay there.

'Absolutely,' she said.

★　★　★

He took her to dinner in a expensive restaurant in Leeds. It was the swankiest place Lily had ever been to. The light was muted and they sat thigh to thigh in a padded banquette and drank a bottle of champagne.

She had never had champagne before. Wide-eyed, she watched Derek fill her glass. 'Isn't it terribly expensive?'

'You're worth it,' said Derek, chinking his glass to hers and watching as she took a sip. 'Do you like it?'

Lily wasn't entirely sure she did, but there was no way she was going to admit to anything so unsophisticated. She took another sip, feeling the bubbles burst on her tongue. 'Lovely,' she said bravely.

Derek smiled and took her hand in his warm clasp. 'You're the one who's lovely, Lily,' he said, his voice dropping to a rumble that seemed to reverberate over her skin. 'Lovely Lily,' he repeated. 'That's what I should call you.'

His eyes roamed over her face and Lily's heart started to beat, so high and hard that she had to put her glass down with an unsteady hand. 'You're so fresh and sweet,' Derek went on. 'That skin, like a peach.' He grazed her cheek with one knuckle, leaving a burning trail on her face. 'Those dark blue eyes.' He traced a line beneath them with one warm finger. 'Put in with a smutty finger, isn't that what they say? And that hair. I don't think I've ever seen such a pure gold. You're more than lovely, Lily. You're perfect.'

The colour rushed up under her skin and she stammered something, not knowing how to reply to such compliments. His touch made her tremble, the warmth in his voice dissolving any last doubts she might have had.

The menu was in French, but even if it had been in English Lily would have been in no state to decipher it. The words danced around on the thin paper that was all restaurants were allowed to use for their menus, and in the end, she handed it back to Derek. 'You order for me,' she said.

He fed her oysters wrapped in wafer-thin slivers of bacon, followed by a pork dish that Derek said was probably whale meat. Not that it made any difference to Lily. Sick with nerves, giddy with anticipation, she could barely eat.

When the meal was over, Derek helped her on with her coat. He let his hands linger on her shoulders as he pressed a kiss to the side of her neck, making her shudder with pleasure.

'I've got a room,' he murmured. 'Let me love you, lovely Lily.'

Lily's knees felt weak as she nodded. 'Yes, please,' she managed, and Derek smiled.

'You are so sweet, darling. I'll take good care of you.'

The fresh air hit Lily when they got outside. She was unsteady on her feet from the champagne, and she clung to Derek as he led her through the blackout with the aid of a torch pointed at the ground. He seemed to know exactly where he was going.

She didn't dare look at the receptionist as Derek signed them in with a flourish as Mr and Mrs Smith. Derek, of course, carried it off with such assurance that no one would have dared question him. 'Not much of a hotel, I'm afraid,' he said as they took a creaking lift to the third floor.

'It seems very smart,' said Lily, who had never been in a hotel before, and Derek threw her a look of amused indulgence.

Unlocking the door, he drew her inside. Lily coloured, suddenly worried about her utter lack of experience. Derek would think her hopelessly awkward. Why hadn't she asked one of the other ATS girls what to do? Connie and Sylvia were always boasting about their experiences. But if she had questioned them, they would have wanted to know who she was going out with, and she was hopeless at lying.

Derek was obviously watching her face and reading her expression without difficulty. 'Stop thinking,' he said as he unbuttoned her coat and tossed it across the chair while all the air seemed to leak out of Lily's lungs. His voice thickened as he looked down at her. 'God, I've been thinking about this since I met you. I think about it every time you put down the clutch and change gear, every time you bend over an engine. You're driving me crazy, Lily.'

His hands were busy with the zip at the back of her dress. Lily pulled away, embarrassed. 'I don't know what to do,' she whispered.

'Don't worry, my darling,' said Derek, his lips drifting over her skin as he eased down her dress. 'I do.'

17

'What's a harvest festival?' Stan was puzzled when Meg asked them to gather up some apples to take to church.

Ruby and Stan had been in Beckindale almost a year now, and at last they were adapting to village life. But there were still times when Meg remembered with something of a shock that they remained city children at heart.

'Well, it's a way of thanking God for being able to harvest all our crops,' she said. The harvest festival was so much a part of life in the village that she had never had to explain it before. It just was, like Christmas or Easter. 'We decorate the church with baskets of fruit and food, and there's a special service,' she went on.

Stan and Ruby looked unimpressed. 'And afterwards we have Harvest Supper in the village hall,' she said, hoping to encourage them. 'It's a party for everyone. We all take something to add to the feast, and there's music and dancing. You'll like it.'

There had been some discussion in the village about whether or not the Harvest Supper should be cancelled in the light of rationing, but Janet Airey soon put a stop to that. 'If we could put on a feast in t'Great War, we can do it now. I say we forget this blessed war for a night and have ourselves a party. The Lord knows, we could all do with a good knees-up.'

Meg, who was no baker, had given their butter rations for the week to Annie to make a cake for them to take to the supper, and Ruby and Stan, in a moment of rare accord, had helped make and decorate some gingerbread men to put on the table too.

The familiar musty smell caught at the back of Meg's throat as she stepped into the church that Sunday. It was the smell of grief to her now, of grief and guilt, inextricably bound up with the horror of watching the coffin that held her twin being carried down the aisle. She had sat here and watched her mother's coffin, too, knowing that she had killed her as surely as she had killed Rosie, and later still, her father's.

Robert Warcup had tried his best to comfort Meg. 'It's not your fault, Meg,' he had said, and Meg had pretended to believe her father to make him feel better. But it was her fault. She had killed her whole family, and now she was alone. In her heart, Meg felt that was all she deserved.

Pushing the memories aside, she made the children sit on either side of her in the pew. At the organ, Len Summers bashed out the opening bars of the first hymn and there was a general rustle as the congregation rose. 'We plough the fields and scatter,' they began in a ragged chorus, as they had sung for every Harvest Festival Meg could remember.

The fragrance of the baskets of fruit placed near the altar drifted through the church as the vicar rose to give his sermon. The Reverend Thirlby was a mild-mannered man, but his voice shook with emotion as he talked about the great battle being waged in the skies above southern England as they had been gathering in the last of the harvests.

Meg listened and couldn't help thinking of another pilot, the enemy with cool eyes and a cool mouth, and she wondered what he would make of the news that the attack launched by the Luftwaffe had failed. Her back had only just stopped aching after the day in the potato field. She had not seen Rolf again, but his face often drifted into her mind, along with a disturbing memory of his skin beneath her hands, the unsettling bump of her heart against her ribs as she watched him drink the tea.

Beside her, Ruby shifted restlessly and Meg dug her elbow into the girl's side. 'Sit still,' she hissed, even as she remembered countless occasions when she had been the one wriggling and squirming and making Rosie giggle until Polly Warcup had leant across her twin and given Meg a wallop. 'Behave!' she had said in a furious whisper.

Meg was doing her best to behave now. Now that it was too late.

★　★　★

The women of Beckindale had taken to heart Janet Airey's demand to put on a good show. When Meg and the children carried Annie's cake and their gingerbread men into the village hall that night, there was already a grand spread on the tables in defiance of rationing. Ruby and Stan's eyes widened at the display: there were

183

jam tarts and fish paste sandwiches, fruit cakes and ginger parkin, oatcakes and pickles and a great wheel of cheese that Maggie Sugden had sent down earlier. There was even a huge ham donated by Clive Skilbeck that Tom Teale was carving into wafer-thin slices so that everyone would get a taste. Jed and Larry Dingle had rolled along a barrel of beer from the Woolpack, and Betsy Middleton was presiding over two great teapots, constantly topped up from kettles boiled by two of the Barlow girls.

The tea was weak, but they were all used to that by now.

The hall was crowded when Meg, Ruby and Stan arrived, but they were not the last to enter. Meg was talking to Sam Pearson, and they were both raising their voices to be heard above the hubbub when the door opened and the three Sugdens stood momentarily framed in the doorway as their eyes adjusted to the noise and light inside.

'Shut that door! There's a blackout on!' shouted Arthur Middleton, taking his ARP duties seriously, and they stepped hurriedly forward as the din faded. It stalled completely when everyone saw who the Sugdens had brought with them.

'What's *he* doing here?' Ruby demanded into the sudden silence, and Meg's heart did a strange somersault as she saw Rolf close the door carefully behind him and turn to face a roomful of hostile eyes. He didn't cringe or even look embarrassed at the attention, but simply looked steadily back.

'Aye, that's a good question.' Janet's son,

one-legged Jim Airey, hobbled forward, his face hard. 'What *is* that German doing here?'

'This is Rolf Schrieber,' said Maggie in a clear voice. 'He's a German prisoner, yes, but he's been working hard to help us bring in the harvest at Emmerdale Farm. We think he deserves to be here.' Her commanding grey gaze swept around the room. 'It was your ma, Jim, who said we should forget there's a war on for tonight, so I say, let's do that. Let's forget Rolf is German for a few hours, and think of him instead as someone who works on the land with the rest of us.'

There was a silence, broken by some muttering, until Janet Airey stepped forward and pushed her son out of the way.

'You're right, Maggie, I did say that, and I stand by it. Those of us who went through t'last war know we need to take folks as we find them, and if your Rolf here is a hard worker, that's enough for me.'

Maggie and Janet were powerful women, Meg thought, able to step up and sway a crowd. In a different world they would be soldiers or politicians, not that Meg could really imagine what such a world might look like. She watched as Janet steamrollered the remaining objectors by turning and opening her arms wide. 'Now, let's get going on this here feast,' she said, and there was a general murmur of agreement.

It seemed that nobody was willing to defy Janet or Maggie outright, but still, no one came forward to greet Rolf, either. He stood to one side, apparently undaunted by the lack of welcome, his face expressionless. Meg didn't think she had ever seen anyone so coolly confident, and she felt an odd shiver go through her at the sight of him.

Abruptly making up her mind, she walked over to him. 'Hello again.'

He turned to look at her. His eyes were a steady grey-blue, she realised, and when they rested on her face, she felt as if he could see right through her.

'Meg,' he said with a nod of acknowledgement.

'It was brave of you to come here,' she said.

'Maggie Sugden asked me. She is an interesting woman, not afraid to be different.' Rolf studied her thoughtfully. 'Like you, I think.'

'You make me sound like a rebel,' said Meg, amused.

'And you are not? You are the only person who has come to talk to me,' he pointed out.

'That's because we know each other so well after you tied me up,' she said with a tart look, and he smiled a little ruefully.

'You will never forgive me for that, I see.'

'Would you?'

He considered that. 'I think I would try to understand why I had been tied up, and be grateful, perhaps, that my bonds were not too tight and that I had been left somewhere warm and dry.'

'Now you're making it sound as if I should be grateful to you!'

'No, not that, but I would be glad if you would forgive me one day, Meg.'

A strange warmth was pooling in the pit of

Meg's belly, and when her eyes met his, her pulse jolted inexplicably. She wrenched her gaze away.

'Perhaps I will, one day,' she said. 'When this war is over.'

'Then let us hope it is over soon,' said Rolf.

Meg shook her head. 'I don't think it will be. You want to invade us.'

'Herr Hitler, not me,' he said. 'I have no hatred for the British. To the contrary, my grandmother was English.'

'Is that why your English is so good?' She had wondered about that.

'I spoke it with her always, yes. I have family in Devon still.'

'I don't think they'll be much use to you there,' said Meg. 'It's so hard to get around nowadays. Devon might as well be Australia.'

'In any case, they don't want to know their German family now.' Rolf shrugged. 'It is sad, but I understand it. I am glad my grandmother is not alive, though, to see her family split and at war.'

'Do you have other family?' Meg asked him.

'My mother, and four sisters.'

'Four!'

'All younger than me,' he said with a faint smile. 'Liesbeth, Hanna, Ingrid and Klara. It was not a quiet house when I was growing up!'

'I can imagine,' she said with a smile. She liked the idea of him with sisters. He would have been the older brother she and Rosie had always wanted.

'And you?' he asked. 'Do you have family?'

Her smile faded. 'Not any more.'

187

'That is sad.'

'Yes, yes it is.'

There was a pause. 'The children . . . they are not your family, then?'

'No.' Meg looked over at them. Stan was tucking into the jam tarts, his cheeks bulging, but Ruby stood apart, watching her talking to Rolf, her scowl burning across the room. 'They're evacuees.'

'But you are fond of them?'

'I think perhaps I am,' said Meg, surprising herself. 'They're not easy children, though. Stan is very quiet and Ruby can be a little madam.'

'She wants to be like you, I think.'

Meg raised her eyebrows. 'What on earth makes you say that?'

'She has your way of lifting her chin and glaring.'

Ruffled, Meg returned Ruby's glare with interest. 'She didn't learn that from me, believe me. She knew all about scowling when she arrived here.'

Jack Proudfoot came over then and asked Rolf how he was finding life in the prison camp. While glad that someone else at least was prepared to engage with Rolf, Meg was conscious of a sense of dissatisfaction as she moved away. She would have liked to have talked to Rolf for longer.

It was soon clear, though, that others thought she had talked to him for quite long enough.

'Oh, Meg, you're so brave,' simpered Elizabeth Barlow. 'I'd have died of fright if I'd had to talk to a *German*.'

Peggy Summers was snide. 'My goodness, Meg,' she said, 'it almost looked like you were flirting with Jerry there.' Betsy Middleton worried, and Mary Ann Teale was blunt. 'You'll get a bad name for yourself, lass, if you're too friendly with the enemy,' she warned.

They might not have refused him entry, but it was obvious that few of the inhabitants of Beckindale were prepared to drop their prejudices enough to actually talk to Rolf. Only the Sugdens, Sergeant Proudfoot and the vicar's absent-minded wife, who probably didn't even realise that he was German, spent any time chatting with him. Couldn't they see that he was just a man like everyone else, Meg wondered?

By the time she had been chastised for fraternising with the enemy yet again, Meg's dander was well and truly up. When the last crumbs of the feast were cleared away, the tables pushed aside and the band was tuning up, she marched over to Rolf and asked if he would like to dance.

His brows went up, but he bowed his head, a ghost of a smile hovering around his mouth. 'I would be delighted,' he said.

'You might change your mind when you see how badly I dance,' said Meg frankly.

Ignoring the shocked whispers that ran around the watching crowd, Meg gave him her hand and let him lead her onto the dance floor.

'See, I said you were a rebel,' said Rolf, evidently aware of the reaction.

Meg put up her chin. 'Hardly,' she said. 'I'm the village schoolmistress. It doesn't get more conventional than that.'

'A conventional woman would never have

asked me to dance.'

'Perhaps nobody else will dance with me.' She was acutely conscious of his fingers wrapped around her hand, of the warmth of his palm against her spine as the band launched into the first number.

'I don't believe that. I can't think of a single reason a man wouldn't want to dance with you, Meg.'

'I'm too awkward,' she told him. 'Too fierce. Too tall.'

'I disagree. You're just the right height. I like to be able to look a woman in the eyes.'

Unable to help herself, Meg lifted her eyes to meet the grey-blue ones looking back into hers. They were cool and amused, but something at the back of them brought the colour to her cheeks. His hand was warm against her back. The silky fabric of her dress slipped seductively beneath his touch and her breathing got so tangled up that she had to clear her throat before she could speak.

'You're unusual,' she managed, and Rolf cast a glance around at those watching them dance with expressions that ranged from doubtful to disapproving.

'You are, too,' he said. 'That is why I like you.'

The band consisted of old Tom Teale and Sam Pearson with fiddles, the cooper Bert Mickleth-waite on his accordion and Len Summers, taking a break from the church organ to bash out tunes on the village hall's battered old piano.

Meg saw Rolf watching them with something like yearning. 'What do you think of our band?'

'I am enjoying listening to music played with such enthusiasm,' he said diplomatically.

'Do you play?'

'Yes, I play the violin.'

'You should have a go on the fiddle,' said Meg, thinking that, like most people, he would protest that he was not good enough. But instead he seemed to brighten.

'Do you think it would be possible?'

When the set ended, Meg took him over to Tom Teale. Gnarled with age and with a seamed face, Tom looked Rolf up and down when Meg asked if he would let him play his fiddle. Tom must have seen something he approved of, for he handed over the instrument.

'Have at it, lad,' he said. 'We're taking a break for a beer anyroad.'

Rolf took the fiddle as if it was something precious. Putting it to his shoulder, he drew the bow across the strings in a long, sweet note that cut through the chatter in the room.

One by one, conversations fell silent as Rolf began to play. His eyes were closed as he played from memory, oblivious to everyone turning to watch him. It was a complicated classical piece, full of yearning, and Meg's chest ached listening to it. Even the children had stopped, caught up in the strange, timeless moment that had the village hall in its grip. The music wove them together, holding them still, making them forget the war and the petty inconveniences and arguments.

I will never forget this moment, Meg found herself thinking.

Maggie Sugden nudged her and inclined her head in the direction of Stan, who had crept closer and was staring up at Rolf with a look of such wonder that Meg felt her heart contract.

When the last, poignant note died away there was utter silence in the hall. Rolf opened his eyes and Meg was sure that for a moment he had forgotten where he was.

There was a taut pause before Clive Skilbeck of all people started clapping, and soon everyone else joined him. Rolf accepted the applause with a restrained bow of his head, but seemed glad when conversations resumed.

Stan, quiet, nervous Stan, was standing before Rolf, tugging at his trousers. 'I want to play it.'

Rolf glanced at Tom, who nodded. Crouching down, he showed Stan how to hold the fiddle and use the bow. Stan's expression was ecstatic as he played a note, and then another. He seemed to know what to do instinctively, and Rolf smiled.

'You have another musician here, it seems,' he said.

'I reckon we do,' said Tom, scratching his head.

Stan could hardly bear to return the fiddle to Tom. 'Can I learn to play it?' he asked Meg beseechingly.

'He should learn,' Rolf said. 'You can tell already he is a natural musician.'

She bit her lip. 'If I ask permission from the camp commander, would you teach him?'

'I would need to borrow Mr Teale's fiddle.'

'All right by me,' said Tom. 'It's a right

pleasure to see a youngster take to the fiddle like that. And as for you,' he went on to Rolf, 'I ain't never heard me fiddle sound the way you made it sound. I reckon you'll be missing music in that prison camp.' He held the fiddle out to Rolf. 'Why don't you take it with you tonight?'

Meg saw Rolf swallow hard, obviously overwhelmed.

'Thank you,' he said simply. 'Thank you, I would like that very much.'

Winter 1940–41

18

Annie couldn't wait to get to the front of the queue. 'I've got news!' she said excitedly to Sarah, who squealed.

'So have I! You go first!'

'Edward's getting leave! Two days, just before Christmas!' Annie hugged herself. 'It's been so long. Can you believe he was posted after his training in June, and now it's December? Six months! I can't *wait* to see him!'

'That's wonderful, Annie.' Sarah beamed at her and Annie smiled back.

'What about you? You said you had news, too.'

'Oh, just . . . ' With exaggerated casualness, Sarah stretched out her hand so that Annie could see the ring with its tiny diamond chip.

It was Annie's turn to squeak with excitement. 'Sarah! You're engaged!'

'Ray asked me yesterday.'

'Oh, Sarah, that's wonderful news! Much more exciting than mine,' said Annie generously.

Sarah glowed. 'We're getting married on Saturday.'

'*This* Saturday?'

'Ray has to join his unit next week, so we're going to get married before then.'

'Good for you,' said Annie.

'I thought you'd tell me I should wait until I'd known him longer,' Sarah said in surprise.

'Before the war, I would have done, but now

. . . if you love Ray and he loves you, why should you wait?'

'That's what I think,' said Sarah. 'Will you be my bridesmaid, Annie?' She leant closer and lowered her voice. 'I have to ask Elizabeth, too,' she said, rolling her eyes in her sister's direction, 'but I'd rather just have you.'

'Of course I will. But Saturday, Sarah . . . that's only three days away! What will you wear?'

'Come with me to Ilkley tomorrow and we'll find something.'

Annie hesitated. 'I don't think I can afford to buy anything new.'

'Oh, come on! You could wear it when Edward comes home. Wouldn't you like him to see you in a pretty frock?'

Annie looked down at her old coat. It had been a cold, grey morning when she set off from Emmerdale Farm, so she had put on sturdy country boots. She wore woollen mittens, and an old balaclava that had belonged to her father covered her head. As an outfit it was warm and practical, to be sure, but a very long way from pretty. Sarah was right: Edward might love her whatever she wore, but it would be nice to make an effort for him.

'All right,' she said with a sudden smile. 'Let's go shopping!'

★   ★   ★

It was fun shopping with Sarah, who bought an ankle-length blue frock and a little veil as her bridal outfit. Annie was talked into a cherry-red dress covered in white polka dots, with a sweet collar and puffed sleeves. It was by far the prettiest frock she had ever owned, and she couldn't wait for Edward to see her in it.

On Saturday morning, she walked down to Beckindale in her old boots, carrying her shoes in her hand. She had replaced the balaclava with her best hat, and the mittens with gloves, but the coat was the warmest she had, so she wore the same one over her new dress. At the Barlows' house behind the shop, she helped Sarah get ready while Mrs Barlow wept and Elizabeth pouted, jealous of the attention her elder sister was getting.

It was a raw December day, but at least it wasn't raining. Annie was glad to keep her coat on as they walked to the church but took it off in the porch. Her dress wasn't nearly warm enough, but she didn't care. It made her feel pretty, and that was enough.

Ray was waiting for Sarah at the altar, running a finger nervously around his collar, but the look in his eyes when Sarah joined him made Annie feel sure that theirs would be a happy marriage, rushed though the wedding might be. She took Sarah's bouquet and stepped back with a smile. Next time, perhaps, she would be the one standing at the altar with Edward, but for now this was Sarah's day.

There was a 'do' in the Woolpack afterwards. Mr Barlow, generally considered to make a tidy sum from the shop, was notoriously tight with his money, but had been unable to withstand

Mildred Barlow's determination to make a show for her eldest daughter's wedding. It was just the kind of comfortingly familiar reception Annie would like for herself, just family, friends and neighbours. The Barlows had laid on a spread of tongue and cold pork, rolls and butter, blancmanges and jellies, and even a wedding cake hidden behind white cardboard as there was no sugar available for the icing. There was tea, with wine or lemonade for the toasts, and games, and Jed Dingle hauled in a gramophone so they could dance.

She was so lucky, Annie realised. Lucky to live in a village like Beckindale. Lucky to feel comfortable and safe in spite of the grim news from the war. Lucky to be young and have a flattering dress to wear that swirled when she danced.

This wasn't like the dance at the Drill Hall. The Sugdens weren't particular friends of the Barlows, so they weren't there, but Annie knew everyone else and they all knew her. There was no need to make small talk. It was Sarah's wedding, and Annie was determined to enjoy herself. She danced with everyone who asked her, with old Tom Teale and with her father and even with Oliver Skilbeck, though she was glad when that particular dance ended. Oliver always held her too close. His grip was too tight, his eyes too hot. Annie couldn't understand what Elizabeth Barlow saw in him.

Her parents left after a couple of dances. Sam's back ached if he stood for too long, and they kept early hours in any case. 'You all right walking back on your own, love?' Sam asked Annie when she said she would stay.

'Of course, Dad.' Annie resisted the urge to roll her eyes. The route between their cottage and the village was so familiar she could have done it blindfold. She had a torch in the pocket of her coat, but she would hardly need it. 'I'll stay until Sarah and Ray have gone and then I'll come home.'

'Hoping to catch the bouquet, eh?' Grace said indulgently, and Annie smiled, thinking of Edward's return. Only ten days until he was back.

'Something like that,' she said.

The happy couple were spending the first night of their marriage at the Woolpack. They were eager to retire, but first there was the obligatory tossing of the bouquet. Sarah winked at Annie and threw it carefully in her direction, only for Elizabeth to barge in and snatch the flowers just as Annie was lifting her hands to catch them.

Sarah scowled as Elizabeth brandished the bouquet triumphantly, but Annie just smiled ruefully. It was only a bunch of flowers. It didn't change the fact that she was going to marry Edward.

Once Sarah and Ray had been waved off to bed, the party broke up. Annie put on her sturdy boots once more and took her shoes in her hand. They wouldn't have lasted a minute on the muddy farm tracks. Glad of her warm coat, she set off for home. It was a familiar route: over the bridge, past Meg Warcup's cottage, up the track

201

to Emmerdale Farm. Then all she had to do was let herself through the farmyard and head up the narrow track that led to the old shepherd's cottage where the Pearsons now lived.

Or, Annie considered, she could take the shortcut up the hill once she had passed Meg's cottage. It was steeper and harder going over the tussocky grass, but she had her torch and she was tired after all the dancing. She wanted to get home as soon as possible.

Imagining how good it would feel when she was tucked up in bed, Annie turned through a gate and set off across the hillside. She kept her torch pointed towards the ground but when she heard panting, she swung it round to see Oliver Skilbeck emerging from the dank night.

She wasn't frightened, not at first, but her heart sank. 'Are you following me, Oliver?'

'I want a word with you, Annie Pearson.'

She sighed as she carried on walking. 'What about?'

'About why you're such a cock-tease.'

Shocked, Annie stopped. 'That's disgusting language, Oliver. And not true, neither.'

'Isn't it? Don't tell me you didn't know what you were doing, putting on that dress and flirting with me and everyone else in trousers.'

'I wasn't flirting with anyone. I don't even know *how* to flirt!'

'You're a slag,' said Oliver viciously.

'How dare you!' Annie's voice shook and she turned to walk away from Oliver, but he grabbed her by the arm.

'Don't you turn your back on me!'

She could smell the beer on him, beer and something darker and more dangerous. Too late, Annie realised the situation was spiralling out of control. With an effort, she made herself speak steadily. 'Please let me go, Oliver.'

'Give me a kiss first.'

'No!' Instinctively she turned her face away as he lunged for her.

His breath was sour on her face. 'Why not?'

'I don't want to. I don't like you.'

'Why not?' he screamed at her. 'You like everyone else! Perfect, pretty Annie Pearson! Always so friggin' happy. Everybody thinks you're so *sweet*, so *nice*, so *good*, don't they? But I know what you get up to with your precious Edward when you think no one's looking.'

Annie was really frightened now. 'Let me go!' she said, beating at him with her free hand, but Oliver grabbed it and shoved her so they fell together into the cold, wet grass.

Oliver was pinning her down, one hand over her mouth so that she couldn't scream. Not that there would be anyone to hear except the sheep huddled against the wall in the distance. With his other hand he ripped her coat apart and jabbed painfully under the dress she had put on so happily earlier.

Annie writhed and squirmed to get free, but he was too strong for her, and as she felt him fumble with the buttons of his trousers, it dawned on her with horror that he was really going to do it. He was going to rape her in the middle of a muddy field in the darkness, and there was nothing at all she could do about it.

She tried to make her mind blank, but she couldn't block out the agonising thrusting and grunting, the foul words he muttered, the rank smell of his hand over her mouth. Annie wanted to gag, but it was ail she could do to keep breathing.

And then, at last, he was off her, hauling himself to his feet, panting and trembling. 'You asked for that!' He spat in the grass beside her. 'If you go whining to anyone about what just happened, I'll tell Edward Sugden and then everyone else that it was your idea, that you were drunk and that you couldn't wait to spread your legs for me like the tart you are. That should make Edward's leave, eh? It'll be your word against mine, and don't you forget it.'

When he had gone, Annie rolled onto her side and retched and retched. Up came the blancmange and the wedding cake and the cold pork. Up came the tea and the half-glass of wine she had drunk to toast the happy couple. She was tempted to stay where she was on the ground with the mud and sheep droppings and the wet, yellowing grass, but she forced herself painfully to her knees and groped around for her hat that had fallen off and the torch and shoes she had dropped when he grabbed her. She was shaking so violently that she could barely stand.

She was very cold, so cold that she could not imagine ever being warm again.

Her parents were in bed when she got back to the cottage. Annie went out to the privy in the back garden. She longed for a bath, but there was no way she could drag the tin bath in and heat water without waking them up. So she pumped some cold water into a basin and, stripping naked, she stood shivering on the paving slabs and scrubbed herself raw. Then she crept up the stairs, her clothes bundled in her arms. She shoved them to the bottom of the chest in her tiny room. She would clean them up later, but she knew already that she would never wear her pretty new dress again.

The next morning when she looked in the mirror, Annie couldn't believe that she looked exactly the same on the outside. Inside, she was ripped and raw, churning with loathing, for Oliver and for herself. How could she have let him do that to her? The filthy names he had called her, the venom in his voice, coated her still like slime, and revulsion clogged her throat.

'You all right, love?' Grace asked her. 'You look a bit peaky.'

'I had some tongue at the wedding,' said Annie. 'I think it disagreed with me.'

She used the same excuse when Maggie Sugden commented on how quiet she was in the dairy later that morning. *It'll be your word against mine*, Oliver had said. He would tell everyone that she had been drinking and had led him on. The very idea of it made Annie gag.

There would be plenty of people who would believe her rather than Oliver, Annie knew, but it wouldn't stop the foul rumours circulating. Even if Oliver didn't confront Edward directly, Edward would hear what had happened. He might not think that she had encouraged Oliver, but he would know that Annie had lain in the mud while Oliver had pushed inside her. He wouldn't feel the same about her. He might pity her, he might be disgusted, but he would feel different, Annie was sure of that. And he would certainly confront Oliver. Edward only had two days' leave. She didn't want him to spend it fighting, or trying to comfort her.

Besides, what difference would it make if she *did* accuse Oliver? Nothing could undo what he had done. Annie couldn't imagine anything that would make her feel better. She would keep her shame to herself, she decided, and say nothing, at least until Edward's leave was over.

★ ★ ★

The morning Edward was due to come back, Annie woke feeling not joy but dread. She had waited so long to see him again, and now she was consumed with fear that he would sense the change in her. He had always known her better than anyone else. Surely he would take one look at her and know how dirty and disgusting she felt, how her stomach churned and turned with the memory she couldn't seem to push away. She could barely force food down her throat without gagging, and the weight had fallen off her in the ten days since Sarah's wedding. Annie told anyone who asked that she had a bug, and although her mother and Maggie eyed her searchingly, they accepted it. But Edward, surely Edward would know at once?

Annie had never been a good liar, and she didn't know how she was going to pretend to

206

Edward that everything was all right. She had to try, though. She was *not* going to spoil his leave. She just had to get through two days and then she could fall apart.

'I'll wait in t'truck,' Jacob said as he pulled up outside the station. 'You'll want to meet Ed on your own.'

'No, you come too,' said Annie, wanting Jacob's presence to stop her blurting out the truth on the platform.

They stood together watching as the train pulled in with the usual gushes of steam and squealing of brakes. Annie felt sick. She had a sudden, irrational conviction that she had forgotten what Edward looked like and that she wouldn't recognise him. She stared frantically at the passengers getting off the train, searching for the dark blue of the Royal Navy uniform, but she couldn't see it anywhere.

Jacob touched her arm. 'There he is.'

'Where?'

Then Edward was there, not in uniform but in a suit with trouser legs that rose two inches above his ankles and sleeves that came well above his wrists. But it wasn't the ill-fitting clothes that made Annie's heart turn over. It was the guarded look in his eyes, the restraint in his smile.

It was Edward, but somehow not.

'Edward.' Annie swallowed. For the first time in her life, she felt shy of him.

'Hullo, Annie, Jacob.'

There was a tiny pause while the three of them stood there, then Annie stepped forward. In the

207

past she would have flung her arms around him and let him pick her up and swing her into a kiss. Now she pressed her cheek against his rough one. 'Welcome home, Edward.'

'It's good to be back,' said Edward, but he didn't sound as if he meant it. He sounded as if he was just saying that because that was what you were supposed to say.

Jacob shook his brother's hand. 'What's this? Where's your uniform?' he said, nodding at Edward's clothes.

'We were torpedoed on our way into Liverpool,' said Edward. 'I was lucky. I got into a lifeboat and we were picked up by another ship in the convoy but everything I own is at the bottom of the Atlantic. They had to find us all new kit when we landed.' He held out his arms. 'We'll get new uniforms when we rejoin a ship, but for now this was the best they could do to send us on leave.'

The old Edward would have laughed as he told that story.

Jacob cleared his throat. 'Well, let's get you home. Ma should be able to do something about the suit.'

'How is she?' Edward asked politely, the way he might ask after a distant relative.

'She's . . . Ma.'

Edward nodded.

Annie had dreaded Edward seeing the truth in her face. It had never occurred to her that he wouldn't really look at her at all.

'You all right, Annie?' he asked as he helped her into the truck, and she summoned a smile.

'Yes, I'm fine.'

Maggie whisked the suit away to let it out as far as possible, and in Jacob's old farm trousers and a heavy jumper, Edward looked more himself. But he wasn't himself, Annie could tell. It was not just his stiltedness with his mother. He listened to their tales of wartime life, nodded understandingly when they told him about the German prisoner of war who helped with the farm work. He even mustered a smile when Maggie told him about how they had outwitted the Ministry of Food man.

'The Skilbecks tried to get one over on us, but Annie wasn't having it, were you Annie?' Maggie was trying desperately to include everyone, but Annie could only nod. Once she had loved this story, but now the mere mention of the Skilbecks was enough to make her throat clog with revulsion.

Maggie floundered on. 'They'd reported us to the Ministry of Food for having killed pigs without a licence, but fortunately Jed Dingle got wind of it and warned us just in time. Annie kept the ministry man talking outside — she pretended to be slow-witted, didn't you, love? — while Jacob and I ran the hams upstairs. Then I got into bed and pretended to be ill, and when the ministry man insisted on seeing me, I was seemingly being sick into a basin. Well, he soon backed away from that, and he never got the chance to realise that I had four hams tucked next to me under the covers!'

Edward kept his smile in place, but Annie could tell that it was an effort. He was there, but

209

not there at the same time. She would catch him looking into space, as if seeing something too terrible to name, but he wouldn't talk about what had happened to him.

She understood.

It was a wretched time. All the light and joy in Annie's life seemed to have drained out of her in that damp, dark field. Her heart still swelled with love for Edward, but when he kissed her all she felt was the ache of a black void inside her. When he said that he wanted her, he needed her, she couldn't bring herself to say no. She told herself that it might be a way to reach him, but it was so different from the first time they had made love by the beck. This time the cold drove them inside to the barn where they had kissed so many times in the past, but there was no tenderness, no excitement, no surging pleasure, just sadness and desperation. Afterwards, she lay beside him in the hay, unable to stop the tears leaking from her eyes.

Edward didn't even notice.

19

Lily hummed as she fastened her jacket. Derek had been recalled to London for some hush-hush meeting, and he'd been away for more than a week, but the day before she had had a message that he would be on the train later that afternoon. How long would it be until they could be alone together, she wondered, with a shiver of anticipation.

Adjusting her belt, she studied her reflection. She was proud of her uniform and made sure that every button was gleaming, every piece of leather polished to a high shine. But it was not the uniform that gave her that glow, she knew. That was what being in love did for you.

Lily was still dazzled by her luck. Derek loved her! She tightened her tie, enjoying the contrast between the stiff uniform and careful demeanour they maintained during the day, and the other times, when they lay in bed together. Derek was an assured lover. He made her feel beautiful and seductive, a woman of the world.

He told her that he adored her, that he needed her, that he couldn't live without her, but they made no plans. There was a war on, as Derek reminded her whenever Lily mentioned the future. There would be time to think about marriage when the war was over. Until then, they should live for the moment.

Lily was glad to go along with that. She even

found the secrecy exciting. She had never imagined herself as someone who had a sophisticated affair with a man like Derek. In Beckindale there were doubtless plenty of couples who anticipated marriage — Lily was fairly sure Sarah Barlow for one hadn't waited until her wedding day — but none of them had what she had. They didn't have secret assignations in hotels, didn't drive up into the hills ostensibly on army business just so they could be alone. Derek had made her life glamorous and exciting. He had made her feel safe and adored. Since that first time he had taken her out to dinner and then to bed, she was happier than she had ever been, and she refused to question what she was doing.

The day dragged until it was time to go to the station. Lily stood on the platform, just as she had when she had first met Derek. What a long time ago it seemed. She was fizzing with excitement as she watched the train chug into the station and stop with a great belching of steam and hissing of brakes.

And there he was, coming towards her with a smile. It was all she could do not to throw herself into his arms, but she stood to attention and threw a smart salute in return to his knowing look.

'Where to, Colonel?' she asked as Derek threw his kit bag into the back of the jeep and got in beside her.

'To the nearest hotel, Corporal,' he said, putting his hand on her thigh, and her mouth dried with desire.

'I know just the place.'

They went to the Red Lion, which had become one of their favourite hideaways. It was a quiet pub, out of the way on the far side of Ilkley where they were unlikely to meet anyone they knew.

Afterwards, Derek lit two cigarettes and passed one to Lily, who didn't really like smoking but felt incredibly sophisticated when she did. 'God, I've missed you, darling,' he said, and she smiled as she shifted to face him.

'How was the meeting?'

'What meeting?' Derek was momentarily disconcerted and then, when Lily looked surprised, his brow cleared. 'Oh, yes, that . . . boring as hell, like those meetings always are. I spent it dreaming of you.' He put his cigarette aside and ran his hand possessively over her hip. 'You're so beautiful, Lily.' His voice lowered suggestively. 'And so exciting.'

Lily laughed. 'I don't think so!'

'But you are. You drive me mad,' he said, nuzzling her neck. 'I see you in your uniform, driving the jeep so competently, or fixing an engine, and you're the ultimate practical Yorkshire lass, and at the same time I know that underneath you're this sexy, passionate woman . . . it doesn't get more exciting than that!'

'Thanks to you.' Lily wound her arms around his neck. 'I love you, Derek.'

'Come here,' he said, taking the cigarette from her and stubbing it out so that he could roll her beneath him and make love so expertly that Lily didn't notice then that this time he hadn't said it back.

She was still glowing the next morning when she went out to the jeep. It was a crisp December morning and she was rubbing her hands together against the cold. Her smile faded a little when she saw Nina waiting for her, swathed in a typically extravagant fur coat.

'The camp sent a car for Derek earlier,' Nina told her. 'There's some flap on, I gather. I said I'd let you know.'

'Oh. Right. Thank you.'

'I was hoping to have a word with you, too.'

'Oh?' said Lily discouragingly. The last thing she wanted was a cosy chat with Nina Lazenby.

Nina hesitated. 'There's something I think you should know.'

Something in her voice sent an chill down Lily's spine. 'Is it about Dad?' she asked fearfully. What if he was ill and hadn't told her?

'No.' Nina shook her head. 'It's about Derek.'

Lily took a step back. 'What about him?'

'Did you know he was married, Lily?'

'What? No.' Lily actually put out her hands as if to ward off a blow. 'No, he would have told me.'

'Would he?' said Nina gently.

Lily stared blindly at the jeep. 'He loves me,' she said, but even she could hear that she sounded as if she was trying to convince herself. 'He would have told me,' she said again, and Nina sighed.

'Oh, Lily. Men like Derek Mortimer . . . they're charmers. They make you think that you're the only person in the world for them, but when you're not there, they turn all that attention onto the next person. They can't help it. I'm sure he'll

214

have told you he loves you, but when it comes down to it, the only person Derek really loves is himself.

'People like that can only deal with what's right in front of them,' Nina said. 'They think about now, not the past and not the future. Unpleasantness gets pushed away, and they tell themselves they'll deal with it later. Derek will have meant to tell you about his wife at some point, but it would have been an awkward conversation and he'll have put it off for as long as possible, probably hoping either that you'll never find out or that someone else will break the news for him. Just as I've done.'

'You seem to know a lot about him,' Lily said in a dull voice.

'I was married to a man just like Derek, once. I understand how easy it is to love him.'

Strangely, she never once thought of doubting Nina. As soon as she heard the word 'married' Lily knew instantly that it was true. Of *course* Derek was married. Why wouldn't he be? While she, blind, stupid fool had believed what she wanted to believe. She had never even thought to ask him. She had thought herself sophisticated! If her heart hadn't felt as if it were tearing slowly, agonisingly, apart, Lily would have laughed at herself.

'I really didn't want to tell you, Lily,' Nina went on, watching her face in concern. 'I knew you wouldn't want to hear it, least of all from me, but Derek told me that she's coming to stay for a while and I wanted you to have some warning.'

'I see.' With an effort, Lily brought her chin

215

up. 'Well, I suppose I should thank you.'

'I don't want any thanks, Lily. I just didn't want you to be hurt.'

'Why? I've only ever been horrible to you.'

'Because I understand your pain,' said Nina. 'Because I love your father, and you're the most important person in his life. Like it or not, that means you're important to me, too.'

Lily drew a steadying breath. She was *not* going to cry and weep and wail and carry on. She had humiliated herself enough, it seemed. It was as if Nina had snapped her fingers in front of Lily's face and jarred her awake from a trance, so she felt disorientated and shaken, but never once doubting the truth of what the other woman had said.

'I . . . think I'd better talk to Derek,' she said, and Nina nodded.

'That's a good idea.'

The unspecified 'flap' kept Derek busy all day, and Lily was glad of the excuse to bury herself in work. With her head over an engine, nobody asked her awkward questions, and it gave her a chance to think. At the end of the day, she presented herself as usual to drive Derek home. He was all smiles, and when she suggested stopping for a drink, he agreed with alacrity. 'Back to the Red Lion?' he said, but Lily shook her head.

'I think the Woolpack will do.'

His brows rose. 'That's a bit close to home, isn't it?'

'We won't be taking a room. I just need to talk to you.'

'Righty-oh.'

They found a quiet corner in the Woolpack. 'Why didn't you tell me about your wife?' Lily asked him.

He barely blinked. 'I wanted to, darling. I've been meaning to tell you, but being with you was so wonderful, I couldn't bring myself to spoil things. There never seemed to be the right moment.'

'You don't think I deserved to know that you were married?'

'You don't understand.' Derek dropped his head in his hands. 'My marriage was a terrible mistake. Hazel is . . . well, she can be very difficult. I've tried to end things, but as soon as I suggest it, she says she's not well.' Lifting his eyes to Lily's, he smiled sadly. 'I can't tell you what it's been like being with you, darling. No dreadful scenes, no hysterics. You're so sweet and loving.'

And stupid, Lily thought with a new bitterness.

'Do you have any children?' she asked evenly and he hesitated.

'Two boys. They're away at school. They're the reason I've stuck with Hazel as long as I have.' He grasped Lily's hand. 'You know it's you that I love, Lily, and I know you love me.'

'I do,' she admitted, 'but your wife is coming tomorrow.'

Derek seemed ready to brush that aside as a minor detail. 'That's true. I couldn't find a way to put her off, but she won't be here long. I'll talk to her and make her see that it's over, and then you and I can be together, I promise.'

'I don't think so.' Lily disengaged her hand and stood up. 'You should have told me that you were married, Derek. It was wrong of you to let me go on believing that you were free. Now that I know you're not, it has to end.'

Derek protested and kept protesting the next day, while Lily behaved with scrupulous correctness. It made her cringe to remember those days when she had returned his secret smiles, or let him caress her behind a door. What a fool she had been!

Ignoring his attempts to talk her round, she drove him back to Nina's the next evening. The moment the jeep drew up, a woman came flying out of the house.

'Derek!'

Hazel Mortimer was younger and prettier than Lily had expected. She didn't look hysterical, either. When Derek got out of the jeep, she threw herself into his arms.

'Hullo, darling,' Derek said in a warm voice. Exactly the same voice he had used to call *her* darling, Lily remembered with a painful twist of the gut.

His back was turned to her and she remembered what Nina had said. *They only deal with what's right in front of them.* Derek had forgotten her already.

Hazel Mortimer pulled back, still smiling. 'How are you?'

'All the better for seeing you.' He put an arm around her and they turned towards the house. 'Have you met the lovely Nina? Isn't she a character?'

'Marvellous,' Hazel agreed. 'What a charming little village this is!'

'Isn't it? All very Yorkshire,' Derek added, putting on a cod Yorkshire accent, and Hazel laughed.

Lily's knuckles whitened on the steering wheel.

Hazel glanced at Lily, her gaze sharpening as she registered that Lily was young and very pretty. 'Do you need a driver again tonight, darling?'

'Oh, no,' he said casually. 'Pick me up at the usual time tomorrow morning, Corporal.'

'Tomorrow's my day off, sir.'

'Oh, right. Of course. Well, carry on, Corporal.'

'Thank you, sir.'

Sick with misery and humiliation, Lily put the jeep into gear. She risked one last look back at Derek, but he was shepherding his wife towards the house, Lily obviously forgotten. Hazel was looking over her shoulder, though, and her eyes were narrowed in suspicion.

20

Annie stood on the platform, saying goodbye to Edward again. This time Jacob stayed in the truck and there were just the two of them, marooned amongst the jostling passengers. It was the busiest time of day for the station, with milk churns and cartloads of potatoes and cabbages waiting to be loaded onto the train, and people coming and going.

Annie and Edward were scarcely aware of the activity around them. It was as if they were separated from the rest of the world by an invisible wall, trapped together in a silence that thrummed with regret.

'Annie,' Edward said suddenly, and stopped.

She made herself smile. 'What?'

'I just wanted to say . . . I'm sorry,' he said. 'These past two days — they haven't been what I thought they would be. I longed and longed to come back and see you, but when I got off the train and saw you . . . I can't explain it. It was as if I had left part of me back on the ship. As if I were still on that lifeboat in the Atlantic and you were at Emmerdale, and I couldn't reach you.'

'I understand,' said Annie, but Edward shook his head.

'How could you understand? You don't know what it's like out there, Annie. The waves are huge and the water's so black, but worst of all is the waiting and waiting, not knowing if a

220

torpedo is going to blow you all to smithereens. When it does, it's just luck as to where you're standing. There's a huge explosion, and if you can, you run for the lifeboats. Last week, the ship was alight and you could see clear as day, and I saw my mate Mike on the ground. I nearly tripped over him.'

Edward stopped, swallowed. 'We joined up at the same time. He was a laugh, Mike. So I stopped to help him but he . . . half of him had just disappeared. Everything below his waist blown right off him.'

Annie didn't know what to say. Edward's eyes were unfocused, and she could tell that he was on that terrifying ship in the dark again. 'The bosun grabbed me and told me to get off the ship,' Edward went on after a moment. 'He said Mike was dead but I keep thinking, what if he wasn't? His eyes were open. What if he was waiting for me to help him?'

Annie's throat was aching. 'Edward, you couldn't have done anything.'

'I know.' He sighed. 'Part of me knows that, but all the time I was here, I was thinking about the expression on his face. Thinking about how small he looked without any legs.'

'And our tales of the war here didn't mean anything to you?' said Annie quietly.

Edward shook his head. 'No. I know it's not fair. I know life has to go on and that everybody's doing what they can, but I've forgotten how to belong. I've only been away six months, but already I'm a stranger. I'd look at you, Annie, and I'd think how pretty you were and I'd tell myself that you were my girl, but it didn't feel real. But just now, I looked at you and suddenly I *saw* you. I recognised you, my Annie.' He took her hands. 'And now I'm going back to sea, and I've wasted these two precious days with you and I am so, so sorry.'

Annie's cheeks were wet. 'You don't need to be sorry, Edward. You think I don't understand, but I do. I know how it feels to stand outside yourself and watch people you've known and loved for years and think: who *are* you? So I'm sorry, too. We thought the war wouldn't change us, but it has. We'll need to get to know each other again when this is all over.'

'Yes.' Edward smiled at last and tightened his clasp on her hands as the train puffed into the station. 'So you'll still be my girl after the war?'

'I'll always be yours, Edward,' Annie told him.

He kissed her then, a kiss full of yearning, and when he released her, tears stood in her eyes.

This might be the last time she saw him, she realised. The last time she touched him. Next time the torpedo struck, it might be Edward standing in the wrong place. And her last memory of him would be of these two wasted days, and a tender kiss shared much, much too late.

Hugging her arms together, she watched Edward climb onto the train. He pulled down the window so that he could lean out. 'Goodbye Annie,' he said. 'Next time will be better, I promise.'

'Yes.' Annie's smile wavered horribly but she kept it in place. 'Next time we'll do it better.'

She waved until the train had disappeared

round the bend, and then she walked out to the truck, oblivious to the bustling around her. Jacob was waiting in the cab. She climbed in beside him and just sat, glad that he didn't start the engine immediately. Together they watched the steam from the train evaporate as it chugged into the distance.

'Edward's gone.' Annie heard the words come out of her mouth as the terrible truth struck her. 'He's gone.' It was as if an unseen hand had cut through a string that had been holding her upright for the past ten days, and she collapsed forward with a howl of anguish. Edward had gone just when she had found him again. Those few precious moments on the platform were all she had to show for his two days of leave, the only time when Edward had really been *there*, and now he had gone again.

She cried and cried, cried for the bitter waste of it. Jacob slid awkwardly across the seat and put his arm around her.

'Come on, now, Annie, don't take on so,' he said. 'Ed'll get leave again. He'll be all right.'

Annie lifted a tear-drenched face to his. 'What if he isn't? What if he never comes back and I've spoiled *everything*?'

'I'm sure that's not true,' said Jacob inadequately, but she wasn't really listening to him.

'I didn't tell him the truth.' Too late she realised how she could have tried to make things better. 'I didn't tell him I was wretched, too. I let us be wretched apart instead of wretched together.'

Jacob frowned. 'I knew you hadn't been well,'

he began, but Annie cut him off.

'I'm ashamed, not sick.'

'Ashamed? What could you possibly be ashamed of, Annie?'

Annie slumped back against the seat and pushed a weary hand through her curls. 'Oliver Skilbeck raped me,' she said, defeated.

The ugly word seemed to reverberate around the cab.

'When?' asked Jacob, dangerously quiet.

'After Sarah's wedding. I was taking the shortcut home and he . . . he . . . ' Her throat closed and she couldn't say it. 'He raped me in the field,' she forced the words past her mouth at last. 'In the mud, with the sheep droppings. And that's how I feel now: dirty and stinking with shame.'

Jacob drew a careful breath. 'Why didn't you say anything?'

'I didn't want to spoil Edward's leave, but it was spoiled anyway,' said Annie, and her voice cracked. 'Everything's spoiled now.'

★ ★ ★

Lily didn't know what to do with her day off. It was a relief not to have to face Derek, but her life had revolved around him for six months now, and the day yawned bleakly ahead, empty of all the love and passion and excitement that being with Derek had brought.

To her surprise, Nina hadn't told Mick about their conversation, so Lily told her father herself that her affair with Derek was over, and why.

224

'You were right about him, Dad,' she said.

'Ah, *mavourneen*, I wish I had been wrong. But I'm proud of you for doing the right thing.'

In the end, she took herself for a walk. It was a bright day, the sky a high, thin blue and the air unseasonably soft. She headed for the river, to a little beach under the bridge where her parents had once met, and where she had gone after her mother died. Half hidden behind a tangle of bushes, it was a good place to think and be quiet.

But when she pushed her way through the undergrowth and skidded down the embankment, she found that the beach was already occupied.

By Jack Proudfoot.

'Oh.'

He was sitting on one of the smooth boulders where she used to sit, but at her sudden appearance, he pushed himself to his feet with a grimace of pain.

'Lily,' he said, an inflection of surprise in his voice.

'I'm sorry. I wasn't expecting anyone to be here.'

'I come here to think sometimes.'

'Same here.'

'I haven't seen you here before,' he commented lightly, but the eyes that rested on her face were shrewd.

'No, well, I've been preoccupied by other things the last few months,' said Lily, realising with shame how absorbed she had been with Derek to the exclusion of everything else.

'And now Mrs Mortimer has turned up.' Her gaze flew to his and he shrugged. 'I'm a policeman,' he said. 'It's my job to know what's going on in Beckindale.'

With a sigh, Lily went to sit on one of the boulders. 'I suppose everyone knows that we were having an affair?'

'It wasn't hard to guess.' After a moment, Jack resumed his seat, stretching out his leg and rubbing it. 'Did you know he was married?'

'I should have done, but I didn't. Not until Nina told me.' She glanced at Jack. 'Did you?'

'I thought it was very likely.'

Lily picked up a pebble and threw it into the river. 'You must think I'm an idiot,' she said bitterly.

'I think you're very young,' he amended.

'And there was me, thinking I was so sophisticated and glamorous . . . ' Lily's face twisted. 'Instead, it turns out I was young and stupid.'

'There are worse things to be.'

She turned her head to look at him. 'You could have said no, no, Lily, of course you're not stupid,' she pointed out, and a smile hovered around his mouth.

'Would that have made you feel better?'

'Probably not.' Her eyes narrowed as she saw him rub his thigh. 'Is your leg painful?'

'It can be.'

'What's wrong with it?' she asked abruptly.

'I had polio.'

Lily looked at him in surprise. 'Polio? I heard you'd been in a car accident. Or tortured by gangsters. That's the other rumour doing the rounds.'

That infuriatingly elusive smile again. 'Is that what they're saying? No, nothing so exciting. Though I'm not sure I wouldn't rather have been tortured by gangsters than go through years of treatment for polio again. I was lucky, I didn't have to go in an iron lung, but it's still not much fun.'

'Is that why you're here in Beckindale? Because of the polio?'

'Partly. I was all set for a career as a detective in Leeds, had been marked as a high-flyer, and then I got ill.' Jack's expression didn't change, but Lily sensed what a devastating blow it had been to his hopes. 'I had years of treatment and rehabilitation until I had to accept that I was never going to have the stamina I needed to go back to what I was doing before. When they offered me a post here, I took it. It's not as demanding being a local policeman, and there's a need for officers who know what they're doing as so many have joined up.'

'You must find Beckindale pretty dull after Leeds,' said Lily sympathetically, and he turned his head to look at her.

'It has its compensations,' he said. There was nothing suggestive at all about the way he spoke, but for some reason Lily felt her cheeks tingle.

'Sergeant! Sergeant!' The voice calling from the bridge made her jump. One of Meg Warcup's evacuees was shouting and waving.

Jack hauled himself to his feet once more. 'What is it, Ruby?'

'Mrs Lazenby sent me. She said to tell you Jacob Sugden is murdering Oliver Skilbeck and can you come right away?'

'Where are they?'

'Outside the Woolpack.'

Lily scrambled up the bank after Jack and they made their way as quickly as they could back into town. They were accompanied by Ruby, who had been on the scene when Jacob launched himself at Oliver and started punching him.

'There was blood *everywhere*,' she told them. 'Jacob was saying 'Annie told me what you did. I'm going to *kill* you', and that's when Miss Barlow — Mrs Merrick, I mean — grabbed me and told me to run and find you, so I didn't see any more,' she added regretfully.

Jack's expression was grim as they approached the Woolpack. Clearly Ruby was not the only one who had been sent running with the news, as half the village seemed to be gathered outside the pub, all talking loudly and gesticulating. Jed and Larry Dingle held a still-struggling Jacob by the arms. He was white-faced and wild-eyed, his lip split and bleeding, but he was swearing and shouting at Oliver, who lay sprawled on the ground, his face so battered that Lily caught her breath. Elizabeth Barlow was on her knees beside him, shrieking that Jacob had killed him.

Lily couldn't help noticing how effortlessly Jack cut through the noise without raising his voice. 'Jed, Larry, take Jacob inside and keep him there,' he said, and when they obediently dragged Jacob into the Woolpack, he glanced at Lily. 'You ever done any first aid?'

'Yes, it was part of our ATS training.'

'Good. See what you can do for Oliver. Ruby,

you go and find Dr Moss and get him to come here straight away. Someone take Elizabeth home,' he added as she collapsed into histrionic moans. His cool gaze swept the crowd. 'And the rest of you, move on. The excitement's over.'

Muttering, they dispersed, many into the Woolpack. Lily knelt beside Oliver. 'He's in a bad way,' she said. 'Oliver, can you hear me?'

To her relief, Oliver groaned. His eyes fluttered open and he turned his head to throw up all over Lily's skirt.

'Great.' She scrambled to her feet with a sigh. 'At least he's not dead. I'll get some water and clean him up.'

She had barely had time to rinse off the worst of the blood before Ruby trotted back, followed by the portly Dr Moss. The doctor tutted and shook his head as he examined Oliver, who moaned in pain. 'A bad business!' he said. 'Whoever did this was vicious. He's lucky things aren't worse.'

A squeal of brakes announced the arrival of Clive Skilbeck. The news had evidently travelled as far as the Skilbeck farm, and he had driven down in a truck which to Lily's experienced eye looked spanking new. How had the Skilbecks managed to get hold of a vehicle like that in wartime? she wondered.

Clive Skilbeck had other things on his mind. 'Oliver!' he exclaimed, rushing over, only to recoil in horror at the sight of his son's face. 'Jesus Christ! Who did this to you?'

'Sugden,' Oliver managed to mumble through swollen lips.

'Jacob Sugden! That bastard!' Clive swung round. 'Where is he?' His gaze fixed on the Woolpack. 'In there? Wait till I get my hands on him!'

Clive was a big man and a powerful one, but Jack stepped calmly in front of him.

'This is a police matter now,' he said. 'I will be speaking to Jacob Sugden. Take your son home, get him patched up. I'll come and see him tomorrow.'

Clive loomed aggressively over Jack, who was shorter and slighter, with a weak leg to boot, but Jack didn't move. In the end, it was Clive who dropped his eyes first.

'Those Sugdens have always had it in for Oliver,' he said, his florid face mottled purple with rage. He jabbed a finger at Jack's chest. 'I want Jacob to go to prison for this.'

'If Oliver wants to press charges, he can,' said Jack, 'but I want to find out exactly what happened first.'

When Oliver had been helped, moaning, into the truck, Jack turned to Lily. 'Sorry about your skirt,' he said.

She looked down at the stains ruefully. 'It'll wash. Are you going to talk to Jacob now?'

He nodded. 'Come with me? It's always handy to have a witness.'

'All right. I need to wash my hands, anyway.'

Lily, having cleaned her hands as best she could, and had another ineffectual go at the stains on her skirt, found them in the Ladies' Lounge. Jacob was slumped at a table, watched over by Jed, who was straddled over a chair, while Larry did brisk business in the main bar.

Jack pulled out a chair and sat down opposite Jacob. 'All right,' he said calmly. 'Tell me what happened.'

Jacob was nursing his hand. His knuckles were bruised and raw, but his eyes were burning with anger.

'He deserved every bit of it,' he said, low and savage. 'I ent never going to apologise for that.'

'What did Oliver do to you?'

'Not to me. To Annie.'

'Annie Pearson?'

'I knew summat was wrong.' Jacob shook his head from side to side like a tired bull. 'One day she was looking forward to Ed coming home. She was happy. She was . . . she was *shining* with it, you know?'

Lily knew what he meant. There had always been a bright quality to Annie, something blessedly uncomplicated. To say that she was pure made her sound wet, but that was what Lily had always felt about her. Everybody else seemed to be a muddled mess of emotions, but Annie was simple and contented and good in a way that should have made her nauseating but somehow didn't.

'She was like she always was,' Jacob went on, 'and the next day . . . ' He snapped his fingers. 'The next it was gone. It was like the light in her was just snuffed out, like a candle.'

'Did you ask her what was wrong?'

'Course I did. I kept asking her, but she just said it were nowt. Then Ed came back on leave. Ever since they were kids, they were a couple. Well, you know that, Lily. Annie couldn't wait for him to come home,' he went on when Lily nodded, 'but when he got here . . . it was like they hardly knew each other. We couldn't understand it.'

'And then?' Jack prompted when Jacob trailed to a halt.

He drew a deep breath. 'Then today I drove Ed to the station with Annie. I shook his hand and said goodbye, and I said to Annie I'd wait for her in the truck. I thought they'd like a few more minutes alone. Well, the train came and went, and eventually Annie came out and got into the truck, and her face . . . ' Jacob's face worked with remembered distress. 'I can't describe it. She started howling and howling. I couldn't get much sense out of her at first. I kept saying that Ed would be all right or some such nonsense, but she wouldn't be comforted.'

Jacob lifted his red-rimmed eyes to look at Jack. 'And that's when she told me. She told me Oliver Skilbeck raped her after Sarah Barlow's wedding and left her lying in a pile of sheep shit.'

'And what did you do then?' asked Jack after a moment.

'What would you have done?' Jacob demanded as Lily sucked in a horrified breath. 'I took Annie back t'farm. And then I went to look for Oliver.'

Jack looked grave. 'Why didn't Annie report this?'

'She said she didn't want word getting round while Ed were home. Oliver told her he'd tell everyone she led him on. As if anyone would believe that of Annie,' Jacob said in disgust. 'I had to do what I did, and I'd do it again. I'm just sorry I didn't kill him.'

'I'm still arresting you for assault,' said Jack.

By the time Jacob had been locked in the village's single cell, Jack was looking weary and his bad leg dragged. Lily had dressed Jacob's cuts, and now watched as Jack rubbed a hand over his face.

'I'd better get up to Emmerdale Farm,' he said, 'and then I'll need to see the Skilbecks. This is a nasty business.'

'Do you want a lift?' Lily asked impulsively and he looked at her in surprise. 'You look tired,' she explained, 'and it's a long bike ride from here. And it's getting dark. I've got the jeep.'

'Isn't that for army business only?'

Lily thought of the times she and Derek had driven into the hills or to a cosy pub where they could rent a room.

'I don't think anyone could object, under the circumstances,' she said.

'In that case, I'd be grateful. Thank you,' said Jack in his cool way.

Maggie Sugden came out to meet them at Emmerdale Farm, her face drawn. 'What's happening? Where's Jacob? I can't get anything out of Annie.'

Jack didn't answer her directly. 'Can I talk to Annie, Mrs Sugden?' he asked instead.

They sat around the kitchen table. Maggie kept a hand pressed to her mouth in horror as Annie confirmed Jacob's story. Her voice was flat, her eyes dull.

'I was afraid Edward would do what Jacob did if he heard the rumours, and he'd spend his leave fighting,' she said.

'I can arrest Oliver if you want to press charges,' said Jack, but Annie shook her head.

'It's his word against mine, just like he said. Not everyone will believe him, but some might and people will start wondering if there's smoke without fire. Next thing I know, I'll be the village slut.'

'Not if we can make the charges stick,' said Jack.

'What if you can't? Oh, what does it matter anyway?' Annie's voice cracked. 'Now Jacob's made a scene, everyone will know that Oliver . . . that he . . . that he . . . '

'I think she's had enough,' said Maggie, putting a hand on Annie's shoulder as she broke into tearing sobs.

'What's the point?' Annie demanded bitterly through her tears. 'It's done now. Nothing will undo it. I didn't want Edward to know and now he's gone, and that's that.'

Lily waited in the jeep when Jack went in to see the Skilbecks. 'What did Oliver say?' she asked when he came out and climbed tiredly into the passenger seat.

'He denied it at first, then decided Annie had 'asked for it'.' Jack's voice curled in disgust. 'Clive Skilbeck wants the book thrown at Jacob, but I've agreed that if he doesn't want charges brought against Oliver, he'll accept that Jacob goes free.' He sighed and dragged a weary hand through his hair. 'So no one is happy, least of all Annie Pearson.'

Poor Annie, Lily thought as she drove Jack

back to the police house. It was slow going in the dark, and she had covered the headlights with cardboard so that only a tiny slit of light illuminated the road.

It was hard to believe that she had been feeling sorry for herself that morning. What did *she* have to feel sad about compared to Annie? Lily asked herself. She'd made a fool of herself over a man who had taken advantage of her. She was embarrassed and hurt and humiliated, but no more than that.

Strange that only that morning she would have said she disliked Jack Proudfoot intensely. Lily slid a glance at Jack's profile in the dim light. Now, she didn't know how she felt. All she knew was that she had barely given Derek a thought all day.

21

'That's pretty.' Ruby spoke from the doorway as Meg held up the locket. It glinted in the wintry sunlight coming through the window.

'It was Rosie's.'

Meg turned to show her as Ruby came into the room. She was fascinated by Rosie and the fact that Meg had had a twin sister. 'Tomorrow's Christmas Eve,' she told Ruby. 'That's our birthday, so I like to wear this to remind me of her. Do you want to see?'

Ruby nodded and Meg opened the locket for her. 'Oh . . . there are people in there!' said Ruby in delight as she peered closer at the tiny photographs. 'Who are they?'

'That's my mum and my dad.' Meg's smile was sad as she looked at her parents. They had been so young and happy once. Until the day she had got bored and made Rosie cycle up Teggs Hill with her.

'They look nice,' said Ruby wistfully.

'They were.'

'Do you miss them?'

Meg had to swallow down the grief that came barrelling up her throat. 'Yes, I do.'

'I don't have a dad,' Ruby said. 'At least, I don't think I do. What's it like?'

'Having a father?' Meg hesitated. 'It depends on the father, I suppose. Mine was lovely. He was quiet, but strong and steady. He never spanked us. My mum had to do that. Dad used to read us stories and do different voices for all the characters.' She smiled at the memory.

'I wish I'd had a dad like that,' Ruby said, tracing the outline of the locket with her finger.

'You've got a mum,' Meg reminded her, and after a moment, Ruby nodded.

She still wrote to her mother every week, refusing to be daunted by the lack of reply. 'Mam's not one for writing,' she had told Meg once, on the defensive when she realised Meg had caught her looking through the post. 'I don't mind.'

Meg's heart cracked for her. At last, Ruby was blossoming. An excellent mimic, she often made Meg laugh with her stories of her friends and of Beckindale's characters. She could take Janet Airey off to a tee, and did an excellent imitation of the vicar's wife. When she was in a good mood, she would chatter away while she laid the table or helped with the dishes. Meg no longer had to nag her to do her share of the chores around the house.

It was encouraging to see how Ruby was letting her guard down, although there were still days when she was as restless and reckless as Meg had once been. Several times she had taken Meg's bicycle without permission. It was far too big for her, and she'd fallen off and had to limp home with cuts and grazes. But she was undaunted. Meg was torn between worry, anger and a reluctant admiration for Ruby's courage.

The only real problem with Ruby now was her refusal to accept Rolf. Meg wasn't sure if it was because she was jealous of the attention Stan was getting since his musical talent had been discovered, or whether she was still traumatised from their capture after the plane crash. She played up whenever Rolf came round to give her little brother a lesson, as he had been doing every week since the harvest supper.

'He's a Hun!' she complained loudly to Meg. 'I wouldn't let him in the house! Ent you heard what them Germans are doing to us?'

Ruby was not the only one who thought Meg was unpatriotic for inviting Rolf to the cottage. His exquisite playing at the harvest supper might have momentarily silenced the people of Beckindale, but there was still plenty of suspicion and dislike of the prisoners of war, especially the German ones. Not so surprising, perhaps, given that every time they switched on the wireless there was news of dreadful bombings, or the terrible toll of pilots and aircraft in the battle for the skies over the south coast. Meg understood, but she was finding it increasingly hard to think of Rolf as an enemy.

She looked forward to his weekly visits to teach Stan. She sat quietly in the corner and got on with the bottomless pile of mending while she listened to them play. Stan's ability was a revelation. Even Meg, knowing nothing about music, could tell that he was remarkable. Rolf had sat down with Meg after the first lesson with a serious expression. 'Stan has a rare talent,' he said. 'I play something and he's able to copy it. You must nurture his playing.'

Meg was proud of Stan, but here was a new

weight of responsibility. How was she supposed to nurture a musical genius in a tiny cottage in Beckindale in the middle of a war?

'I will teach him what I can,' said Rolf when she expressed her doubts. 'But I think me coming here may be difficult for you.'

Meg soon found out what he meant. Word quickly got round that Rolf was going to the cottage on a regular basis. Working on a farm was one thing; cosy chats with the local school-mistress quite another. She began to notice people avoiding her eyes, or crossing the road rather than stopping to talk to her. There was often silence around her in the queue at the shop.

Oh, it wasn't everyone — Meg could count on the Sugdens and the Dingles, and Nina Lazenby had never been one to follow the crowd — but there was enough bad feeling to make her uncomfortable. Still, Meg had been the focus of horrified interest before now, and attempts to warn her about the consequences of fraternising with the enemy only brought her chin up.

It was too late to see Rolf as a faceless enemy. She thought sometimes she could draw him with her eyes closed: the precise angle of his jaw, the glimmer of cool amusement in his eyes, the long musician's fingers. The line of his mouth . . . just thinking about his mouth set a humming beneath Meg's skin.

After the lesson, Meg gave him tea and a slice of admittedly unappealing cake. He was reserved at first, but as they got to know each other she learnt more about his family in Germany. He told her about his sisters, practical Liesbeth, sensitive Hanna, clever Ingrid and Klara, who loved her food. There had been tension when Rolf had announced that he was going to be a musician. His father, he said, had been an engineer and wanted Rolf to follow in his footsteps. Rolf had persisted and had begun to make a name for himself as a violinist. He had even been invited to join an orchestra in America.

'Why didn't you go?'

Rolf had sighed. 'Because when I had the chance to go, it felt like running away. I am not a supporter of the National Socialists, but Germany is my home. It is my country, my family are there. The politics there, it is . . . difficult. I blame myself. I was too busy thinking about my music to realise how ugly things were getting. I could have got away, it is true, and I would be fine, but what about my mother? My sisters? How could I live with myself knowing that I was safe and they weren't? So I volunteered to learn to fly,' he said, 'and there is a bit of me that is ashamed because I love it so much. It is so . . . so *free* up in sky.'

'It must feel wonderful.' Meg could imagine it, the space and the light and, yes, the freedom. 'I'd like to go in a plane one day.'

'You would not like to be in a plane at the moment. In the camp we have been getting news of great battles between the Luftwaffe and the RAF. It has been bad, I think?'

'Yes, we haven't seen much of the war here, but in the south, and in the big cities, it's been very bad. We were all thinking we'd be invaded,

240

but so far we've beaten you back.' She hesitated. 'Would you have been part of that attack if you hadn't crashed?'

'No, I was on reconnaissance,' he said. 'But it is all part of the same thing. War is a bad business.'

'Are you glad to be out of it?' Meg had asked, and Rolf's eyes had rested on her face.

'I begin to think I am.'

★   ★   ★

Now Meg made her way downstairs. Stan was fidgeting, running backwards and forwards to the window while he waited for Rolf.

'Rolf's going to teach me some carols,' he told Meg. 'We're going to play them at the Christmas party in the hall tomorrow. When's he coming?'

'He'll be on his way,' said Meg, although she was nearly as anxious. To get to the cottage, Rolf had to walk from the camp, through the village and across the bridge. He had a big circle sewn on the back of his jacket to identify him as a prisoner of war, and was allowed out on his own within five miles of the camp. There simply weren't enough guards to keep an eye on all the prisoners, but the system seemed to be working pretty well. Yet there was always the chance someone would take exception to a German walking free, and things could turn ugly very quickly.

Like Stan, Meg found it hard to settle. The next day was Christmas Eve, and her birthday. Hers and Rosie's. Once it had been a day full of excitement. The Warcups hadn't had much, but Polly and Robert had always made a fuss of them, and told them again the story of the snowy night they had been born in 1915. Meg and Rosie had always longed for it to snow again on their birthday.

And perhaps this year it would. It was certainly cold enough. The sky was an iron grey and a bitter wind moaned around the corners of the cottage. Meg hugged her cardigan around her. She should get some more wood from outside and build up the fire. Neither Rolf nor Stan would be able to play if their fingers were too cold.

Opening the back door, she hurried over to get some wood, biting down a shriek of fright as a figure loomed from behind the woodshed.

'Oh, you gave me such a fright!' she sighed, recognising Rolf. 'What on earth are you doing out here?' she said, dropping her voice to a whisper as he laid a finger against his lips.

'I have brought the presents for the children. I was just hiding them out here. You can take them in tomorrow morning.'

Meg had been appalled when she discovered that neither Ruby nor Stan knew when their birthdays were. 'Mam never told us,' Ruby had shrugged.

'In that case, you can share mine,' Meg had said impulsively. 'We'll have our birthdays and Christmas together.'

The previous Christmas had been a blur. Meg had been lonely after her father's death, and struggling to cope with the two half-feral children who had been landed on her. This year, though, she was determined it would be different, and she had discussed how to get hold of a gift that would mean the most to Ruby and Stan.

It was Rolf who had come up with a solution. There were skilled craftsmen at the camp, he'd pointed out, all more than happy to have a reason to use their skills in return for an extra packet of cigarettes. 'There's an Italian who is a fine woodworker and a musician, too. We will see what he can do.'

Now Rolf unwrapped a perfect half-size violin to show Meg. 'For Giuseppe it was a labour of love. I am going to ask if he can come to the hall tomorrow to listen to Stan play it.'

'I'd like to meet him,' said Meg, already planning how she could negotiate an extra packet of cigarettes from Jed Dingle.

For Ruby there was a bicycle, built from pieces cannibalised from broken ones. Rolf had made it himself. Meg pressed her fingers to her mouth in delight when she saw it.

'Oh, you are clever! How can I ever thank you?'

'It is I who thank you,' said Rolf. 'If it were not for you, I would be sitting lonely and miserable in the camp on my own.'

Meg's eyes met his for a moment and then slid away. 'Well, come in. It's freezing out here, and Stan's waiting for you. Thank you again for the bicycle and the violin, Rolf. I'll bring them in after the children are in bed, and they can be a surprise in the morning.'

Ruby slammed in when Stan was practising and stomped straight upstairs when she saw Rolf was there. Meg was content to sit by the fire and work through her sewing pile. She was not a natural needlewoman, but both children were growing so fast and she couldn't afford to buy them new clothes. Maureen Airey, one of Janet's five daughters-in-law, had three lads, the youngest a couple of years older than Stan. She had given Meg a selection of shorts, shirts and jumpers her boy had grown out of, and Meg was now occupied turning up the shorts and mending frayed collars and assorted tears. She had knitted some more socks for him, too.

Stan had been pale and scrawny, but he was starting to put on weight and his cheeks wore a healthy glow. The new clothes should keep him going for a few more months, and then she could let the shorts down again. He had stopped wetting the bed, which was a huge relief, and not just because it meant less washing. Meg was convinced that discovering music had trans-formed him, and as she listened to him playing 'In the Bleak Midwinter', she marvelled anew at his talent.

Later, she made tea and warmed some apple mincemeat tarts. The children, ever alert to the possibility of food, gobbled down a tart each and then ran off, and Meg wasn't sorry to see them go.

Rolf bit into one of the tarts. 'These are good.'

'They're meant to be mince pies, but there's so little butter for pastry now, and I was too late to get any more dried fruit from the shop.' Meg took a cautious bite herself. She had used dried apples with cinnamon and mixed spice from the larder, and mixed in a few cooked prunes that she had left over. The result was not nearly as bad as she had expected. 'They're all right, aren't they?' she agreed, relieved. 'Not exactly a mince pie, but sort of Christmassy.'

'In Germany we have *stollen* at this time of year,' said Rolf. 'It's a cake, made with fruits and nuts and spices, and sugar on the top. It is Klara's favourite. She likes her cakes. And *lebkuchen*. That's a kind of gingerbread, I think you would say.' His nostalgic smile faded. 'I don't suppose she will get many sweet treats this year.'

There was a pause.

'Have you heard from your family?' Meg asked.

'Yes, the Red Cross forward letters for prisoners. I had one from Liesbeth. They were glad I was safe. I am safer than they are,' he said with a trace of bitterness. 'Your pilots are dropping bombs on Berlin whenever they can.'

'I'm sorry,' said Meg. 'This war . . . it's awful. I don't know why it seems worse at Christmas somehow. It's supposed to be about peace and goodwill to all men, and instead we're dropping bombs on each other.'

'You're right.' Rolf nodded his agreement. 'But what can we do? We cannot stop the bombing, but we are doing what we can by sitting here together, thinking about Christmas, even if we are drinking tea instead of *glühwein*,' he added in an attempt to lighten the atmosphere.

Meg smiled. 'I wish I had something more

exciting to offer you.'

'Right now, I am happy to have peace instead of excitement,' said Rolf. He looked around the room. There was a wireless on the sideboard and a rag rug in front of the fire. The mantelpiece held a gently ticking clock and was crowded with knick-knacks collected by Polly Warcup that Meg couldn't bring herself to move. His gaze came back to Meg, sitting on the other side of the fireplace, a sewing basket on the table beside her and a pile of mending on the arm of her chair.

'It feels very peaceful here,' he said as if it had just struck him.

'It won't last,' said Meg. 'Ruby will be on the rampage again soon enough, and then it's anything but peaceful!'

'We should enjoy the moment then,' said Rolf, and they exchanged a smile that caught and held for a startling moment. The silence lengthened as the air shortened, and Meg had to force her eyes away from his, her heart hammering uncomfortably.

'Yes, we should.'

22

'What are you making?' Rolf said easily enough after a moment.

Meg looked down at the dress on her lap. She had been looking through her wardrobe to see if she could find something to cut down for Ruby, and she had come across Rosie's favourite dress at the back. It was one Polly hadn't been able to bear to give away. Meg's first reaction had been to push it back into the wardrobe, but what was the point? Material was scarce and the colour would suit Ruby beautifully. She had brought it down and had been trying to summon the courage to start unpicking the dress. Ruby was much smaller than her twin had been, and the seams would have to be taken in.

'Oh, just something for Ruby . . . ' Without thinking, she stroked the material, remembering how much Rosie had loved it.

'You look sad,' said Rolf quietly.

'Do I?' Meg mustered a smile. 'I suppose I'm remembering my twin, Rosie. This was her frock once.'

'You were a twin?' Rolf looked interested. 'I didn't not know this. Were you . . . what is the word? The same?'

'Identical,' she told him. 'No, we were completely different, and not just in looks. Rosie was the nicest person you could imagine. She was sweet and pretty and kind and everything

247

that is good, and I was . . . not. We were opposites in every way, but we were also the same, if that makes sense.'

'I think so. And I think you are not very kind to yourself, Meg. You are not ugly or unkind or bad in any way. If you were, you would not look after two unhappy evacuees the way you do.'

'I do that because I have to, not because I'm a nice person. Rosie was nice to everyone because she genuinely liked them, while I'm cross and crotchety. I know what they say about me in the village: I'm the strict, sour schoolmistress. I'm the bitter, repressed spinster.'

I'm the one who killed her sister.

Rolf actually laughed. 'I do not recognise that person at all!' He sobered. 'What happened to Rosie, Meg?'

She smoothed the material over her knee. For a wild moment she was tempted to tell him the truth, but the words stuck in her throat. 'She . . . died. When she was fourteen.' It was all Meg could manage.

'I'm sorry,' said Rolf simply.

'Don't mind me. It's my birthday tomorrow, so obviously it's Rosie's too, and it always makes me maudlin, I'm sorry.' Determinedly, Meg put the frock aside and glanced at the clock on the mantelpiece. 'You'd better get back for roll call.'

'Yes, I must go.' He got to his feet. 'I'll see you at the hall tomorrow?'

'Of course. Thank you again for the children's presents, Rolf,' Meg said as he reached the door, and he stopped.

'Oh, I nearly forgot. I made you a present too.'

From the inside pocket of his jacket, he took a necklace and held it out to her.

The chain glimmered in the firelight. It was warm from his body as Meg held it in her hands. She had never seen a necklace like it before. It was made of what looked like beaten silver, and hanging from it was a polished stone pendant. When Meg held it up to the light, she saw swirls of grey and green and tawny brown.

'It's beautiful,' she said. 'So unusual.'

'Like you,' said Rolf.

The colour rushed to her face. 'Thank you.'

Was he going to kiss her? Meg wondered with a jolt of anticipation, but in the end he turned to open the door.

'Happy birthday for tomorrow, Meg,' he said. 'I'll see you at the hall.'

He slipped out and Meg was left staring at the door, the necklace clasped in her hand. Of course he hadn't been going to kiss her. Nobody would want to kiss her, awkward, brusque spinster that she was.

But he had told her that she was beautiful, un-usual. *Like you*, he had said. Meg ran her fingers over the smooth surface of the stone and smiled.

⋆ ⋆ ⋆

Ruby and Stan were wild with excitement the next morning. 'It's snowing! Can we go outside?'

'Well, you can . . . ' said Meg, 'unless you'd like your presents first,' she added casually.

'Presents?' Suspicion mingled with hope in Ruby's voice.

'We decided this would be your birthday as well, remember? I've got you both a present. It's for your birthday and for Christmas. But if you'd rather go out and play . . . '

'No,' said Stan firmly. 'We'll open our presents.'

'All right, but you must stay here and promise to keep your eyes closed until I say you can open them.'

'Promise!'

Meg made them wait in the kitchen while she carried the bicycle and the violin into the tiny parlour. She put the violin on the table and propped the bicycle against one of the chairs.

'Ready?' she said, going back into the kitchen. 'Don't open your eyes yet.'

They were both trembling with excitement as she led them into the parlour. 'All right, you can open them now.'

Their eyes flew open, and they stared, taking in the bicycle and the violin. There was a moment of utter stillness and wonder. Meg found that her throat was aching at their expressions.

Stan moved first, touching the violin reverently. 'Is it for me?'

'Yes.' Goodness, she would cry if she wasn't careful! 'A friend of Rolf's made it at the camp. Do you like it?'

Stan's face answered for him as he lifted the violin and put it to his shoulder as if it was part of him. He drew the bow across the strings in a note of wonder and Meg smiled.

'I guess you do.'

Behind Stan, Ruby was approaching the bicycle from the side as if it were a wild animal she was determined to catch unawares. Meg sat on the arm of one of the easy chairs by the fire and watched her. 'I thought if you had a bicycle of your own, you might stop borrowing mine,' she said.

'It's mine?'

'Yes, it's yours. You can take it with you when you go home.'

Ruby looked at Meg and then at the bike, and her mouth wobbled before she clamped it into a stern line with a scowl. 'I never had no present like this before,' she said, almost aggressively.

'I know.'

'Can I ride it now?'

'Well, it's snowing . . . oh, why not?' said Meg, giving in abruptly. What was the point of having a bicycle if you couldn't ride it straight away? She remembered the Christmas Eve when she and Rosie had been given bikes. They hadn't been able to wait to go outside and ride them.

* * *

Ruby was persuaded with some difficulty to leave her new bicycle behind when they walked down to the Christmas Eve service in the church. It had been snowing on and off all day, and the fells stretched white into the distance, broken only by the sharp lines of the stone walls.

Afterwards, there was a party in the village hall. Maggie Sugden, Janet Airey and others had organised the first one during the Great War, and it had become a tradition. At the very first Christmas party, food had been in scarce supply and now it was rationed again, but as at the harvest festival, treats were found for the children, and somehow the tables were laden with jellies and trifles and gingerbread while the adults consoled themselves for the scarcity of food with a bowl of punch concocted from a secret recipe by Jed Dingle.

As schoolmistress, it fell on Meg to organise games for the children. Nina Lazenby had lent her gramophone and they played boisterous musical chairs and statues, pin the tail on the donkey and Simon Says, until Meg's ears were ringing.

'I think you deserve a break,' said Maggie, bringing her a glass of punch. 'Careful of this! It's lethal. I don't know what Jed's put in it.'

Released from the constraints of rules, the children, by now all thoroughly overexcited, ran around the hall and when they were tired of that, outside to throw snowballs at each other, much to the exasperation of the ARP warden on duty, who shouted every time they opened the door and let a sliver of light show.

'Come and sit down,' Maggie went on. 'Annie could do with seeing a friendly face.'

Maggie might also have noticed that once the games were over, there was nobody rushing over to talk to Meg either. Grateful for the thought, she followed Maggie across the hall.

'How is she?'

'Brave,' said Maggie. 'Of course, since Jacob's fight with Oliver, everybody knows what

252

happened. Annie keeps her head high but it's not easy. There'll always be those who'll wonder if Oliver is right and she was leading him on,' she went on angrily. 'Jacob was a fool to go for him like that, but in my heart I don't blame him. I could cheerfully kill Oliver myself. He nearly broke Annie. She's getting better, but when a man does that to you, it breaks something in you. I know,' she said grimly when Meg looked at her in surprise.

Annie was looking better than when Meg had last seen her. There was more colour in her face, but she had lost that sunny sweetness that had been so much a part of her before.

'Need a rest?' she said as Meg sat down beside her.

'You could say that.' Meg eyed the rampaging children as she took a slug of Jed's punch and nearly choked at the strength of it. 'Why did I ever think I wanted to be a schoolteacher?' she said as Annie patted her on the back. 'I can't control children at all. I'm not even sure I like them,' she confessed.

'You're better with them than you think,' Annie said. She paused. 'Why *did* you decide to be a teacher?'

Thrown by the seriousness of the question, Meg swirled her punch in the glass. 'The truth? Because that's what Rosie always wanted to be. She had it all worked out. She was going to teach and then she was going to get married and have four children.'

Meg risked another sip of punch. 'But I didn't really know what I wanted. To do something

253

exciting, be something exciting. A writer, a pilot, an explorer . . . anything that would shock my parents, I suppose.'

'I remember you being a rebel,' said Annie with a smile, and Meg felt a pang of sadness for her younger, more interesting self. 'Did that change when Rosie died?'

'I suppose so.' Meg sighed. 'Rosie was always the golden child. I don't mean my parents didn't love me, but Rosie was special. They would have been so proud if she'd become a teacher. So when she died, I suppose I felt I had to try and . . . not replace her, but be the good daughter, the sensible daughter they'd lost.'

Annie looked at her. 'It must have been hard for you, Meg. So you became a teacher to please your parents?'

'That's right. I had to do something, anyway, and I don't suppose I'd have been much of a success as an explorer.' Meg tried to make light of it, but Annie seemed to be considering the matter.

'We don't have much chance to do something different, do we? It's not like we can choose to do whatever we want here. I never even thought about it before,' she confided. 'I was just grateful to have a job at Emmerdale Farm. I never wanted to go anywhere else, do anything else. But now . . . '

'Now?' Meg prompted when she trailed off.

'Now I'm wondering what it would be like to go somewhere where not everybody knows all your business.'

'Well, that's one thing about the war,' Meg

said. 'You can get away from village life.'

'Why don't you do that?' Annie asked. 'You're clever. You could join one of them services, like Lily Dingle.'

'I could,' said Meg slowly. 'But now there's Ruby and Stan to think of, and I can't leave the school in the lurch and . . . I suppose I'm making excuses, aren't I? The truth is, I'm just boring. I'm not a rebel any more.'

Annie laughed. 'Says the girl who's thumbing her nose at the world and carrying on with an enemy prisoner!'

'I am not *carrying on*.' Meg coloured. 'It's just . . . nothing. Rolf's giving Stan violin lessons, that's all.'

'I'm not criticising you,' said Annie with a half-smile. 'I admire the way you don't care what anyone thinks, Meg. I want to be more like you that way.'

Meg hesitated. 'I'm so sorry about what Oliver did to you, Annie.'

Annie lifted her hands and let them fall in a gesture of hopelessness. 'The worst thing is I feel that somehow I deserved it. Up till then, I had a charmed life, I suppose. I liked everyone — well, not the Skilbecks, but I didn't hate them — and I thought everyone liked me. I had Edward, and I couldn't imagine ever wanting to be anywhere else or do anything else. I couldn't see how that could ever change. But then it was the war, and then . . . and then Oliver . . . ' Her soft mouth set in a hard line. 'Well, it turns out there are plenty of people more than ready to think the worst of me, so I've decided I have to grow up, stop caring about things so much.'

'It's not easy,' said Meg. 'I don't understand how people can be so judgemental. We've all got something that makes us feel bad, but that doesn't seem to stop them. Look at Lily Dingle. She's beautiful and smart. She can drive a car and fix engines. She's doing her bit for the war effort. But all anyone can talk about is the fact that she had an affair with that colonel, and now he's left with his wife.'

'Poor Li — ' Annie broke off. 'Look, isn't that your German?'

Meg swung round in her chair to see Rolf step into the room, followed by a wiry older man she presumed was Giuseppe. Rolf was carrying Tom Teale's fiddle and made no attempt to draw attention to himself, but everyone stopped talking and stared at him.

Rolf looked across the hall and when his eyes found Meg's something in his face made her heart start to thump erratically. Without realising it, her hand went to the pendant around her neck. For a moment, there were just the two of them in the hall.

'Nothing?' said Annie beside her. 'Right.'

Her gentle words snapped Meg out of her trance and she registered the outright hostility in some of the faces that were turned to Rolf. 'Bloody German,' said someone, loud enough for Meg to hear.

Getting quickly to her feet, she clapped her hands. 'Children! Children! Get everyone in from outside. We're going to sing carols now.'

Stan came running across to collect his violin

while Meg sorted the children until they stood in a couple of ragged rows. Then, at a nod from her, Rolf and Stan started to play. They began with 'Once in Royal David's City', and after the first few bars, the children started to sing to the music, the adults joining in.

As they sang their way through all the favourite carols, the atmosphere in the hall changed. The bristly suspicion leaked out of the air and the mood became more reflective. They left Meg's favourite carol until last: 'Silent Night'. As the voices died away, Rolf left Stan to play the music once more on his own. The sweet, clear notes filled the hall until he lowered his violin and smiled with the simple joy of making music.

Meg's throat tightened unbearably at his expression. She could see her own sense of amazement that such a small boy could produce such a beautiful sound reflected in the faces around the hall. His performance was followed by a telling moment of silence before the spell was broken with a joyous round of applause. Chairs were pushed back, glasses chinked. Children were called and taken home. A baby cried and was shushed as conversations began again.

After all the excitement, Ruby and Stan were exhausted. Stan sat next to Rolf, clutching his violin. Out of the corner of her eye, Meg, who was clearing away the debris from the games, could see him keeling slowly towards Rolf's shoulder as his eyelids drooped. A little further away, keeping her distance from Rolf, Ruby tried to maintain a protective watch over her brother, but her own eyes were struggling to stay open.

Maggie followed her gaze. 'Annie and I will finish up here,' she said. 'That little lad needs to be in bed.'

Stan didn't wake when Rolf lifted him up. Meg took Ruby's hand and for once the girl didn't pull away. 'Come on,' she said, 'let's go home.'

Jack Proudfoot had been keeping an eye on proceedings all evening, and now he stood at the door. 'Have you got permission to be out of camp, Schrieber?' he asked pleasantly as Rolf made to pass with Stan lolling over his shoulder.

'Until six thirty.'

Jack looked at his watch. 'You're cutting it fine.'

'I would like to help Miss Warcup take the children home.' Rolf tilted his head down to Stan. 'As you can see, this little one is too tired to walk.'

'All right, then.' After looking from Meg to Rolf, Jack made up his mind. 'I'll go round to the camp and have a word with the Commanding Officer there. I'll say I gave you permission to stay out until nine o'clock.'

'Thank you, Sergeant.'

Jack gave him a hard look. 'You be back by nine, and not a minute later, or you'll be on bread and water for a week.'

'You have my word,' said Rolf.

They put Stan to bed fully clothed, and Meg helped Ruby into her pyjamas. For once Ruby put up no protest and was asleep too before Meg had closed the door.

Rolf was waiting when she went downstairs. He had stirred up the fire, and was turning the dial on the wireless which hissed and crackled gently.

He looked up and smiled as she came in and the air thickened. 'I don't have any *glühwein* — is that right? — but I can offer you some of last year's sloe gin,' said Meg, smoothing down her frock in an unconsciously nervous gesture.

She poured the gin into two glasses and gave one to Rolf. 'What shall we drink to?'

'To you, of course. Happy birthday, Meg.'

'Thank you.' She swallowed. 'And happy Christmas, of course.'

'That too. Let's drink to peace, as well,' he suggested as he touched his glass to hers. 'And to a time when we will no longer be enemies.'

'To peace,' Meg echoed.

He had found some music on the wireless at last. A big band was playing a popular slow number. Rolf drained his glass and put it down. 'Dance with me?'

'There's not much room to dance in here.' But she let him take her glass so that she could put her hand in his and succumb to the temptation of leaning into his lean, solid body. Rolf held her close and rested his cheek against her hair.

'This is enough for us,' he said. 'For now.'

Spring 1941

23

'Hazel will be gone soon,' Derek had said when Lily drove him to camp for the first time after his wife arrived. 'I'm going to talk to her about a divorce, I promise, but now isn't the right time.'

'I don't want you to divorce her,' said Lily.

But Derek refused to believe that the affair was over as far as Lily was concerned. He was indulgent with her over Christmas, assuming that she was sulking because he hadn't told her that he was married.

'As soon as Hazel's gone, we'll go to the Red Lion and talk about things,' he promised. 'I miss you, darling.'

Lily missed him, too, but she missed believing that he was a decent, honourable man more. She missed his touch, missed the expert way he could drive her to mindless pleasure, but harder still to bear was losing the innocent happiness of loving him and thinking that she was loved in return.

But she wouldn't change her mind. It was too late for that.

She was cleaning spark plugs one day when her fellow ATS corporals, Connie and Sylvia, came into the garage. 'Hey, Dingle, we were just talking about this Colonel Harrison,' said Connie. 'What do you know about him?'

Lily straightened, wiping her hands on a rag. 'Harrison? I've never heard of him. Who is he?'

'But — ' Connie and Sylvia exchanged looks.

'You mean, you don't know?'

'Know what?'

'Delicious Derek is being transferred. Colonel Harrison is taking over from him.'

Derek hadn't even bothered to tell her that he was going. Another difficult conversation he had avoided.

'Oh, I'm so sorry,' said Sylvia, reading Lily's expression without difficulty. 'We just assumed you knew,' she went on with honeyed sweetness.

Too late Lily realised that everyone must have been aware of her affair with Derek. She had been so blissfully happy that she hadn't thought of what anyone else would think, and now she read a spark of malicious satisfaction in Sylvia's eyes.

'No,' she said evenly. 'I didn't know. When's Colonel Harrison coming?'

'Tomorrow, I think.' Connie slid a knife skilfully under her sympathetic smile. 'We'll all miss Delicious Derek. It'll be especially hard for you, though, Dingle, you being his personal driver and all.'

Lily waited until they had returned to work on their own vehicles before she knocked on Derek's office door. 'Come in,' he called. He was sitting behind his desk, looking impossibly handsome, and in spite of herself Lily felt the old tug of lust in her belly. He glanced up to see her standing to attention and smiled the old seductive smile. 'At ease, Corporal. What can I do for you?'

'I understand you're leaving tomorrow, sir.'

'Oh, yes, I've been meaning to tell you,' he

said ruefully. 'I just haven't had a moment since the order came through. The usual rush job! I'm being transferred to York. I'd hoped we could have a word on the way back to my billet,' he added with a meaningful look. 'I wouldn't mind a last look at the view from Teggs Hill.'

Lily felt sick remembering how many times she had driven eagerly up to Teggs Hill so they could be alone. How thrilled she had been by the secrecy of those encounters in that isolated barn. How pleased with herself to be having such a passionate and exciting affair! Now those times seemed cheap and sordid.

She looked out of the window. Heavy snowfalls in January had left huge drifts piled along the lanes, and although February was proving warmer and wetter, the fells were still white.

'I don't think there'll be much of a view today, sir,' she said. 'Will you be needing a lift to the station tomorrow morning?'

If Derek was afraid there might be some awkwardness in having his mistress drive his wife to the station, he gave no sign of it. 'Super,' he said, clearly deciding he had brushed over a potentially difficult conversation and already moving on. 'Oh eight hundred hours sharp, please.'

He couldn't even spare her that last humiliation.

Steeling herself, Lily made sure that she was looking composed in her uniform when she presented herself at Nina's door at eight o'clock the next morning. Nina answered, looking worried, but Lily kept her face expressionless.

'Car to take Colonel and Mrs Mortimer to the station,' she said.

Nina sighed. 'I'll tell them you're waiting.'

For all his insistence on punctuality, Derek and his wife kept Lily waiting ten minutes in the cold. She snapped a salute when he appeared and opened the rear door.

'Thank you, Corporal,' said Derek, ushering his wife into the car. As if he had never told Lily that she was perfect. As if he hadn't kissed every inch of her body. As if he hadn't told her that he loved her.

Lily's heart clenched, but she kept her face a mask.

'The station, please.' Hazel Mortimer tossed the request as Lily got behind the wheel, evidently seeing her as a glorified taxi driver.

Lily could see Derek and his wife in her rear-view mirror. Hazel was fidgeting with the fur collar of her coat and she kept darting glances at Lily's back.

'I won't be sorry to leave here,' she said to Derek. 'Beckindale's a rather dreary little place, isn't it?'

'There'll be more for you to do in York,' Derek consoled his wife.

'There certainly couldn't be less!' Hazel looked out of the window, unimpressed. 'The scenery's pretty enough, but the village itself is so backward! And that ghastly accent!'

Lily's accent, in fact.

Lily held tightly to the wheel. She was fairly sure that Hazel's remarks were addressed

directly to her. Hazel might not have acknowledged her, and she might only be able to see the
back of Lily's head, but she clearly knew exactly
who Lily was. Part of Lily couldn't blame her.
This drive must be as bad for Hazel as it was for
her. Lily wanted to turn round and say that she
was sorry, to tell Hazel that she hadn't known
Derek was married, but what would be the
point? Hazel presumably knew what her
husband was like.

At the station, Lily caught Hazel's eye as she
opened the rear door for her. It was the first time
she had looked at the older woman properly.
Derek's wife had clearly been a pretty woman
once, but now Lily could see the lines dragging
at her eyes and at the corners of her mouth.
There was a charged moment where it seemed to
Lily that she stood outside herself and could see
how young and fresh she must look compared to
Hazel. She could see the bitterness in Hazel's
expression, and she almost understood it. Once
Lily had dreamt of being married to Derek, but
now she could see that it would be purgatory,
constantly waiting for him to be unfaithful to the
next pretty girl, never able to trust him out of
your sight.

'Thank you,' Hazel said in a clipped voice. She
might have been referring to the drive, but
perhaps she meant that she was grateful to Lily
for not making a scene.

Lily nodded a brief acknowledgement before
opening the boot to lift out their two suitcases.
'Would you like me to take these onto the
platform for you, sir?'

'Oh, I think we'll manage.' Derek smiled warmly, careless of his wife's presence. 'It's been a pleasure, Corporal.'

Lily could feel herself shrinking like a snail from the innuendo in his voice. 'Thank you, sir,' she said in a monotone, and as she turned, she caught Hazel's eye again in something like sympathy.

'Goodbye, Mrs Mortimer,' she said. 'Have a good trip.'

⋆ ⋆ ⋆

Colonel Harrison turned out to be pompous and short-tempered, but in a way Lily was relieved. There was no temptation to relive the intimacy of driving Derek around. To Marcus Harrison, she was just a driver, and that suited Lily fine.

He was billeted in the neighbouring village, and Nina was sent an inspector from the Ministry of Food instead, much to the dismay of almost everyone in Beckindale, who enjoyed the benefits of a farming community and relied heavily on a barter system to relieve the dreariness of food rationing. Hasty plans were made to hide hams and cheeses passed on by the likes of the Sugdens at Emmerdale Farm. Arthur Middleton, the butcher, showed the inspector an ostentatiously clear counter and was shocked — *shocked!* — at the suggestion that he might have some packs of sausages concealed some-where. The Barlows in the village shop were equally virtuous, issuing an invitation to the inspector to drop in at any time and see how scrupulously they stamped ration books.

The news that February was grim, and getting grimmer. Some of those who had left Beckindale to serve in the forces or help with the war effort would never return. Ted Micklethwaite was killed in Abyssinia; George Ransome's tank was hit by a shell in Libya. Doris Webster had gone to work in a munitions factory and was badly injured in an explosion. Sally Briggs was run over during the blackout, and Violet Pickles died when a bomb fell on the house where she was billeted.

There was renewed talk of invasion, and the very real possibility that there might be German troops driving into Beckindale led to urgent meetings of all the local volunteer groups. Fuel was strictly controlled for fear of it falling into enemy hands, and Lily's father had to endure regular checks of how much petrol he had at the garage.

Lily listened to the complaints about how strictly rationing was suddenly enforced, but she hardly cared. She felt faintly nauseous, and Derek's leaving had left her with a dragging weariness. It crossed her mind that she should work out when she had last had a period, but as she had never been regular and Derek had always been careful, she dismissed the dreadful suspicion that she might be pregnant from her mind. She couldn't be. She *wouldn't* be.

No, the idea was nonsense, Lily told herself firmly. Of course she wasn't pregnant. She was just tired and depressed after a humiliating break-up, just like anyone would be. What she needed was to get a grip and cheer up.

There was a dance to raise funds for the war

effort in the village hall that night. Connie, Sylvia and some of the other girls from the camp were all going. Lily had been so absorbed with Derek that she hadn't wanted to go to many dances, but that would have to change. She would go, she decided. She would go, she would have a good time, and she would *not* be pregnant.

Her flowered voile frock was really more suitable for summer than February, but Lily put it on anyway as it made her feel confident. Carefully, she painted her legs to look as if she were wearing nylons, and wished she had a friend she could ask to draw a line up the back of her legs for the seam. She rolled her hair, powdered her face, painted her lips a bright red.

The dance was in full swing by the time Lily got there. The hall was crowded with recruits and others from the camp, but there were a few familiar faces from Beckindale, too. She spotted Elizabeth Barlow dancing with Oliver Skilbeck, of all people. Hadn't anyone warned her what a creep the man was? He was one of the few men not in uniform, and Lily fully intended to give him a wide berth.

There was no band, but a gang from the camp were standing over a gramophone and making sure the music kept coming. With the ratio of men to women so far weighted in her favour, Lily was soon dancing. Possessed by a feverish gaiety, she set out to be the life and soul of the party, dancing and flirting with whoever asked her, drinking whatever was put in her hand. Someone had brought a bottle of gin and was spiking the blander options on offer. The result was delightfully numbing, and Lily's inhibitions loosened. She danced faster, laughed louder, held out her glass for more. Why hadn't she done this before? She felt wonderful!

'Come and dance with me.' A good-looking recruit called Tony (she thought) dragged her back onto the dance floor and Lily went willingly. They were putting on a pretty good show, she thought, until Tony swung her round and she crashed into Oliver Skilbeck, who turned angrily.

'What do you think you're doing?'

'Sorry, mate,' said Tony, preparing to move on, but Oliver was clearly in the mood for a fight.

'Don't you 'mate' me,' he snarled, ignoring Elizabeth Barlow's attempts to tug him away.

'Leave it, Ollie!' she said.

Oliver shook his arm free. 'No, I won't leave it. I'm sick of this lot throwing their weight around just because they're in uniform.'

'At least we're ready to go and fight,' said Tony. 'What are you doing?'

'Farming's a reserved profession,' Oliver said, bristling. Like many of the local farmers, he was defensive about not being in uniform.

Tony was unimpressed. 'Right. So you milk a few cows. Very brave.'

'Ignore him,' said Lily, who had drunk too much to be cautious. 'He's a bad man.'

'Oh yeah? And you're not exactly Miss Goody Two Shoes either, are you?' Oliver sneered. 'You think you're so special in your uniform, but everyone knows you've been shagging that colonel.'

'Hey!' Tony's face darkened. 'Don't talk to her like that.'

'Why not? It's true.'

'Leave it.' Lily put a hand on Tony's arm, but he was as angry as Oliver by now. He put her rudely to one side and dived for Oliver.

The next minute, half the men in the hall had piled into the fight. For many of the dancers, it was all part of the fun. The men were ready for a punch-up. As far as Lily could tell, half of them were fighting each other for the hell of it, and they were deaf to the pleas of the organisers to calm down.

It was not until Jack Proudfoot arrived that order, was restored. He separated Oliver and Tony and broke up the other fights. 'You can all leave now or I'll put you on a charge,' he told them. 'Your choice.'

'Uh-oh,' said Lily, leaning tipsily against the wall between two recruits who were cheering their pals on. 'Fun's over.'

Jack came over and frowned. 'What are you doing here?'

'Having a good time,' she told him with a defiant smile.

'Well, it's over now.' He glanced at her companions. 'Hop it.'

'But we weren't fighting,' they protested.

'I don't care. The dance is over. I want you all back in camp.'

Grumbling, they took themselves off. 'Goodbye!' Lily called, sliding slowly down the wall with a fatuous smile on her face.

'You're drunk,' said Jack.

'No, I'm not,' she said. 'I'm just . . . relaxed.'

He sighed. 'Wait here. I'll just have a word

with the blokes tidying up and then I'll take you home.'

'I don't need to be taken home. I'm more than capable of taking myself,' Lily declared, but her steps wove across the floor and her head was spinning as she struggled with the door. The bitter cold outside helped a little, but it was pitch-black. Fumbling her torch out of her bag, she dropped it on the ground.

'Oh, bother.' She bent to grope around for it, only to topple over completely. 'Bother,' she said again, and struggled to her hands and knees. Where was that torch? She felt around and encountered not the torch but a pair of shoes, and was patting her way over them and up a trouser leg before she sat back unsteadily on her heels.

'Come on.' There was a smile in Jack's voice as he put a hand under her elbow and lifted her to her feet. 'Let's get you home.'

'I can't go home like this,' said Lily. 'Dad'll kill me.'

'Well, I'm not leaving you here. You can go home or sober up in the police house.'

Lily dithered. 'I think I'd better sober up,' she decided at last.

She was glad of Jack's firm grip on her arm as she stumbled.

'How much have you had to drink?' he asked.

'I'm not sure. I'm not used to it,' she told him owlishly, and then paused. 'I don't feel very well,' she confessed.

'I was afraid of this.' Jack steered her over to the ditch and let her go so that she could throw up. 'Better?' he said when she straightened at last.

'No,' she told him. 'I feel awful.'

'Come on, let's get some coffee down you. You must be frozen,' said Jack as they headed up the lane. 'Didn't you bring a coat with you?'

Lily patted herself as if she could have put it in a pocket. 'I must have left it in the hall.'

'You can get it tomorrow. Here.' Jack shrugged out of his jacket and hung it around her shoulders. It was warm from his body as Lily clutched it around her.

'What about you?'

'I'll be fine, but let's step on it.'

Even hampered by his limp, Jack could walk fast and Lily found herself trotting to keep up. She was glad when they got to the police house. The front of the house was the police station with an office and two cells, but Jack led her round to the back.

'Wait while I check the blackout,' he said.

Lily stood stock-still in the darkness. Not being able to see anything made her preternaturally aware of the weight of his jacket over her shoulders and the faint, not unpleasant smell that clung to it. Jack's smell, she realised; and when he put on the electric light, she stared at him, suddenly, shockingly aware of him as a man.

'I'll put the kettle on,' he said.

They were in a functional kitchen with little in the way of cheery touches. The parlour was even worse. There were two armchairs, one with a lamp beside it, a table piled with books and a wireless, but otherwise the room was bare. Nothing on the mantelpiece, no pictures on the wall.

'Hmmm,' said Lily. 'It's not exactly homely, is it?'

Jack looked around as if seeing the room for the first time. 'It could probably do with a woman's touch,' he agreed.

'You should get married,' she said.

'You think?' he said in a dry voice.

'I'm surprised you didn't get married before you came here.'

'Well, that was the plan.'

The kettle was whistling. Jack turned back to the kitchen to spoon some coffee into two mugs.

Lily followed him. 'What happened?' she asked from the doorway, and he lifted his shoulders as if the answer was obvious.

'Polio.'

She frowned as she watched him pour water into the mugs. 'So . . . were you engaged?'

'Yes.' Jack said it on a downward breath as if he wished he had never mentioned it.

'What was her name?'

'Carol.'

'What was she like?' Lily wasn't sure why it was so important to know. 'Was she beautiful?'

'Yes,' he said. 'I thought so, anyway.'

He had called Lily beautiful once, she couldn't help remembering.

'Oh.' She took the mug of coffee he held out to her.

'No milk, I'm afraid,' he said. 'Not very nice, but it'll help sober you up.'

Lily took a cautious sip and made a face. He was right. It wasn't nice.

'So . . . Carol. She just left you in hospital?'

'I don't blame her.' Jack gestured Lily back into the parlour and they sat in the two armchairs. 'I was the one who broke it off.'

'Why?'

He didn't answer immediately. Looking down into his mug, he seemed to be remembering the past. 'I didn't want to be a burden to her,' he said at last. 'Carol's very . . . lively. She's sharp and funny and intelligent and always doing something. She gets bored reading a book or even watching a flick. What she likes to do is dance, and when I first got ill, I wasn't sure I'd ever dance again. I didn't want her to tie herself to a man who might be paralysed.'

'And she let you break it off?' Lily was outraged.

'It was the best thing for both of us,' said Jack firmly.

There was a pause.

'So you haven't got a broken heart?'

He swirled his coffee in his mug. 'I don't think hearts really break. They just get . . . sore sometimes. But if the person you love doesn't love you, you just have to accept that and get on with it.'

'It's not that easy,' said Lily, thinking of Derek, and Jack glanced up at her with a twisted smile.

'I didn't say it was easy.' He put down his mug. 'Now, drink up and I'll take you home.'

24

Annie sat with her legs up on her bed, a pillow cushioning her back against the wall. Sooty had made himself comfortable on her lap and was purring loudly as she unfolded Edward's latest letter and read it again. Since that dreadful time in December and that all too brief conversation on the platform, their letters had been more honest, more thoughtful, almost as if they were getting to know each other properly.

Strange to think that they had known each other all their lives and yet it was only now, after those wretched two days, that they were taking the trouble to talk about what they really felt. Annie had loved Edward for as long as she could remember. Now it felt as if she were falling in love with him for the first time.

Everything had been so easy until the war. Too easy, perhaps. Their love for each other had never been tested. Well, now it had, and Annie hoped that it would be stronger than ever as a result.

It hadn't been easy, but she was determined to put that awful thing Oliver had done to her behind her. She couldn't forget it, or forgive him, but she could refuse to let herself be broken by it. There were so many dreadful things happening in the world right now. Already two of her school friends had died in the war, and everyone in Beckindale had grown to dread the arrival of Frank Swainby on his bicycle. Once the telegraph boy had brought good news and excitement; now Frank and his like were called angels of death.

The war seemed to be going badly. The authorities were making preparations for invasion, and what would happen then? On the wireless they heard about bombs dropping on cities. Annie shuddered to imagine what it must be like to spend night after night in shelters listening to the world exploding, and then to go back and find that your house had been obliterated. What happened to those people who had lost all their possessions? Where were they all living? How did they have enough to eat? How did you start again when you had lost everything?

And though Annie knew it wasn't important to most people, she couldn't bear to think of how terrified the animals must be. Those that had survived the terrible cull at the beginning of the war, anyway. She had heard that over a quarter of a million pets had been destroyed in a single week as it was feared there would not be enough food for them. Annie stroked Sooty and he twisted with a murmur of pleasure as he let her tickle his furry tummy. Another reason, if she needed it, to remember how lucky they were to live in the country where pets like Sooty were well able to fend for themselves.

She wasn't the only one dealing with an awful situation, Annie reminded herself often. She just had to toughen up and accept things as they were. Oliver was not going to leave Beckindale.

There would always be people who would believe that she had led him on, or asked for it in some way.

Well, there was nothing she could do about that. Annie was just glad that she hadn't been a virgin. At least she had the memory of that first time with Edward, so she knew what it was supposed to be like between a man and a woman. She tried not to think about that last time when she had cried. Instead she made a point of remembering the happy times she and Edward had spent together. She pushed the jumble of memories of that awful night into a box at the back of her mind and slammed it shut. Usually it worked, but the smell of sheep droppings still made her stomach turn in a queasy mixture of remembered terror and revulsion.

Folding Edward's letter carefully, Annie tucked it back under her pillow. She would read it again before she went to sleep. It was Saturday and she had a day off. She had promised to go to the pictures with Sarah that afternoon, the first time she had felt like going out. But Sarah was missing Ray, and for once the grey clouds had cleared to leave a watery blue sky. When Annie had walked into Beckindale that morning, the air had been surprisingly soft and laced with a promise of spring at last after the bitter winter. She had spotted buds on the thorn trees and daffodils trembling on the edge of bursting into flower. And so when Sarah had asked if she would go to the flicks with her, Annie had said yes.

Sarah was waiting at the bus stop in Beckindale. She was watching Frank Swainby prop his bicycle back outside the Post Office. 'I shiver every time I see him get on his bike,' she said when Annie joined her. 'I keep thinking: what if the next time it's a telegram about Ray?'

'Have you heard from him?'

'He's somewhere in North Africa,' said Sarah. 'Says it's hot as hell. What about Edward?'

'I think he'd probably like a bit of heat. There's not much of that in the Atlantic. He says he might get leave again in the summer.'

They chatted easily as the bus rattled along the country lanes. Sarah was still living with the Barlows and told Annie how worried they all were about her sister Elizabeth, who was infatuated with Oliver Skilbeck and wouldn't listen to what anyone else said.

'I think she's mad,' said Sarah frankly. 'Apparently he started some fight at a dance the other day. He's a troublemaker.'

Annie shuddered. 'He's worse than that.'

But she wouldn't think about Oliver. That was over.

They bought themselves a half-pound box of chocolates to share and sat in the shillings to watch *Pride and Prejudice* with Greer Garson and Laurence Olivier. 'I think he's ever so handsome,' Sarah confided.

It had been good to get out. Annie told herself she would do it more often in future. She had spent too long hiding wretchedly in her room, afraid of meeting Oliver or of facing down anyone who might have heard the rumours about her. The evenings were getting lighter now that spring was on its way. Things could only get better, Annie thought optimistically.

Mentally composing a letter to Edward telling him all about the film, Annie walked home. No shortcuts for her, not now, but she was happy to walk up the track to Emmerdale Farm. It was just starting to get dark as she cut across the farmyard, and she stopped to put her head round the kitchen door to say hello to the Sugdens.

'I had such a nice afterno — ' She broke off at the scene, icy premonition snaking down her spine. Maggie was sitting at the kitchen table, staring down at a telegram. Joe had his hand on her shoulder, while Jacob stood by the fire, looking lost. Nobody spoke, they just looked at Annie.

'What is it?' she asked. Her voice sounded strange in the heavy silence.

Maggie tried to speak. She opened her mouth but no sound came out, and the devastation in her face was like a cruel hand closing around Annie's throat.

'No,' she said. Inside, she could almost hear the snap of her core breaking. 'No, not Edward.'

Maggie's hand trembled as she lifted the telegram, but Annie refused to take it. 'It's a mistake,' she insisted.

Jacob found his voice. 'Edward's ship was torpedoed,' he managed unsteadily. 'He didn't make it. There's no mistake.'

'But . . . ' Panic clutched at Annie's chest, making it hard for her to breathe. 'But he's coming back,' she said with a blank face, unable to accept what Jacob was saying. 'He promised. It's going to be better next time.'

Jacob just shook his head.

Annie stared from him to Joe and then to Maggie, whose straight spine seemed to sag beneath a weight too great to be borne as she pushed back her chair.

'Edward,' she whispered. 'My baby.'

Her hands came up to cover her face, and a cry of pain seemed to be wrenched from her. Joe's ruined features twisted with grief. He gathered Maggie into his arms and she slumped against him, howling.

Jacob took a step towards Annie, but she backed away. *No mistake*, he had said.

She turned and ran.

Edward was dead. She would never see him again. Never lie next to him in the grass. Never hear his laugh. Never run towards him and feel his arms close around her.

Never, never, never.

★ ★ ★

Much later, Jacob found her in the stable, curled up in the straw by Neddy's feet, her body still heaving with sobs. 'Annie . . . ' His voice broke. 'Annie, I'm so sorry.' Dropping onto the straw beside her, he gathered her into his arms and rocked her, and this time Annie let herself be comforted. 'I'm sorry, I'm sorry,' he murmured against her hair.

Annie wept until her breath was ragged and

painful and then she lay her aching head against Jacob's shoulder.

'I don't want to believe it, but I do,' she said. 'How can that be? One moment I was thinking I could be happy again, that everything would be all right, and the next, it's all over. Edward's gone. He's *dead*.' The awful word burst out of her as if it had a will of its own, and the truth of it made her start crying again.

'I keep thinking of him in that cold water,' said Jacob in a low voice. '*Lost at sea*,' they said. 'What does that even mean, lost?'

'Don't,' said Annie, pulling away from him. She couldn't bear to think of it, and yet she couldn't think of anything else. Had Edward drowned in the black, restless sea, or had he been blown apart like his pal Mike? Had it been quick, a flash and then done, or had he sunk slowly into the water, getting colder and colder, knowing that he was going to die? Had he been afraid? Had he thought of Emmerdale then? Had he thought of *her*?

Pain twisted viciously inside her, tighter and tighter around her heart until she thought it would shatter.

'He should never have been at sea.' Jacob was following his own train of thought. He sounded angry. 'He should have stayed here, in the Dales. What did he want to join the Navy for anyway? It was a damn fool thing to do. Typical Ed.'

He was grieving, too, Annie understood that. He had lost a brother, and a friend. Maggie and Joe had lost a son. But she, she had lost the love of her life. Her future, her happiness, the other half of her, all lay at the bottom of the Atlantic under that black, black water.

★　★　★

Emmerdale Farm was in mourning. The dogs drooped, the horses hung their heads as they plodded to the fields. Even the dairy cows seemed subdued, their great brown eyes sad.

'You don't need to go to work today, love,' Grace told Annie the next morning when she appeared dressed as usual. 'Maggie'll understand.'

'What else will I do?' Annie asked, and to that Grace had no answer.

Maggie looked hollowed out by grief when Annie went into the kitchen. She was standing at the sink, staring out of the window, her hands stilled in the middle of washing up. Annie knew exactly how she was feeling, as if the task of wiping the cloth across the next plate was too enormous to contemplate. Annie's own limbs felt as leaden as her heart. The air was dense, like mud that she had to push her way through.

Tying on a pinny, Annie went to take the cloth wordlessly from Maggie's hand. 'I'll do it,' she said.

'Annie.' Maggie turned in slow motion, registering Annie's presence for the first time. 'Annie, what am I going to do?' she asked brokenly.

'Go on,' said Annie. 'That's all we can do.'

Maggie wrapped her arms around her waist, almost as if she were holding herself together.

'I'm not sure I can, not again. Not after this.'

'You must. Jacob needs you. Joe needs you. Emmerdale Farm needs you.' Annie abandoned the washing-up and put her arms around Maggie, finding it easier to comfort than be comforted. 'And I need you, too,' she said.

Maggie, strong, stoical Maggie, collapsed against Annie. 'My baby,' she wept. 'My boy.' Annie held her and the two women cried together until they could weep no more. Then they drew shuddering breaths, wiped their faces and got on with the washing-up, because there was a farm to run and jobs to be done and nobody else to do them.

The relentless routine of the farm helped Annie through the weeks that followed. She had thought that she was wretched after Oliver had raped her, and Edward's leave had gone so horribly wrong, but that was nothing compared to the desolation she felt after Edward died. It seemed so cruel to have despaired and then learnt to hope again, only to realise that all hope was gone.

Edward would not be coming home.

They would not fall in love again.

Things would not be better.

Annie's grief was bone-deep, a physical ache that pinned her down. The mindless tasks of cooking and cleaning and helping in the dairy got her from one hour to the next. She moved through the day as if sleepwalking, her senses deliberately muffled. She wouldn't let herself feel; she wouldn't let herself think. If she thought, then she had to face up to a world going on without Edward in it; to a future stretching bleakly ahead, a dreary, empty plain she would have to trudge across alone.

Better not to think at all, Annie decided.

25

Lily sat back on her heels and wiped her mouth with a trembling hand. For the fourth day in a row she had been sick in the morning, and she was terribly afraid of what that might mean.

The first day she had thought it an embarrassing reminder of how much she had drunk at the dance. The second, a bug seemed a plausible option. By the third day, a horrible suspicion was making her feel even more nauseous, and now . . .

Desperately she tried to remember the last time she'd had the curse. Everything had been such a blur since Derek had left in December, and she had never been regular. But not this year, she realised. Not once.

Forcing herself shakily to her feet, Lily rested with one hand on the privy wall. Dear God, what was she going to do?

She had thought making a fool of herself in front of Jack Proudfoot was shameful enough. Lily cringed whenever she remembered how she had thrown up in the ditch in front of him. How she had practically forced her way into the police house and interrogated him about his private life. *You should get married*, she had told him. What if he thought she was angling for the role?

Mortified at the memory, Lily covered her face with her hands. Even if she had had hopes of Jack — which she definitely *hadn't* — they

287

would be doomed if what she suspected was true.

Perhaps it wasn't true. Perhaps it was just a bug after all.

But one look at Dr Moss's face when he had finished examining her put paid to that hope.

'You're nearly four months gone,' he told her gravely. 'Will you get some support from the father?'

'I . . . I don't know,' said Lily, still reeling from the confirmation of her worst fears. She supposed she should be glad that he hadn't asked her if she knew who the father was — but then, pretty much everyone in Beckindale would have a pretty good idea, and Dr Moss would be no exception. All that time she had fondly imagined that her affair was secret, it had been discussed over cups of tea or pints of beer all over the village.

Fumbling with the buttons of her coat as she finished dressing, Lily thanked the doctor and somehow made her way outside, but she stopped by the gate and stared blankly ahead as she pulled on her gloves. Now what? She had absolutely no idea of where she should go now or what she should do.

The sky was a pale blue and a watery sunshine washed over the fells. The air was laced with a hint of spring and new growth. Lily thought of the baby growing inside her and felt dizzy at the enormity of the change ahead.

Frank Swainby cycled past with a bag of letters. In the queue outside Middleton's the butchers, Anne Micklethwaite and Ellen Webster had their heads together, their hats bobbing up and down as they swapped the latest scandal. Squeals and shouting came from the school playground. Sarah Barlow and Annie Pearson were waiting for a bus.

Life was going on as normal all around her, Lily realised, but there was no normal for her now.

'Lily?' Mary Ann Teale stopped beside her. 'You all right, love?' Her bright eyes flickered from Lily's face to the brass plate at the doctor s door and Lily could practically see her putting two and two together. She could imagine the conversation with Janet Airey already.

Saw that Lily Dingle coming out of doctor's this morning. She looked very peaky. If you know what I mean.

And Janet would purse her lips, immediately making the connection. *That colonel, I suppose? Poor Rose, it's a mercy she never knew.*

Lily put her chin up. 'I'm not feeling very well, Mrs Teale.'

'Want to sit down and have a brew?' She nodded at her cottage across the road and Lily mustered a smile.

'Thanks, but no, I think I'll just go home to bed.'

'You do that, love. You need your rest,' Mary Ann added with a meaningful look. *In your condition*. The words hung unspoken but unmistakable in the air.

So that was it, Lily thought. The news would be round Beckindale in no time. She would have to tell her father first before the gossip reached him, but she quailed at the thought of it. He would be so disappointed in her.

Tears burned behind Lily's eyes. Never had she missed her mother more. Rose would have been disappointed, too, but she would have known what to do and how to break the news to Mick. Lily wouldn't have felt so horribly, desperately alone.

Blindly she began to walk back to the garage, but as she turned down the lane past Pear Tree Cottage, her steps slowed.

If you ever need any help, I'm here.

As if Lily's thoughts had summoned her, Nina's front door opened and she emerged with a basket over her arm. She was wearing a jaunty scarf tied in a bow around her red hair and was in wide slacks and a flamboyant green jacket cut fashionably short. In the past Lily would have decided that Nina looked vulgar. Today, she seemed vivid and stylish and next to her, Lily herself felt wan.

'Lily!' Nina turned from closing the door and spotted Lily hovering at her gate. 'Were you coming to see me?'

'No . . . I mean, I don't know . . . you're going out. I don't want to hold you up.'

'I'm only going to see if there's anything more exciting than a tin of pilchards for dinner, and that can wait.' Nina went back up the step and opened her door. 'Come in.'

Numbly, Lily followed Nina inside and into a comfortable, colourful room that looked out over the garden at the back. The walls were covered in bold paintings and there were books piled up everywhere. A desk was pushed in front of the window. Spread out on it were quick, clever sketches of cooking, sewing and other household tasks.

'My contribution to the war effort,' said Nina ruefully. 'They're to illustrate Ministry of Information pamphlets. The patriotic way to mend socks and cook without sugar, that kind of thing. I do quite a lot of posters, too. It's not what I'd call art, but it feels like something useful I can do.' She paused. 'But you're not here about my drawings.'

'No.' Lily swallowed. Nina was watching her with such concern that she had to turn her head away. 'I need your help,' she heard herself say, appalled at her abrupt tone.

'Oh, my dear . . . ' Nina seemed to know what Lily was going to say already. 'Sit down,' she said. 'I'll make you a cup of tea and we'll sort it out.'

Lily dropped down onto the sofa, feeling unutterably tired and defeated by Nina's kindness. She had despised and resented the older woman, but what had she ever done to Lily other than make her father happy? Lily added shame to the queasy mixture of bewilderment and fear and exhaustion and regret sloshing around inside her.

When Nina came back with a tray of tea, she put a spoonful of precious sugar into Lily's cup before stirring the tea and handing it to her. 'Drink that up. You look like you need it.' She waited until Lily had taken an obedient sip. 'Now, tell me.'

Lily put down her cup and saucer with an unsteady hand. 'I'm going to have a baby,' she said starkly. 'I don't know what to do.' Her voice cracked and she burst into tears.

'Well, you're doing the first thing, which is to have a good cry,' said Nina, coming to sit beside her.

'I want my mum,' Lily wailed.

'Oh, Lily, of course you do.' Gently, Nina pulled Lily's head onto her shoulder and held her while she cried, murmuring soothingly and stroking her hair until she had subsided into hiccuping sobs.

'I'm sorry, I'm sorry,' Lily managed at last, scrubbing tears from her face with the back of her hand as she straightened up. 'I don't know why you're being so kind to me when I've only ever been horrible to you.'

Nina's smile was understanding. 'Lily, I know how much you miss your mother, and how hard it's been for you to see your dad get together with someone else. It's natural for you to resent me, but I hope you know that your dad has always, always put you first.'

'How am I going to tell him?' Lily's voice wobbled again. 'He'll be so ashamed of me! Everyone's going to say that they knew I was a typical Dingle all along, sleeping with a man before marriage, causing a scandal. All the busybodies are going to love this,' she finished bitterly.

'There are worse things than being talked about,' said Nina mildly. 'I think you'll find that your father understands. Mick's never been a prig. Do you really think he and Rose waited until they were married?'

Lily gaped at her, momentarily shocked out of her misery. 'What?' she said, and Nina smiled.

'There's nothing new about sex, Lily. You may have discovered it in 1940, but it's been around for a lot longer than that! It's a natural part of loving someone, and it always has been. What?' she said, amused, when Lily coloured at the casual way she talked about sex. 'You think your dad comes round here to hold hands?'

She laughed outright at Lily's expression. 'Nobody likes to think of their parents having sex, do they? All I'm saying is that Mick isn't going to blame you. He'll understand that you loved Derek. You did, didn't you?'

Unable to speak, Lily nodded, her eyes brimming with tears.

'Have you told Derek yet?'

'I only went to the doctor this morning,' she said miserably. 'I was hoping it wasn't true.'

'Derek needs to know,' Nina pointed out.

'But he's married. He's not going to divorce his wife and marry me — and I wouldn't want him to,' Lily added, earning an approving nod from Nina.

'So I should hope not,' she said. 'But Derek is still the father of this child you're carrying. He still has some responsibility. Most of the responsibility, in fact.'

'Should I write to him?'

'I'd go and see him if you can. Where is he now?'

'In York, I think. But I don't know where exactly.'

'We can find that out. You can ring him and tell him you want to talk to him, but meet somewhere public,' Nina warned. 'Don't let him talk you into a cosy tête-à-tête where he'll be able to weasel his way out of his responsibility.'

Lily hesitated. 'Would you come with me? I don't mean when I talk to Derek, but for afterwards? I think I might need some moral support.'

'Of course I will.' Nina patted Lily's hand. 'It'll be all right, Lily. You'll see.'

For an artist, Nina was surprisingly practical. She found out where Derek was based and gave Lily his telephone number so that she could ring and arrange where to meet him. It was Nina who looked up the times of the trains, too, and Mick used up some of his precious fuel allowance to drive them both to station, 'Are you sure I can't come with you?' he demanded.

'I'm sorry, Dad,' Lily had whispered when she told him she was pregnant. 'Are you very angry?'

'I'm angry all right,' Mick had said. 'But not with you, *asthore*.' His face hardened. 'I'd like to thrash that colonel to within an inch of his life, though.'

He had wanted to accompany them to York, but Lily was afraid that he wouldn't be able to restrain himself from punching Derek.

'No, Dad,' she said, hugging him at the station. 'This is something I need to do by myself.'

An icy drizzle was falling when they got off the train in York and needles of rain stung Lily's cheeks. The tantalisingly springlike warmth had been vanquished as the direction of the wind swung round to the north and winter was firmly back in charge. She huddled into her coat as they walked across the bridge leading towards the Minster, where Nina planned to look around while Lily was talking to Derek.

He had suggested meeting at Betty's Café, so Lily took a table in the window to wait for him. Feeling conspicuous on her own, she studied the menu, that was typed on flimsy paper. The choice looked appetising enough, though she was pretty sure the fishcakes would be made with snoek, the virtually inedible fish that was all they seemed to be able to get nowadays. She doubted the steak pie would have much steak in it, either. The filling was likely to be heavy on the offal, she thought with a sigh.

Lily fidgeted with her gloves. She was nervous about seeing Derek again. What if it turned out that she still loved him? But just then a car drew up outside the café and Derek got out, looking as impossibly handsome as ever. He bent to say something to the driver, a ravishingly pretty young woman who wore her uniform with a stylish air.

Lily could imagine the conversation; knew exactly how Derek would be smiling at her. They were probably having an affair, she thought dispassionately. Oddly, it made her feel better that she wasn't the only girl to have been seduced into thinking she was special. There had doubtless been others before her, and there would be still more after his York driver.

She was able to smile coolly when Derek arrived, oozing charm. 'Lily, darling, I hardly recognised you out of uniform.' He winked at her. 'I wish you'd given me more notice. We could have found somewhere to . . . be alone,' he added with a meaningful look.

'A room, you mean?'

'Well, you have to admit that we were very compatible,' he said with a mock-wolfish smile. 'I miss you.' And then, without missing a beat, he glanced around. 'Nice place, isn't it? I usually come to the bar downstairs. The Dive, they call it. Terrific parties.'

The waitress came over and asked if they were ready to order. Derek glanced at the menu, grimacing at the choice. 'I think I'll have the savoury macaroni. What about you, Lily?'

'Just coffee, please.'

When the waitress had gone, Lily took a deep breath. 'I asked to meet today because I need to talk to you,' she said. 'I'm pregnant,' she added baldly.

Derek's expression stilled. 'Oh, dear, I was afraid of that.' He lit a cigarette. 'That's inconvenient. You know my situation, Lily.'

'That you're married?'

'Yes. And I'll be honest with you, this isn't the right moment for me to talk to Hazel about a divorce.'

'I'm not asking you to marry me. I just thought you should know.'

'Of course, of course,' he said hurriedly. 'But there's nothing to get in a state about, darling. I've got a doctor pal here in York who can sort you out, quick as anything. In fact, go along this afternoon,' he said, clearly relieved that Lily didn't intend to make more of a fuss. 'I'll write you a cheque to give him. It'll be perfectly painless and over in a trice. Problem solved!'

He pulled out his chequebook without waiting for Lily to reply. She watched him numbly as he scribbled out the figure and signed with a flourish. A problem, that was all her baby was to Derek. How could she ever have loved this man?

But what choice did she have? She couldn't bring up a child on her own. When Derek proferred the cheque across the table, she hesitated but took it.

Thank you trembled on the edge of her tongue. Rose's training in manners was strong but Lily swallowed the words. She wasn't going to thank him. She nodded instead and pushed back her chair.

'Goodbye, Derek,' she said as he rose, a gentleman on the surface if not in behaviour.

'Going already?' he asked, surprised. 'What about your coffee?'

'I'll pass on the coffee. I don't think there's anything else to say, do you?'

His eyes fell and something like shame crossed his face. 'I suppose not.'

Afterwards, Lily met Nina outside the Minster and showed her the cheque. Nina kept her face carefully blank. 'What are you going to do?'

'What can I do?' Lily folded the cheque and put it back in her purse. 'It's sensible. Derek said it would be quick and easy. He seemed to know all about it.'

'I'll bet,' said Nina in a dry voice.

Lily forced a smile. 'Well, let's get it over with.'

They found the doctor's surgery in a backstreet outside the city walls. A slab-faced woman showed them into a waiting room and said she would let the doctor know they were there. Lily clutched her handbag in her lap, depressed by the room's grubby air of defeat.

Problem solved. Quick as anything.

She thought of the baby growing inside her. A child, not a problem to be solved. *Her* child.

Was it a boy or a girl? She would never know, if she went ahead with the termination. Never know if it would have her blonde hair or Derek's warm brown eyes. It would be a wretched secret that she would carry for the rest of her life, instead of a child that laughed and loved and played in the streets of Beckindale. A child that would run to have its grazed knees kissed better, that would hold up its arms to let Mick swing it up onto his shoulders.

It might be shameful to bear a child out of wedlock, but was it not shameful, too, never to let it live at all?

'I can't do this,' Lily said, and got to her feet. 'I want to go.'

'Then we'll go,' said Nina with alacrity.

'Oy, where are you off to?' The receptionist came downstairs as Nina opened the front door. 'The doctor's just ready for you!'

'I've changed my mind,' said Lily, tearing the cheque into pieces and dropping them onto the sideboard. 'I'm going to have the baby after all.'

Summer 1941

26

Ruby came clattering down the stairs as Meg bent to pick up the letters that had just dropped through the front door.

'Is there one for me?'

Meg looked through the bundle, knowing already what the answer would be. 'Sorry, not this time, Ruby.'

'Oh, well.' Ruby managed a careless shrug. 'Stan's playing his violin again. I'm going out on my bicycle.'

'Where are you going?'

'Just around. I'll see if Edna wants to come out.'

'I don't want you going near Teggs Hill, Ruby.'

Ruby rolled her eyes. 'Yes, yes, it's too dangerous, I know. You say that every time I go out on my bike.'

'I mean it,' said Meg seriously.

'I *know*.' Ruby shot Meg a mischievous look. 'Don't you trust me?'

'No,' Meg said, but she couldn't help laughing. 'Go on, have a good time.'

She carried the letters through to sit on the bench outside the kitchen door. It was a beautiful Saturday in May, and she stretched like a cat in the warmth, leaving the letters in her lap for a moment while she enjoyed the peace. She felt strangely content. Stan was blossoming under Rolf's tuition, and Ruby seemed to have found her place in

Beckindale, too. Somehow they had all rubbed down together and become a little family.

Stan was practising in the front room, and the sound of the violin floated out into the summer air to mingle with the drowsy hum of bees and the burble of wood pigeons. Meg smiled. If it weren't for the occasional booms and shots from the training camp in the distance, she could almost believe that the war wasn't happening.

Two of the letters looked dully official, so she read the first from her friend Elsa, who had been at teacher training college at the same time and was now, it seemed, married and in India. When she had read the letter through to the end, Meg let the flimsy pages drop back into her lap. Elsa's excitement at her new life was obvious, and while Meg was glad for her friend, she couldn't help feeling a pang of envy at the same time. What could she write back to Elsa about? She was still teaching at the village school, still living in the same cottage, still unmarried. There were no exciting developments in her life.

Perhaps when — if — the war ever ended, things would change. She would have no ties then. There would be nothing to stop her going overseas if she wanted. She could go to Australia, perhaps, or Canada. She could teach. You didn't have to be rich to travel any more. Look at how Dot and Jonah Dingle had set off for South Africa. Meg had envied them that freedom, without realising that she could have it too.

As for Ruby and Stan, well, they would go home to Hull, and Rolf, to Germany. That was what they all longed to do. The thought was unexpectedly depressing.

To distract herself, Meg picked up the official-looking envelope and opened it. It was a letter from Mrs Wood, chair of the billeting committee in Hull who had liaised with Meg over the evacuation of the children from the city. She had bad news, Mrs Wood wrote, and Meg read on, aghast. Brenda Dubbs had been killed in an air raid. Reading between the lines, none of the relations they had been able to trace wanted the bother and expense of taking the children back, and it appeared there had never been a Mr Dubbs. Would Meg be prepared to keep Ruby and Stan with her in Beckindale for the longer term, as they seemed so well settled? Naturally, she would continue to receive the government allowance to cover the cost of providing food and accommodation for the evacuees for the duration of the war.

Dismayed, Meg read the letter twice to make sure she hadn't made a mistake, and then dropped it onto the bench beside her so that she could press the heels of her hands against her eyes. How was she going to break the news to Ruby and Stan? She suspected Stan's memory of his mother was hazy, but Ruby had kept Brenda stubbornly in mind, in spite of the fact that there was never any reply to her letters. She was going to be devastated.

★ ★ ★

Telling Ruby that her mother was dead was one of the hardest things Meg had ever done. She waited until Ruby came back, and gave her a drink and a couple of oatcakes smeared with blackberry jelly. It was a treat, and Ruby was too intelligent not to sense that something was up.

'What's going on?' she asked suspiciously.

'Come into the front room,' said Meg.

'I don't have to listen to Stan playing his stupid violin again, do I?' Ruby said, but she followed Meg in.

Stan put down his violin reluctantly when Meg said she wanted to talk to them both.

'I'm afraid I've got some bad news about your mum,' Meg began.

Ruby tensed. 'What? What's happened?'

'There was an air raid.' Meg moistened her lips, hating the way Ruby seemed to be crumbling before her eyes. 'Your mum . . . I'm sorry, she couldn't get to the shelter in time. She was killed.'

Her heart cracked as Ruby's rigid expression seemed to collapse in on itself, but still she wouldn't cry. 'A bomb?' she said in a harsh whisper. 'A bomb killed Mam?'

'Yes. I'm so sorry, Ruby. And Stan,' she added, although Stan was looking puzzled rather than distraught.

'A German bomb?'

Meg let out a sigh. 'Yes.'

'How can you have that Hun here when he killed our mum?' Ruby's expression twisted as all the hatred and confusion she had felt when she first arrived in Beckindale boiled back to the surface. 'You should be ashamed of yourself, consorting with the enemy. I've heard them say that about you in the shop. That's what it means, isn't it? Being all friendly, even when he and his kind are dropping bombs on us!'

'It wasn't Rolf who killed your mother, Ruby.' Meg kept her voice even with difficulty.

'He's a German, in't he?' Ruby flung herself over to the window, her thin shoulders rigid with distress.

'What will happen to us?' Stan quavered, and Meg rested a hand on his head. He wasn't grieving the way Ruby was, but he was frightened.

'Well, you're going to stay here,' she said.

'With you?'

'Yes, with me.'

'Can we stay for ever?'

Looking down into his anxious face, Meg couldn't bring herself to hedge around with ifs and buts and talk about when the war would end. 'You can stay as long as you want, Stan.' She glanced at Ruby. 'Both of you.'

'Will I still be able to play the violin?'

She smiled as Stan homed in on what was, for him, all that mattered.

'Yes, of course you will.'

It was too much for Ruby. She turned on him. 'You and your stupid, stupid violin!' she said savagely. 'I wish you'd never picked it up! It's all you care about, you and that horrible German! I don't want to stay here, I never have. I hate it! Meg doesn't want us!'

'Ruby, that's not true!'

'It *is* true!' Ruby slammed out of the room, and Stan's eyes filled with tears.

Torn between the two of them, Meg hesitated.

'She's just upset,' she told Stan. She needed to catch Ruby, but she was too late. By the time she reached the gate, Ruby was pedalling furiously along the lane. She slowed as she met Rolf, walking towards the cottage to give Stan his music lesson. For a terrible moment, Meg was afraid that she would ride straight at Rolf, but she swerved at the last minute. 'I hate you!' she cried. 'I hate you, I hate you, I hate you!'

Watching helplessly from the gate, Meg saw her cycle out of sight, while her bitter words echoed through the soft summer air.

★　★　★

Meg tried, but she couldn't reach Ruby. Something in her had shut down at the news of her mother's death. Her face was set, her body clenched. She wouldn't be touched. If Meg tried to comfort her, Ruby slapped at her hands and ran off. When Meg talked to her about grief, she turned her face away. Stan had happily accepted that his home was now with Meg — Meg suspected that he had forgotten that he'd ever had another one — but Ruby couldn't, or wouldn't. As the weeks passed, Meg worried more and more about the unhappiness in Ruby's eyes.

'She needs time,' Rolf said. 'How did you react when your sister died?'

'Like Ruby,' Meg admitted. 'But that was different.'

'How?'

Because that was my fault, she wanted to cry,

but she didn't. 'It just was,' she said, and even she could hear how like Ruby she sounded.

It was a beautiful summer, as if to offset the grimness of the news. Too many familiar faces already would not be returning to Beckindale. Worst for Meg to bear had been the news that Edward Sugden had gone down with his ship, and her heart ached for poor Annie, who now had to go through life without him.

One day she left the cottage just as Annie was passing with a big shopping basket, and they walked across the bridge into Beckindale together.

'How are you?' she asked Annie, who didn't bother to pretend that she didn't know why Meg was asking.

'Sometimes I'm all right. It's like I'm looking down on myself and I'm kind of numb. But other days, it's as if I'm only just managing to hold myself together, and if I relaxed even a fraction, I would simply shatter. So I just tell myself that I'll get through the next hour, or the next day, and if I can do that without falling apart, that will be enough. I can't think beyond that.'

'I remember how that feels,' said Meg. She felt it still sometimes, the terror that she would simply break into a thousand little pieces of grief and guilt.

Annie didn't look at her. 'Does it get any better?'

'Yes. I know it's a cliché, but time does help. But the sadness and the missing them, that never goes away completely. It just becomes part of you.'

On the long June evenings, Meg sat in the garden and listened to Stan playing the violin. She wished Ruby could appreciate her little brother's remarkable talent, but Ruby refused to have anything to do with him while he had a violin in his hand.

Worn down by Ruby's refusal to be comforted, Meg looked forward more and more to Rolf's visits. She knew that Ruby hated him being in the cottage, but Stan needed him, and Rolf had become a dear friend. She needed him, too.

He could never be anything more, Meg knew that. He was a prisoner; the enemy. She was responsible for two children, and he had to be back in camp in time for the roll call every evening. Most people in the village shared Ruby's view of Rolf, but Meg refused to give up the friendship. For the first time since Rosie had died, she had found someone who seemed to understand her. She could say whatever she thought and Rolf would consider it, narrowing his eyes thoughtfully. He might disagree with her — he often did — but he was never shocked, always interested. In his presence, Meg could feel the hard shell she had built around herself after Rosie died begin to fracture at last.

So she was hurt when he arrived one afternoon in a distant mood. 'Is something wrong?' she asked.

'Apart from the fact that I am a prisoner in an enemy country?'

It was so unlike Rolf that Meg stared at him. 'Apart from that,' she agreed slowly.

He walked over to the window. 'I hate this war.'

'We all do.' She went over to join him and they stood together, looking out at the golden afternoon light slanting over the fells. 'It will end one day.'

'What if 'one day' is too late?'

'Rolf, what is it?' Meg asked quietly. 'Something's wrong, I can tell.'

He let out a long sigh. 'I had a letter from home. A letter from my sister Liesbeth, I should say,' he corrected himself. 'My home does not exist any more. It was hit by a bomb.'

Meg's hand crept to her mouth in horror. 'Are your family safe?'

'Liesbeth was working, and Ingrid had gone to meet her but my mother, Hanna, Klara . . . they are all dead.'

'Oh, Rolf . . . ' Meg felt helpless. She knew something of all of his sisters now: about Klara's sweet tooth, and Hanna's love of dogs. She wanted to touch him, but she didn't dare. He was holding himself rigidly, only a nerve jumping in his jaw betraying his emotion.

'I have to get back there,' he said. 'I am ashamed.'

'You've got nothing to be ashamed of,' she said hotly, but he shook his head.

'Yes, I do. I have got too comfortable here. What am I doing? The camp is not barbaric. I have somewhere to sleep, somewhere to wash, decent food. I like the work at Emmerdale Farm. And most of all there is you, Meg, and Stan. Playing music with him, seeing how talented he is . . . I have forgotten that we are at war. I have started to feel at home, to take pleasure in this captivity of mine, and all the while, my family have been suffering and dying while I'm teaching Stan how to hold the violin! Of course I should be ashamed.'

'But what can you do? You're a prisoner.'

'I can try to get back.'

Meg caught her breath. 'You mean escape? Rolf, you can't! It's too dangerous. You don't have any papers, and how far would you get wearing those clothes?' she added, gesturing at the large yellow circles that marked out the prisoner of war's uniform.

'You could lend me something to wear.' Rolf turned to her and grasped her hands. 'Do you have something of your father's? Anything? I hate to ask you, Meg, but I must try and do this. The thought of my sisters all alone in Berlin . . . I must do something!'

'Even if you can get rid of your uniform, where will you go?'

'I'll head for the coast. I can get a boat somehow.'

'You'll never make it.' Meg was on the verge of tears. 'I'm so sorry about your family, Rolf, but they wouldn't want you to put yourself in danger, would they?'

'I've thought about it,' he said, 'and all I know is that I must try. It is light until late at the moment, which means I can cover a lot of ground.' His grip tightened on hers. 'It is a lot to ask of you, Meg, but I am begging you to help me.'

She gave in at last. 'I'll have a look through Dad's clothes.'

She didn't want to involve the children, so they agreed to pretend that everything was as normal. Stan came rushing in, delighted to find Rolf there early, and they started the lesson. Meg blinked back tears as she dug in a chest of drawers for an old jacket of her father's. She found a shirt and a pair of trousers with braces, together with some socks.

What would they do to her if they found out she'd helped a prisoner to escape? Meg bit her lip. This was wrong — but how could she turn her back on a friend? Rolf was desperate. If she sent a message to Jack Proudfoot or the camp, he would never forgive her, and she would never forgive herself for betraying him.

But how was she going to say goodbye to him?

I just tell myself that I'll get through the next hour. Meg remembered Annie's words and made herself take a steadying breath.

Downstairs, she found Ruby in the kitchen. From the front room came the sound of the violin. How would she comfort Stan when he discovered Rolf had gone?

Who would comfort *her*?

Meg plastered on a bright smile. 'Let's make some tea,' she said to Ruby as she put the kettle on the range to boil. 'You can give me a hand.'

'Shall I cut some cake?'

Meg was too anxious to wonder at Ruby's sudden helpfulness. 'Yes, thank you. Be careful with that knife, though,' she said, noticing what Ruby was holding in her hand. 'It's very sharp.'

Rolf was sitting in the armchair listening intently to Stan playing when Meg carried in the tea tray. 'Here we are,' she said with forced cheerfulness. She was vaguely aware of Ruby moving purposefully behind her, and of Rolf starting to rise courteously at her entrance, but after that everything got confused. There was the flash of a knife in Ruby's hand, a cry of shock and pain from Rolf. Stan's bow scraped to a jarring halt and Meg turned in horror to see Rolf collapsing, grey-faced, back into the chair, a hand clapped to his shoulder near the neck, while Ruby stood aghast, staring at the bloody knife in her hand.

'Rolf!' Meg threw the tray onto the side table and dropped to her knees beside him. 'Ruby, what have you done?'

'I wanted to kill him, but I couldn't . . . I couldn't!' Ruby dropped the knife and burst into hysterical tears.

'How bad is it?' Meg asked Rolf urgently.

'I will survive.' His face was screwed up in pain. 'Look after Ruby.'

'No!' Ruby cried when Meg made to go to her. 'No, I don't want you. I want Mam! He's a filthy Hun and he killed her! I hate him and I hate you!' Whirling round, she ran out of the room, and the next moment Meg heard the door slam.

She would be long gone before Meg could catch her, and anyway, she needed to run off her shock and fury. She would come back later and Meg would talk to her then. For now, she had to see how Rolf was.

Stan was white-faced and shaken at the drama. Meg had him help her find a bowl of clean water and a cloth and some bandages, keeping him busy to take his mind off the terrible thing he had seen.

She nearly fainted when she saw how close Ruby had come to fatally injuring Rolf. If the knife had been a few inches closer to his neck . . . Meg couldn't bear to think of it. In the event, the cut was not as deep as she had feared, and she suspected Ruby had lost her nerve at the last minute. Even so, it was a nasty wound. Meg cleaned it and dressed it and Rolf talked cheerfully to Stan throughout, though by the time she had finished they were both sweating.

Eventually Stan was reassured enough to run off and Meg was left alone with Rolf.

'You can't go now,' she said. 'You're injured.'

'I must. I may never get another chance as good.'

Nothing Meg could say would change his mind. With a heavy heart she gave him her father's clothes and he changed into them quickly. 'They'll ask you if you know where I've gone,' he warned her. 'You must lie. Tell them I stole these clothes. Tell them I tied you up again,' he suggested with a crooked smile.

At the back door, he stopped and looked at Meg. 'Thank you, Meg,' he said. 'Thank you for everything.'

'Will I ever see you again?' she asked bleakly.

'After the war,' said Rolf. 'I'll come and find you. I promise.' He took her face between his hands and kissed her, a long, heart-shaking kiss.

'I promise,' he said again as he raised his head.

He slipped out of the door, lifted a hand in farewell and was gone.

Numbly, Meg went back inside to clear up the mess of bloody cloths and spilled tea in the front room. She wanted to howl, to throw herself on the floor and beat her fists in anguish, but she couldn't do that. She couldn't afford to think about the fact that Rolf had gone. She had to look after Stan and she needed to talk to Ruby.

Where *was* Ruby? As the hours ticked past, Meg grew more and more concerned. She was used to Ruby running off and sulking for a while, but she'd never stayed away this long. Supper time came and went and the shadows lengthened, and as the golden light faded from the sky, Meg faced the awful truth at last: Ruby had gone too.

27

Lily winced as she straightened up from the engine and put a hand to her back.

'Everything all right, *mavourneen*?' Mick was instantly alert. He fussed and fretted over her like a mother hen nowadays, and it was driving Lily mad.

'Yes, Dad,' she said with a sigh. 'I've got a stiff back, that's all.'

'Perhaps helping me in the garage isn't a good idea,' he said worriedly.

When her pregnancy could be hidden no longer, Lily had had to resign from the ATS. She had hated handing back her uniform, but she knew that she had made the right decision to keep the baby. Every time she put a hand on her stomach and felt the child growing inside her, she felt a rush of love so intense it literally took her breath away. She missed the ATS, missed feeling as if she were doing her bit for the war effort, but the baby was what mattered.

Still holding her spanner, she wound her arms around Mick's neck and kissed him. 'I love you, Dad,' she said. 'I'm so grateful to you for not throwing me out the way some fathers would have done, but you have to stop treating me as if I'm made of glass! I'm pregnant, not ill.'

'I just worry about you,' he said. 'Like I worried about your mother when she was expecting you.'

'I know you do, but you have to let me work. What else am I going to do with myself?'

'You could rest.'

'I don't need to rest, Dad. I need to be doing something, and at least here in the garage I can do something useful.'

'I can't deny it's been a help having you here,' said Mick. All the young mechanics had been called up, and although the fuel rationing meant that there were far fewer cars on the road, he was still overwhelmed with work. Farm machinery needed repairing. The doctor had a car that had to be kept in good working order, as did the man from the Ministry of Food. There were delivery trucks and farm vehicles and the occasional bus to be fixed when something went wrong. Everybody else used a bicycle to get around, and Mick mended those too when they broke. He also had a limited supply of fuel for those entitled to it, carefully guarded.

'Well, then, let me help while I can,' said Lily, stepping back. 'I won't be able to get under a vehicle for much longer,' she added with a rueful glance down at her expanding belly. 'I'll rest then.'

The truth was that she needed to keep busy. She didn't want to think beyond the baby being born, and closed her mind to all the questions that would come after that. How was she going to afford to feed her child? Where would they live?

She would have to make some decisions soon, Lily knew. She couldn't hide in the garage for ever. Somewhere along the line she would have to face the village. She wasn't the first to fall pregnant out of wedlock, that was for sure, but it usually led to a hurried marriage and an 'early' baby. Lily would have no husband to give her respectability, and she was well aware of the disapproval her decision to have a baby alone would arouse.

Well, she deserved it, Lily told herself. After all, she had been the first to judge Nina Lazenby for her divorces and her unconventional dress and her noisy parties, before she had understood that they went with a kind and generous heart.

At the end of the day, she and Mick washed together at the pump and changed out of their oily overalls. Mick had plans to spend the evening with Nina.

'Why don't you come too?' he said to Lily, but she shook her head. He and Nina needed time alone together.

'I need to stretch my legs,' she said. 'It's such a lovely evening. I think I'll go for a walk.'

Already she had had to let out her dresses twice. Lily put on her coolest frock and a pair of her most comfortable shoes, and walked slowly up the lane, absently swishing her hand over the tangle of long grass and cow parsley. The road was dusty beneath her feet and the hills shimmered in the warmth of the long afternoon.

At the bottom of the lane, she paused, then turned deliberately towards the village. Everybody seemed to be out enjoying the weather. A group of boys were playing football in the street. A couple of girls had chalked hopscotch onto the melting tarmac and were hopping up and down, while the older ones whispered and giggled together.

Neighbours gossiped over walls or tended their gardens, and almost all turned to look as Lily walked past. Some stared openly or nodded coolly to make their disapproval known, but there were plenty of others who returned her greeting. Still, Lily was glad to see Jed lounging outside the Woolpack with a cigarette.

'Nice not to be the Dingle giving the old pusses something to gossip about,' he said with a grin, and then cocked a brow at her. 'You all right, Lil?'

'Yes, I'm fine. I wrote to Aunt Dot about the baby,' she told him. 'I don't know what she'll say.'

'Oh, Ma'll be fine about it. She's not one to cry over spilled milk.'

That was true. Dot Dingle had always been reassuringly practical. 'I wish she was here,' Lily sighed.

'I reckon she does, too. They can't get back now,' said Jed. 'She'll be giving Pa hell for taking them to Africa if I know her, but it looks like they're there for the war.'

There was no sign of the war on this golden evening, Lily reflected, but it had changed everything. If it hadn't been for the war, Derek would never have come to Beckindale. She wouldn't have fallen in love with him, and she wouldn't be pregnant. Strange to think how Hitler's decision to invade Poland could have had such a profound effect on the life of an insignificant young woman in Yorkshire.

Her steps were taking her up the hill and she paused to mop her brow. It was very hot still, and she wasn't as fit as she had once been. Perhaps it was time to go back. Belatedly, Lily realised that she was almost at the police house. She could see Jack Proudfoot sitting outside on a bench. His leg must be sore, as he had stretched it out in front of him and was rubbing it.

Lily had seen little of Jack since that mortifying evening when she had been sick in the ditch. Truth be told, she had deliberately avoided him. Those cool grey eyes saw too much for comfort, and always made her feel twitchy.

Oh Lord, he had seen her! It would look too obvious if she turned round now. Lily made herself walk on and lifted a hand in greeting. If she was lucky, Jack would take the hint and just wave back. But no. He got up and limped towards the gate.

'Where are you off to?'

'Just for a walk. Is that allowed?' Lily was startled at the sharpness in her own voice. What was it about Jack that rubbed her up the wrong way?

'You look hot,' he said.

Lily put her hands to her cheeks, which were suddenly glowing. She could see herself too clearly through his eyes: red-faced, sweaty, damp hair plastered to her forehead. And that was before he took note of her bulging belly and frumpy shoes.

'It is a bit warm,' she said. 'I was about to turn back.'

'Sit down and have a drink,' Jack offered.

She wanted to refuse, but she was hot and thirsty and now she thought about it, her feet were aching. It would be good to rest for a moment. 'Thank you,' she said awkwardly.

'Come in.' Jack held open the gate and gestured Lily to the bench. 'It's nicer out here. I seem to remember you didn't think much of my decor inside,' he added with a dry look, and Lily flushed.

'I was rather hoping you didn't remember anything about that evening,' she said. 'I've been trying to wipe it from my memory, anyway. I'm sorry if I was rude.'

'You weren't rude. You were unhappy.'

'And drunk.'

A ghost of a smile hovered around his mouth. 'That too.'

Lily forced her gaze away from that tantalising almost-smile. 'I learnt my lesson. I haven't touched a drop since.'

'I think you'd be safe with beer,' said Jack. 'It's so weak nowadays you could drink a barrel of the stuff without it having any effect.'

'That's true, but I'd just as soon have water now, if that's all right.'

He disappeared inside, coming back a few minutes later with a stone flagon of water and two cups. The water was deliciously cool and Lily drank deeply. Lowering the cup at last, she caught Jack's eyes on her face. Something in his eyes made her touch a finger self-consciously to the corners of her mouth in case she was dribbling water down her chin.

'Thanks,' she said. 'I was thirstier than I thought.'

Jack leant down to pick up the flagon from the

ground and refilled her cup. 'I haven't seen you for a while,' he said in a neutral voice.

'No, well, I'm not in the ATS any more, as you probably heard.'

'Yes, I did.'

'I've been keeping a low profile,' Lily admitted.

'Hiding?'

'No,' she said defensively, before her shoulders slumped. 'Well, maybe. I suppose I was afraid of what everybody would think.'

'Does it matter?' said Jack. 'Isn't what you think of yourself more important?'

Lily turned the cup between her hands. 'Derek gave me money to get rid of the baby,' she found herself saying. 'It would have been the sensible thing to do. I was going to, but when I got there, I just couldn't go through with it.' She couldn't look at him. 'So now for ever after I'll be 'that Lily Dingle who got herself knocked up'.'

'Do you regret it?'

'Derek, or deciding to keep the baby?'

'Both, I suppose.'

Lily thought about it. 'I regret being stupid and naive, yes.'

'Are you still in love with him?' Jack asked.

'I don't think so. Maybe I still love the man I thought he was, but not the man he turned out to be. As for the baby, if you had asked me six months ago if I wanted a baby, I would have been horrified, but now . . . ' Instinctively, she laid a hand on her belly. 'Now I can't imagine a future without one. With so many people dying in this awful war, it feels important to have new life, too.'

Jack put down his cup and leant back against the wall to stretch out his leg. 'Are you going to stay with your father at the garage?'

'That's the question.' Lily sighed and set her own cup on the ground. 'He's been wonderful, of course, but I don't want to be a burden to him. He's got his own life with Nina now.' She glanced at Jack. 'I think they might get married, and I don't think it's a good idea for them to do that with me and a baby hanging around. I'd like to leave and get a place of my own, but I don't see how that's going to be possible. Basically, I've got no idea what I'm going to do,' she admitted with a twisted smile.

'You should get married.' Jack quoted her own words back to her and she acknowledged it with a half-laugh.

'Right, who's going to want to marry me?'

'Lots of men, I should think. You're beautiful, smart, capable — '

'And I've got an illegitimate baby,' Lily finished for him.

'Can you cook as well as fix an engine?'

She laughed. 'Why, are you in the market for a wife?'

Jack looked at her. 'You were the one who said I should get married,' he reminded her.

'I was joking!'

'It's not a bad idea, now you come to mention it,' he went on, head tilted to one side as he considered it.

Lily's smile wavered uncertainly. 'Now you're joking,' she said.

'Am I?'

'You don't want to marry me!'

'Why wouldn't I?'

'Because . . . because you don't love me,' she said, still more than half convinced that he was teasing her.

'And you don't love me,' he pointed out after a tiny pause. 'But I need a wife, and you could do with a husband. It might not be very romantic, but successful marriages have been built on less. We wouldn't have any unrealistic expectations of each other.'

Lily looked at Jack, and then away at the view. The sky was flushed with colour in the west where the sun was angling down towards the fells at last. 'You're not serious,' she said finally.

'But I am,' said Jack. 'The more I think about it, the better the idea seems.'

'You don't even like me!'

He looked surprised. 'What makes you say that?'

'It's the way you look at me, like I'm irritating you.'

'I think you'll find that I'm irritated with myself for not being able to be completely professional when I'm with you,' he said. 'You're very, very pretty, you know. It's more distracting than it should be.'

Lily blushed. 'Still, it's a long way from thinking someone's pretty to wanting to marry them.'

'True,' said Jack. 'But I've been thinking about what you said when you were here that night, about the house not being comfortable. It's not really a home, it's just a place I sleep. It feels temporary, the way everything has felt temporary since Carol left me.'

Lily sat up straighter. 'I thought you broke off the engagement?'

'I did, but only because I could tell she wanted out but felt too bad to tell me while I was ill. I did the noble thing,' he said with a self-mocking twist of his mouth. 'I just didn't count on how quickly she would accept my offer of ending the engagement.'

Lily imagined him lying in a hospital bed, ill and in pain, watching the relief in his fiancée's eyes as he released her. Somehow she didn't think she would like Carol very much.

'You see?' said Jack. 'You're not the only person who's been naive. Carol was one of the reasons I came here. I wanted to get away from all the memories. It was bad enough being with friends who remembered Carol and I together, and who felt awkward whenever her name was mentioned, and when I came out of hospital I was always seeing her in town with her new fiancé. Coming here was a chance to start again, but after you were here that night, I realised that I hadn't started anything. I was stuck.'

'And you think getting married would unstick you?'

'Yes. It can be lonely being a village policeman. Everyone is always on their guard with you. I'd like someone to come home to at night, someone to talk to — and if that someone could also cook, that would be a bonus.' Jack shifted on the bench to face her. 'I'm not much of a catch, Lily, not with my leg, but if you marry

324

me, I'll look after you and your baby. I'll be a father to him or her, I promise.'

Lily searched his face. If anyone had asked her as she set out for her walk if she would end up considering marriage to Jack Proudfoot, she would have laughed in their face, and yet, incredibly, she *was* considering it. Her baby would need a father. And why not Jack? It wasn't as if he were distasteful to her. Far from it, in fact. Lily's eyes rested on his mouth and felt warmth pooling inside her.

'If we got married, would we . . . ' She trailed off, flustered, when he raised an eyebrow.

'Would we . . . ?'

'You know,' she said, her colour rising once more.

That smile was hovering around his lips again. 'Touch?' he suggested, taking her hand, and she let out a breath.

'Yes.'

'Kiss?'

'Yes.' She cleared her throat before he suggested anything further. 'How would we know that we were . . . compatible?'

'We could try it and see,' said Jack solemnly.

Lily shot him a quick look. Was he laughing at her? 'All right,' she said.

'Let's try now.' Jack shifted further along the bench and slid one hand gently under her hair to the nape of her neck. His fingers were warm and sure and Lily's heart began to thud against her ribs. His eyes moved over her face as if learning her by heart while his thumb traced the outline of her mouth.

Very slowly, he lowered his head to touch his lips to hers and Lily was leaning closer, ready to melt into him, when the sound of an engine approaching at speed made them jerk apart.

'Jack!' Jacob Sugden jumped out of his old truck. 'One of Meg Warcup's evacuees has gone missing. We need to put together a search party.'

Jack was on his feet, instantly alert, while Lily was slumped on the bench, her pulse drumming with frustration. But the news that one of Meg's children was missing brought her to join Jack at the gate.

Meg had come to Emmerdale Farm in a right state, Jacob told them. She'd brought the little boy, Stan, and asked them to look after him while she went after Ruby. 'She was off before we could stop her,' Jacob said. 'Now there's two of them running around t'fells.'

'How long has Ruby been missing?'

'Hours, Meg said. There was some kind of set-to — I didn't get what — and the girl ran off. Meg thought she'd come back later, but she never did.'

'Any idea which way she went?'

Jacob shook his head. 'Could be anywhere.'

'Right,' said Jack crisply. 'I'll call the LDF out and organise a search party. We'll use Emmerdale Farm as our base, as you're closest to Meg's cottage. Can you go back and set things up there?'

Jacob nodded and drove off. Jack turned to Lily. 'It looks as if we'll have to finish our conversation another time. Are you all right to go home on your own?'

'I'm coming with you,' said Lily, and when he began to protest she threw up a hand. 'I'm not suggesting I trek across the fells, but I can drive a vehicle. I'll get one from the garage and take you up to Emmerdale Farm. We need to find Ruby — and Meg.'

28

'Ruby!' Panting, Meg bent and rested her hands on her knees while she gulped in deep breaths. 'Ruby!' she called again when she was able to straighten.

No reply. Just the gusty sigh of the wind over the grass and the thin call of some distant bird. The setting sun was turning the clouds on the horizon a fiery red that was darkening by the minute. Meg eyed the sky with trepidation. It looked as if rain was coming in, and soon, judging by the way the wind was picking up, and that meant Ruby, and Rolf, would be out on the hills with little to protect them from the elements. Rolf at least would be sensible enough to take shelter, but Ruby . . . where *was* she?

'Ruby!' she shouted again, bracketing her mouth with her hands to carry the sound further.

Maggie had tried to persuade her to wait for the search party when she dragged a distressed and bewildered Stan to Emmerdale Farm, but Meg couldn't bear the thought of hanging around while Ruby might be hurt or terrified. As soon as she was sure that Stan was safe, she had headed out with Joe Sugden. They had agreed that he would search down by the beck, while Meg went uphill to get a better view of the area.

Where would Ruby have gone? She had taken her bicycle, so she would surely stick to lanes and tracks, but with several hours' start, she could be anywhere. There would have been plenty of time for her to cycle to Ilkley, or even further. Meg felt cold at the thought of a twelve-year-old girl alone at night in town. Jack Proudfoot could organise a search further afield. She tried to calm herself with this thought. There was still a possibility that Ruby was hiding nearby.

Meg tried to think like Ruby. She had been a rebel, just like Ruby, so where would *she* have gone when she was twelve? Meg answered her own question: to the one place she was forbidden to go, and she raised her eyes to Teggs Hill and the lane winding steeply up the fell.

It's too dangerous, she had said. *You must never go there.*

'Oh, no,' Meg whispered, and began to run.

It felt quicker to cut across the fell rather than backtrack to follow the winding route of the road, but she soon regretted it. The going was rough, and she kept stumbling over the clumps of grass and heather.

She was aiming for an isolated barn near the top of the fell, but the clouds were already overtaking her, blotting out the long summer twilight and spitting rain as the temperature dropped. Meg hadn't stopped to change, and was just in the frock and shoes she had put on that morning. It felt like a lifetime ago.

Stupid, she told herself. She knew better than to come out on the hills like this, but it was too late to turn back now. Convinced that Ruby had decided to go up the hill, Meg ploughed on. She remembered her own determination to ride down the other side of the hill, to dare to do what even the boys wouldn't do.

I don't want to, Rosie had said, puffing from the exertion of pushing her bike to the top of the hill. She had looked down the precipitous road with its twists and turns. *I'm scared.*

Oh, come on, Rosie. It'll be fun.

Meg felt sick. Staggering to the barn, she leant against the wall while she got her breath back. 'Ruby!' she called again. 'Ruby, where are you?'

'Meg?' A figure appeared out of the gloom and spoke softly. 'Meg, are you alone?'

She spun round, holding a hand to her chest to stop her heart leaping out. 'Rolf!'

'What are you doing up here?'

'It's Ruby. She's missing. She never came back after she ran off. I thought she was just sulking, but she's been gone too long. I'm afraid she might be . . . ' Meg couldn't say it. 'I have to find her,' she said instead. Realising she was gabbling, she made herself stop and take a breath. 'Why are you still here?'

'I needed a rest.' He had a hand to his shoulder where Ruby had stabbed him. 'My feet got wet crossing a stream, too, and my boots are rubbing. I thought I would hide until it was darker and try to dry out my socks. I was just going to move when I heard you calling.'

Meg frowned at his bare feet. 'Have you got blisters?'

'That is the word I could not remember,' said Rolf, clicking his fingers.

'Let me see.'

She was appalled when she saw what a mess his feet were in, with two angry blisters on his heels and others on his toes. 'You can't walk to the coast like this!'

'I'm not going to the coast now,' he said. 'I'm coming with you.'

'Rolf, you can't.' Because she wanted so very badly not to say goodbye again, Meg made herself step away. 'There'll be other people looking for Ruby, too. You can't risk anyone seeing you,' she said urgently. 'You need to get as far away as you can.'

'I'm not going to leave you wandering around the hillside on your own,' said Rolf, sitting down to pull on his socks and boots once more. 'What if Ruby is hurt?'

'This could be your only chance to get away,' Meg reminded him 'What about your sisters?'

'Right now, Ruby is more important.'

'She tried to *kill* you.'

'She's an unhappy little girl. Do you think I will walk away from her because of that? Come,' he said briskly, taking Meg's arm. 'We're wasting time arguing. What makes you think she came this way?'

As they climbed up to the road, Meg explained why she thought Ruby would have been drawn to Teggs Hill. 'It's my fault for telling her the road is too dangerous. I should have known it would only make her more determined to come here.'

'Is the road really so bad?'

'Yes.' It was easier going on the road, and they were able to switch off Rolf's torch, although Meg hated to think of how painful his feet must be. 'It's where my sister died.'

'What happened?'

Meg was very conscious of Rolf's warm fingers on her arm. 'I killed her,' she said, and waited for him to drop his hand.

'Why do you say that?' he asked.

'Because I did. I was the one who insisted Rosie come with me. She didn't want to come. She was happy reading a book, but she always gave in, and I never did. She was sweet and I was stubborn.' Meg's voice cracked. 'Why didn't I just leave her be?'

Their eyes had adjusted to the darkness and she felt Rolf glance at her. 'So she agreed to come cycling with you. How does that mean you killed her?'

'Because I wanted to cycle down the other side of Teggs Hill. We were forbidden to come up here because it was dangerous, but of course that just made it more exciting for me. We had to push our bikes most of the way up the road here. Rosie kept saying that she was tired and why didn't we go back, but I was determined.'

The feel of the handlebars, the exhilaration of pushing off down that dizzyingly steep slope. Meg could still feel the wind blowing her hair back, the thrill of hurtling down at such speed.

'We set off together,' she told Rolf. 'I was screaming with excitement and then I looked and I realised that Rosie wasn't there, so I . . . I stopped.'

Eventually. It hadn't been easy at that speed and the bike had skidded, throwing Meg off and skinning her knees.

'I ran back up the hill,' she went on. 'I could see her bike on its side, its wheels still spinning, and Rosie lying beside it.' She swallowed. 'I thought . . . I thought she was playing a game at first. I thought she would open her eyes and laugh.'

Ha, ha! Come on now, Rosie. I'm sorry, OK? It's not funny any more. Open your eyes.

Meg had faltered to a halt, but she had come this far and she would need to finish it. She had never told anyone about those long, desolate minutes trying to shake her sister awake.

'But she never did open her eyes,' she said. 'The silence just went on and on. Her neck was broken. I couldn't even cry. I just sat and held her and eventually they found us. They must have come looking along this road, just like we're looking for Ruby.'

'Meg.' Rolf stopped and let go of her arm but only to pull her comfortingly close. 'Meg, it was an accident. It wasn't your fault.'

'It *was* my fault.' She made herself step away from the comfort. She didn't deserve comfort. 'My mother never recovered. Rosie was their golden child. My parents never said they blamed me but I knew they did.'

She started walking again, and Rolf fell into step beside her. 'I did everything I could to make up for what I'd done,' she said. 'I was never naughty again. I never broke the rules. I was as good as Rosie had been. But none of it brought her back. My mother died a year later. I'm sure it was of a broken heart, so that was my fault too. After that, it was just Dad and me, but he was like a ghost, a hollow version of what he'd been before. And all because I wouldn't let Rosie read her book in peace,' Meg remembered bleakly. 'All because I was bored and wanted a thrill.'

'How old were you?' Rolf asked after a moment.

'Fourteen.'

'Meg, you were a child.'

Meg barely heard him. 'And now there's Ruby,' she said, distractedly. 'What if the same thing has happened to her? That will be my fault, too.'

'You didn't chase Ruby off. She ran away.'

'If I hadn't told her it was dangerous, she wouldn't have come this way.'

'You don't know that she has,' Rolf pointed out. 'Come, let's find her first before you start taking the blame for something that may not have happened.'

They paused at the crest of the hill. 'Ruby!' Meg called again. 'Ruby!'

Rolf cocked his head. 'Wait! What was that? Call again.'

'Ruby!'

And there it was, a faint cry. Meg began to run down the hill. The road had twisted only twice before they found the bike on the edge of a precipitous slope, its wheel buckled.

'Oh my God, *Ruby!*'

'I'm here.' Ruby's voice came quavering from the darkness and Rolf shone the torch down the hill in search of her.

'There!' Meg clutched at him as she caught sight of Ruby's white face. She was clinging to a clump of bracken to stop herself tumbling further.

'Ruby, are you all right?'

Ruby started to cry. 'I'm frightened and my ankle hurts,' she wept.

'You're going to be fine,' Meg called down in a hearty voice, adding in an undertone to Rolf, 'How are we going to get her up?'

He was examining the slope with his torch. 'It's not too bad,' he said. 'I will go and get her. You keep her calm.'

Ruby's voice quavered when she heard that Rolf was coming to get her. 'He hates me!'

'No, I don't hate you, Ruby.' Rolf's voice came reassuringly calm through the darkness. 'Nobody's cross with you. We just want to get you home.'

Very cautiously, he climbed down the slope, testing each foothold to make sure it was secure, before he reached Ruby.

'Take my hand,' he said, stretching out his good arm towards her.

'I'm scared.'

'I'll be right behind you,' said Rolf. 'You just need to crawl and I'll stop you falling. We'll take it slowly.'

Inch by inch, they coaxed Ruby up to the road on her hands and knees. It seemed to take a very long time, but at last Meg was able to reach down and help her up the last few feet.

'Ruby! Oh, Ruby!' she said, hugging Ruby to her. 'I thought I'd lost you!'

'I'm sorry, I'm sorry.' Ruby burst into incoherent tears. 'I'm sorry I'm so horrible!'

'You're not horrible, Ruby.'

'I am! I hurt Rolf, and I don't know why. I was just so angry, and then so frightened. I wish I hadn't.' Ruby dragged an arm under her nose and sniffed. 'I'm sorry, Rolf.'

'Maybe you should say sorry to Meg, too? She is the one who came to find you.'

She hung her head. 'I'm sorry, Meg.'

'It's all right, Ruby. I'm just glad to have found you. Why did you run away like that?'

'I thought I would go to prison for stabbing Rolf, and you would hate me because I'm a bad person.'

'Oh, Ruby, of course I wouldn't.'

'I was jealous,' said Ruby, determined to make a clean breast of it. 'Stan was so happy with his violin, and you like Rolf, and I was sulky and bad-tempered.'

'You've just lost your mum, Ruby,' said Meg. 'I understood why you were unhappy.'

'But that's just it. I *wasn't* sad when I heard about my mum. I thought I would be, but when it happened, I was relieved because it meant I could stay with you,' Ruby said. 'I felt so guilty and I don't know why, it was like I needed to be angry with someone instead of being angry with myself.'

Meg's throat closed, and she gathered Ruby back into her arms and let her cry out her fear and distress as they sat together in the road.

'You're both going to get cold,' said Rolf, squatting beside them. 'We should get moving.'

'I'll take her home,' said Meg. 'You . . . you go on.'

But when they helped Ruby to her feet it was

clear that she had injured her ankle so badly she would be unable to walk.

'Then I will have to carry you,' Rolf said. 'How do you call it when you're on my back?'

'Piggyback,' said Ruby, letting him hoist her onto his back. Only Meg saw the spasm of pain that crossed his face as she wrapped her arms around his neck where she had stabbed him only hours earlier.

'Rolf.' Meg spoke in an urgent whisper as they set off up the hill. 'Rolf, you can't come back. They'll know you tried to escape. They'll punish you.'

'So be it,' he said.

For ever after Meg would remember that walk through the June night. They stuck to the road, but it was the long way round, and her shoes pinched so painfully that in the end she took them off and limped barefoot beside Rolf and Ruby, step after agonising step. Rolf's feet must have been in an even worse state, but he wouldn't stop to take his boots off. They were almost at Emmerdale Farm when Lily Dingle, who had been out searching with Annie Pearson, spotted them and came running to help while Annie called for the others.

After that it was a blur. Jacob Sugden took Ruby from Rolf's back. Meg saw Rolf sway for a moment and then pitch forward. Jack Proudfoot only just caught him in time. 'He's bleeding,' Jack said sharply. 'Joe, give me a hand and let's get him inside.'

The kitchen at Emmerdale Farm seemed to be full of people. Maggie was examining Ruby's swollen ankle, but she shot a worried look at Meg, who was too exhausted to do more than stand numbly.

'Annie, get Meg to sit down before she falls down, too,' she said briskly, and Meg found herself pressed into a chair and a cup of sweet tea put into her hands.

Rolf was barely conscious. Lily was helping Jack to take off his boots and socks. They fell silent when they saw the state of his feet. 'How far has he walked like this?' Jack asked after a moment.

'From Teggs Hill,' Meg said, and he shook his head. 'And before that, from my cottage.'

'Dear God,' said Jack. 'That must be almost ten miles altogether. He's not going to be walking any further on these feet for a while.' He turned back to Rolf's limp body laid on the rag rug. 'Lily, give me a hand with his jacket, will you?'

When the jacket was off, Jack inspected it. 'Care to tell me why he's not in prison uniform, Meg?'

She shook her head dumbly. 'He saved Ruby,' she whispered.

Jack gave her a searching look but laid the jacket aside and returned to his examination of Rolf. He could hardly miss the bloody bandage around Rolf's neck once they had the shirt off, but he waited until Rolf had been washed and patched up. Between them, Jacob and Joe managed to get him upstairs and into Jacob's bed, while Ruby was put to bed in Edward's old room.

Looking tired, Jack came back downstairs. 'I don't see any need for a guard,' he said. 'He's not going anywhere for a while. I'll just stand down the LVF. I think everyone can go home now. Not you, though,' he added, pointing at Meg, who was still sitting numbly in the chair where Annie had first put her.

'I think we could all do with something stronger than tea,' said Maggie firmly and produced a bottle of Scotch from the back of a cupboard. 'I was saving this for Edward's next leave.' Grief washed over her face but she pressed her lips firmly together and set the bottle down on the table, while Annie fetched some glasses. 'We'll have it now,' she said. 'If the war's taught us anything, it's that there's no point in saving for the future. Pour it out, Joe,' she told her husband. 'Don't hold back.'

Meg took a sip of the whisky that was put in her hand, choking a little as it burned comfortingly down her throat.

Jack took the seat opposite her and accepted a glass with a nod of thanks. He took an appreciative sip and then set the glass carefully back on the table. His cool eyes settled on Meg's face.

'That looks to me like a stab wound in Rolf s neck,' he said conversationally, 'and he's wearing civilian clothes. I think you'd better tell me what's been going on, Meg.'

29

Annie watched Meg take a slug of whisky as she finished her story. She put the glass down and looked defiantly around the table. Her face was white with exhaustion and there were dark smudges under her eyes, but Annie thought she could see the old Meg in the combative tilt of her chin.

Strange how the war was paring everybody back to their essential selves, Annie reflected. Since Rosie's death, Meg had withdrawn behind a brittle shell. It was as if she stomped down on all the rebellious instincts she had had as a child and deliberately refashioned herself as cold and conventional. But the war had cracked that carefully created image. It seemed to Annie that Meg was rediscovering not just her wildness but the sweetness that had always been part of her. Schoolmarm Meg would never have defied convention to befriend an enemy prisoner of war and help him try to escape. She wouldn't have run headlong into the hills for a troublesome evacuee either. That night's adventure had been the old Meg through and through. Annie was glad to see her back.

Look at Lily Dingle, too. Annie's gaze moved on round the table. Plenty of times Annie had heard Maggie shake her head over the way grief over her mother's early death had crushed Lily's joyful, passionate spirit. It had closed her down,

340

made her fearful of change and quick to judge others. But now Lily was pregnant and glowing, despite the shame of not being married. Annie remembered how anxious she had been in case she and Edward had made a baby before he left; how she had quailed at the mere thought of the scandal and what everyone would think, even though there would have been no question that they would be getting married. She couldn't help admiring how Lily was facing them all with her head up.

And what about *me*? Annie asked herself. For as long as she could remember she had been part of a pair with Edward. The war had certainly changed that. Edward was dead, and there would always be an empty space beside her now. Annie felt as if she were unbalanced, forced to walk leaning to one side to avoid falling into the dizzyingly deep void where Edward should be. She was still trying to find out what kind of person she was in her own right — as Annie, not half of Annie-and-Edward.

Annie had seen Meg's face when she saw the terrible state of Rolf's feet. She was in love with him, whether or not she realised it. Lily, too, was looking at Jack Proudfoot in a way that made Annie mentally raise her eyebrows. So that was the way the wind was blowing! Who would have thought it? She knew how they both felt; remembered the dark tug of desire, the certainty that only that one man's touch would make you feel complete; the relief of knowing that he was there beside you, someone to hang onto when the world swung uncertainly around you.

Out of nowhere, fresh grief squeezed Annie's heart and surged into her throat. Closing her eyes, she took a slug of whisky to dull the pain. Meg might face an uncertain future in love with an enemy prisoner, and Lily's unborn child meant that her situation would always be complicated. Neither could enjoy the sweetness of a straightforward romance, but at least the men they loved were alive, were there. Annie was glad that her friends seemed to have found love, but oh, how she envied them too, and how agonisingly she missed Edward.

But Edward was dead, and she had to learn to accept it. She had had her chance at love. It had been perfect, but now it was over. Opening her eyes, Annie looked around the kitchen. The range with the battered kettle; the dresser where she carefully set the plates after washing them up. The ticking clock on the mantelpiece and the old-fashioned copper warming pan hanging on the wall. The cupboard bed under the stairs. The rag rug in front of the fire. No hams hanging from the beams as they had before the war, but otherwise everything at Emmerdale Farm was so familiar, the same as it had always been since Annie was a small girl.

She had clung to that familiarity, Annie realised. She hadn't wanted anything to change, but war had come and things had changed anyway. If she didn't know who the real Annie was, perhaps that was because she had been afraid to be by herself, afraid she might find out that there was nothing to her without Edward.

Perhaps, thought Annie, it was time to

discover who she really was, and whether she was brave enough to leave everything that was familiar behind and follow Edward out into the world.

'So that's it,' Meg finished. She looked at Jack Proudfoot. 'What will happen to Rolf?'

'That's not up to me, I'm afraid,' said Jack. 'Clearly he's not going anywhere tonight, but I'll have to inform the prison authorities. I imagine there'll be punishment for attempting to escape. I'm sorry, but they can hardly let it go.'

'But he saved Ruby — and me,' Meg protested. 'I don't know what would have happened to us without Rolf. He gave up his chance to get home to his country to help us.'

Jack shook his head. 'I'm sorry,' he said again. 'I saw what it cost him to bring you both safe home tonight, but the fact remains that he's an enemy airman trying to make an escape.'

'He won't be able to escape now,' Meg said bitterly.

'They're not going to shoot him, Meg. He might be put in solitary confinement or on bread and water. It's not the end of the world.'

'It is when he's desperate to get home to his family. His mother and two of his sisters were killed by our bombs,' she pleaded. 'His other two sisters need him. Wouldn't you try to escape?'

'I would, yes,' said Jack, 'but I'm not in prison. I'm a policeman and I have to uphold the law, whether I like it or not. I'm not going to turn a blind eye while an enemy prisoner escapes back to Germany. Even if Rolf were to make it, which I doubt, he would be sent back to the front line to fight against us again. Do you really want that?'

Meg slumped in her chair, defeated. 'No,' she muttered. 'I just don't want him to be punished any more. He's a good man.'

Maggie leant forward. 'How would it be if we said that we'd asked Rolf to work late here and forgot to ask permission?' she suggested. 'It was a fine evening, and we were saying we wished we had more help to get the hay in, weren't we, Joe?' She sent Joe a meaningful look and, after the tiniest of pauses, he nodded. Jacob caught on belatedly, too.

'Yeah, we were,' he said. 'Rolf was a big help.'

'And then while he was here, we heard about Ruby going missing, so he volunteered to search with Meg, and that's how his feet were so torn up,' Maggie went on persuasively.

'So you, what, gave him civilian clothes to work in during the evening?' Jack's voice was dry but Meg had straightened.

'I can bring his uniform from the cottage. Nobody else need ever know.'

Jack sighed. 'What about the stab wound in his shoulder?'

'Couldn't we just say it was an accident?' Meg asked. 'Please, Sergeant Proudfoot — Jack — it's bad enough that Rolf has to go back to camp, but I can't bear for him to be punished for trying to escape as well, not when he gave up his attempt for Ruby.'

There was a long pause. Jack looked round the table. 'I'm certainly not going to tell anybody,' Lily offered. The Sugdens all nodded, and then everyone's eyes turned to Annie.

'I'll say Rolf was here if anyone asks.'

'Very well.' Jack pushed back his chair. 'I'll go and ring the camp commander now. I'll be back in the morning to escort Rolf to the camp, and he'd better be here,' he added with a warning look at Meg.

'He will be,' she said. 'Thank you, Jack.' She looked at each of them in turn. 'Thank you all.'

★ ★ ★

Jack Proudfoot came back the next day with a military escort to take Rolf back to the camp, and Lily turned up a short while later in one of Mick's cars to drive Meg, Ruby and Stan back to the cottage as Ruby's ankle was still swollen and Meg's feet horribly blistered.

The farmhouse felt empty when they had all gone. Annie helped Maggie clear up after their unexpected guests. 'D'you reckon Rolf will be allowed to come back and work here?' she asked Maggie as she washed the breakfast dishes. In spite of her initial reservations about employing the enemy, Annie had come to like the quiet, hard-working German.

'I hope so.' Maggie dried a cup with brisk efficiency and hung it on its hook on the dresser. 'Jack Proudfoot's got his head screwed on right. He'll talk the camp commander round. He knows we need the labour, specially at this time of year. Talking of which, can you help with the strewing after this, Annie? I'll see to dinner.'

'All right.' Annie wasn't sorry to be out in the

345

fields with the sweet smell of cut hay. It was a grand day to be outside. Last night's clouds had cleared, leaving a high blue sky, but the air was fresher, with a welcome breeze. She took a rake and joined Jacob and Joe turning the hay. It was a mindless task that gave her a chance to think.

Maggie brought dinner out to the field. It was just rabbit pie and some pickled onions, but Annie guessed that they were luckier than most. She would miss the farm food, she thought, realising that she had made up her mind.

'I'm thinking of joining up,' she said, nibbling at an edge of pastry as she sat with the Sugdens on the grassy bank at the edge of the field.

'What?' Jacob had been lounging beside her but at that, he sat up. 'Annie, you can't!'

'It's time I did my bit for the war effort.'

'You're doing your bit here!'

'It's not the same,' said Annie. 'Besides, I need a change.'

Maggie looked sad. 'We'll miss you, Annie, but I understand.'

'Well, *I* don't understand!' Jacob leapt to his feet and stalked back into the field. Snatching up his rake, he started furiously strewing, his expression thunderous.

'Don't mind Jacob,' said Maggie. 'He'll get over it. Where are you going to volunteer?'

'I thought the Navy, like Edward. I'm going to apply for the WRNS.'

Grief arrowed through Maggie's eyes at Edward's name. 'I'm glad,' she said. Her gaze rested thoughtfully on her angry son. 'It's not a bad idea for you to see a bit of the world, Annie.

346

Giving young women like you a chance to travel and try new jobs is about the only good thing to come out of this cursed war.'

'That's what I thought.'

'When are you thinking of going?'

'I'll wait till you've got the hay in, and have got a new girl to help. I'll give a hand at the summer fete next week like I promised Mrs Airey, too, but after that . . . '

'I'd forgotten about the fete.' Maggie sighed. 'Well, we'd better put on a show, though God knows, we've little enough left in the larder. We always used to have a few extra jars of jam or a ham we could donate, but with the war on, there's nothing left.' She turned to Annie. 'What's Janet got you doing?'

'Donkey rides for the children. I said I'd take Neddy down. That's all right, isn't it?'

Maggie nodded, smiling. 'I always think of Neddy as yours, Annie.'

All at once Annie was struck with the enormity of what she had said she would do. She would be gone, and Emmerdale Farm would carry on without her, because the animals needed to be fed and the cows milked and the crops harvested, however broken human hearts were.

'You'll look after Neddy while I'm gone?' she asked Maggie, suddenly wobbly, and Maggie put her hand over hers.

'Of course we will. We'll still be here when you come back, Annie. It doesn't have to be for ever.'

★　★　★

347

Jacob was silent over supper, but when Annie had finished clearing up and was untying her apron, he got up abruptly and said he would see her home. Annie bit her lip, but nodded. Jacob was her friend. She was afraid that he was going to try and persuade her to stay, and she hated upsetting scenes. She didn't want to hurt anyone. It had been hard enough telling her parents, although they both said they understood that she wanted a fresh start.

'All right, then,' she said, pulling on her cardigan against the evening chill. She wished Maggie and Joe goodnight, and at the front door stooped to tug the collies' silky ears.

'I'll miss you two,' she told them, and their feathery tails thumped.

'I wish you'd change your mind about going,' Jacob said as she straightened up and headed across the yard to the track that led to the shepherd's cottage.

'I've thought about it, Jacob, and I need to go,' she said as gently as she could. 'There are too many memories of Edward here.'

'Edward!' he repeated bitterly. 'Edward, Edward, Edward! It's always about him! Poor Edward, how will he feel now that he knows he's a bastard? What about the rest of us? What about me? How do you think I felt, knowing Ma had had an affair?' His fists clenched and unclenched.

Annie stared at him. She had never heard Jacob talk like this before.

'What is it, Jacob?' she asked.

His shoulders slumped. 'You're going,' he said. 'After everything I've done, you're leaving me.'

348

'Everything you've done?' Annie repeated, puzzled.

'I beat up Oliver Skilbeck for you,' said Jacob after a moment.

'I didn't ask you to do that, Jacob,' she said gently.

'Someone had to protect you! Ed didn't even notice how wretched you were, did he?'

That shot went home. Annie hugged her arms together. 'I can't talk about Edward,' she said.

'You can't think about anything but him either, can you, Annie?'

'You know how I feel about Edward,' Annie said, not understanding the intensity in Jacob's voice.

'Oh, yes, I know,' he said bitterly. 'I've always known. Why do you think I cheated?'

Annie stopped. 'What?'

'I cheated,' said Jacob.

'Cheated how?' she asked. Her eyes searched his face and he turned it away in shame. 'Jacob?' she prompted.

'Ed and I agreed to draw straws to see who would go and fight and who would stay and farm,' he began heavily.

'I remember.'

'Ed made a big thing about choosing which straw to draw, but it wouldn't have made any difference. I only had short straws in my hand.'

A pulse began to beat in Annie's temple. 'So Edward was always going to be the one to go and fight.'

Jacob couldn't meet her eyes. 'Yes.'

'Why?'

'Why? Because I loved you, of course!' he burst out. 'I've always loved you, Annie, and you barely knew I was there! You only ever had eyes for Edward. So when the war came and we decided that one would stay on the farm, I knew he wanted to go, and I thought . . . I hoped . . . that if Ed was gone, you might turn to me.'

Annie's eyes were burning. 'You wanted him to *die*?'

'No! No, of course not. I just wanted you to *see* me. Ed would never have settled down, you know. He were always restless. I hoped that in the long run you'd realise you were better off with me,' Jacob ploughed on, ignoring the way Annie was backing away from him. 'You still would be. Please, Annie, don't go away. Stay, and marry me.'

'*Marry* you? How could I marry you when you've admitted cheating on your own brother? I thought we were *friends*,' said Annie, close to tears. 'I trusted you, Jacob, and you've betrayed me in the worst possible way.'

She began walking fast up the track, but Jacob kept pace, raking his hand through his hair in despair.

'Annie, I'm sorry, I'm sorry! You don't know what it's been like for me, mad with love for you and knowing that it's been for nothing. And all the time feeling guilty about Ed dying . . . I didn't torpedo that ship, but I might as well have killed him by not giving him a choice about going.'

'You *should* feel guilty,' Annie shouted on a sob. 'Cheating! If you'd done the decent thing,

Edward might still be here! We could have been married, and instead . . . ' She choked back her tears. 'How *could* you, Jacob?'

'I did it for you, Annie.'

'No, you didn't,' she said coldly. 'You did it for yourself. If you'd done it for me, you'd have made sure Edward stayed at home. He'd still be alive instead of at the bottom of the Atlantic'

'He wanted to go,' said Jacob. 'He wanted to pull the short straw, Annie, you know that he did.'

'That's not the point! You *cheated*, Jacob.'

'I'm sorry,' he said wretchedly again. 'Will you ever forgive me?'

'I don't know,' said Annie honestly. 'One day, perhaps, but not yet, Jacob. Not yet.'

30

Lily grunted as she twisted the spanner, and swore out loud when it slipped off the nut.

'Language!' Jack tutted from behind her, and she jerked upright, only just avoiding banging her head on the bonnet of the car she was fixing.

The near miss could have been the reason her heart was lurching uncomfortably in her chest. She hoped it was that, and not that this was the first time she had seen Jack since the morning at Emmerdale Farm when he had escorted Rolf back to the prison camp and she had taken Meg and the children back to the cottage.

That had been a week ago, a week when Lily had convinced herself that she had misunderstood that whole strange conversation about marriage. Jack couldn't possibly want to marry her and take on another man's child. He must have been joking, and how mortifying to think that she had almost been taken in by it. Not that she had really been considering marrying him, she always added quickly to herself when her thoughts drifted back to that evening, which they did more than was comfortable. It was an absolutely ridiculous idea.

But he had been going to kiss her. He wouldn't have done that unless he was serious, surely? Again and again, and much to her annoyance, Lily found herself reliving that moment when he had slid his hand under her hair and pulled her towards him. Her pulse pounded whenever she thought about the heat in his eyes, the way her skin had tingled under the graze of his fingers.

If Jacob Sugden hadn't driven up then, what would have happened?

Lily had barely been able to concentrate on Meg's tale when the bedraggled group had finally made it back to the farmhouse that night. She had sat around the table with the others, but she had been aware only of Jack. Every time he turned his head, every time his lips moved, her stomach dipped alarmingly. All at once, she was excruciatingly aware of him: his hands, the angle of his jaw and the precise point where it met his neck, the heart-shakingly cool line of his mouth.

Lily felt as if she were tumbling over and over down some slippery slope. She wanted to grab onto something to anchor her and give her a chance to catch her breath, but instead all she could do was churn with a queasy mixture of lust and confusion and embarrassment. She was pregnant, she kept reminding herself. She shouldn't be feeling like this, especially not when the man in question wasn't even the father of her child.

This wasn't how she had felt about Derek. That had been infatuation, she could see that now. She had adored him and been dazzled by him but she had never felt this disturbing hunger before. Lily wasn't even sure that she *liked* Jack, so why did she want him that much?

And what was the point of wanting him when he clearly wasn't that bothered about her? A week had gone by, and he hadn't shown any interest in resuming their conversation — or that kiss.

He must have changed his mind. Well, fine, Lily told herself. What man in his right mind would want her in her current condition? She looked down at her bulky body and sighed. At least that would be a reason she could understand. She hated the lowering thought that Jack had just been amusing himself. What if he'd assumed she was easy? That because she had had an affair with Derek she would be quick to jump into bed with the next man who came along?

Was that what she was doing?

All in all, Lily was unsettled and short-tempered that week, and in no mood to give Jack a warm welcome now that he had finally deigned to turn up.

'What are you doing here?' she demanded.

'I thought it was time we finished our conversation,' said Jack, quite unfazed by the chill in her voice.

'What conversation was that?' asked Lily snippily. 'It's so long since we spoke, I've quite forgotten!'

'I'm sorry,' he said, holding up his hands in a gesture of acknowledgement. 'I've been busy. A series of break-ins, a theft of building materials and last night a fight at the Woolpack . . . not to mention negotiating a pass for Rolf Schrieber so that he can go back to work at Emmerdale Farm, and continue Stan's music lessons. Every time I wanted to come and see you, something else happened, so I decided to wait until things had calmed down and we could talk without interruption.'

Lily sniffed. 'So you thought I'd just be hanging around, waiting until you were ready to have a chat?'

'No,' said Jack. 'I hoped to see you at the fete, but when I met your father just now, he said you'd decided to stay here.'

'I thought he and Nina would like to be on their own. Did you hear, they're getting married.'

'I did,' he said. 'It's good news, isn't it?'

'Yes.' Realising that she was fiddling with the spanner, Lily put it down and wiped her hands absently on her overall. It *was* good news about her father and Nina, but she couldn't help feeling a little doleful. 'It'll be a big change, though. Dad's going to move in with Nina.'

'Ah. Does that mean you'll be able to stay here?'

'Only temporarily. Dad'll need someone to help in the garage eventually, and that person will need somewhere to live, too. Nina says I can live with them if I want, after the baby is born.'

'*Is* that what you want?' asked Jack.

'Not really. I don't want to be a gooseberry.'

'Which brings us back to the conversation we never finished last week,' he pointed out. 'Have you thought any more about marrying me?'

'I didn't think you were serious,' Lily said. 'I mean, it's a ridiculous idea. We hardly know each other!'

Jack came over to take her hands. 'That's easily solved. We can get to know each other. In fact, why don't we start now?'

Lily's fingers seemed to have acquired a will of their own and were twining around his.

'This is crazy. If you'd asked me a week ago if I liked you, I would have said no!'

'And now?'

'Now I . . . I don't know,' she admitted.

Jack smiled. 'That's a start.' His grip tightened. 'Come on, Lily. Leave this. Go and put on a frock and we'll go to the fete together.'

'I don't really want to go,' she grumbled, but he wasn't having any of it. 'Of course you do. Everybody loves a summer fete, and this one is in aid of the war effort. It's our patriotic duty to put on a good face and enjoy ourselves.'

Lily looked down at her swollen stomach. 'Everybody will gossip when they see you with me,' she warned, and Jack's smile warmed as he drew her closer to him.

'In that case, let's give them something to gossip about,' he said.

★   ★   ★

Meg wasn't entirely surprised when Ruby caught a chill after her hours out on the damp hillside. Her fever was worrying enough to call out Dr Moss, but worse was the lethargy that followed. Meg closed the school for a week and did her best to tempt Ruby's appetite with jelly and a sponge cake made with real eggs that Mary Ann Teale had dropped off.

Between Ruby's hacking cough and Stan's neediness, Meg was kept busy, and perhaps it was just as well that she had little time to fret about Rolf. Stan asked constantly when he would be able to resume his lessons, but there was little Meg could tell him — until Jack Proudfoot came round one evening.

'I've been able to persuade the camp commander that Rolf should return to agricultural work,' he said. 'I'm not sure he entirely believed that Rolf had been at Emmerdale Farm the whole time that evening, but it suits everybody that we all pretend he was. With shipping under attack, farms are under pressure to up production, and they can't do that without labour.'

'So he'll be allowed out again?' Meg asked eagerly.

'Eventually. I'm sorry, but the camp commander feels he has to make an example of Rolf, too. He's to spend two weeks in solitary confinement first. It was the best compromise I could negotiate, I'm afraid. It's not too brutal,' Jack added, seeing Meg's dismayed expression. 'He'll have his fiddle and books, and it'll give his injuries a chance to heal. It could have been a lot worse.'

'I know. I'm grateful, Jack — truly, I am.'

At least Rolf was safe, Meg told herself. Stan missed him terribly, and she did, too. She hadn't realised just how much Rolf's visits had come to mean. Still, as Jack had said, things could be worse, and they would see him again.

'Word seems to have got out about the way Rolf carried Ruby down the hill,' Jack went on casually. 'I think he'll find more of a welcome in Beckindale than he did before.'

Meg suspected that Jack was responsible for

357

the change in attitudes, and was doubly grateful. It wasn't just Rolf who would benefit. Any number of people found an excuse to drop in, like Mrs Teale. Others brought the little they could spare: an egg or two, a couple of sausages, and even from Jed Dingle, an orange that Meg carefully peeled and divided into segments for Ruby and Stan. She was touched and humbled. Beckindale might be riven by rows and feuds and gossip, but when it came down to it, it was a community that pulled together, especially when one of its own was in trouble. Until now, Meg had always felt as if she wasn't a real part of the village, and the sense of belonging gave her a warm glow. She was looking forward to the summer fete in a way she never had before.

Now it was just a question of whether Ruby would be well enough to go.

Fortunately, Annie had told Stan that she would be taking the donkey to the fete, and the prospect of a ride on Neddy was the first thing to have sparked his interest since he had picked up a violin. Even Ruby was roused from her lethargy to admit that she would like to ride on the donkey, too.

The day of the fete dawned a pale grey but it was not long before the sun burned through the clouds.

'I thought you would like a new frock to wear to the fete,' Meg told Ruby at breakfast. She had retrieved Rosie's old dress from the bottom of the sewing pile where she had thrust it, cut down so that it would fit.

Ruby's eyes widened. 'A frock? For me?'

'It's time you had something new,' said Meg, her throat tightening at the wonder on the child's face. 'Why don't you go and try it on? I can always alter it if it's not quite right.'

Adept by now at hopping up and downstairs on her good ankle, Ruby took the dress silently and went up to the bedroom she shared with Stan. Meg gave her a few minutes while she cleared up after breakfast and listened with one ear to Stan playing the violin. Hanging up her apron when she had finished, she went upstairs and put her head round the bedroom door.

Ruby was standing by the bed, her eyes on the floor, stroking the frock as if she could hardly believe it was real. Her lips were pressed together in a perfectly straight line as if to stop her mouth from wobbling.

'Does it fit?' Meg asked, and Ruby nodded. 'You look very pretty in it,' she went on, swallowing the lump in her throat. 'It's not new, of course. It was my sister's dress. I altered it for you.'

Ruby looked up at that, her expression stricken. 'This was Rosie's?'

'Yes, I kept it.' Meg tried to smile. 'It was silly, I know. It wasn't doing any good in the back of the wardrobe and — what's the matter?' she asked as tears spilled down Ruby's cheeks. 'Do you feel ill again?'

'No,' sniffed Ruby. 'I don't deserve this! I feel so bad about what I did, Meg. I'm so sorry for all the trouble I caused. I thought nobody liked me, and then everyone came out to find me.'

'It turns out we like you after all,' said Meg, but Ruby would not be comforted.

'You shouldn't,' she said. 'I've got summat to tell you.' Digging under her pillow, she drew out a familiar locket. 'I stole this from you,' she said, almost shoving it into Meg's hand. 'I took it with me when I ran away because it was yours and I wanted . . . I don't know what I wanted.'

'Oh, Ruby . . . ' Meg turned the locket in her hand.

'It's your sister's,' Ruby went on. 'I know you miss her. I know you wish she was here, not me, and you won't want me to stay now.' She lifted her chin, ready to take her punishment. 'I'll go away, but I want you to keep Stan,' she said. 'He'll be happy with you.'

'He won't be happy without you, Ruby,' said Meg. 'And nor will I.'

'But . . . but,' Ruby stammered.

Meg went to sit on the edge of the bed and patted the space beside her. 'Sit down,' she invited and, bemused, Ruby sat.

'You shouldn't have taken the locket,' Meg went on. 'You knew how much it meant to me and you knew it was wrong. I hope you'll never steal again.'

Ruby shook her head. 'I won't!' she said fervently.

'But now you've given it back to me.' Meg looked down at the locket in her hand. It was only a cheap trinket, but it had been Rosie's. 'Here,' she said, passing it back to Ruby. 'I want you to have it.'

Ruby gaped at her, the locket dangling from her hand.

'It's true that I missed Rosie terribly when she

died. I still do. I always will,' Meg said. 'But now I've got you and Stan — and I've got a necklace of my own,' she added, and touched the pendant Rolf had made her. 'Just because I loved Rosie doesn't mean I can't love you just as much, Ruby. You're not a replacement for Rosie, you're you, but I think she'd have wanted you to have her locket. She would have liked you,' she added, smiling a little as Ruby flushed with pleasure. 'There is one condition, though,' she added.

Ruby looked up from the locket in her hand. 'What?'

'That you and Stan stay and live with me. We'll be a family, and we'll see this war through together. Will you do that?'

'Yes!' Ruby threw her thin arms around Meg's neck and hugged her. 'Oh, yes, I will!'

'Good, that's settled.' Meg hugged her back. 'Now, let's get ready. Mrs Sugden will be here any minute. She's going to give us a lift to the fete in their pony and trap to save your ankle.'

They were waiting outside when Maggie drew up. Jacob was sitting beside her but he jumped down as the trap slowed and to Meg's astonishment, lifted Ruby's bicycle from the back.

'My bicycle!' Ruby cried in delight. 'Thank you, Mr Sugden!'

'Jacob walked up the road until he found it,' Maggie said in an undertone to Meg. 'He carried it all the way back.'

Meg could have hugged him but Jacob shrugged off all attempts to thank him.

'Thank Lily Dingle,' he said. 'She's the one that fixed it.'

Annie was scratching Neddy between his long ears when she saw the Sugdens arrive with Meg squeezed between them on the seat, and the children with their legs dangling over the back of the trap.

The past week had been awkward. She couldn't forgive Jacob for cheating, but there was a little voice inside her reminding her that he'd been right when he said Edward had wanted to go and fight. Edward would have gone anyway, Annie knew. If there had been a long straw to pull, and he had chosen it, she was sure that he would have bargained to change places with his brother.

Worse was the feeling of having been foolish and blind. How could she not have known that Jacob loved her like that? Oh, she had sensed that he liked her more than he should, but not that he would cheat his own brother for her. It seemed to Annie that she had lived her whole life without a clue about what was going on around her. That was going to change, she vowed.

The fete was in full swing already. A committee headed by Janet Airey and Betsy Middleton and Mrs Thirlby, the vicar's wife, had been planning for months, determined not to let the war spoil one of the highlights of the village year. There was a tea tent, as always, and cakes for sale, even if most had had to be made with dried egg. A WI stall, with not such a lavish display of jams and preserves as previously, but still a good effort. Annie had been roped in to give the children donkey rides, but there were plenty of other activities, too: toss the ring, guess the weight of Fred Airey's enormous marrow, a lucky dip with prizes buried in a packing case full of sawdust curls. Competition for the largest onion was as fierce as ever, as were the cakes, flowers and vegetables being solemnly judged.

Most popular of all was the raffle, with prizes provided by Jed Dingle on the understanding that no questions would be asked about where they came from. The biggest prize was a bunch of bananas, closely followed by a pair of nylons and a bottle of Scotch. Annie saw Jack Proudfoot, Lily Dingle beside him, wander over to study the table with raised brows before moving on with a resigned smile. Perhaps Mrs Thirlby had persuaded him to look the other way, just for a day. Or more likely it was something to do with what Lily had whispered in his ear, she decided.

Stan clambered down from the trap and rushed over to Annie, who he had made firm friends with the night his sister had run off. 'Annie! Annie! Can I ride Neddy?'

Annie saw Jacob's shoulders tense at the sound of her name and looked quickly away. 'Course you can,' she told Stan. 'Hop on.'

Stan was already proudly clutching Neddy's mane when Ruby hobbled up, slowed by her bad ankle. 'Can I ride him, too?'

Patiently, Annie led Neddy round the field with his eager riders. The donkey rides were popular with the children, but most of the adults were more interested in the other stalls, so she was unprepared for Oliver Skilbeck to come up beside her as she was helping Stan off.

'I haven't seen you around for a while,' he said, sneering.

The sound of his voice was enough to make Annie's stomach tilt with disgust, but she managed to keep her voice even. 'Leave me alone, Oliver,' she said. 'I don't want anything to do with you.'

'That's not very friendly — ouch!' Oliver broke off with a yelp of pain. Neddy, recognising his old tormentor, had leant forward and taken a bite of his rear end.

'Why you — !' Furious, Oliver swung between Annie and the donkey, his clenched fist raised threateningly. 'Bloody donkey!'

'You leave Neddy alone,' said Annie, her heart hammering with fear. 'Serves you right if he took a chunk out of you after the way you treated him. He hasn't forgotten, and neither have I.'

Oliver lunged for the donkey, but all at once Jack Proudfoot was there. 'I wouldn't advise you to hit the animal,' he said calmly to Oliver. 'I wouldn't want to arrest you for animal cruelty.'

'It bit me!'

'I'm sure Neddy had his reasons.' Jack's voice was cool and Oliver stared at him in disbelief, one hand clamped over his buttock.

'You should arrest *her* for having a dangerous animal,' he said, jerking his head in Annie's direction.

'I think it's probably best if you move along now,' said Jack. 'Nobody wants a scene at the fete. Why don't you just go on home?'

'There's nothing worth seeing here anyway,' sneered Oliver, and with a last vindictive glance at Annie, he limped off.

'Thank you.' Annie smiled gratefully at Jack.

'A pleasure,' he said. 'Let me know if he causes you any more trouble.'

'I will, but I'm leaving tomorrow.'

'I'll just make sure Oliver's on his way without giving any more grief,' said Jack with a farewell nod to Annie.

Lily lingered. 'Leaving?'

'Yes.' Annie helped hoist Ruby onto Neddy's back. 'I'm joining the WRNS.'

'What's that?' Meg had come up in time to hear Annie's announcement. 'Are you really going, Annie?'

Annie nodded. 'Tomorrow. I've made up my mind.'

'Beckindale won't be the same without you! Everything's changing,' said Lily dolefully.

'In a good way, for some,' said Annie, nodding at Lily's swollen belly. 'You'll be a mother soon, Lily.'

'I know.' Lily put a hand on her stomach, a smile trembling on her lips. 'It's an incredible feeling.'

'And maybe you'll be a wife, too,' Annie probed gently.

Lily coloured. 'I don't know what you mean.'

'You and Jack Proudfoot?' Annie prompted, and Meg raised her eyebrows.

'Aha! Is that so, Lily?'

Lily's blush deepened. 'No . . . maybe . . . I haven't decided,' she muttered.

Annie and Meg laughed. 'We'll take that as a

yes,' said Meg. 'Why don't you make it a double wedding, with Mick and Nina? I just heard they're getting married, too.'

'That's right.' Lily couldn't disguise her relief at the change of subject. 'I'm going to be Nina's maid of honour.'

'I'm glad you're friends now,' said Annie, and Lily nodded.

'Nina's been wonderful to me. The best thing about being such a fool over Derek is getting to know her, and to realise that she's not trying to replace my mother. She's just herself. She doesn't care what anybody thinks, so I'm trying to be more like her.'

'There's nothing like a wedding to change minds,' said Meg. 'Now that Nina is going to be Mrs Dingle, I notice all the old gossips are starting to change their tune. I heard Brenda Lane tell Peggy Summers that Nina was 'refreshingly unconventional', which must be a good sign. She'll be accepted in no time and asked to join the knitting circle, and then there'll be no going back for her!'

Lily couldn't help laughing. 'I hope so, though Nina doesn't care one way or another.'

'What about you, Meg?' Annie asked. 'Is your life changing, too?'

'Well, it looks as if I'm adopting Ruby and Stan,' said Meg with a smile. 'I've gone from spinster schoolmistress to having a family of two, so that's quite a change, I suppose.'

'I'm glad they're staying with you. They've really blossomed since they've been in Beckindale, haven't they?'

Meg's eyes followed Ruby and Stan, who were fighting over whose turn it was to go on Neddy again. 'They really have,' she agreed. 'I'm not saying it's perfect, but I can't imagine life without them now.'

'And Rolf?' Annie asked.

'Jack says they'll let him out soon and he can go back to work at Emmerdale Farm. I'm hoping he'll be able to give Stan lessons again.'

'You love him, don't you?'

Meg didn't answer immediately. 'Yes, I do,' she admitted at last. 'If I could have chosen who to fall in love with, it certainly wouldn't have been a German prisoner of war, but it turns out that he's the one for me. I have no idea if we'll ever have a future together, so all we can do is make the most of now.'

'That's all any of us can do,' Annie agreed.

'And you're going away,' said Lily. 'I didn't think you'd ever leave Beckindale, Annie.'

'Nor did I, but the war is making us do a lot of things we never thought we'd do before,' she said, thinking of Jacob and how he had cheated with the straws.

'It won't be for ever, though, will it?' said Meg. 'Beckindale wouldn't be the same without you.'

Annie looked around the fete, at the familiar faces and the backdrop of the grey stone village and the green hills behind. Her gaze moved from her parents, to Maggie and Joe, to Janet Airey and Mary Ann Teale and so many others who had been part of her life for as long as she could remember, and came to rest at last on Jacob, who was looking back at Emmerdale Farm as if he wished he were there.

'No, not for ever,' she said. 'I'll be back.'